RETURN

Haf

THE CHILDREN'S WAR

But it isn't unborn children, it's unborn boys, he reminded himself, falling into somber thought.

And while he didn't want to follow that line of reasoning, unless there was something physiological, medical, or chemical that he knew nothing about, the fact that *one* sex was singled out for "error" made incompetence the most modest and innocuous of terms.

Which could mean, terrible as it was to contemplate, that what had happened to Mark—and to Eddie Dugan's boy, the Italian's son, hundreds of others—was surely intentional. Not accidental.

But who could possibly have such a fury against people as helpless as newborn males? Richard frowned, yanked the steering wheel to force the old Camaro back into its lane as a Chevy whined past. This damnable thing was almost *Biblical!*

J.N. WILLIAMSON
JOHN MACLAY

WARDS OF ARMAGEDDON

LEISURE BOOKS ∞ NEW YORK CITY

Dedication

For Mary; for Joyce;
and
for two sons named John,
one born on an Army post in 1968

A LEISURE BOOK

Published by

Dorchester Publishing Co., Inc.
6 East 39th Street
New York, NY 10016

Copyright ©1986 by J. N. Williamson and John Maclay

Printed in the United States of America

WARDS OF ARMAGEDDON

AN INTRODUCTION

By Richard G. Lugar
United States Senator, Indiana

J. N. Williamson is a talented and prolific writer in whom his fellow Hoosiers have justifiable pride. Jerry and I were classmates in Indianapolis and enjoyed the competitive stimulation of a class which produced an internationally recognized composer-pianist and another often-published novelist.

The Shortridge *Daily Echo* gave us all an opportunity to publish news stories and columns of opinion, and to appraise the work of others. Jerry displayed imagination and discipline. He was tenacious and he demanded notice.

Even so, I was surprised to watch a stream of J. N. Williamson books find eager publishers and wide audiences over the decade past. I was deeply pleased to see the growing success of a friend I had not anticipated would stay at the demanding literary craft for the years required to establish a full-time career.

Many of Jerry's books have been entertainments playing successfully to the readers' needs for mystery, shock, or a fictive introduction to

the occult. His characterizations and his storylines
were involving. He discovered formulas that work
and he will write and edit many more books to
satisfy a growing body of readers.

Wards of Armageddon is much more ambitious.
With Baltimore's John Maclay, a publisher as well
as a new writer to reckon with, Jerry has written a
substantial novel. They have set the story in Washington and Indianapolis and at military facilities
and it is peopled by military families, a Washington
journalist, citizens of the Broad Ripple and Baltimore suburbs—and others whose personalities and
locations, in slightly different circumstances, are
well known to me.

I admire his imagination, but must point out,
as he surely would, that J. N. Williamson is
describing activities which did not happen and could
not happen under current checks and balances.

The Select Committee on Intelligence of the
United States Senate, of which I am a member, is
charged with oversight of all intelligence activities,
overt and covert. The President of the United
States, each military service, and all other independent government entities must share news of their
work with the Intelligence Committees of the
Senate and House in a timely manner and they have
done so since 1977 when I first became involved.

This requirement for sharing has not obviated
extraordinary proposals on occasion, but citizens
who read *Wards of Armageddon* must know that
their anxieties have been created by the imaginative
work of J. N. Williamson and John Maclay, and not
an arm of the Federal government.

I salute my friend and his collaborator for a
superb book of fiction which will merit a much larger
readership for their work!

Prologue

Saving Civilization

(On the second day of January the American air offensive launched the biggest aerial battle so far in the war. When U.S. planes attacked surface-to-air missile sites, seven Communist MIGs went screaming from the skies.)

General William Westmoreland said: "The only language that Hanoi understands is the language of force."

(Three days later, there was an official report: In Vietnam, the number of Americans killed and wounded—respectively—totaled 5,008; 30,093. It was not over.)

Antiwar poster pressed on countless American bumpers like a goodbye kiss: "WAR IS NOT HEALTHY FOR CHILDREN AND OTHER LIVING THINGS."

(Late in February, that year, it was learned that Vietcong guerrillas were using rockets. The rockets bore Russian and Chinese markings.)

President Lydon B. Johnson declared that the bombing would cease if he could find "just almost any step" to justify, not merely rationalize, the action.

(Before May ended, more than 10,000 Americans had expired during the fighting in Vietnam.)

Colonel H. E. Opfer, air attache at the U.S. Embassy in Pnom Penh, argued disdainfully: "You always write it's bombing, bombing, bombing. It's not bombing. It's air support."

(Public protests against the war were mounting. In the spring, draft cards were burned during demonstrations in both New York and San Francisco.)

Spiro T. Agnew, soon to become Vice President of the United States, later observed: "Yippies, Hippies, Yahoos, Black Panthers . . . I would swap the whole damn zoo for the kind of young Americans I saw in Vietnam."

(August, same year—buildup of U.S. troops in Vietnam reported; 45,000 to 50,000 additional forces would, in less than a year, mean a total of 525,000 men serving.)

General Westmoreland: "A commander must learn to live with frustration, interference . . . and criticism so long as he can be sure they do *not* contribute to failure."

(President Lyndon Johnson pledged, that November, no increase in the Vietnam troop strength of Americans serving there poor 506,000 Within a week, Dak To was the scene of the bloodiest battle yet in Vietnam. Outcome: Jets and ground troops captured something called "Hill 875.")

During the year in question, Americans learned to watch the evening news in unprecedented numbers. There was so much going on in the world that some Americans even began reading newspapers again. The right-wing army in Greece seized power and, later, one George Papadopoulos headed up a new military government. Admirers of strength, of might and daring, smiled . . . Civil war broke out in Nigeria . . . The United States, U.S.S.R, and Britain barred the use of nuclear weapons in space . . . There was rioting in Hong Kong . . . People who had a narrow interest in eventually celebrating their own thirtieth birthdays collected, marched, protested, with the result that many others scowled . . . An Indonesian *coup d'etat* ousted less-than-beloved President Sukarno . . . Clearly, this was a time of grand-scale muscle-flexing; numerous smiles returned.

Alone, the Middle East produced enough headlines—or those feature stories mentioned meaningfully ahead of the opening commercials—for a more typical decade. With tension ever increasing between still youthful Israel and her grudging Arab neighbors, Egyptian president Gamal Abdel Nasser asked for the withdrawal of the United Nations' essentially euphemistic peace-keeping border forces. Dreading Arab attack, Israel engaged in the "Six-Day War," succeeding in occupying the Sinai Peninsula, the Gaza Strip, and the Golan Heights—not to forget all Jordanian territory west of the fabled river Jordan. Those who were nourished by thrills, bolstered physically by displays of power or graphic death—whatever their particular partisanship, or absence of one—reveled in a year marred only by those they saw as weak, ineffectual, collectivist, and —worst of all—obstructionist.

It was the year 1967, a time prefatory to the Tet offensive in Khe Sanh in January, 1968. But one man, at least, would never see Saigon again.

"Riots," said the soldier, "break out. Fighting breaks out. War breaks out and guys break out of jail." Richard Grant, corporal, spoke sourly in the home to which he'd been returned. During his second tour of combat duty he had suffered his first wound. Watching Walter Cronkite made him feel he'd never left Nam. "And now," he said, giving his wife a glance of mystification, "fire has broken out in *Apollo 3*, killing three astronauts. Remember, Molly? Remember when it was only pimples that broke out? Or is it all on the same scale, do you think —all this 'breaking out'?"

She didn't reply, not immediately. She was feeling guilty because of being glad, not much more than that, that her husband had returned in time for the delivery of their first child. Hard to think of anything else, so hard; except his wound, his limp. "I don't think I follow you," she said.

Richard sank into a chair by the window. He was careful as he propped up his freshly gimpy leg. Then for a moment, he looked out the window, saying nothing. He made out the high gate encircling Fort Christopher; it would be his final military station before honorable discharge.

His gaze moved to Molly's great belly, his eyes softening. "Let's just say I hope somebody's found a cure for blemishes by the time Junior grows up."

PART ONE

THE TIME OF MOLOCH

"Out of this war are going to come some of the finest people this country has ever seen."

—General William C. Westmoreland

1

At some unclear instant during his ceaseless and painful pacing, Richard had cast aside the encumbering crutch—unsought souvenir, mere weeks back, from an overworked M.A.S.H. unit in Nam—and settled for limping without its eternal, bleak reminder. Bad enough, looking now like every comedian's stalest cliché—the expectant father.

He didn't want to emphasize it by seeming to beg for pity.

Besides, there had been enough unwelcome melodrama in his young life during recent years to last Corporal Richard Grant a lifetime. Maybe there had been no way to avoid that, but there was no need to advertise the fact that he was internally turbulent as he waited for his first child to be born.

The more he paced, however, thinking it over— this protracted rerun of a hundred billion fatherly vigils—the more Richard didn't care much if the fey, khaki-clad orderly smirked inanely each time he and the others passed the open waiting room. Some events were simply too full of human caring and its suspense to honor the modern ritual of Cool. He felt

that he should not be expected to perch calmly in a
chair, his lap piled high with dog-eared magazines
and reenlistment propaganda. If a bunch of faded
funny-men found an expectant dad to be a mother
lode of satirical nuggets, hell, let 'em laugh. To hell
with them! Because they didn't know one thing
about Richard Bruce Grant. Or Molly Skylar Grant.
And when the kid came—raise thumb to nose in pre-
discharge salute—they'd never have that chance!

Richard paused, realized he was ranting mentally,
and forced a smile.

Shortly after the baby was born and released from
the Fort Christopher Hospital, all three Grants
would be abandoning the military lifestyle forever.
Well, the *older* Grants, anyway; for it occurred to
the pacing Richard—not for the first time—how
much he hoped there'd be no need for a military at
all, by the time this child was eighteen or nineteen.
The best thing about having a girl, if things worked
out that way, was probably the likelihood that she'd
have to endure army life only if she sought it.

Which, Richard ranted again to himself, would be
over his dead and buried carcass!

Next swing around the drab, otherwise isolated
waiting room, the curly haired little man in the
faded corporal's fatigues paused long enough to
return the icy stare of a bearded male orderly at the
entrance. The latter, biting his lower lip, tucked a
bedpan beneath one thin arm and fairly flew down
the outer corridor, feet making light scuffing
sounds. *He'll need to raid the narc cabinet for
Valium after that,* Richard decided with a grin. *A
quart bottle!*

He glanced down, toward the crutch he had discarded, and his smile fell away with his gaze. Until
now, he'd scarcely put the thing down, all but un-

consciously fearing that his leg would snap off if he rested all his weight upon it. Now he felt he'd tossed it aside harried hours ago; relived panic made him think of retrieving it. But it had slipped beneath a phony leather chair across the room and only the tip of the spiny bottom segment was in view, like a dog's rubbery snout. Or one dark toe. Richard shuddered; he filled once more with imminent death. He'd come within Cong rifle shot of winning his very own, state-of-the-art artificial leg, and the perspiration turning cold on his forehead this moment was what lingered from one second of hasty Cong zeal, yards outside the DMZ. His eyes wouldn't shut, remembering. But he stared anyway, recalled the familiar sweet scent of blood, sounds of screaming that was his, shock that he had killed the Cong who'd hurt him with his own return shot through one instantly technicolor eye.

Had he really shouted, "Got the sonofabitch!" before passing out? He'd reached the point that handful of weeks ago when he could no longer be sure whether all the screaming came from himself, plummeting bombs, or from hard, narrow little women with bronze heads thrown so far back that their coal-colored hair lapped the small of their unbending spines. So the last scream he would ever hear in Nam, Richard had issued, consciously— loudly enough to pierce the tuned-out awareness of a surgeon who asked sharply what he meant, Corporal, surgery would only waste additional taxpayer money. He'd replied through teeth fixed as any skeleton's that if the doctor amputated and then proposed something fashionable in prosthetics, Corporal Grant wouldn't be alive long enough to wear it. *Mais certainement,* and how'd you like another suicide to explain, Doc?

What was taking his baby so *long?* Was the kid looking for him in Nam?

I was silly, Richard decided abruptly, *turning down the leg.* The ongoing sweating and recurring nausea said he'd been overdramatic. The way drama always found him out, insisted he play with it —like a kicked-out dog who had just enough smarts to find you, regardless of where you were.

But all he had ever wanted was time to ease into some hopeful, creative regimen, even the kind of routine many men saw as boring. Consciously, he was utterly different from the people and experiences that engulfed him. He had yearned to be a writer of some kind for as long as he could remember and writers weren't athletes, they didn't have to have two legs.

And after the surgeon had explained those things to Richard—"It's not as if you're giving up an *eye* or something"—and shown clearly that he no longer understood why this short-of-stature corporal made such fuss when amputation would be so much quicker, more eco*nom*ical—Richard had really felt he was being ridiculous. Obstinate.

Probably he had insisted upon keeping the leg because he'd doubted that he owned anything else except his body.

Or because, if he'd been sent to a stateside hospital to accustom himself to the new "device," Molly would have had to have their baby without him.

Richard had felt obliged to be present. He'd picked the wrong time for her to get pregnant, that first time back after his initial taste of infantry combat. She'd had to carry the child alone for most of the first two trimesters, and Molly didn't actually cope with this kind of thing especially well.

For the first time, Richard stopped pacing
entirely, stood with his legs—good and bad—apart
but braced. Portions of his mind were always oddly
detached, observant even of himself, and he knew he
resembled a drunk with quite a different choice than
the one confronting him. He had to find a better way
to stay afoot, or pitch forward on his face. Or fetch
the crutch.

Dragging his foot, Richard raised his left wrist,
saw that his watch had stopped running.
Exhausted, he felt a second's panic when he
wondered if time might truly have ceased, leaving
him—always—to wait for Molly, and the kid.

He was so deep in the recesses of the enormous
post hospital that he saw no windows anywhere. It
wouldn't even be possible to tell if the sun had come
up. Maybe this portion of the building was a
dummy, a military mock-up; perhaps it was, in fact,
a secret missile silo and the effete looking orderly
he'd chased off was a Pentagon agent, sitting now,
before a panel of evilly brilliant lights, one nervous
finger resting on the button.

Swearing, awkwardly wheeling to face the
corridor, its illumination banked and imaginatively
ominous, Richard made a face. The child, on its way
now, had never been part of Richard Grant's game
plan for life. Yet neither had Molly and certainly not
Vietnam and never the United States Army. Point
of goddamn fact, the infant human being he'd sired,
fighting to get into the crazy world, wouldn't have
been conceived, but for Nam.

Nam, ungodly father and unholy son, slayer of
spirits and plans, wrapped into one.

Or did the very existence of any army somehow
summon a war in which it could grow like some
warped and perverted child? Or could the nation's

problems involve the attitudes and assumptions of
the permanent uniformed personnel? There were
still plenty of decent officers, like Richard's latest
company commander, regardless of what people on
the outside preferred to believe. Yet even they—
when they learned to *know* the Richard Grants of
every rank instead of seeing them only as so many
strips of ranking cloth—had only one decent option
during a war like Nam. Waving a treasonous, dismissing hand, murmuring ruefully, "Go home. Get
out of this hellhole."

But each man *was* an individual. A real and
independent person, whether impersonal wars concealed the fact or not. Anybody seeing Richard lurch
around the hospital waiting room in his carbon copy
fatigues mightn't believe that he and Molly were
different, but that changed nothing.

What the hell had happened to a guy who prized
independence so much that live-and-let-live had been
the first article of his creed? In Richard Grant's
twenty-four years, he had never minded how folks
handled their own affairs if they didn't bother
people whom Richard, himself, cared about. He'd
even concluded recently that this was a logical,
mature extension of his own intense preference for
privacy, a deep-seated craving for freedom to do
what he wished with his own life—if he harmed no
one else.

Indeed, in his young philosophy, people who did
not demand that liberty—and those who denied
other people their inclinations, however cockeyed—
happened to be the constant, the real foe. Anytime.
Anywhere. A foe Richard wished to steer clear of,
since any encounter even with those who restricted
their own lives would surely inform him how little
they minded when enforced limits were placed on

others.

Which, then, left him no choice but to try to change their minds.

Vietnam, like such necessities, violated all Richard's principles and he had come to suspect that whether the men fighting beside him had thought it all the way through, they were the generation that agreed with him, the last to be deceived in the slightest. His own child, coming now to life, would *know*—with electric clarity—when anyone else threatened his intimate liberties—and deal with that enemy any way that was swiftest.

This place they'd called Nam was an artful device, a prosthetic on which the enemy had propped its stumped soul, then staggered forward with bayonets pricking the backs of free men. It was an invention of officialdom in many parts of a complex world that was old, maimed, and dying. When, at last, it toppled to ground, a new growth of Richard's kind would be fertilized—a flowering of those who *had* thought it through, and always would.

Maybe I shouldn't have taken it so personally, the corporal reflected, making his way haltingly to the door, through it, and down the corridor. *I do that a lot.*

He hadn't gone out there to find out what was wrong, consciously. But he gazed off, down the hallway, and shivered. Back when he'd left poor Molly entangled in a flutter of neat, efficient hands, he hadn't realized how long this damned corridor was. Reminded Richard of the tunnels men near death claimed led them toward paradise.

Edging forward, he doubted he would find God at the other end.

Part of his impression of interminability stemmed from the fact that it was dark but for the periodic illumination of recessed ceiling lighting and doors left ajar. It was also quiet as a chagrined whisper. His heels clacked with each step, the sound of his limp reminding Richard of old "Mummy" movies.

Farther down or possibly up—basic directions in huge buildings went awry; shadows and corners made bizarre insets and angles—Richard detected the start of carpeting. *To cushion the feet of doctors and nurses*, he thought at once, then frowned.

Wrong, he corrected himself. *To cushion the gurney carts with unconscious, helpless human beings, pushed God-knew-where.*

Richard half stopped. At the far end of the hallway, a door was opening, silently.

A uniformed man stiffly filled the frame. He'd stopped to stare back at Richard, as motionless as if someone had spray-painted his erect, distinguished image into the gap. With a crown of laurel leaves instead of his crushed military cap, he might have been Alexander, or Caesar, flushed after departing the vomitorium and hungering for freshly conquerable worlds. Richard shuffled faster, tried to peer past the officer, see him only as an image from old books or art museums.

"*There* you are, Corporal!" Unreadable blue eyes shining from shadow traced Richard's short, square body appraisingly. "But I'd heard you were a sergeant."

Then how do you know it's me? "I'm entitled to the third stripe." Reluctantly, Richard approximated a stockstill stance, unwilling to mutter "sir."

"Battlefield promotion, I think?"

"Yes. But I am getting out." Evenly, mind on his family. "No need to sew it on."

"Nonsense." The heartiness diminished, but

lingered. "You take what you have coming in this man's world. The Army must have taught you that much."

"Oh, it tried." Richard, with mild surprise, realized that the other, older man had led him nearly all the way back to the waiting room—merely by being smotheringly close; confident. That instant he stopped walking. "Sir, my wife, Mrs. Grant—our baby? D'you have news?"

The officer's eagles flashed into view as they passed beneath a chip of shorting electricity that flickered semaphore signals on the officer's face and long forehead. The cap tugged down made the features uncertain but the eagles were ready to vault right off the colonel's shoulders. "The surgeon will be along any moment, Grant. I'm sure. I did check things myself; personally. And your little lady was conscious, giving it hell."

Richard was incredulous. If the colonel wasn't a doctor, what right had he to go where the husband wasn't permitted? This Army! "What does 'giving it hell' mean? In this case, sir?"

"Why, here comes Captain Witsell now, if I'm not mistaken." The taller man was gazing down the hall toward the room he had exited. The strong fingers on Richard's shoulder pinched. "We take care of our own, Corporal, count on it! None of this costs you a red cent, boy. Life can be rather good for the career soldier."

Richard, drifting, nodded. He saw the figure in doctor's whites approaching at a fairly brisk pace but he was staring up the corridor at the colonel.

"Corporal, you have a remarkable service record; remarkable." The voice was warm and furry like a sleeping bag after sentry duty. "Looked into your file myself, personally. That bad leg—since you showed the guts to keep it—needn't take you out of the game, Grant.'' Richard nodded and began drifting uneasily toward the nearing surgeon. He tried to tune out the officer. "You will think it over, won't you?"

The man in whites—Captain Alfred Witsell—was the doctor Molly had been seeing. During Richard's absence in Nam, she'd had the whole burden of deciding where to go for prenatal care and treatment. Only now did Richard understand how trying the time had surely been for young Molly. He longed, abruptly, to tell her so.

Molly's father was a respected, even renowned physician in private practice, who'd lately moved to the Indianapolis home town of his new second wife. Molly had infuriated him by remaining, finally, at Fort Christopher to have the baby instead of going "home." Doctor Skylar had told her that "military medicine" was a "disgrace to the profession" and had otherwise indicated how hurt he was when she refused to go to him in the Midwest. The Skylars were originally from Washington, D.C., where she'd met Richard; Molly had believed she would feel alien enough around her new stepmother, let alone a wholly unfamiliar city. Eventually, Richard sensed, they'd have to make peace overtures to Doctor Skylar. The doctor had demonstrated just how stubborn he was when, as Molly changed her mind at the last minute and offered to join him in Indianapolis, he would have none of it. "Dad told me just to forget about it," Molly'd informed Richard, "that he was really much too busy to tolerate a whining, pregnant woman anyway." That had surprised even Richard. He hadn't thought Doc Skylar would cut off his nose to spite his face.

Witsell's face hove into view as they met outside a

partly opened hospital room door. Through it, Richard glimpsed the effete orderly, changing sheets for a boy with his leg immobilized in a cast.

"I want to inform you at once," the captain said, swiftly capturing Richard's attention, "that Molly's doing well. A-OK, point of fact."

Richard heard the message but saw the grim expression. It was an expanse of noncommital, sallow solemnity, that face, plus another quality that was hard to place. Something subtle, indistinct; an element, Richard believed, of anxiety. But when he tried to frame a question, words didn't come and his studied balance upon his wounded leg sagged. He needed to throw out his right hand to the surgeon's snowy, solid shoulder.

For a second, Captain Witsell said nothing, didn't seem to notice. Then, with a sigh, he slipped his arm round Richard's shoulders, led him toward that room from which the senior officer had emerged. Glancing back, Richard saw that the colonel was nowhere in sight.

"There are . . . challenges," Witsell said. "Problems. Even in the ultramodern medicine of the sixties." His voice was toneless, unadorned. "For them, I fear, we remain . . . unprepared. There have been tremendous advances, *yes*. And who knows, in the seventies, certainly by the eighties, we shall have the knowledge and the means of coping with all but a few dread diseases." Rather absently, he squeezed Richard's shoulder. "Count on it."

"I don't mean to be rude, sir, but my wife is giving birth *tonight*." Just before entering the fluorescence flooded room, he caught familiar odors he'd hoped to forget; others which he wanted no one to explain to him. "What, exactly, are you trying to tell me?"

For the first time, beneath Richard's intense

scrutiny, Captain Alfred Witsell's face acquired distinct features. Brows so fine they mightn't have shown except they were the color of bad burns. A small nose of no greater prominence, indefinite side-burns and an ambiguous pursing of lips so wide he seemed ravenous. Eyes that couldn't have been said to dance, except for the inference of vivacity; this man's colorless eyes moved restlessly, as if his unsought tour of military duty had condemned him to an eternity of inspections. Only the nose, hungry mouth, and small chin were centered upon Richard Grant's face. "Being blunt, Corporal, I have to tell you something I don't want to say at all." The rest-less eyes paused. "Your child was stillborn."

2

They had been cleaning up in one of the colorless, shockingly illuminated, germ-free rooms through which Witsell led the stunned Richard, and they were very good at it. He noticed that much as he passed through the first room. There was no evidence whatsoever of mess, sorrow or drama, no sign of a vulnerable young woman's pointless ordeal or even of that life which would not be. Such considerations had not been permitted to cause the faintest disruption of sanctified routine, and Richard dully supposed he was meant to be impressed. Surely if industry and tidiness were the universally admired qualities everybody said were the next things to God, someone ought to have applauded. Why else would human beings strive to become machine-like?

But except for the sibilant sough of papers being shuffled into a crisp manila folder by a silent youth fixed before an O.D. desk, it was cathedral-quiet, and Richard Grant's shredded nerves whined to him about strangeness. He felt distinctly weird about the way he was being thrust politely among the un-

27

speaking aides, almost like something distasteful
left too long on a gurney. Perhaps the fact that he
had lost all track of time had something to do with it.
He'd temporarily forgotten, anyway, how the
adjustment of stateside living was made, and
becoming enervated in the intestines of a structure
without windows or timepiece, with no people with
whom he could conceivably identify, he felt abruptly
as if he were wandering into a Kafkaesque prologue.
What was it Kafka'd said? "You are free and that is
why you're lost." But while he could bolt, run from
this building's steaming bowels, Molly could not.

When he was passed between two distinguished
men in white, neither physician appeared to see
Witsell or him; they ranged apart without breaking
a conversational flow, then relocked behind them.
Nothing anywhere, Richard thought, could be as
efficient or methodical as the combination of
military and medical routines.

Or as cold, as impersonal and unnoticing.

Alfred Witsell swept him out into a new hallway,
this one shorter, better lit than the one emptying
into the waiting room. The corridor was used
principally by the hospital staff, the rooms were
better marked, and Witsell appeared to be heading
Richard toward one with a single word of identification: RECOVERY. In economically blocked
military lettering.

That was when Richard felt the first burn of tears
flooding his eyes. How in the world did a woman like
his Molly, a few years out of high school and the
stern protection of a patrician father, recover from
this? From any of "this," if you saw it whole, looked
at it properly. Because it had been a swift courtship,
by order of Vietnam, a quick marriage, quicker con-
ception—none of it normal for Molly or for him,

little of it what either of them had planned. None was even remotely idyllic, little was romantic, all was only marginally fulfilling. Then, ponderous months on her own.

There were women to whom marriage, and childbirth, were novelty, no more than that. Molly wasn't like that. Considering life as a series of stages and all those they'd known together twisted or disfigured, could she recover at all from his loss?

If there was a chance, for her, for them, it began in the lonely hospital room ahead of Witsell and him. "What *was* it?" he asked the other man; but apparently Witsell did not hear him, because there was no hesitancy in his brisk pace.

As the ramifications kept coming to mind, Richard saw that the only outcome of his marriage, aside from his memories of sex with his bride, would be a fruitless pregnancy and a prolonged period of sadness and recrimination.

He wasn't sure he was up to it.

A door was opening ahead and Witsell was stopping. Richard halted, too, aware in a distant way of a clock to his left, mounted against the whitewashed wall: 5:59.

For a second, it meant nothing to him. Presumably, morning; presumably he'd been there all night. Now he saw an orderly emerging from a room, shoving a cart. Richard saw covered plates of food, inhaled the unmistakable fragrance of hot coffee and scent of eggs. He was hungry; promptly cursed himself for thinking of Richard Grant. He read the time again: 6:00—straight up.

Suddenly it was important to note and record the time, always to know when the terrible loss had occurred to Molly and him. Hobbling after Witsell again, he tried to guess how long it had been since

. . . the child. He slipped slightly, swore; he wished he had taken the crutch with him. Blood pumped like pummeling fists against the walls of his temples. Demanding that he sit. *No,* he had to find out what the baby had been; *no,* he'd keep walking somehow. Why was it people never memorized the minute a truly fine party started, or came to a close; the exact minute a raise, or promotion, was announced? What was intrinsically wrong with people that they never recorded any but the bad, the troubling, miserable human things?

Was it linked somehow to being burdened by guilt, or welcoming it?

Had he, and Molly, in point of fact, done something wrong?

He looked up and cleared his throat.

"What was it?"

The doctor, Captain Witsell, glanced over. He'd been lost in his own thoughts, making marginal notes on a printed paper. "I beg pardon?"

"What *was* it?" Richard, angry, tensed. What did the fool think he'd be asking about at a time like this? The name of the newest Presley record? "I am assuming my dead child had, at least, a sex of one kind or the other. I asked you to identify it for me. Sir."

"It was a boy." Witsell's gaze locked with his, nothing in the eyes, the shark's mouth narrowed, almost pursed. The physician was unperturbed, arguably unconcerned. "Its sex was male."

Richard nodded, as if someone had told him the date. Give Witsell credit, at least, for answering questions and not rushing him toward the room, the way a lot of civilian doctors like Molly's Dad would. Alfred Witsell was all right; he'd stopped without protest, he was watching every expression of

Richard's attentively, he was presumably prepared to wait until Richard got his guts together. None of this was fun, no, it was agonizing, it left a guy dazed, confused; but he mustn't take it out on Witsell, or the United States Army, or even this goddamned hospital. Because things simply went wrong, they happened despite the best of care; he could be certain that this stony-eyed, fishfaced automaton had done what he . . .

Richard whirled and hit the wall with his fist as hard as he'd ever struck anything. He watched his fist pop away from the wall and didn't feel real pain until he saw dots of redness freckling his knuckles. Then he struck the wall again, moaned, fought a nearly thrilling desire to weep. "Does Molly—does Mrs. Grant—*know?*"

Blank stare. "That the child was stillborn?" He stood erect, looking disapprovingly. "Certainly not, Corporal! I would not usurp your husband's role. What *others* may have done . . ."

Richard, feet braced, resumed his waiting stance. Questions milled, tried to surface; one concerning the question of what had been wrong with the child wouldn't take logical form. Because he didn't let it. "His name was Mark. D'you like it?"

Witsell's glance at his watch wasn't surreptitious at all.

"See, I didn't want my son—if it was a boy—to be stuck with a name he hated. I wanted it to have some dignity yet be slightly different. It was Molly who came up with Mark. D'you see, Captain? You can't turn 'Mark' into anything stupid, not even a nickname! Isn't that wonderful?"

Witsell's eyes closed as if he'd gotten smoke in them. Reopening them, no more human expression showed. "But he's dead, Corporal. He didn't live."

"For God's sake, Captain, I mean, for *God's sake.*" Richard shook his head, laughed. It trailed off a sound longer than it should have lasted. "I was just telling you my son's name—if he'd been all right." And Witsell's cool gaze met his; held. Richard felt perspiration dripping from his forehead, stinging his eyes. Shuddering, he moved forward, taking the point. "Let's go."

"A moment."

Richard stopped. He heard the sounds of other people moving around elsewhere on the floor, and sensed the size of the building. Dozens, hundreds, of people, maybe, would be arriving for the day shift. Ready to work with human machines, like Molly or him; men with serial numbers, dogtags, and wives who got in free because a government arrangement grudgingly agreed to it. Richard understood that the captain behind him had paused only because he had something of his own to say.

"Corporal, your wife is behaving somewhat irrationally. Now, don't let that concern you. It will pass, I'm sure; but I felt we should coordinate our approach to her."

Molly was his wife, not a military objective; what did this presumably well-meaning fool mean? Sweat along his spine and over his shoulders turned to ice. "Molly is not irrational. She's inexperienced. She can be foolish sometimes. She is never irrational. Tell me what you're talking about."

"Actually, I'd rather you saw for yourself, but I thought you should be warned. Prepped for it." Witsell drew abreast, reached around to put out a palm against Molly's door. "It isn't uncommon to fantasize in situations of this sort."

Richard put out his own hand and clamped it on the other man's wrist. The skin was amazingly cool and pliant. His blood pressure, his heartbeat, not one damned vital sign had registered the slightest stress in this process of informing Richard, he'd have bet on it. "Captain. Where—is Mark?"

A daring blank expression. "What?"

Richard's eyes shut but he held to the arm, moved it faintly. "Sir, I had to hurt human beings. In Nam. I wasn't proud of it but I wasn't ashamed, either, even when I got back, read the papers, saw the placards." He swallowed. "A man called me a baby killer, but I wasn't that, not knowingly at least."

"Release me."

"Sir, the point is that I won't be able to forget how to hurt people for a long, long time and right now I'm exceedingly tired." Just then he realized how his fingers had tightened, how he'd shuffled his feet for leverage, and threw the officer's arm away. Pretty streaks of scarlet and cream showed already on the man's wrist. "What have you done with my son?"

"The remains," Witsell said, "were destroyed." He made no attempt to massage his dangling hand but there was expression in his face now. "It's procedure."

"How?"

"The usual way. Cremation." The physician's eyes were as hard and relentless as Richard's grip. "It's in Army regulations, Corporal, so don't touch me again."

"Captain, doctors *tell* people first. We might have preferred burial—decent funeral services, a few words—"

"Take my word for it, Corporal Grant," said Witsell, bluntly, "it's better that you didn't see it."

He pushed Molly's door open then.

How *naked* she looked. Richard hesitated, fractionally, then began limping toward the bed. His feelings seemed appropriate now and tears slid down his cheeks, but the finely honed, detached mind Richard was coming to despise worked better than ever under pressure. They'd seen that about him early on, and liked it at once, the way he did what he had to do better when his emotions were aroused than when he wasn't especially interested. Something about his unique way of transforming an automatic, gut response to instant action. Molly had been clad in a nightgown of her own, and her hair briefly brushed; the covers were up over her restored belly, but she looked naked anyway. Maybe it was the absence of makeup and the sallow and clinical look of the light on her blonde hair, but probably it was the way in which she was also showing him the way she felt inside, holding nothing back.

He dropped to his knees beside her, careless of his bad leg, taking her outflung hand.

"Did you see him?" she asked, eagerly. "Isn't our Mark the most beautiful thing in the history of the universe?"

Richard's upward, darting glance caught the expression on her doctor's face. Part of it was sheer I-told-you-so. Part of it was a smile. Then there was no expression at all.

"Oh, Molly," Richard gasped, leaning forward solicitously to press his cheek against hers. "They didn't tell you, did they?"

To his surprise, her chin bobbed. Her light, nearly violet eyes were solemn, only distantly mirroring the slightest anxiety. "Yes, another man was in here after Doctor Witsell and everybody left, and he t-told me Mark was stillborn." Her fingers closed on his hand, squeezed. He realized that the effects of the anesthetic lingered. Her breath was foul. "Isn't that perfectly ridiculous?"

The man in white loomed above them. He withdrew her hand from Richard's, let it hang limply from the wrist; he counted. His glance was brief, but studied as well as firm. "Mrs. Grant, I'm afraid it's true. Your baby was stillborn." Richard's turn, then, to feel the frigid gaze "Isn't it, Corporal Grant?"

Molly spared him from making a choice. "But that's absurd!" She frowned, clearly trying to concentrate. Abruptly, she tried to sit up. "It's absurd because I *saw* my little boy being born!"

Richard inhaled sharply, froze. She was twisting to face him, panic rising now into her familiar, delicate features. He had no idea what to say.

"Richard, listen!" She leaned toward him with growing desperation. "The other man was mistaken. I told him that, told him he was confusing our baby with—with some other poor woman's baby. Mark is *fine.*" Her nails pierced the flesh of his hand. "He is, I *know* he's fine."

"Sweetheart; Molly, honey." He searched furiously, frantically, for the proper words. From the corner of his eye he watched Captain Witsell head silently toward the door, his stride purposeful; then he was murmuring to someone in the corridor. He extricated his hand with difficulty. "Dear girl, the doctors . . ."

A male orderly came into the room, a methodical, feline wraith with fine cat's whiskers. He carried a small tray, a half concealed syringe. Richard saw him approaching, appearing bored as he regarded Molly. Richard's leg muscles tensed, bunched. But this was all routine, it was "something" that "happened." It wasn't uncommon. Because she'd wanted this child so badly she couldn't give him up. Stretching past Richard, the orderly was efficient with his jab, and plunge; the husband turned away.

"*Damn* you!" Molly slapped, awkwardly, hazily; but the man was already near the door, chore completed, disappearing. "*Damn* you!" she called after him, unaware perhaps that he'd gone. "Don't you dare treat me as if I'd gone crazy, do you hear me? Do you?" Bewildered but intense, almost fevered, she took Richard's face between her slim, hot palms. "Honey, tell them I don't imagine things! Tell them I *saw* our baby! Darling, I *heard* him, I *heard* him!"

"Molly—"

"I heard him, I *heard* our baby, I *saw* him, *I heard him!*"

He parted his dry lips to speak. Then, she wasn't there. Losing consciousness from the sedative's swift influence, it was as if she had turned to liquid and flowed away. She sagged and Richard eased her back to the bed, watched her blonde hair fan out on the pillow like so many golden rivulets returning to some shining, ancient sea.

Richard stood. Witsell was watching, just inside the door. He went to the doctor. "My wife doesn't imagine things." There was nothing mechanical in his voice, but the conviction in it grew as he continued to speak. His curly, dark hair felt as if it had been tugged to expose an incipient headache. He'd bathed twice a day since getting back, scrubbing, but everything about him smelled incessantly sour. "She saw our baby and she says Mark was born alive."

"Don't touch me," the doctor said levelly, "or I'll summon someone."

"I only want to know what's going on here, Captain, what's happening." Tears of exhaustion smarted and Richard blinked them back. "You're asking me to take your side against my wife, the only person who's given me any happiness for years. Tell me how I can do a thing like that."

"You can do it because you respect truth, and facts. Corporal, what conceivable purpose would we have in lying to you?" The words reflected more concern than the officer's inflection. But as Witsell stretched his neck, craned it, and rubbed it, his own weariness was clear and disarming. He, too, had been there all night. "I'm a doctor, remember? I don't want to throw a lot of clichés at you, but it's a fact that I swore an oath to save lives. You can relate to that, can't you? You understand it?"

The inclination was to nod, to give it up. Molly, asleep across the room, seemed so small. He looked back miserably. "Explain."

"I can't explain what went wrong inside Mark; I won't lie to you about that. Nature has a way, from time to time, of showing good sense, of disposing of those who would be insupportable burdens on the parents and never be able themselves to enjoy a productive or pleasant life. Fundamentally, Grant, what the hell difference does it make *what* was your boy's problem? Knowing wouldn't give him so much as a single breath of life."

Finally, Richard did nod. He got out a handkerchief and blew his nose.

"This, Richard, I *can* tell you: You'll be able to have more children. If the two of you decide you want to try again, Molly's perfectly capable." He revealed the bruised wrist; lightly touched Richard's bicep. It was a gesture of ordinary humanity so late in being offered that it came close to reducing Richard to tears. "I repeat, there's nothing wrong with Mrs. Grant except for what she is fantasizing, and that, as I said before we entered the room, is not uncommon."

"But what do I do about that?"

Captain Alfred Witsell raised his injured wrist, inspecting it with medical expertise for the first time. He wriggled his fingers, grunted. His eyes glittered as he glanced at Richard. "There are procedures," he said, "but let's figure on starting with psychiatric counseling." He started for the door.

"How's the wrist?"

Witsell looked back, smiled. "I'll live. We all will."

3

The summer of 1967 came into the Grants' one
story, sparsely furnished house with the breathy
familiarity of a fat and wheezing old woman who
had failed to phone first. It was thickly oblivious to
their already unmanageable assemblage of demanding, psychic boarders; reeking, it settled heavily
upon the sagging furniture with its legs straddled
steamingly, fanning itself as it droned an intolerable, ancient history—a midsummer night's
memoir of all the service families since Truman, and
Hiroshima. Like any uninvited, garrulous neighbor,
the summer-woman reveled in the private fears of
the prior tenants, drawing narrow satisfaction from
knowing its own turgid part in sending them on
their way. The season was clearly a conspiratorial ally of the nearby Army post, and Richard Grant
longed to acknowledge his abject surrender and flee
with Molly into a more comfortable, civilian life.

But they could go nowhere until she made an
acknowledgment of her own and displayed evidence
of her healthy adjustment to it—to a realization
and, at the least, an embryonic acceptance of the

fact that her firstborn, Mark, had never seen her or any portion of the world of living beings.

Several days ago, with joy, anticipation, and a swollen belly, she had left the drab government owned house, peopled already in her imagination with all those dear persons whom her child was intended to become: from cuddly infant to adorable toddler, from the brave little boy beginning the first grade to a lanky teenager making her so deliciously proud when he earned all A's and B's, then came to consult her on the question of which college scholarship to select. Molly hadn't doubted that the child growing in her womb would be male. Even when those first, really sharp pains of labor came, she'd known that the tiny house a stone's throw away already was filled with young Mark's spirit, his indomitable essence.

But she had returned empty-handed, instead, her aching arms at her strangely fleshless sides; and no place in her experience had seemed so deserted, so devoid of human life. When she'd steeled herself to enter the bedroom, Richard clumsily consoling in her wake, Molly had scarcely suppressed a shudder. Mark's crib and blue basinette, miniature potty chair and several leering, stuffed toys bunched almost resentfully against the wall, trailed attenuated shadows like fingers of dark entreaty. Peculiarly haunted, Molly traced the outline of the snowy bedsheet of a chubby, cherubic form, and yearned for his small, pale ghost to reach up, beseeching her ready, maternal comfort.

Then she'd reminded herself secretly that sweet little Mark might not have died at all—that he had certainly been born alive with the primary article of faith—but been accidentally misplaced, probably swapped for another mother's stillborn baby.

Military inefficiency, their stupid carelessness with people's lives, was legendary. Her physician father, Doctor Skylar, had said so, often enough. She'd felt both Richard's caring hand upon her arm and his uncomprehending distance, and loathed him. Someday she would get him to believe her—him, or somebody—and a search would be instigated. Someday, then, Mark would be restored to her and the others could see what fools they had been to doubt her.

She couldn't let Richard remove Mark's things because he'd be needing them.

She thought about it all, mostly, at nights.

But for the time being, Molly was doing her best to find and to tread a difficult, narrow line—one intended to accommodate both her husband's emotional needs and her own. Raising her head slightly from her pillow, she gazed down at the still healing wound in Richard's leg. Frowning, vaguely disgusted, she turned away from him, on her side. Understanding that he had little choice except to go along with Doctor Witsell, Molly refrained from discussing the baby at all. Even when, out of apparent concern for her well-being, he broached the matter, Molly grunted something terse. She was not about to be placed in the position of choosing between husband and child. She'd read enough magazines this past year to know how dumb that would be!

Besides, she could not voice her conviction that she'd seen Mark born, anesthetics or not, without an upwelling of her emotions, even her tears, and Molly definitely did not wish to hear some cold, masculine lecture on logic from one Richard Bruce Grant!

It was bad enough, trying to tolerate the persistently calm, detached questions posed by Doctor Maxwell Silverstein, the Army shrink. She'd seen

him daily in the hospital and had had to agree to
visit him in order to be released. The same hospital
that swapped helpless infants around as if they were
old M-14s or fatigues!

Sighing, hot, Molly kicked the sheet from her own
legs. Richard's nonstop snoring proclaimed his own
acceptance of their terrible loss, Molly felt, and his
easy-as-pie adjustment to it. Sometimes she
wondered why a word had been invented—
"father"—to designate the male part of the birth
process. It was she who'd carried the child in her
own body for nine months while its "father" was
thousands of miles away, shooting a gun like a boy
who'd never grown up. And worse, taking the lives
of other mothers' sons! She wondered if he'd ever
given a thought, or had a truly sad feeling, about the
fact that his own flesh-and-blood offspring had been
misplaced or died, that he would never have a
chance to watch the wonderful ways of a growing
child. When they'd talked about it that one time,
before Doctor Witsell and Doctor Silverstein said
she might become an outpatient, all she had seen in
Richard's overgrown boy's face was his worry for
her and his perfectly obvious yen to resume their old
life, as if nothing had happened to change it! As if
having another child would somehow replace Mark,
and all the unique qualities he had, qualities never
possessed by any other human being since the dawn
of time!

Her one consolation was how much Richard
despised both her doctors and how angry he'd been
after the balding, impeccable Silverstein inter-
viewed them both and asked a lot of questions about
their life together. Worse, from Richard's point of
view, had been the fifty minutes he spent along with
the psychiatrist, answering questions about his

boyhood and his parents. "What in the hell that has
to do with *your* pregnancy and beliefs, I'll never
know!" Richard had nearly shouted, turning red-
faced below his fringe of tight, dark curls. "He's
just trying to get a bunch of cheap jollies!" Where-
upon Molly had giggled, barely hiding her smile to
keep him from getting angrier.

   She craned her neck, and studied Richard in sleep.
That silly, curly head of his was what had drawn her
to him at the start. Now, even after fighting in Vietnam, he still seemed like a teenaged boy to her, with
a crazy kind of innocence and naiveté that Molly
could never have put into words. She knew, vaguely,
that he'd learned a lot about hand-to-hand combat
and she suspected he might have had to defend
himself, but that seemed so unlikely, when she
looked at his sleeping form. He claimed he was five
nine and weighed one seventy-five but she doubted
if he was five eight and one sixty-five. He had a
rounded, almost hairless jawline, bony shoulders,
and big feet. Awake, his light-colored eyes ranged
from an apologetic and melancholy severity about
life, which was apparently uncharacteristic of the
Richard she had adored for the time they'd been together, to a glibly ribald, sometimes manic joy for
virtually everyone and everything upon this
plundered and plundering planet. Liberated and
uninvolved, Richard showed an exuberance of affection which was, at such times, all encompassing, as
well as the soft, vulnerable outer shell beneath
which he worked at disciplining his boundless determination and cocky, male self-assurance.

   How *smart* Richard might be, since he cared
about being liked and often force fed himself hip
custom and slang the way less intelligent young
men taught themselves history or sentence

structure, Molly was only beginning to perceive. It did not necessarily cheer her, especially now. Intelligence didn't count for a lot with Molly, except when it seemed capable of alarming, even terrifying. Her father's citations and plaques did not include an award for Best Husband or Dad of the Year. If there was a meaningful connection between intelligence and success, she could not see it. Once, laughing, Richard even had called her, "My favorite stereotype," and then had been obliged to reassure her that he hadn't meant to insult her. She still wondered if he had.

Molly always had tried to keep most things on the surface instead of dangerously plumbing the depths, even where her own values and attitudes were involved. What fascination Richard found in probing the complexity of human motivations, especially on paper, escaped Molly totally. What he read or tried to learn, what story lines he developed from his analysis, and what he might or might not believe in had nothing to do with what she loved about her husband. The fact that he was "talented," too, a term she linked with her father's medical skill, with sewing by hand and preserving jams, merely complicated things.

What I love about him? She framed the words with her lips, tasting them, almost marveling and certainly surprised by the unbidden, unconscious thoughts. *The Richard I've adored . . .*

Smiling, shifting her slight weight in bed carefully to avoid awakening him, Molly put out a small hand to touch the dark, damp hair curving at Richard's temple. *I do love you, you silly, stubborn man,* she remembered with a sheen of tears that veiled her eyes like rain brought by chanted prayer.

And, *You would have made a marvelous father.*

* * *

Two further days passed. With them, also, two further meetings between Molly and Doctor Maxwell Silverstein, and twenty minutes of Richard Grant's life placed in that worthy's care. After he'd taken Molly home, he went to see Captain Henry McCaffrey, his company commander.

"The experts are getting nowhere at the speed of light," he asserted. Although he had been on good terms with Captain McCaffrey, it was only now, when he was definitely leaving the service, that Richard felt free to express his true thoughts. *Some* of them.

"The age of miracles was a few centuries ago, Dicky-bird." McCaffrey, somewhere in his middle thirties, looked trim even when he slouched. "I suspect you're one of those literary chaps who regard writers as the superiors of psychologists when it comes to understanding the workings of the human mind."

"I'm certain of it, sir," Richard replied with a nod. He felt his belly tense the way it always had when he found it a matter of pride to support his convictions in the face of authority figures. "People have always had mental disturbances. Before Grandfather Freud came on the scene, it was writers who tried to solve their problems—in books, at any rate. Have you ever noticed, sir, how the leading modern shrinks can't wait to put their views on paper?"

McCaffrey's frown, with his chin sucked into his uniform collar, turned the lower portion of his face into a mass of creases, crevices, and pale lines. Richard thought of a cream-horn. And that the captain must have sampled some saucy little wine at the officers' club last night. "Feelings of superiority are awf'ly important to you, aren't they,

Dicky-bird? Those questions about your sex life diminish you in some way?''

"There's more to Molly's unconscious, or mine, than what we've done in the sack. Or the idea that one of us has a thing for his parents.''

"You've always resisted authority, haven't you?'' McCaffrey was laboring to avoid lifting the lid of his right eye more than the marginal needs of vision. "Witsell remarked upon your aggressive ways, Dicky-bird.'' Suddenly the eye was visible, stark and staring with owlish ferocity. "One might almost believe you question the probity of your betters.''

An hour later, allowed to leave, Richard reminded himself that it was only a matter of weeks before he'd no longer have to suffer such abuse without civil, civilian resources. Alone, he told himself that, if his separation date rolled round and Mrs. Richard Grant then remained unwell and military treatment was withheld, he might look to the filing of a lawsuit. One that would definitely be widely inclusive.

Molly, the day after, saw Richard grinning broadly as he left her in the office of a new psychiatrist, a woman. Captain Lenore Bianchi.

But for the next three days and a trio of sessions which excluded him, Molly said little about her discussions with Bianchi. There was only the whispered comment, "Making progress.'' It sounded almost like a reproach. If it was true, Richard wasn't able to see it; Molly had taken to arising in the middle of the night and smoothing the unused sheets in the baby crib, sometimes standing at the bedroom window to stare out at nothing Richard could see.

Because he'd been given no duty assignment aside from showing up for roll call in the mornings, he employed the time alone to investigate the train of thought which he found instantly agonizing and difficult: What if Molly could not be persuaded to accept little Mark's stillbirth—*because she was right?*

Changed to civilian garb, an old sports shirt from his personal dark ages open to the sweaty waist, Richard sipped good German beer, tried to sort it out. It occurred to him immediately that, had he suffered some brain injury, nothing in this world would persuade him that he hadn't been in Vietnam, hadn't come close to losing his leg.

Then there were the other matters, each in itself minor, which disturbed him about that night of his interminable hospital waiting. Some appeared improbable, anomalous, at first: the fact that a colonel had not only inquired about the progress of a corporal's pregnant wife but approached him personally about reenlisting. Neither, clearly, was drastically out of line; some career officers were bachelors, long divorced or widowers; without a convenient war to keep them busy, they surely walked their commands at odd hours.

But what of the fact that his wound was so bad it couldn't make him a prime recruiting catch? If he re-upped, it would mean a desk job, probably stateside. Why would they want him to stay in?

And there was the fact that the colonel in question never had removed his hat, a breech of courtesy, inside a building, even in the military.

Richard pressed the beer can against his forehead, aware that his nerves were taut. He recognized the feeling; he'd known it, often enough, in Nam. The only thing lacking was the accompanying urge to evacuate his bowels.

Pouring with a trembling hand, he paused to frown at the lowering summer sky beyond their front room window. That orderly, the one who'd seemed effete, and secretive—he'd been assisting a *male* patient, down the corridor from where Mark was born dead. That seemed strange. Were there rooms for female patients off the corridor one reached through the operating areas? He'd gone to visit Molly, of course, but she'd seemed to be the only patient on that part of the floor. Was it possible there were operating surgeries and recovery rooms specifically for women patients elsewhere in the hospital, and, if so, why had they taken Molly into an area that seemed reserved for male patients?

That evening, after he'd picked up Molly at the hospital entrance and brought her home, she was exceptionally quiet. He was on the verge of cross-examining her concerning her memory of the emerging child, when she called him to the kitchen.

She was wearing an apron, preparing dinner. She had tears in her eyes but she was smiling, putting out her arms to him.

"We talked about it today, Doctor Bianchi and I," she said.

He buried his face in her mass of yellow hair and hoped she wouldn't hear his thundering heart. "Darling," he began, hesitating. "About what, exactly?"

"The chance that I might just be deluding myself, because I wanted to." She hugged herself against him from head to toe as if she might never willingly release him. "About the possibility that my unconscious mind made it all up."

"Oh, baby," he said in a breath, kissing her neck.

"Doctor Bianchi is simply wonderful, I have the impression I've always known her." She stopped talking, tensing. Before he could ask what the matter was, she continued. "I feel guilty as sin."

"Why, exactly?"

She shrugged, against him, and it was his turn to hold on forever. "I dunno. Because—because now I'm actually starting to consider it myself." Molly made a strangling sound. "And it makes me feel like I'm *abandoning* Mark."

Later, she told Richard that Doctor Bianchi wanted to speak with him the next day.

"There was no reason for you to be surprised by Molly's reaction to the death of your son."

Richard looked at her across an expanse of desk which, quite clearly, Doctor Lenore Bianchi had paid for with her own money. He felt miles distant from her, but it wasn't the size of the desk alone. She sat well back from it; on her side, there was a gulf between her and it. Whether it was because she was farsighted, felt confined when she pressed against the desk, or wanted her patients to see how lovely she was, Richard couldn't be sure.

But he'd have put twenty dollars on the idea that Lenore Bianci knew what an impression she made, and rather liked it.

"Why shouldn't I have been surprised?" he asked tonelessly.

"It doesn't require testing to determine how masculine you are, at least in your primary attitudes, Corporal." She gave him a smile which passed smug and veered sharply, on an incline, toward superior. With her forest of deep red hair, the smile was like something shining in a fireplace.

"Is that bad, Captain?" His own heavy, massive leather chair felt unbudgeable and it, too, was two feet back from the gleaming desk. "Seeing that I am a man?"

"Not if your attitudes are an accurate reflection of your hormonal balance and all that." She held an ornate desk lighter to a filter cigarette and he hadn't seen her hands move. "None of us is entirely feminine or masculine, you know."

He gave her a brittle smile. "Yes, I do, but it's hard to believe, looking at either one of us. Captain."

"I'll take that as a compliment, I believe."

"Do," Richard coaxed.

"We are, as well, programmed by our environment, particularly during the first, crucial years when what we see pleases or displeases us. All that goes into the psychological mix to produce preferences of sexual and other kinds."

"I'm a writer. Writers must be observant, and thoughtful, to be any good." He'd lit a cigarette of his own, but when he leaned forward to tap the ash in a tray, his arms were too short. He paused, then let the ash fall to her carpeting. "I'm reasonably certain Molly's preference is for men and mine is for women. Sexually, that is."

She didn't appear to have heard him. "As females grow, we tend to learn, unconsciously, in the main, how essentially frail we are and how we are encouraged to be unstable emotionally. We have, you see, had an opportunity to witness the struggles of our fathers, brothers, and those we begin to date. We've learned to walk that precarious mental tightrope which needn't concern maturing males."

"What tightrope is that, Doctor Bianchi?"

She looked back at him, frostily. He wondered if he'd ever seen a better-looking woman. Standing, she was tall without being presumptuous about it; standing or sitting, even her Army uniform could not make her magnificent figure altogether shapeless. Surely, he thought, the buttoned jacket was snug enough to pinch. "The tightrope strung, and

sustained for women, by the males of society.
Consider the way a growing female observes the
scarcely suppressed sexual hostility which her
father directs not only toward his wife but his
daughter. His rare, even daring moments of human
warmth contrast sharply with the attitudes his
daughter senses about his business concerns—for
Business, with a large B, is the last, vestigial battlefield of the aggressive, death-fearing but death-dealing male."

"I'm not hoping to go into business, with a large
or small B." Richard had used up his cigarette in
record time and wanted to grind it into the rug.
Instead, he rose, put it out in Lenore Bianchi's ash-
tray, and drew within five feet of her glittering,
green eyes. "I'm the creative type." He paused.
"Death-dealing male?"

"I'd heard that you regarded writers as superior
psychologists." She tapped the file simply marked
GRANT with a blood red nail, and held his gaze
until he'd taken his seat. "Are you aware that
certain behavioral psychologists and others perceive
female human beings as living symbols of life, males
as living symbols of death? A death males are
utterly compelled to attempt to inflict, however,
um, representationally?"

"You'd give a whole bunch to see me lose my
temper, wouldn't you, Captain Bianchi?" He folded
his hands behind his head, and tried leaning back
indolently. It hurt his neck but he stayed that way.
"To prove how much I want to hurt people, right?"

"A woman who is pregnant, Corporal Grant,
regardless of how well she had made progress in
male-oriented society, is especially prone to the
primitive attitudes which people of your sex
continue to endorse and promulgate—consciously as

well as unconsciously. Those views, demands, call
them what you wish, come rushing in at the
pregnant woman. The impact is more than a
command, however: it is an imperative. And she
does not even resist, in most cases." The redhead
nearly beamed. "Molly Skylar Grant did not offer
even token resistance."

"For the record," Richard murmured, "I don't
like you much, Captain. Which keeps that record
straight, I believe. Even."

"Do I scratch your vanity, Corporal?" She arose,
briskly, believably military as she drifted around
the desk without looking at him. "Pity, when I
speak professionally, not personally. You see, the
validating requirement to reproduce becomes as
urgently important to the pregnant female as it is to
any animal. If she fails to deliver the *ideal,* the
perfect human child, she is lost; defeated."

"By what?" As he craned his neck to peer up at
her, the pain was worse, but the doctor was easily
the most pleasing one to see in Richard's experience.
"Or by whom? The husband?"

"Only in part." Bianchi turned to him, leaning
against the front of her desk. Somehow she had
another cigarette in one long, slender hand, but
there was little suggestion of intimacy. The desk
was too wide for that. "Pregnant, a young woman is
plugged into eons of racial consciousness. Generally,
it is still more clearly spelled out for her by other
females, from Mama to Auntie, from Sister to Girl
Friend. And this, Corporal, is the message: *Nothing*
except producing the healthy, ideal child—prefer-
ably male—will authenticate a claim to ordinary . . .
worthwhileness." She smiled. "I'm obliged to coin a
word, you see. It is something rather beyond simple
acceptance, because, by the time the child is born, it

is what she feels, herself."

For the first time Richard realized he had heard something informative. "Are you confirming, then, that Molly imagined—fantasized—that our son was born alive?"

"Come, Corporal!" She faced him and he shoved himself to his feet, his leg gone numb. She was taller than he was in flat military heels and she was even more beautiful close up. It was too bad, he thought, that she was probably a Lesbian. He might have been tempted. "You didn't seriously believe what she said, did you?"

"I guess," he replied, aware of her nearness, "I was willing to try."

"Perhaps you'll make it as a writer," Bianchi said softly. "I've been trying to make you understand that women of Molly's kind and background are incessantly tested by male-dominant society and that she has felt responsible for an ultimate failure. I've managed to implant the tiny nugget of reality in her mind by dealing, first, with getting her to understand that she needn't be quite so *cooperative* with the imperatives of society. I'll be seeing her again but, in one sense, I've done all I can for Molly. The rest will be up to you."

"How?" Richard asked, spreading his hands. "How can I help her?"

Lenore Bianchi rested the palm of her hand on his chest, and left it there. "By making sure she has another child as soon as possible, a fine, healthy, living child." She paused as if waiting. "I've always enjoyed tests, personally—intriguing challenges. They bring out the best in me. What about you, Corporal?"

He chuckled, and turned to limp toward the door. " 'Women of Molly's kind,' I think that was your snide little term, also happen to be women of *my* kind, Captain." He looked back at her, rather ruefully. "They're quite enough challenge for me."

"How did it go?"

He glanced up from the newspaper and smiled at Molly. "Actually, it was pretty stimulating."

"I'm glad you like Doctor Bianchi."

Richard met her gaze, thinking how pretty she looked in the doorway to the small kitchen, and wondering how to help her the rest of the way.

Very possibly, he reflected, the stunning redhead had outsmarted him after all. Because it wouldn't be in the least surprising if Captain Bianchi had administered her own test, to him—to learn if he was the kind of man whom Molly needed during this period of transition.

Undressing for bed, it occurred to Richard to wonder if he'd passed the test or flunked it.

When Molly remained disinclined to make love, he wondered the same thing all over again.

4

Agreeing to consider the possibility that she'd been
self-deluding about the events surrounding her
delivery proved to be a powerful stimulus toward
recovery for Molly Grant. She astonished herself by
beginning to drive again and, by the close of that
week, she was going alone to her appointments with
Doctor Bianchi—not without trepidation, but with a
resurgence of courage and the vague realization that
she needed to start helping herself.

Richard, standing in the early afternoon sunlight
to watch his young wife pull away from the curb,
breathed a deep sigh of relief and grinned with fresh
hope. Nothing about it was over. He understood
that. It might take a year or more before there was
anything normal again, about the marriage, and
years before Molly could again agree to try—to try
to become the mother of a healthy, living child.
After all, she was bravely attempting to do something certain psychiatrists had claimed to be impossible: she was setting out purposefully to forget,
when trying not to think about a matter of
importance was a contradiction in terms.

That was why getting Molly to inch forward toward accepting the nature of her understandable, maternal fantasy had been so vital. Without it, she might never have crawled slowly to a standing stage: consciously agreeing with him, with Doctor Lenore Bianchi and Doctor Witsell, then repeating it to herself sufficiently for her unconscious mind to begin approaching conviction. Becoming persuaded that little Mark's death was a pitiable but unarguable fact.

To Richard, Molly's request to take their old car and cope with her own daily psychiatric sessions was an outstanding, even amazing evidence of her progress. That day, buoyant, he dug out his old Royal 440 and began writing once more. Soon the burden of earning a livelihood would become entirely his. It was high time to look to his responsibilities, as well as his needs.

His initial efforts bore fruit as his first short story in years. Eagerly criticizing it, a few hours after finishing the yarn, he saw at once that it was unpublishable in terms of the major magazine markets. Nonetheless, his creative labors had furnished him with other delights.

In the first place, it wasn't actually an awful story. The premise wasn't particularly fresh but he'd developed it with originality. Richard saw that he'd lost little of his facility with words and was pleased. Simply attempting to create again enabled him to discover that he was fairly bursting with ideas.

Which meant the best news of all: that he enjoyed writing more than any other of the potential money-making enterprises he could imagine pursuing after his imminent discharge from service. Yes, it would be an arduous climb to the level at which his work was consistently published; but it wasn't impossible and he believed Molly was the ideal, supportive wife to provide encouragement when the inevitable rejection slips began flowing in.

Or would be, once she was herself again.

At the end of one lengthy afternoon session in late August, Molly finally heard what she'd longed to hear. Speaking calmly, deliberately, Doctor Bianchi said there was nothing more she could do to help the younger woman, and tomorrow would be the last fifty minutes of psychiatric evaluation—God willing —in Molly's life.

That night, Richard rejoiced with her, and did what he could to assure her that it was really the time to begin anew—to leave the Army behind, and every miserable, lonely moment the two of them had experienced.

Molly's farewell to the beautiful Bianchi was more tearful than she'd intended and she clung to the psychiatrist until she realized what she was doing. Still blinking, but sniffing and smiling at the same time, Molly started the car and headed toward their rented house. In only a couple of days, Richard and she would be driving to Washington and the realization of it brought a sense of overwhelming love for him. In return for her agreement to get a job and pitch in financially until his writing began to be productive, Richard was offering her the gift of returning to the D.C. area of her girlhood. Although Dad Skylar was with his second wife in Indianapolis now, the neighborhood Molly had chosen was near to many old friends and not a few members of her family.

Nearing the little one-story, she found her heart bursting with the kind of feelings she'd experienced after graduating from high school—an elation born of impending freedom, of dazzling change, or going home again.

She stopped the car at the curb, bowing her head. Whatever else was true, she wouldn't be returning in triumph with her own baby son carefully pressed to her heart. It was neither a victory nor, she saw for the first time, a defeat. It was simply starting over. And trying neither to cry nor to think, Molly wasn't aware, for half a minute, of the music fairly dinning from her old, rented Army property.

Then she caught a glimpse of Richard through the window, wearing some kind of crazy hat and gesturing to her to come inside. *What in the world . . . ?*

Curious despite herself, Molly slipped out from behind the wheel and walked quickly up to the door.

Grinning like a madman, Richard threw open the door and, when her startled lips parted, thrust a party horn into her mouth! *"Surprise!"* he shouted, plunking a screaming-red paper hat on her head and snapping the rubber band beneath her chin. He reached out, violently hugging her and pulling her into the house at the same time, nearly making her choke on the toy horn. To her utter astonishment, he executed a perfect cartwheel, threw out his arms in lunatic gesture, and cried, "It's *parrrrrrrr-ty time!"*

Cued up with the wonderful precision of a radio station engineer, a recording began blaring a sentimental Irish melody—"Sweet Molly Malone"—on their twenty-dollar 45 player.

Breathless, alternately laughing and fighting back tears, Molly stared at the decorations Richard had strewn around the tiny house.

MERRY CHRISTMAS! shrieked a red and green banner above the door leading to the small kitchen. A grinning, orange, plastic pumpkin sat squatly on a table. Beside it, collapsed in a chair, a Halloween dummy Richard had hastily constructed from an old jacket and pants, plus a grocery sack for the head, seemed to give Molly an affable wave. On the curtains hung before the front room window, when Richard pranced over to close them, was a streamer depicting a naked girl in a champagne glass and the legend, HAPPY NEW YEAR!

"You idiot!" she cried, pivoting.

Everywhere she looked, Molly encountered the trappings of holiday—a stuffed groundhog with a goofy grin; lifesized cutouts of Thanksgiving turkeys; a poster saying HAPPY ST. PAT'S from the twisted smile of a sozzled Irishman; several toy bunny rabbits two feet high, with Richard's home-made sign—HAPPY EASTER!—pinned to their plump undersides.

Molly's nose twitched like those of the stuffed bunnies. "What do I smell?" she demanded. "Richard Bruce Grant, what are you cooking?"

"A real turkey!" he exclaimed, looking maniacally proud. He blew his own toy horn at her and it turned into an absurd tongue, which licked her cheek. "With all the fixings, although"—he paused, giving her a rakish wink—"they may require a little *further* fixing by the lady of the house."

"You don't know how to roast a turkey!" She pointed her index finger at him, accusingly, trying not to laugh. "You don't know how to cook *nuttin'!*"

"Didn't!" he protested, wiggling his eyebrows and raising his paper hat from his curly head. "I didn't know how, but today, I learned!"

"But what—"

He saw her bewildered expression, her helpless wave of a slim arm, and then he hopped like a bunny to a chair in the dinette. "But what is all this for?"

he demanded, finishing it for her. "'Why did a
reasonably talented, fairly normal, average kind of
husband like yours truly go to *absolutely no* expense
and trouble to produce such a miracle as greets your
incredible orbs?'' He hopped back to her with two
gaily wrapped boxes, put one in her unprotesting
hands. "*This* box of candy is for Valentine's Day,"
he said, momentarily hiding the other behind his
back, "and *this* marvelous, massive, utterly
delicious box of the finest chocolates known to man
is for the two anniversaries we didn't share
together!"

Molly shook her head, thunderstruck. Then, her
arms starting to ache, she had an inkling of what he
was up to and leaned forward to kiss him. "I think I
get it," she said softly.

"I think you're gonna!" He reached over the
boxes she was holding to kiss her back, and reached
around her with his hands to pinch her bottom.
"This crap is my humble best shot at making up for
all the holidays and assorted good times we've
missed, and I don't think I overlooked a thing." He
pulled a ragged calendar from his hip pocket so she
could see the dates he'd checked off with a black
marker. "Elsewhere in this mess I've made of the
house you'll find an American flag for Veterans
Day, a checkered flag your father sent me for
Memorial Day—remember, they have the 500-mile
Race in Indianapolis then—and a couple of boxes of
highly illegal fireworks, so that we can celebrate the
Fourth of July."

"You're still an idiot," Molly murmured, putting
her gifts on a chair and turning into his arms, "but a
wonderful idiot."

"Hey, I wondered when you'd figure that out!"
He was grinning but she saw that his eyes were

moist. "But I did this for another reason, too, babe.
Because we're truly starting out on our own, the
right way at last, and I figure that's reason enough
for a celebration." He stretched on tiptoe to kiss her
eyelids. "Maybe life isn't exactly the way either of
us would choose, but it's not over and we're
together. I hope you'll give me a chance to prove I
can still make it a nice life, for both of us."

The turkey was, to no one's surprise, the next best
thing to inedible. After Richard had chewed in-
dustriously on a leg and Molly had fought her way
through a rubbery breast, which she referred to as
"the worst falsie I ever saw," he arose and excused
himself. Ruefully, he produced an unopened package
of Stark & Wetzel hotdogs, pointedly placing them
next to Molly's plate.

She began to giggle. "If you ever waste our hard-
earned money like this again," she swore, filling a
pan and turning on the gas, "I'll lay you low!"

"Speaking of laying," Richard intoned in his best
Groucho Marx, flicking imaginary ash and inclining
his head in the direction of their bedroom.

There was the briefest of pauses. Then Molly
looked over from the stove with a tremulous smile.
"I can take a hint, Ricardo." She crossed to where
he sat at the wooden table, reached down to take his
hands. "A person would have to be thick as a
damned mountain to miss *this* enormous hint.
Idiot!"

They made love tentatively, gropingly, then with
an urgent desire to please the other. That night was
the first time in months and it served the purpose
which each of them had in mind. Although it wasn't
especially fulfilling, because it verged upon the
mechanical and because Richard was fearful he
would hurt her, the act itself created a bridge

between them, one they hoped would remain long after they'd physically pulled apart. They didn't express it in words, but each of them silently prayed it would be a bridge not only for accessibility to one another, but to the new, or altered, frontiers they were slowly starting to envision.

In the middle of the night, Richard found himself sitting up in bed, sweating profusely. Without adequate time to wonder what had brought him to abrupt wakefulness, he heard Molly whimper.

She was sound asleep and crying with no more passion, or vehemence, than a little girl. He saw that when he leaned over to inspect her tear-swept face, and whispered "child-woman," not for the first time. She was bathed by a shower of white moonlight falling from a window edged by the sweltering summer's night, her yellow hair pressed back at one side by her much-tugged pillow. Molly had the kind of appeal in her features that appeared at once achingly youthful and vulnerable, yet knowing and eager to know more. His gaze swept to the rise of her pale flank, to the five o'clock shadow of her lately shaven underbody, then back to adore the way her rather frail arms were folded over her breasts. Molly was having a nightmare, but she would have called it a dream.

He lay back down, both affectionately and physically aroused, and knew he did not need to ask her why she wept. Even then, she was questing for a son lost in a limbo which, like little Mark himself, could not truly exist.

Except in a mother's empty and unforgetting heart.

Some men who are pushing fifty have presumably sipped from a fountain of youth, possibly during that strange phenomenon called Out-of-Body-Experience. Rather than being seized and taken aboard a UFO, doomed forever to find their names trailing such words as "Abductee" and "Neurotic Hoaxter," whatever finer credentials they might boast, such men know only that they are "blessed with looking young" and that nothing they've done, in terms of not drinking or smoking, will explain their luck.

Doctor Conrad Skylar was far too dignified to have permitted himself unseemly flight of any kind, whether in his psychic undergarments or in the unsuitable company of three-foot-high aliens with globular skulls. As a rule, he drank not from deLeon's fountain of youth but a bottle of mineral water or, on special occasions, a good Scotch. Neat.

Molly's father, Doctor Skylar, who would technically turn fifty on his next natal day, also did not look thirty, forty, or, for that matter, fifty. At a casual glance, the most he generally vouchsafed all but a handful of intimates, the renowned and talented Conrad Skylar had appeared a ruddy, straight-spined fifty-eight since he was half that figure.

Skylar had thought it all through, once, a long while ago, arriving at an interesting conclusion: without consulting one of the newfangled computers, which he saw as a clear and present danger to independent cognitive activity, he reckoned that fifty-eight was the ideal age for a noteworthy physician. Thereafter, he had seemed to be precisely that age—no more, no less—up to the present time.

Perhaps that is why Doctor Skylar was balding before he turned thirty, yet possessed, in 1967, precisely the same short supply of sparse, hedge-like black.

In August of that year, however, the good doctor found that his usual iron control of his life and those of the people whom he considered his intimates appeared to be suffering a minor mudslide. He was irascible and short-tempered, more than was customarily the case, because—and Doctor Skylar knew it—he felt a quantity of covert guilt. Since the emotion was utterly fresh to him, he didn't know how to cope with it except by yelling at nurses and, for the first time, turning away from his second, much younger wife.

Conrad Skylar wished badly that he had offered to pay for his daughter's delivery of a child, just so long as she had gone to some private, "real" baby doctor. Whether young Mark (for that was to have been his name, and it was, by coincidence, the first name of his favorite grandfather, also a physician) might have been born alive with appropriate medical attention, he could only surmise. His guess, which was a professional one, after all, was that there would be a new Mark in the family if he, arguably the finest doctor practicing now in the Midwest, had done the right thing by Molly.

Doing what he could to learn the truth, Doctor Skylar had just this week commanded and received —thanks to the understanding of peers on the board of the American Medical Association—a copy of the Mark Grant death certificate. Now that he was coming off a twenty-hour stretch of charitable medicine at Wishard Hospital, he let his disciplined curiosity have its head and lay back on his office couch to study the certificate. It was, he saw immediately, completely in order, properly signed and witnessed; simultaneously the first and the last

question he wanted to pose were instantly
answered.

Skylar did something else, asked more questions,
anyway. It would have been Molly's kid, and now
that he finally took the time to think of it, he was
fond of her. He might even love her, he realized,
rising to make several brisk phone calls.

His professor friend from Johns Hopkins, with
whom he'd split many a fee during his long years in
Baltimore—D.C., phoned less than two hours later
with a report. "It doesn't actually seem to have been
anybody's sin of commission or omission, Conrad. I
spoke with Witsell. You were right; he was once a
student of mine. I'll grant you he seemed nervous as
all get-out, but that probably means he's worried
about a patient, losing sleep, or felt apprehensive
about one of his old instructors knocking him out of
bed."

"Then you feel as well that everything possible
was done for my daughter and the fetus?" Doctor
Skylar posed the question, then listened attentively
for the reply.

"I'm not going to step into that one, Conrad," the
colleague said with lazy camaraderie. "I wasn't
there. As a matter of fact, Witsell mentioned somebody else in Delivery with him at the time, but *I* had
no part of it. My guess is, with the modern research
going on at military facilities these days, your
grandson-to-be had his best shot right where he
missed the target."

Skylar grunted something, tugged at his long
upper lip. Already he was formulating another
approach, to another contact. Doctors weren't
doctors because they had intuitive flights of mystic
knowing, but because they knew enough simply to

be thorough. To keep poking around until the truth popped into view.

"I am sorry about your grandchild, Doctor." A sympathetic note, as phony as the professor's long forgotten bedside manner. "Can Molly have others?"

"She can," Skylar retorted, snapping off the words. "The question is whether or not she will."

He rang off, jotted a name on the prescription pad in front of him in his indecipherable scrawl, and made another call. Surely somebody could be found who would make a simple declarative statement: *Had* the swiftly cremated Mark Grant been stillborn, or had something else happened?

Not long after he received a portion of the answer he sought, Doctor Conrad Skylar decided to drop the issue for awhile. Say, fifteen or twenty years.

He hadn't often been threatened, intimidated, and the balding physician wasn't sure about the proper response.

Doctor Skylar hoped cowardice was suitable.

PART TWO

THE UNFORGOTTEN

"We are going to have peace, even if we have to fight for it."

—General Dwight D. Eisenhower

5

On the verge of winter, the brick colonial's collected silences threw clinging shadows upon the three-decade-old floors; like a salesman's samples of unwanted wallpaper. When the man in his early forties started, in bed, stood and moved out into the folds of quiet, he was unsure why he'd awakened, and piqued. There was the disturbing impression of responding to a secret summons.

He did not go all the way to the second story landing where he could have craned his neck and glanced over the high railing to see if a prowler had entered. Instead, quiet in his bare feet and rumpled p-js, the middle-aged man paused beside his wife's family highboy in the hall. Its size reassured him.

Inside of it, old things lay in disuse and a pretense that it wasn't permanent; textile bones waiting for reassemblage. Absently, the man ran his fingertips over a burnished urn set atop the costly piece.

He shivered. It was conjured, fairly obligatory. He wasn't especially cold from the contact, not any more, but something freezing within him saw old recollections starting to drag across the attic of dusty memories.

The effort to make them scatter was conscious, and considerable. Perhaps, Richard mused, he'd been called to consciousness by the season change which paid scant homage to man's calendars, obeying instead some more harrowing imperative, one a creative person might share, somehow, in troubled sleep. Coming awake, parting from sleeping Molly, he'd been drawn instantly to the windows and seen the thin lace of snow patterning his small lot. It was that time, but he'd been newly surprised. In Washington, D.C., snow always seemed to come initially at dusk. Kin of the city's inconstant women, it stretched its pale slip over the contours of evening, and, by daylight, concealed nothing. Washington winters were more than merely feminine, though; they were shape-changers, succubi, frigid of body and spirit.

He sat on the steps full of sweetly singing similes, magical metaphors, and a terror at trying to put them on paper.

Because he didn't dare fail again.

Over the past three years, Richard Grant had known the bubbly triumph of a true bestseller. It had enabled the Grants to move into this neighborhood of government and military families of similar rank on the career ladder. He had also endured the id-fracturing failure of a second book. New ideas, possible plots and sparkling characters skyrocketed around inside his head whether he was awake or asleep.

But if the choice was wrong, this time, they'd plunge to earth and leave a crater deeper than the 1908 explosion in Siberia!

Publishers saw a writer as commercially viable on the strength of a recent, winning book, but the reading public had mashed Richard's confidence so

flat that he'd considered moving into nonfiction.
Any flop this time put Molly, their two daughters,
and this charming white pachyderm in the
Maryland suburbs—in charming Montgomery
County—in peril, along with him.

They'd gotten used to Nice Things. *And frankly,*
Richard mused, padding to the landing and lowering
his pajama clad buttocks to the top step, *I'm not
much in favor of the classical artistic life. Sacrificing
simple pleasures for surviving in a tenement, or
garret!*

He stifled a sigh and groped in his pajama top
pocket. He never went anywhere, these days,
without smokes, not even in the middle of the night.
No, there was small appeal to poverty, once one had
tasted success. Mass communication—bilking
bucks by exposing the plight of poor people, who
really had little choice about being either exploited
or penniless—had turned the nation reality crazy,
and he hadn't escaped. Just look at how awful you
are; dammit, you owed it to the Unborn to feel
lousy! Not that you spoke of it, to anyone; you
remained still for fear something certain might be
changed. The fact that a busy leveling went on,
incesssantly, Richard thought, seemingly so necessary that no one could know if it were social or
socialistic, involuntary or arranged, kept one quiet.
Once you had enough Things, paid for or not, you
kept your yap shut; you settled.

Richard, blinking, looked blankly at the generous
unfolding of his carpeted stairs. It was two decades
or more since he'd been young enough to fancy that
something ineffably compensatory—some well-
balanced, cosmic redemption—throve in the
poverty-as-purge pursuit of Big-A Art. Yet no one
wanted art, any longer; they scarcely thought to

pretend they did. And it was twenty years since
Mark . . . hadn't been born.

He glanced up, toward the direction of their
bedroom and Molly, sleeping now in golden panties.
An internal writer's vision came of cool lemonade
turned tart with a dash of bitters, and fruit lying
heavy against the sides of a frosted glass.
Externally, Molly had changed so little Richard
could only marvel, feel grateful sporadically, alternately guilty, and inadequate. Whatever was
importantly different about his girl had all
happened inside, and seeped through only enough to
tighten the fair skin over her cheekbones and wide
forehead, and turn her fine, yellow hair tawny. His
fingers shook as he slipped a cigarette between his
lips. He supposed that one did not meet Molly,
today, and think in the slightest of age, but rather of
some inaccessible painter's point in infinity, an
Elsetime of her private past from which Molly
threaded a graceful reach into the present. Her con-
temporaneous existence was as tenuous and frail as
coils of drifting smoke, and it could be brushed
aside, but it always returned. In a sense, he saw,
Molly could never be harmed *here;* the genuine heart
of the woman dwelled in dismal memory seven
thousand days ago in a crystalline container which,
while cracking, would never truly shatter.

Richard knotted a fist, let his arm dangle between
his legs. Why was he sitting here thinking, if that's
what it was, in the middle of the night? Did he
honestly feel the Grant family was moving onto
winter ice, or was he thinking like a writer again?
Below, heavy draperies covering the high, downstairs windows cloaked the first floor in nearly total
darkness and Richard, raising his bare heels above
the top step to stretch, felt enough sudden vertigo

to drop his feet and clutch with one hand for the banister. *Big deal war hero,* he sneered at his own past, and finally lit the cigarette. And why did so many men have the inclination to blame material desires, understandable preferences for the nicer, the better and the safer life—read: Get enough Things and you could pretend to a security which held death at bay indefinitely—on their wives?

As a rule, that simply wasn't his style. He knew it was a fact that there would never have been either a briskly selling novel or a second book abject flop, or even the hazardous and hurrièd move from her family's former neighborhood to Wheaton, Maryland, this pretty poppy pinned on Washington's lapel, if it hadn't been for Molly keeping her word. She'd been all guts. Despite the enduring, agonizing questions about their stillborn son which surely continued to plague her, she'd stayed achingly silent on the subject and kept her part of their bargain.

Remembering, drawing neat connection, Richard drew in smoke and tried not to smile. After his honorable discharge, she had gone right to work and stayed with it. Thank God, he'd done his part! Because the thing men hated about women was the way they unfailingly kept their words, and despised utterly their men who did not. In arrangements between the sexes, he'd learned, "couldn't" was the obscenity which made their hairless lips curl. "Trust" was the first word sewn into the bright banner of marital fidelity, and it was all-encompassing, it didn't even have as much to do with sex as with time-honored commitment. Well, eventually he had come through! Since sales jobs were ideally suited for a man who sought a decent draw and wanted to check in with the boss in the morning,

then be on his own, Richard had bluffed and huffed
his way through a series of selling positions. The
goal was not to be a great success at it, since making
too much income would have made it impossible to
quit, and write. The goal was to keep the job, and
the draw, while he honed his creative skills.

It had worked, narrowly. Gradually, his part-time
writing became so fascinating to him that he could
see only with passing panic that he was running out
of easy-to-get sales jobs. That was when *Terror in
the Eye of the Beholder* sold, earning a remarkable
advance.

By that time, Molly had used her family name,
Skylar, for all it was worth, and its cash value had
made her upwardly mobile enough to be starting
work on her third job.

Experimentally, Richard raised his feet again
against the downstairs darkness, sighted between
his two big toes. He blew out smoke as if firing it
across a rifle sight. The dizziness passed and was
replaced by a wakefulness which was unbearably
familiar. He could not replace it, he knew, unless he
could pick the topic for his third book, research and
outline it. *If I knew* what *to write,* he thought, *I
could write a whole chapter tonight.*

He heard the slight sound of Molly, up the hall,
flopping over in bed; it was her distinct, tiny
unhappy sound. He hoped she wasn't awakening.
There was money in the bank for the immediate
future but Molly went on working, in a way Richard
thought obsessive, and she'd been promoted
recently. Still a bank teller, first job opportunity
offered by Doctor's Skylar's friend, years ago, she
was "over" (Molly put it that way) the other tellers.
She was so proud of that!

Suddenly, he understood, his Molly represented a

variety of upper-middle-class America, a kind that disturbed Richard because of the tendency to accept limitations; the kind he saw as wholly self-made. In the early days of their marriage, after leaving Fort Christopher behind, he'd been concerned that she would see how tolerant he was; the strings of open-mindedness strangled as quickly, on occasion, as the ligaments of bigotry. But keeping her position at the bank over a period of years—even while less attractive women were advanced around her—had built a measure of confidence in Molly. He grinned at the glowing tip of his cigarette. Now, promoted, she was inclined to display a slightly condescending attitude. Last week, in fact, she'd gone out of her way at dinner to mention airily to him how unstable his creative career could be, and how stable (and consequently, in the Skylar family terminology, how superior) banking was.

He'd thought about the stock market crash and then not argued the point. Molly was turning forty, and she'd have died before confessing how miserably insecure it made her feel. The fact that he'd felt precisely the same several years ago, that he understood how disturbing it grew if one brooded over it, could not be his sympathetic gift. Because he'd tried to give it when Molly followed him into her thirties and she'd reminded Richard that men were still regarded as handsome, virile and distinguished, at thirty, forty or fifty—but that women merely got old. She, of course, had been one hundred percent right: but he hadn't understood why it mattered so much to Molly, when each of them was already married.

He tugged on the banister and clambered to his feet, under the injunction of the shrinking cigarette he now pinched like a marijuana joint between index finger and thumb, and silently padded back up the softly carpeted hallway. Did second-story men go into this line of work because it was so peaceful, so quiet? After listening to the cigarette's dying sizzle in the commode, he left the roomy bath on a sudden impulse to make sure the girls were all right.

Michelle, ten, had kicked off her covers. Richard began to replace them, the way he'd seen Molly perform the maternal task a hundred times. But Michelle appeared perfectly comfortable, and gave no indication of turning blue for at least another few decades. He chose to share his younger daughter's independence but had to resist the temptation to stoop and kiss her temple. At the door, he paused, glancing at her again, and smiled. He knew he did so partly because he really thought she was cute, and partly because it was the sort of thing a father was supposed to do.

Mary's door was closed. Stock still, he stopped with his hand outstretched, filled with wonder for the incalculable number of worlds that spun invisibly within others. Without trying the knob, he knew the door would be locked. Mary was twelve.

Two daughters—two females—flesh of Molly's flesh, but not yet and perhaps never to be mind of his mind.

At the end of the hall, the urn atop the highboy gleamed dully.

He retraced his measured steps to the bathroom, entered, hesitated before the commode with his hand on the superfluity of flannel at the fly. He frowned, changing his mind. He did not have to go, and Michelle, despite the fact of December, had boldly kicked off her covers. He switched off the soundless bathroom light and went in to rejoin Molly.

She was sprawled on her back and naked to the

waist, and her breasts did not flatten as much as those of younger women he had recently observed in R-rated motion pictures. Nor did they slump meatily to the side, and he felt filled with admiration. Just inside the bedroom door, he studied her with fond closeness, wondering if Molly would see his new grading system as high praise. Probably not; his was probably the last masculine generation that wouldn't lightly discuss bodily parts and considered "titties" the ultimate in grossness.

And his, Richard decided, was the final male generation to venerate the feminine bosom with a mesmeric and compulsive ardor bordering upon idol worship. He grinned. Molly saw his affection for breasts as asinine. But it had nothing to do with the fact that, in his early teens, titties were the worst-kept secret of smuggled masculine periodicals. Boys then saw fondling them at will as the major part of the meal before the relief of mechanistic coitus. They were the sun and moon of any young male's fantasy universe, never quite seeming the same twice. For Richard, they represented the freedom of functionlessness not unlike chrome. Dual exhausts.

And breasts had symbolized a life in which anything lay within the realm of possibility—and in which eternal beauty existed as a reachable relic, a tangible award for the workday.

But with the renaissance of breast-feeding, Richard's kind of man had felt threatened, even dispossessed. With the do-it-yourself craze, with packing crates delivered to the door containing everything from machines for a ster-e-o-phonic sound system and miniature automobile assembly kits to dried foods for communal living and inflatable rubber women, it seemed the everything had been changed. Overnight, men's magazines' photographers lost the strength or will to frame a graceful dip or rising tilt and instead let their X-ray cameras plunge for the practical, drop into a cavernous passion for the functional, the mechanistic and down-to-earth, the utilitarian and monotonously pragmatic. Women's lib types asserted that women were people too, which was shocking, since Richard's generation had imagined them to be so much more than that.

None of them had ever gone in for natural childbirth and gagged at the notion of watching.

He fell with intentional clumsiness to the edge of the mattress, then hovered over Molly with the singlemindedness of a Kali-worshipper. He wrapped his adoring hand round the closest cup of ephemeral but beatific libation, and lowered his profane lips to sip fantastic nectar.

"Oh, Richard," Molly wailed, "don't you ever sleep anymore? I have to work tomorrow!"

Instantly he dropped over on his back, offended. He yanked at the sheet and blanket, wanting to cover his unacceptable offering at once; Molly's weight was heavy upon them.

When he turned his frowning face to demand, at the very least, his right to simple covering, she amazed him by rising lithely over him. Her breasts dangled before his lips—like ripe fruit, precisely as his books had said. Smile restored, Richard put out his eager hands again.

"*Mama?*"

The two of them froze at the strident young voice from beyond the bedroom door.

"Mama, I can't sleep! I have a simply blazing fever again, I think."

Michelle Grant had not truly reached the age of independence. Neither, Richard realized as Molly's

warmth rushed from him and disappeared into a
stern maternal robe, had he.

With the promotion she'd recently won, Molly
didn't have to be at the bank near White Oak and
the Naval Ordinance Lab until ten. Since Christmas
vacation began that day for Mary and Michelle, she
gave Richard a fond squeeze of the hand as he went
back upstairs to his study, and decided to dawdle
over coffee. The girls seized every opportunity for
sleeping late and Molly only wished she had their
dedication. Her own mother, first wife of the
renowned Doctor Conrad Skylar, had been acutely
conscious of her status, which was fundamentally
the first and last good fortune in her brief life, and
insisted that "everyone" rise when Daddy did.
"Everyone" meant Molly, and Mom. Since Daddy
was at times obliged to be on hospital rounds by five
A.M., Molly had learned to be a morning person—
something for which she had not been cut out by
nature.

Yawning, she glanced at the morning paper. Her
nose crinkled with distaste. Another politician, a
mayor somewhere in New Mexico, had been myster-
iously murdered. No one seemed to know if the
attack was linked with other assassinations of
people in politics around the nation, but once again
there were no clues. Or, if there were, the authorities
weren't admitting it. Carefully, steadily, she filled
her coffee cup halfway and pursed her lips in
thought. Maybe it was true that most politicians
were corrupt, the way lots of her friends were
saying, but it wasn't right to take the law into your
own hands. Daddy had always been strong for doing
things properly, legally, and taught her that the
United States was a nation based upon laws—that it

would endure as a free country only so long as everyone respected that fact.

Sounds from the front door alerted her that the
mailman had come, and Molly arose, wearing the
stylish new suit she'd bought to celebrate her
promotion to assistant manager, and started
through the house. How surprised Richard would
be, she thought, if he knew how much she hated
going to work. It was his small conceit that he
believed he continued to "let" her work, and she
appreciated the fact that he was grateful to her for
making his own little success possible. Originally,
she had gone to cousin Meg for an entrée to the bank
because she prided herself on being a sensible person
and she'd known that she didn't dare remain idle,
not after Mark. In time, it had become a habit; and
then, when Richard actually sold his novel and
earned all those royalties, two years later, she'd
realized that she would have to keep working
indefinitely. Because there was no way she could
depend upon Richard continuing to sell his stories,
and when you figured it was five years between the
time he began writing them and when he finally got
a royalty check, it only worked out to ten thousand
dollars a year! She'd longed to point it out, and to
stop him from buying this massive mausoleum of a
place, but . . .

Her hand, squirming in the mailbox, felt the
familiar square envelope used by her father, and
Molly brought it and the rest of the mail inside,
relieved to hear from him yet simultaneously angry
that it had been so long. *He'd write regularly, if it
weren't for that woman he married,* Molly mused.

Tears started as she studied the square envelope.
His *hand,* it had been so elegant. Now it was
scrawled, like Richard's, but shaky; more so than
she could recall.

Deciding to read it later, she dropped the lesser mail in a chic container and paused with an envelope addressed to Richard. In longhand. The name in the lefthand corner meant nothing to her, so Molly squinted at the letter in the light falling from the long bay window. No use.

"Surely it's not from one of those Army friends," she said, aloud, softly. She swept upstairs with it and down the hallway. *Surely* it's not more brooding about those dreadful days. The notion of it physically sickened Molly.

Passing the highboy, legacy from Mother's estate, Molly scarcely saw the burnished urn. Within the urn, pale ashes of a long dead infant reposed like sand in a theater cigarette container. Without knocking, she opened the door to Richard's study.

Since they had risen before dawn, in the spartan barrack, they had done as they were expected to do: moved, reacted, with incredible speed and alacrity, at once physically and mentally. Despite the early hour—which was now and then varied, to keep them prepared—they'd been perfectly sharp in every thought or deed, because their superiors believed in paradox, and the near-impossible. There was almost constant screaming, and shouting; the hills absorbed the sound, accepted it as one more pollution of their majestic and detached existences.

Occasionally, a human being died.

Less occasionally, one was murdered. Never under the slightest pretense that murder was the accurate word, rarely unintentionally, and never without a practical, purposeful point to be made and an advantage gained, or planned.

No one noticed the passing of the occasional human being except him whose task it was to defend his reasoning, or to demand that the remains be efficiently removed and disposed of.

That night, they would be awakened when it was least expected, often after the last of them had finished his written studies and staggered his way to sleep. At times, these latenight kock-ups would be momentary, seemingly purposeless; other times, blame for failures would be affixed before the others and cruelties administered to all. This night, certain tests were given which combined the needs for physical and intellectual adroitness in a way that less equipped and amateurishly trained men might have found rigorous, or arduous at midday. They were allowed to wear their skivvies.

At dawn, those who failed to pass the late night tests with the highest of marks were obliged to don most of the clothing and work tools they owned in the world and jog to an artificial pool which could not be observed from the surrounding hills. Once there, under closest scrutiny, they were bidden to do something extraordinarily dangerous—without the time to ready themselves or the option to decline the bidding.

Occasionally, a human being just died.

No one, to speak of, noticed.

6

"You busy?"

Molly smiled breezily. She'd stopped a single pace into his *sanctum sanctorum*, gripping the frame of his study door with her slim, red-tipped fingers and leaning all her weight in his direction. She knew that her blonde hair fell forward, framing her carefully arranged face. Richard thought the pose was especially feminine and it made him less likely to bite her head off. His rule, which neither she nor the girls paid much attention to, was that he could be interrupted only when an arising matter was urgent. Hers was not, but she'd slipped his letter into her suit pocket.

"*Am* I *busy?*" he mused. He'd glanced up from his fast deteriorating typewriter, an aging Royal non-electric standard. When he'd begun writing on it, several years ago, it had simply been a typewriter. Richard swore to go on repairing the damned thing the rest of his life rather than succumb to the blandishments of a word processor sales rep. Now he made a face. "Actually, my sweet, it's much too early in the day for troublesome questions. I was just on the verge of creating a genuinely insightful, memorable paragraph, doubtlessly destined for immortality. Probably by being banned from some rinkydink library."

So far, so bad, Molly believed. She'd never understood Richard's humor, even under the best of circumstances, but hated it when he yelled at her. At work, he appeared a total stranger; but she headed across the room toward him with a firm, wifely sense of prior right. "Are you making any progress at all?" He looked, she thought, sallow and bleary eyed; the sheet of paper rising from his machine appeared to be sticking out its tongue. His curly hair, gray-speckled at the temples, had a dark sheen on top from the effort he had made since breakfast, but a surreptitious peek over his flannel-shirted shoulder told her he'd written nothing.

"Certainly, I've made progress! You don't think I'm one of those writing pretenders, who sit before their super costly WPs and try to recall Chaucerian quotations?" He gave his pencil a ferocious nibble, then tossed it in the general direction of the wastebasket beside the desk. He missed. "Let's say I have narrowed down the possible themes for my next book to something between ninety-nine and a thousand. The next step is to arrange them in a circular design and throw *darts* at them."

"That's something, eliminating a lot of other ideas." She wasn't about to commit herself to a morning of hearing out his authorial complaints, trying to soothe his nervous creative spirits. That would make her late to work, and, if she said anything, he'd stare at her as if all her values were wrong, and then pout. "Isn't it?"

"Well-l-l, yes," he agreed with faked judicial reflection. Abruptly he stretched his short neck to kiss the tip of her nose. "It's a sure sign I have writer's block, or terminal insecurity, *or* incipient schizophrenia. Which would you prefer in this best of all possible worlds, our nation's capital?"

He was impossible. She drew the letter from her suit pocket, tossed it on the desktop beside the typewriter. "I have to get packing. Big workday calling."

Richard snatched up the letter, waved it in circles. "Maybe I've heard from my fan!" he exclaimed without reading the envelope. "I'll bet she's finally overcome her timidity at the notion of contacting someone as famous and fabulous as I!"

"You would conclude that your 'fan' is a woman, wouldn't you?"

His light-hued eyes narrowed. From Richard's standpoint, she knew he was loyal to her so the remark had to be her standard implication that he was oversexed. His outflung hand stopped Molly before she could leave. "Who else but a woman would be that damned interested in terror and terrorism? Hell, I wrote the book for a female audience. They're the ones who see conspirators and assassins under every bed—or maybe, on *top* of them!"

Her gaze, cloudy and guarded, upset, met his briefly. Then she wrested her wrist free and started toward the door. "I'd always heard it was women who liked to dredge up the ancient past and throw it in their husbands' faces."

A beat. "No, it's neurotic, stupid writers." He'd called out quickly. "Writers who are scared shitless they will turn out to be one-novel successes. Hey, kid, I'm sorry; that was a cheap shot. Okay?"

She'd hesitated at the door, facing away from him. For a moment it seemed she would not turn back.

"Sure." Her voice lacked assurance, but rancor as well. She looked over her shoulder, managing a smile. "I gotta run." And she was gone.

He saw her close the door softly behind her and promptly felt miserable. When he had written the first, the *successful* book—before they had a dime—he'd enjoyed his work more than anything he tried before in his life. Yet, even then, he'd snapped at Molly for invading his little world; sometimes he'd brought up topics he knew would cause dissension. For a while, he'd believed it was because he subconsciously liked trying out dialogue on Molly. Then he'd believed he was just so unsure of his developing talent that he'd welcomed testing the rhythms and inflections of spoken words.

But during the creation of his second book, Richard had realized how much he enjoyed thinking of himself as the Royal ruler of an island bordered by a back-space key and margin release. Absurd and selfish as it was, he merely resented it whenever Molly demanded that he lower the drawbridges and throw wide the castle door—to reality.

Then, gradually, he'd come to understand that it was *specifically Molly* whom he sought to keep off his magic island—and why: Because she carried the past around like a goddamn Ichabod Crane, with a head full of terrifying memories tucked under her heart. Ludicrous ideas that they had somehow mislaid a baby son twenty years ago. And he'd worked as brilliantly hard on Book One because it had meant an escape from her never-voiced, deadly paranoia—her insistence upon forcing him to rise, dizzily, to exchange his innocuous fantasies for her hurtful ones.

Always, too, there was *something else . . .*

Back already stiffening from his tendency to

hover over a typewriter as if pounding it into sub-
mission, Richard groped for the feathery, free-float-
ing piece of puzzle about Molly, him, Mark's lumpen
emergence. He wasn't quite seeing *all* the facts, or
the truth, not even now; he was still placing the
blame on Molly when, once more, the built-in shit
detector in his mind was always Down.

Reaching out, scarcely noticing or remembering
the letter that had arrived, he typed out the words I
AM KIDDING MYSELF BECAUSE, and paused.
In 25 anguished words or less.

Raising his eyes, Richard looked studiedly out the
window, across the room he'd worked so hard to
acquire; he shivered. Would he never be away from
them for good?—men in Army uniforms, ranks on
shoulders instead of souls, leaving their homes now
and climbing into their civilian automobiles to make
the drive to D.C. proper. Neighbors; career military
men, wives not and perhaps never young, wives who
did not go to the door to see them off. Still, unlike
himself, men who left the house to go to work.
("Why did you tell your teacher I'm unemployed,
Mary?" "Because you never go to work like the
other daddies." A wistful sigh. "You're always here
so I can't give you a kiss when you get home.")
Christmas coming eventually; holidays peculiar on
the outskirts of Washington, whole neighborhoods
emptied as if there'd been a warning siren he'd
missed and all the working dads and moms had been
evacuated. In the distance, Richard saw, a man he
knew to be a three-term Congressman was leaning
on a shovel, probably trying to decide whether there
was enough snow left to give him a workout.
Important men, or men who believed they were; men
who had assignments, so unarguable and so clear-
cut there was nothing to be gained by thinking

about them. How much sense it made that politicians and professional Army personnel dwelled side by side, here; yet Richard could never remember seeing a man of one kind speak to a man of the other kind. *Closed* encounters, if any.

Troubled, holding his breath, he looked back down —not at the letters but at the words he'd typed on the white sheet of paper, and his two hands paused briefly above the keyboard before sending it again into noisy, laborious operation:

BECAUSE I COULD NEVER PROVE IN A MILLION YEARS THAT MOLLY HAS GIVEN ANOTHER SECOND OF THOUGHT TO MARK. SHE IS NOT MY CREATIVE MOTIVATION; I AM. BECAUSE IT IS I WHO NEVER FORGOT, WHO QUITE POSSIBLY CANNOT FORGET.

"Psychologists call it transference," he said aloud, softly. He went back to strike through the superfluous "BECAUSE" and underline the words "SHE," and "I." "And reporters call it passing the buck." He lit a Pall Mall regular and poked at the bright red pack with the index finger of his left hand. " 'Warning: The Author-General has Determined That Being Born is Dangerous to Your Health.' " Incipient headache accompanied Richard on his journey to the center of the truth.

Fact, he wasn't conscious of thinking about the son he'd never seen. If, indeed, it might be said that he'd ever had a son at all. The memories were often like those of another man entirely; as if he'd suffered a brain, or memory, transplant. He did not—could not—miss Mark Grant. If anything, he missed, Richard surmised, what he'd never had the chance to learn *how* to miss.

Maybe it had to do with being in his forties, knowing there would not be a living, male child, because

getting Molly pregnant again was unconscionable at
her age. He ignored the incoming letter again,
looked up, instead, at his framed book jackets; said
"Hell." Age wasn't it. His father, unprotestingly
dying at seventy-three, had seemed more to leave
life, than die; nothing left interested him. And
today, folks died from bizarre, fresh maladies—
sparklingly healthy new viruses and industrial
plagues flashing brash, idiot smiles at you before
burying their cavity-free fangs right in your jugular.
Or died from overcrowding, and unwantedness;
future shock and inability to cope with a fluctuating
government that couldn't decide whether you were a
treasury of golden-age wisdom or Sam and Sarah
Senility with a cerebellum chockful of newly named
nuts. You died aborted, abandoned, or armed these
days, and they stuck you an extra six feet deep to
prevent the radiation counter from flicking right off
the dial; but you didn't really get old, you got bewildered.

Which was what had happened to Richard Grant,
he told himself, grabbing the letter Molly had
brought up to him and opening it without looking at
the name or address on the envelope.

He nearly crushed it in his hands and threw it
toward the wastebasket, because he noticed, at
once, that it wasn't a personal letter. It looked like
something that might have been photocopied at a
neighborhood PIP, but the fact that it was also full
of typos and one or two handwritten afterthoughts
kept Richard from discarding it.

He read it through once, grunted, put it down.
Then he picked it up again and read it more thoroughly, remembering Sergeant Eddie Dugan and,
because Eddie had only existed for him as an
element of an environment he could never fully

forget, the tangled weeds and stunningly sudden open spaces of Vietnam. The clearer Eddie's red, leathery face and sideways grin became in Richard's mind, the more he recalled of the alien land on which they had fought. *Crazy,* he thought, *the way the memory widens—like seeing a regular movie screen sweep out at the sides for Cinerama. And it just keeps going, fanning out the way the squads did, a world of color so vivid and abrupt, sound so deafening you were okay until it became real to you, because that meant you were adjusting to it.* And Hell couldn't become Hell, and hurt you, so long as you thought it was Toledo, or Anaheim.

Eddie was planning a reunion. He'd clearly spent weeks, perhaps months, assembling the list of names and addresses at the top of the homemade page. Which was like Eddie Dugan, who was more efficient and thorough with a flamethrower than other men were with wrenches and screwdrivers, factory machinery, or computers. He'd written his telephone number, at his home in the very same little Georgia town he'd talked about longingly for over a year in Nam, six times, urging the men on the list to call him. SOON, with three harsh lines beneath the plea. Call him to plan a twenty-year reunion of "the old bunch," the squad in which Eddie and Richard had served.

Richard's shoulders shook with silent laughter until he felt the tears in his eyes.

Reunions were for old high school classmates, people who'd been to college together, for families—and they were generally painful enough to send a guy after a bottle of Geritol. Or something stronger. Reunions were for people who had enjoyed something together, and cared about remembering it, pumping it full of life for a few short hours while the wives or husbands who had not yet belonged were bored out of their minds.

The only similar ingredient Richard could see in
Eddie Dugan's idea was boredom, because that, too,
they had shared, the men of Grant's and Dugan's
squad.

I wonder if I'll go. As the thought ended, Richard
peered around as if someone else had spoken. Why
would he even consider doing a stupid damned thing
like that? Well, why was he considering it?

Could it be because, of all things, he felt bored?

A part of the answer was contained in a sentence
of ex-Sergeant Dugan's group letter, just a few
words that Richard felt everyone getting the invita-
tion would understand: " . . . it's us who know what
it was like . . ."

By the time he'd dialed Eddie's phone number,
Richard was certain he would not attend. *Too much
water over the damn dam,* he mused, hardening
himself against Eddie's pleas; *gall bladder patients
know what's it's like, too, but they don't travel
several hundred miles to toast their surgery.*

"So what else is new?" he asked, when Dugan
finally let it drop. The disappointment in Eddie's
tone (only two of the other squad members had even
agreed to think it over) brought Richard to his feet,
and he carried the phone to his study window in
order to get a breath of fresh air. One Christmas tree
was already up, he observed, diagonally across the
block. The year was winding down, drawing to its
familiar close. "You were married, correct? About
the time I was?"

"Right on, good buddy!" A note of heartiness
crept back into Eddie's voice, but it somehow
sounded spurious, present to cover something.
"Alma was the sweetest li'l ole woman I'd ever seen,
up to then. I was lucky to be first. Got me a gawdamn southern harem of lookers now, let me tell

you!''

"Yes, I remember Alma now." Richard frowned. With the familiar rasp of the noncom's confidence in his ear, the Vietnamese landscape was shrinking, narrowing in until Sergeant Eddie Dugan's face and his long forgotten remarks rose to Richard's mind. He sensed something coming, wished he hadn't phoned. "Sorry you two broke up. But what happened to the kid that was on the way? I remember, now, Alma was due not long after my Molly."

"Well, now." Eddie paused and Richard felt his own heartbeat beginning to accelerate. "The ole fortune cookie crumbled all over m'head, Rich." Heartiness was slipping away like a shawl from arthritic shoulders. "And the message inside, buddy, well, it was right easy t'read: 'Gotcha again, sucker,' *that's* what it said!''

Richard turned slowly from the window, his gaze raised, drifting across the morning floor. "I don't think I read you, Sarge." Why was he finding it hard to breathe evenly? "Don't tell me it wasn't your kid Alma was carrying?''

"Oh, I 'spect it was mine, okay." The sigh was short, but audible. "You and me both got discharged from Fort Christopher, y'recall. Well, that's where the poor li'l bugger got hisself born dead, Richard. We never even got a peep at him, 'cause the brass cremated him. Y'know, to spare us the grief? Well, ole Alma and me couldn't make it over th' hump after that." Sounds of energetic throat clearing. "Hey, Rich, I never did hear what happened to your young 'un? Why, he must be nearly twenty years old by now. What'd you name him?''

Richard's ears were ringing. "Mark," he said, pushing the receiver away from him, "we called our son Mark."

7

Everyone knows that some days begin badly, then go skidding off downhill from there, and no one knows how to explain it. Richard realized by mid-afternoon, when he went downstairs, starved, to help the girls fix lunch, that he had innocently stumbled into just such a nightmarish day and would have been happy to bypass an explanation and go straight for the cure. Under the happiest of circumstances, he was a completely inept cook. He'd known it ever since he ruined a perfectly respectable turkey on the All-Holiday celebration he'd arranged for Molly, many years ago, sacrificing both bird and chefly reputation on the altar of Going On From There.

But usually he was able without hurting anyone to toast several slices of bread for peanut butter and jelly sandwiches; and generally, he did not shove the peanut butter jar off to its messy death on the linoleum floor in the kitchen.

As a rule, too, he wouldn't have shouted silly names at his daughters and made grotesque faces at them when they were inclined to tease him.

Ignoring the light brown catastrophe with the jagged glass in the unspoken hope that serious minded little Mary would magically make it vanish, he gave both girls a huge hug and a quarter apiece for apology, then moved briskly ahead to Plan B. This contingency involved opening a large can of Vienna sausages, a meat Richard and Michelle regarded as a sumptuous luxury while Molly and Mary found the greasy delicacies inedible. He intended to use the younger daughter's shared relish as a weapon with which to overpower Mary, but the sausages never reached the table.

The can slipped out of the clutches of Molly's beloved automatic can opener—Richard had never shown mechanical aptitude except with military weapons, when the alternative was grinning good-humoredly at armed foes—and struck Richard's toe hard enough to mash it, and create a beady little string of blood drops. He'd taken recently to wearing thongs during working hours.

"What? *What* did you say?" Squinting through tears of pain, he confronted Mary, already close to Molly's height but cursed with an especially juvenile, perpetually-smirking face. "Are you laughing at me again?"

"No, Dad," she lied, hiding her mouth behind wriggling fingers. "I wouldn't do that when you've been wounded in action." His hard look of suspicion sobered her. "I was just going to say not to worry about the urpy sausages, either. I can warm up some soup for Michelle and me."

"Sure, that's fine!" He yanked at the apron he'd donned, further exasperated when he heard the strings ripping behind his back. He threw his arms to the ceiling, beseechingly. "Soup's absolutely wonderful for you two women, but the breadwinner goes hungry again!''

It was thirty minutes later when Mary knocked timidly at his study door, and entered bringing him a toasted jelly sandwich and a glass of ginger ale, that Richard relaxed and began trying to figure out why he was so upset. Mary generously accepted his second set of apologies—and another quarter—and left the bestselling author to his gradually cooling thoughts.

Part of it was that he was ashamed of himself to learn it had been he, instead of Molly, who was incapable of forgetting the details of their first child's death. *Absence of life,* he corrected himself. Splitting hairs had always been important to him; he saw it as his way of remaining in the real world, by virtue of insisting upon facts and an anti-euphemistic approach to life. Burping and tasting toast, he rose from the desk and went over to slump back upon the couch from their first house. When they had moved to Wheaton, Molly'd gone on a furniture-shopping binge that seemed, for awhile, likely to expend every cent of his first royalty check. He'd demanded that they keep a few of their older pieces, including the couch, manfully lugging them up to his study; and when Molly had finally asked him why he was cluttering up his first really satisfactory working-space, Richard had told her that the fancy stuff downstairs wasn't entirely paid for. ''If everybody stops buying books,'' he'd added, ''or I become a pariah in the authorial marketplace, we'll always have the old crap we own to fall back upon. Literally!''

Since even before that, he realized, he had believed a day did not pass without Molly wondering if little Mark had been accidentally killed, or worse, for her peace of mind, swapped for the infant who'd been born dead. (If you could do so, he wondered, was it possible to "Die alive?") All that time, it had been he who questioned the story given them by Doctor Witsell. Lord, it was so logical, so obvious, when he stopped to think about it! If Mark's name wasn't mentioned, if Molly never commented, which she didn't, the only way the entire situation could be a part of his conscious thoughts was if *he* were thinking it!

Now the past was refusing to stay dead, as if Mark himself rejected it, and weatherbeaten ex-sergeants from the South were making impossible demands upon his time! Well, not impossible, exactly. As a self-employed, full-time writer, he could even agree to go to the reunion if he wished. Heaven knew he was getting nowhere fast with Book Three. And that Book Two, when the royalties were finally owed to him, couldn't possibly provide the Grants with as much working capital as Book One had done. Not that he knew how many copies of Two had sold, since publishers never seemed to have the figures—or *any* figures—at their fingertips; and not that he was ashamed of Two, if it came down to that. Publishers and wives worried about decent profits; writers and the Federal Government never gave a thought to how much money was coming in or how much was being spent. Helluva tandem that was, he grumbled; wordsmiths and Uncle Sam, Above it All while other people struggled to survive. Well, dammit, it was a fact that Book Two—*Perdition's Not a Nice Place to Visit*—was an excellent piece of literature! Book critics had said so, in West Kingston, Rhode Island, Boca Raton, Florida, and Columbia, Pennsylvania; the service had sent them right to him, and for a while it had been nearly enough, feeling that he was "critically acclaimed."

Criticism. Cutting deep. Doctors. Dead babies.
Sergeant Eddie Dugan. Richard's brain made connections; and he sat up, watching early winter gray
the skies beyond his window. What if Eddie'd had
the same doctor, or rather, Eddie's wife? Would that
mean anything? Dear sweet God, was it actually a
remote possibility, after all these years, that he'd
have to wonder, consciously, this time, *again?*
Wonder if Molly's first, intensely personal doubts
contained the slightest validity? Crap, it was he who
should have gone to the shrink regularly, all those
years ago—not Molly!

Dinner was badly strained. Despite that, it stayed
thick as pea soup, largely because while Molly was
genuinely trying to forget the morning squabble
over her delivery of the letter to Richard, she soon
had the distinct impression that Richard was trying
to keep it going.

It came as a total surprise to him when Molly,
warming up one of her older tactics, broached the
matter by way of twelve-year-old Mary. "Sweetheart," she said, fractionally louder than called for,
"would you mind terribly asking that gruff old bear
at the end of the table if he could conceivably break
his creative reverie long enough to pass the damned
gravy?"

"Why do I get that kind of treatment?" he demanded. He'd been lost in thought but had heard
the last part, from "old bear" on. "What'd I do?"

"You haven't said two words to me since I got
home from work!" Her fair skin flushed. She
grasped a knife in one hand, fork in the other,
squeezing them as if trying to decide upon open
attack. "And I think that's pretty petty, over a
little thing like taking you your mail!"

"It's not about that," Richard protested, shaking

his head.

"*Will* you pass the gravy!" Molly clumped the silverware on the table, jarringly. When he rushed the bowl toward Michelle, his thumb disappeared and the spoon sank out of sight. "What other horrible things have I done, master?"

He sucked his thumb, began grinning around it. "Say those two words three times in a row."

"What two words?" she snapped. But she sounded curious.

" 'Pretty petty.' You know." He motioned with his hand. "Go on, try it."

" 'Pretty petty, pity pretty,' " Molly began laughing, despite herself, " 'pritty pritty!' You ass!" She stared at the gravy bowl. "You pushed the spoon inside!"

His eyes twinkled; he'd gone boyish again. "Gravy's fattening anyway."

"I wasn't going to *eat* it," she argued, poking at the submerged ladle with the point of her knife, aware that the two girls were laughing. "I was going to throw it at you!"

That night, as if she were more relieved that they weren't really fighting than she had expected, Molly instigated lovemaking.

Afterward, he lay with his head on her belly. "That was champion," he said, effecting a bad British accent. "Simply champion!"

"Good-o," she murmured above him. Her blonde head was propped on a pillow, against the headboard of the bed. At times she rather liked being naked with a second person, largely because nudity itself seemed to Molly an offering of trust. Richard's legs were off the mattress, from the knees down, and she couldn't imagine how he could be comfortable. "Isn't it always simply mah-velous with the Princess of Passion?"

"Uh-uh." He shook his head, the spackled curls tickling her stomach. He looked studiedly at his rising toes. "Sometimes you aren't here, Princess of Passion. Or may I call you PP?"

"I am so!" She pinched his nose. "What did you mean by that?"

He peeked from the corner of his eyes. "Just that it's not surprising more women than men experience out-of-body travel. You know, that weird stuff about sending your mind or your soul or something free of this rugged travail, so you can get a look into ladies' gymnasiums!" He craned his neck, nibbled on the southernmost curve of her right breast. "Is that where you've gone those times it isn't good for you?"

Molly paused. "Uh-uh." She stared at him, hard. "I'm not the only one. Only I don't think you leave. I think you're imagining I'm some twenty-five-year-old broad with—with really *large* ones, and a liberated libido."

"I wonder if Mark's soul left his body before he was born, or afterward." He spoke so softly she could scarcely hear him. "Or—or if he ever had a soul, at all?"

"Of course, he had a soul!" She kept her tone of voice light but he'd felt her stomach muscles tense and was already sitting up. "And it went back to God."

Richard turned on the mattress to face her. "You really did adjust to it, didn't you, Moll?" he asked, wonderingly.

"You wanted me to," she replied, sounding hurt. "You and all the shrinks in the United States Army. Why do you bring it up now, of all times?"

He did his frown as he reached for his cigarettes, tapped one out. "What do you mean by 'now of all times'?"

Molly shrugged. "Life's okay. Things are going well, aren't they? I mean, sure, we have little tiffs like this morning. All married couples do. But we're, well, growing old together the way it's supposed to be." She hesitated. A moment later, she squeezed his bare shoulder, meaning it to hurt. "Aren't we, Richard?"

"Mary was the ghost-buster, wasn't she?" He kept his back turned, wisps of smoke rising toward the ceiling. "We waited a long time for her, and then she came along and zap, everything was okay. For you. Isn't that the way it goes?"

Molly flattened her breasts against his back, wrapped her arms around him. Something damp touched his temple. "Wasn't that the way it was supposed to go? You tried for years to talk me into trying again, and you were right. Richard, you were *right!* Our little family makes up for almost everything, now, and I—I don't see why you'd rock the boat by d-dredging up the past."

"What would you have done," he asked in the most shockingly normal of voices, "if Mary had been stillborn?"

"Killed myself." It was a fact, he knew, because of the way her body felt on his; because of how distant she sounded. "Richard, you can't *know* how dreadful it was for me, back at Fort Christopher—and don't say you can! I—I almost lost my *mind.* And I mean that." The muscles in her arms tightened, grew vise-like. "Don't let's talk about . . . him . . . ever again. I really can't go through it. Promise, me, honey. Promise you won't mention—Mark?"

"Yeah," he said, a full count later. He crushed his cigarette in a tray on the table next to his side of the bed. When he turned to look at her, his eyes were

shining but his smile was radiant, reassuring.
"Right."

*We're growing old together, life is "going well."
Are we really ready to look at ourselves that way?*
He looked toward his own lower portions, noting
with distaste how oversatisfied they felt. Honey-
moon multiplicity of sexual sessions might have
been ten thousand eras ago . . .

It was almost four in the morning when ten-year-
old Michelle started crying and Richard went to her.
Mary, he thought, his mind instantly churning, *is
really Molly's regardless of what I do. She's her
medal for surviving. The independent one's mine.*

He stood just outside the half-shut bathroom
door, at the request of the independent one, who had
suffered "the *worst* dream I ever had in my *whole*
life" and found it difficult to shake her memory of
the "worst monster I ever saw in my whole *life.*"

Sleepy, holding a palm against an apparently endless series of yawns, he waited as patiently as
possible, the melodic music of tinkling nearly
soothing him to sleep. When his head jerked,
Richard looked up in startlement and found himself
staring down the second story hallway.

At the Skylar family highboy. *No,* he admitted,
shaking his head; *scratch that.*

At the gleaming urn atop the highboy.

"Okay, kid," he muttered, aloud, "I remember."

"What did you say, Daddy?" called Mary.

"I wasn't talking to you, sugar," he replied. And
before she could protest that no one else was up, he
added, "Be sure to flush. Okay?"

He didn't sleep well the rest of the night.

8

Maybe it was partly imagination, but it seemed to take Molly an interminable length of time to leave for work the following morning. Richard found himself practically biting his tongue to avoid giving her the entirely accurate impression that he was rushing her away. Tagging after her in the kitchen, while she made coffee, he was distantly aware that he resembled some kind of quasi-cogent mental patient, shuffling around in his oversized pajamas and yellow thongs, pretending to help. When Molly had finally demanded to know what in the world was wrong with him, he thought fast, took her into his arms, and muttered inanely about how romantic he was after last night's lovemaking. Her stare said she believed him mad so he tried to back off.

The delay in Molly's departure was created by an argument between little Michelle and Mary. Their mother had arisen half an hour ahead of red-eyed, sleepless Richard. She'd bathed and dressed rapidly, even skipped using the dryer on her hair. Observing her haste as she devoured a pecan breakfast roll and gulped down black coffee, Richard knew at once that it was his wistfully ill-considered remark of the preceding evening—that impulsive wonderment about the disposition of their stillborn son's soul—which was bothering Molly today.

Which was why it was important to get her out of the house before he made a furtive, second phone call to his former Vietnam sergeant in Georgia. He didn't blame Molly for reminding him of her terrible ordeal decades ago, and how it had been exacerbated by the torturous sessions with the psychiatrist, Doctor Bianchi. He understood why Molly would want to let sleeping children lie, now. It had almost cost her her sanity and he had no moral right to open the old wounds.

Then, with the morning atmosphere already strained, Mary had "accidentally" read a Christmas want-list assembled by ten-year-old Michelle and concluded, quite wrongly, that the younger sister would get everything she desired. Mary had felt neglected enough to slap Michelle's face when told that the list was none of her business.

And as usual, Richard observed, it had done no good for Molly to remind Mary that *she* was the one her parents counted on, or point out that Mary was nearly a teen-ager. But the notion of that filled Richard with terror, after what he had heard from friends concerning the hazards of raising a child from twelve to twenty. He wondered for the hundredth time what fool had coined the term "teen-ager," since it was so mutually exclusive.

What almost made him abandon his morning's covert plans was a welling up of ambivalence toward his elder daughter. At Mary's birth, both he and Molly had been tearfully grateful that she lived; he'd spent hours making sure the baby girl was well, often phoning the family doctor in D.C., a colleague

of Molly's father, with the smallest infantile
complaints.

Molly had never quite accepted the fact that Mary
was healthy. As her concern for Mark faded along
with the haunted shadows on her face, Molly's
concern for Mary had grown, and brightened. And
by the time Molly's interests had partly switched to
her work, Mary was spoiled.

Not that it was Mary's fault, Richard felt. The
parents had done it, again. And now the child could
not understand why she no longer received all of
Mama's attention. It was only natural that she'd
eventually reached the conclusion that Michelle, her
sister, was the guilty party behind the closing doors
of the Mom-and-Pop Goody Store of Plenty.

Despite the child's present attitude, Richard
believed he could put her on an ideal path, but for
his wife's way of coping with Mary's occasional
problems. Because Molly really did fairly worship
Mary and had made it completely obvious to everyone that she preferred the surviving miracle-child,
to the accidental afterthought, Molly felt mercilessly guilty any time Mary felt remotely blue.

Today, for example, Richard reflected, instead of
smilingly explaining that Michelle's want-list had
more to do with wishful thinking than the real
world, and making sure Mary didn't hit Michelle
again, Molly had permitted Mary to "request *one*
more gift for Christmas"—so that the only person
left in the house in a mood of misery was the old
breadwinner himself, who saw Molly out the door
and who watched their darling daughters hold
hands as they skipped off to play.

He tromped up the steps to his study with the
feeling that the day was already trying to clone
yesterday, and a serious, covertly welcome doubt

that he'd get much writing done today.

"Eddie? This is Rich Grant again." He leaned back from his desk, trying to be utterly casual as he spoke into the telephone. "Sorry to bother you, buddy, but I wanted to ask—"

Interrupted, he froze the way he was, hand behind his neck, second hand tracing smoke-pictures with the Pall Mall it held. "No, Sarge, I didn't call to tell you I'd changed my mind about the reunion."

Silence. Eddie Dugan wasn't answering and Richard eased his typist's chair forward, leaned on his elbows. He felt acutely embarrassed, wished he hadn't put either of them through this a second time.

"She-it, what's the matter with folks these days?" Dugan, whom Richard remembered as a valorous and powerfully muscled non-commissioned officer, sounded old, and it was sad-making. "Time was, a man could be proud of doin' his duty, serving his country. I know, 'cause my daddy was in Double-yew-double-yew-Two and that man never stopped talkin' about it. Not what he did, but how it kind of set him up in life, if y'follow me." A tremorous sigh. "It all started goin' bad during Nam, didn't it, Rich? When all them yellow weaklings chickened out and pissed their guts away in Canada! Well, don't you worry, your not comin' won't make a licka difference. Other men wrote me, said they're too busy puttin' their lives back together to remember their buddies."

"Eddie—"

"I mean to *remember* what we did, Corporal." Dugan's voice was louder, suddenly; there was a slight slur to his speech. "I ain't *ashamed* of fightin' the enemies of my country, and they's a lot of other fellas feel just the way I do!"

"Damn it, Sergeant," Richard snapped, angered partly because his cigarette had burned down and scorched two fingers. "I'm not ashamed either! You hear me, Eddie? Don't you dare tar me with that brush, pal. *I* was there too, remember?"

"What'd you want?" The voice was fading now, not so much lost in the past, or even hurt or angry, as tired. Weary; deflated. It also sounded softer, somehow, but Richard doubted it was a tone of resignation.

"Your first wife, Alma, when she delivered your child stillborn, the way ours was. D'you remember who her doctor was?"

"First wife?" Eddie Dugan exclaimed. He still sounded distant but a measure of his former heartiness was back. "I may not be no literary genius like you, Rich, but I don't make the same mistake *twice!*" He chuckled heavily. "No, man, I don't remember nobody from that time. Leastwise, not stateside." A pause. "Might know his name if I heard it, I reckon."

Richard held the telephone mouthpiece with both hands. "Captain Witsell was Molly's physician. Does that—"

"Sure! Alfred Witsell, *that* was it! Horseshit puke usin' his captain's bars t'keep from answering our questions!" Eddie's voice had grown loud enough that Richard had to hold the phone from his ear. "And now I remember, Rich, they was somebody *else* in that Fort Christopher Hospital who had the same gawdamn thing happen to his young 'un!"

"It was stillborn?" Richard asked quickly.

"Best as I recall," Dugan replied, sounding as if he were nodding. "Never did hear his missus' name but he was a real fuck-up, name of Carliacca—a private, he was, brave as a grizzly bear's balls but just as dumb."

"Eddie," Richard said, keeping his voice as light and level as possible, "you don't remember where Carliacca was *from*, do you? Or what his first name was?"

"Other boys called him Tony," Dugan responded at once, "and he was all the time yakkin' about the Cubs, a real baseball nut. Reckon he might hail from Chi-town."

"You've been a big help, Sarge." Richard uncrossed his ankles and leaned forward. He hesitated. "Someday, maybe, I'll get down South—and—"

"Sure, sure," Dugan said brusquely. Then he gave a bitter laugh Richard felt he might remember for a long time. "Just remember the Alamo, okay, Rich? S'far as I've heard, it's still popular to appreciate the boys in *that* war!"

Moments later, sweating heavily despite swirling snow making transient designs against his study window, Richard had telephoned Chicago information and written down the numbers of two men named Anthony Carliacca.

He reached the right one on the first try.

It was difficult, explaining why he'd phoned, without sounding paranoid. But Tony Carliacca's initial suspicion vanished by the time Richard had stammered his way through the story, to be replaced by an attitude that infuriated the writer.

"Baby, that was a long time ago! You know Ernie Banks was still playin' shortstop for the Cubbies then? I don't remember no Doctor Witsell, and I ain't a guy to hang crepe for some kid I never even seen!"

"All I want to know, then," Richard pressed him doggedly, "is if you think the hospital at Fort Christopher handled the delivery of your child competently?"

"How the fuck would I know?" Carliacca demanded. "Look, it's Christmastime, aw right? I got other kids—real, live, breathin' kids—to think about now; and with the price of clothes and toys what they are, I can only draw a couple of conclusions about you, pal."

Richard squeezed his eyelids together. "Which are?"

"Either you've got your mitts on a money tree or you didn't have no more kids." Tony Carliacca sighed conspicuously. "Aw right, sure, we was shot down when Tony, Jr. didn't make it. But I ain't about t'put my cock on the chopping block for no frigging lawsuit against Uncle Sammy, got me?"

"I think I have. I think I know you very well."

"Baby, that was *twenty* Christmases ago! A couple thousand sleds, fourteen gross of gawdamn diapers, maybe a trillion pairs of shoes—enough material for a Christmas stocking t'cover the whole fucking boot of Italy! Pal, I got seven kids now!"

Richard's muscles tensed; he stared hopelessly at the phone cradle on his desk. "Sorry to bother you. I didn't—"

"Hey! Hey, it's like *okay*, you read me?" Carliacca's relief turned the man almost jovial. "Aw right, look, I don't think it was the Army's fault about what happened to your boy or mine, anyhow."

"Why not?"

" 'Cause the medics at Christopher delivered our *second* child, Belinda. Just a year later, afore I got discharged—and she's healthy as a horse! I wish the Cubbie pitchin' staff was as healthy as that kid! So have a cool Yule, aw right?"

Dismal, absently nodding, Richard put out his hand with the phone—ready to hang it up—

And *heard quite distinctly, the telltale click of a third person, listening in, hanging up the moment*

Anthony Carliacca had.

For half a minute, Richard couldn't move. Was his phone line tapped? Eyes wide with shock, his hand shaking, he picked up the phone, carefully, and listened as if his life might depend upon it.

Nothing. He shook his head. No one there, now.

Then, somewhere else on the second story, somebody was sobbing . . .

He took Mary into his arms, conscious of her tear streaked face, how miserable, how heartbroken, she looked. From the corner of his eye he could see the phone that belonged to his elder child, another of Molly's tangible efforts directed at proving to her daughter that she was still Number One.

The term, in his thoughts, told Richard what was the matter with Mary.

"Kitten, he has nothing to do with you." He took her heart-shaped face between the palms of his hands and smiled as reassuringly as he was able. "He was a long, long time ago."

"But you c-called those men about him," she protested, tears still coming. "Oh, Daddy, I always thought I was first—that I was your oldest kid!"

"But you *are!*" He put her face against his shoulder, hugged her. He'd never smelled anything as fresh in his life as Mary's soft, light-brown hair. She wasn't a new Molly, or an imitation of her; with her hair a tone darker, Mary was the next dimensional step in some logical but lovely progression, a chromatic shadowing of the hues and rhythms of a rainbow. "Mark never drew a breath of air, never actually *existed* on this silly old planet. Listen to your old man, puss, check it out with Mom if you don't believe me: Mark was *never alive.*" Awkwardly, he kissed her forehead and got part of an eyebrow. "You're our firstborn, our oldest kid, and you always will be."

"Is that him in the big vase out in the hallway?"

Richard didn't exhale. His mind raced, tried to shrink from the outflung fingers of his daughter's question. Mute, he nodded.

"Okay, then that's why Mom always makes me and Michelle leave it alone, right?" She'd pulled back, looked questioningly at him. He realized for the first time that Mary was leagues brighter than her mother. "Mark is *inside* it, isn't he, and that's why we don't dare touch it?"

He raised her from his lap, found her heavier than a week before, plopped her down on the bed and knew she went on staring up at him. Standing, his curly head was circled by posters of rock musicians who were no older than some of his neckties, by blue Smurfs with the expressions of sadists and Schulz-sold cartoon dogs looking pleased at being dim-witted, and mildly deformed. Mary had spilled some cheap perfume on her miniature makeup table and he knew suddenly that her curving knees would not fit beneath it much longer.

Mark was well named. He'd marked them all, poor dumb Snoopy that he was, and now he was really trying to defeat the Red Baron.

Richard nodded at Mary, fumbled with her door-knob, and stumbled into the hallway. He saw the urn, not far off now, gleaming dully. He covered the distance in four strides and put out his hand to it. No one had ever looked inside, not to his knowledge. There were some things people didn't do, not even these days.

It took awhile, partly because he kept glancing back anxiously in the direction of Mary's room.

Then the lid *gave,* with a tiny sound of hissing, and he was looking into the urn before he could change his mind forever.

The urn was empty.

9

A curious and attentive stranger entering the clamorous city room of the great metropolitan newspaper and discovering the regal woman sitting with her long, sleek legs crossed, at a littered desk nearest the managing editor's glass-partitioned office, would have been surprisingly wrong in what he came to think. Compelled to stare, because the woman was possessed of the kind of affable but careful beauty good breeding is said to produce, the newcomer might have concluded that she was a Very Important Person from the Maryland suburbs, coming perhaps to file the most delicate and tasteful of complaints—the wife of a famed senator from Massachusetts, Connecticut, or New Hampshire, possibly, or the Vassar or Bryn Mawr educated daughter of a four star general with high political aspirations.

There was an ornate name plate atop the desk which read COURTNEY RANKIN, presumably identifying the male reporter whose desk it was and who would be so very, very sorry that he had missed his lovely caller. Even should her complaint prove to

have been directed at Mr. Rankin, because of some
trifling oversight or misinterpretation of detail in
his story about her latest party for the foreign
ambassador, Rankin would have considered himself
fortunate to meet a woman with such self-possessed
intelligence burning independently in her challenging blue eyes, such an arrestingly aristocratic tilt to
the pert nose, such a taunting, oddly sensual smile
upon a wide mouth consisting of a short, determined
upper lip and a full, eminently kissable lower one.
Although she wore a pale blue suit with severe lines,
intended to de-emphasize her figure, Mr. Rankin
might well have observed what a striking bearing
she had, the generous thrust against the bodice of
the white blouse beneath the suit jacket.

Except that no man named Rankin toiled for that
prominent Washington newspaper, aside from a
half-Thai printer downstairs who enjoyed boasting
about his bisexual proclivities. The fascinating
woman seated at the desk, alternately scribbling
shorthand notes and poking a yellow pencil thoughtfully into her modishly styled, chestnut hair, was
hard at work on the preliminary development of a
major news story; and *she* was COURTNEY
RANKIN, a generally well-favored reporter at said
prominent newspaper for almost seven years now.
Favored, except that Courtney's way of running up
unwieldy expense bills on the stimulus of a sudden
creative hunch tended to leave her managing editor
on the Perry Whitish ledge of economic suicide.

She raised the top sheet of her lined notebook
again, again studied the rather dogmatic and terse
psychological profile she'd requested. It described,
as if by arcane Freudian magic, the likely mindset of
certain anonymous and unidentified terrorists who
were currently cutting a systematic swath—plus the

throats of minor officials—across the country. The
assassinations appeared to be haphazard, random
except for the politicized nature of the unsuspecting
victims. But that was precisely what made Ms.
Courtney Rankin feel sure of something: that the
last thing motivating the unknown terrorists was
randomness. Obviously, there was nothing casual or
accidental about the way they had left no clues
whatsoever. According to the authorities in the
towns and cities where they had struck, unless they
lied to make the culprits feel overconfident, there
wasn't enough left behind even to indicate their
point or points of origin, or what they had hoped to
gain.

And to Courtney, that element was especially
intriguing. Until today, she'd had the impression
that they were professional killings. After all, no
demands had been made and none of the usually
voluble terrorist groups had claimed responsibility.
Until today, too, she'd theorized that organized
crime, discerning the public's growing concern
about domestic and foreign terror alike, had simply
chosen to cast suspicion elsewhere. That might have
explained why no other journalists were attempting
to link the random killings spread throughout
America. If a certain, cynical type of newspaper
person believed that the Mafia had acted to take the
lives of various doubtlessly corrupt political figures,
low or high, he or she might then see little cause for
alarm. Still disaffected by Watergate, that reporter
might view organized crime in the light of doing
what the public electorate should have been doing
all along.

Such narrow thought, however, was anathema to
Courtney Rankin. Even if she hadn't been a woman
who tried hard to go on believing in law, and due

process, she was first a reporter, and a significant story was a significant story. Which was why she'd chosen to determine if it were possible to reconstruct a provable link between these widely spaced, cold blooded murders, and wind up breaking it via the wire services—after, of course, her exclusive story had appeared in Washington.

But the expensive shrink's psychological profile had not corroborated Courtney's theories. Instead, it had astonished her. This morning, she found herself stuck with the need to justify its exorbitant cost when the report denied any connection at all with any professional fraternities of dispassionate killers.

Far worse, Courtney was deeply touched by what her behavioral psychologist acquaintance had suggested in his well paid profile. Not that she automatically thought he was wrong; his credentials, which included testimony in half a dozen major criminal trials in D.C., disposed her to believe he must be right.

If he was, however, the implications were profound. Rather more than what Courtney Rankin had reckoned on—and a rather larger story, than the important one she had imagined.

Now she looked up from her notebook with the familiar feeling of surprise which comes from the obligation of leaving one's thoughts for the world around one. She found the people working at the fringes of the city room and at the other desks peculiarly dreamlike, not nearly so real as what she'd been running through her own mind. Almost in a mood of relief, she saw the stack of books on the corner of her desk, some of them purchased from a bookstore and some borrowed from the Forest Heights library, and tentatively threw out her hand,

regaining a measure of contact with her previous
line of careful thought. They were books concerning
various aspects both of psychology and crime—
Abraham Maslow's *Toward a Psychology of Being*
and *The Farther Reaches of Human Nature;* Colin
Wilson's priceless *The Outsider, Order of Assassins,
New Pathways in Psychology* and *Encyclopedia of
Murder;* Jesse's *Murder and Its Motives;* Richard
Grant's *Terror in the Eye of the Beholder;* Carl
Jung's *Undiscovered Self;* David Reisman's *Lonely
Crowd;* Moore's *The Lawbreakers*—and she knew
abruptly that her next stop was to interview a
bonafide expert.

Jung and Maslow were dead, she knew. Wilson,
whom she really wished to discuss it with, was in
England. Courtney idly opened one of the books,
saw a photograph of a smiling, curly haired writer
whose work she'd found fresh and perceptive, even
while he wrote in the novelistic form. Grant, according to the bio on the dust jacket blurb, lived in
Washington!

"He won't be in the phone book," she told herself
aloud, conversationally, drawing a thick volume of
white pages from the center section of her desk.
"He's bound to be unlisted."

But he wasn't. Her flame-tipped index finger
skimmed the line; Richard Grant lived in driving
range, out in nearby Wheaton. She couldn't believe
her luck.

Instantly she rushed for her phone, buried
beneath read-outs of her next column.

But what was the best way to approach him?
Courtney Rankin was the kind of newspaperperson
who tended to think that hers was the finest job in
the United States, until she met a published author,
someone who had not only enjoyed the luxury of re-

searching his material until the last frail fact was
unearthed and had then constructed a fat, juicy
enduring book, but who also had achieved the
dignity of relative permanency, as contrasted with
the ephemeral nature of the daily newspaper. If
anything would ever pry her away from the paper, it
would be the comic's unforgettable reference to
newspapers as liners for garbage cans.

Or the New York *Times*.

For a moment, then, she peered out at the others
working in the city room, and their outlines became
sharper, familiar, much more real. This was not
merely three column inches about some peccadillo-
prone junior senator from an uninfluential state,
whose heated displeasure would be expressed as a
simple denial, she reminded herself. The people at
the heart of this story—if Doc was correct in his
profile, and if she were right in what she was beginning to deduce—could make this the most
dangerous assignment of her career.

He couldn't remember when he'd felt more foolish,
and the book lying on the car seat beside him only
underscored his low valuation of himself.

The tome was his own, first published novel, and
Richard meant to use it as a bold means of cutting
through red tape, if he had to. He just hoped the
people he was going to see would be the right kind,
and, wending his way through post noon traffic on
16th Street, he decided that the world could, again,
be divided into two kinds.

Some people weren't impressed if you were the
author of a book or, for that matter, if you'd written
a book that remained atop the best-seller list for a
solid twenty-six weeks. They were the modern kind
who swooned at the boots of rock musicians, and

stood in line for autographs from anybody who had
ever appeared in a movie or on network television.
They would, however, be courteous to you and
possibly let you affix your signature to their sweaty
autograph books if you'd succeeded in selling your
book for "the motion picture version."

Then there was the other kind of human being,
Richard's favorite. Generally the type of person who
could not leave the room without reading matter in
hand, linked by their common belief that each of
them "has a book inside" and that someday they
will be magically driven to express their hearts on
paper, they had only to learn that you'd been
published to queue up and meet you—whispering to
one another in line, "What did you say he wrote?"
and "Have you read it?"

It was hard to figure which group properly housed
government bureaucracy, Richard reflected. Most
such workers were old enough to have outgrown
juvenile music and probably had graduated from
high school, theoretically with the precious
acquisition of an ability to read. But on the other
hand, if they'd worked in Washington political
circles long enough, they stood an excellent chance
of being able, now, to read nothing but their
own unique gobbledegook-bureaucratese. Richard
grinned, as he passed through Kensington and
realized he was nearing his destination. *If I
remember to add the suffix* 'icize' *to enough words,
and use all the parts of speech wrong but
importantly, they may nominate me for the
Presidency on the spot!*

His goal was the Army Medical Center, due north
of the nation's capitol, and his purpose, as
competently as he could define it, was to scrutinize
the birth statistics of military hospitals for a rough

period including the year 1967. The year Mark
Grant became a legal name, a statistic to be
retained, a male Caucasian citizen of the United
States who was nevertheless as much an
"unperson" as any of those described by George
Orwell. Because he'd never known a microsecond of
actual life.

By the time he'd left his doddering car in an
enormous parking lot and started with hollow footsteps down a fluorescent lit corridor on the strength
of nothing more than giving permission to record his
name, address, and social security number in a
frightening ledger, Richard's earlier doubts were
starting to leave him. If Mark's vulnerable young
life, his human rights, his civil rights, whatever the
glossy title this government might have given them,
had been taken by unarguable carelessness, surely
Mark could not rest until somebody *paid*—paid, at
the very least, by a guarantee that other military
deliveries would not be botched.

But Richard was also aware of how he'd lost his
nerve and not mentioned his profession to anyone at
the information counter. He'd even put his book into
his jacket pocket, next to an easily procured table of
civilian statistics, a list against which he could
compare the Army records, if he was allowed access
to them. Following a crisply uniformed young
attendant past an open door through which he could
detect a bristling battery of computer hardware,
Richard shivered. *Thank God,* he thought, *Molly's
at the bank and doesn't know where I am. If she did,
she'd be sure I was in the clutches of terminal
paranoia.*

He took his seat where he was directed, sliding
gingerly into it as if the chair might be electrified, or
a gas pellet might drop from its underside. Flat out,

his palms lowered slowly to the top of the table; he essayed a hideous grimace meant to represent nonchalance and, audibly humming, raised his glance to look around the room. Just as surreptitiously, Big Brother surveillance cameras took his picture and that of a round, military-straight individual he now noticed at the other end of the table. *I don't blame them for taking his picture,* Richard thought. *With that Adolf mustache and those weepy eyes behind sunglasses, he's obviously a spy from the NKVD.*

The weepy eyes rose, in Richard's direction, the man's reflective sunglasses returning to the writer a distant, dual image of his own instinctive palm wave and ghastly amiable smile. Then the uniformed attendant was back with two massive volumes, one of which he slid beneath the nose and Hitler mustache of Richard's companion in espionage. "Thank you," said the spy. "If you want anything else, General, just call," said the youth.

Richard was thoroughly abashed, his nerves sizzling like bacon in a frying pan, when the other large volume was politely placed on the table before him. "Thank you," he said weakly. "You're welcome," said the attendant, glancing obviously at a card, "Mr. Grant."

Molly turned her chair almost completely in a circle, away from the very young, very beautiful teller whom she had been disciplining.

Management, at whatever rung in the ladder, did not dare allow the managed to see them crying.

She also did not want the other woman on the phone with her to know exactly how badly her heart was breaking.

"I certainly appreciate your going to all the trouble of tracking me down at work," she said

softly, glancing back, through tears, at the
impatient beauty on the other side of her desk. She
pressed her fingernails into her palms, fighting for
control. "That was very considerate of you."

"And of your father," came the all-but-unfamiliar
voice of Molly's stepmother. "We should have
expected that he'd fall this ill when his grand-
children were on Christmas vacation."

Oh, Christ, Molly thought desperately, *that's
bringing it right into the open!* Clearly, she would
have to get to Indianapolis immediately, while there
was time. Despite the way her dad had become a
seething chaos of recrimination, doubt, longing, old
love and old hate, Molly had known at once that she
would go to her father. That was what people did.
But now this woman, this stranger on the phone,
was calculatingly insisting that Molly put Mary and
Michelle through the awful mill, too, and she wasn't
at all sure they were old enough for it. Or if *anyone*
were ever old enough for dying.

"I don't know if we can handle the air fare for all
of us," Molly said aloud. Her handkerchief was
pressed near her mouth and the telephone, simultaneously, but she'd been surprised by how level her
voice was. The younger teller, Molly could see from
the corner of her eye, wore that long-suffering
expression of those people who are so mercifully
removed from dying-ages that they can afford to be
bored. Molly made up her mind to fire the impudent,
calloused creature just as soon as she hung up.

"I thought your husband was doing fabulously,"
said Mrs. Skylar. It was almost a question, but not
quite. She sounded wonderfully adjusted to what
was happening to her own mate. "But don't let's
worry about finances, dear. Your father gave me
instructions for just such an emergency, and I have

already wired an ample sum of money to you."

Then the conversation was over without Molly fully realizing it had ended, with the words, "Don't call me 'dear,'" still on her lips. She turned her poised face back to the younger woman, said, "It's Daddy," simply, and her expression became tortured and abjectly lonely.

"Oh, you poor thing!" The pretty teller, startled by tears, was immediately around the desk, taking the older woman into her arms. "Is he . . . ?"

"No, not yet," Molly said through her tears; "Soon." She looked at the mournful beauty consoling her and patted the young cheek. "You're going to be okay, honey," she sobbed. "You're coming along just *fine!*"

Richard had to put his fingertips on his forehead, let the fingers and his palms conceal the expression dawning in his eyes and taking shape in his expressive features. He'd forced himself not to jump, or twitch, not with the surveillance cameras watching and recording every move. Now he tried to breathe shallowly, get full control of himself, before copying the stunning facts he'd found in the book of statistics.

Footsteps! The general—was his name mentioned or not?—leaving the volume he'd used on the table, open, striding past without a single glance in Richard's direction.

He lifted the hand he'd automatically pressed over the significant portion of the page, and studied it again.

There were three sets of figures; he should have anticipated that. He'd sneaked a look at the civilian table he'd brought along, seen at once that the Army stats of surviving infants, male and female,

was somewhat lower by ratio than that of nonmilitary births. Then he'd found that the survival
rate of females delivered at Army hospitals was
actually somewhat *higher* than the same data for
girls born to civilian-related mothers.

Which, clearly enough, left the final military
statistics for *male births* a terrifying if slightly
altered substantiation of Richard's worst fears.

Because, during the period running roughly from
1967 through 1970—*the approximate period of
major American involvement in the Vietnam war*—
it appeared that *boy babies born in a number of
Army hospitals,* not just Fort Christopher, but other
military hospitals scattered throughout the United
States, *were born dead at a rate almost twice that of
the national average!*

What in hell was going on—or had been going on,
just at the right time to cost Molly and Richard
Grant their firstborn, to seize from them the only
male child they would ever have?

Richard realized he was looking blankly right into
the unblinking camera lenses studying him with
brotherly concern, and quickly looked away. He had
to get out of there, and *soon!* The audacity of it,
leaving the statistics precisely as they were,
suddenly seemed to Richard a worse, balder thing to
do than the revisionist history of Orwell's famous
book. Was the totalitarian Big Brother in America
less cautious than he of 1984—or had he succeeded
so well, moved so much more quickly toward mind-
control of the United States version of Oceania, that
there was no need to alter the books? Was the
typical American that accepting, that brainwashed?

Or was it, in some unguessable fashion, only one
more example of the bewildering, screwed up world
of Nam and Watergate, and was Richard wrong in

thinking the single, paralyzing word that leaped to mind: *Experimentation?*

"Need anything else?"

Richard half rose to his feet, yanked there by the materialization of the courteous uniformed youth who stood inches away, reguarding him with a bland, lineless face and cool, efficient gray eyes. He tried not to stare down at the book, which was still open. He knew he should not draw attention to it, and to himself. But he hadn't copied the statistics yet, and he wanted badly to do that, to copy them word for word.

"Did you find something you'd like to photocopy?" asked the youth. The question was like a blade of steel prying at Richard's nerves. It was eerily as if the boy had read his mind. "If so, we—"

"No!" He shook his head, too hard; smiled, and sweated. He couldn't risk the possibility that a record would be made of what he'd photocopied. "Thanks, I'll only be another minute."

Doubtful, possibly even concerned, the youngster went to the door, stopped to look back. Richard nodded, smirked; he waggled his fingers, and the soldier stepped stiffly out of sight.

The surveillance cameras went right on gurgling. Richard sat down again, remembering movies, TV programs, in which the hero—James Bond, likely as not; maybe Napoleon Solo—had thrown his coat over such damnably constant, curious, silent observers. Heavily perspiring, he copied the page of statistics on the reverse side of the sheet bearing the civilian birth data, wondering if he shouldn't have photocopied them. If Big Brother decided to take the book away now, and change it, it would be Richard's word against the All-Powerful, and he knew how that would end.

When he'd finished, acting on impulse, he got slowly to his feet and, carrying the statistical volume, strolled to the other end of the table. He turned his back to the high-banked cameras, put the book down beside the one used by the general, and opened his coat. For a moment, Richard braced himself, as though for machine-gun fire, then dropped the sides of his jacket and again picked up the book of birth data.

The same one he'd used himself.

I didn't read Sherlock Holmes mysteries for nothing, he thought, dizzy with daring as he put the volume back where it had been. *Take that, Moriarty!*

When he started back through the dank, long corridors toward the front of the building, he required all his will power to keep from running.

But he also had to admit to himself that he hadn't felt so wonderfully stimulated in years.

10

"Must I remind you that you have two beautiful daughters? Honestly, Richard, I would have thought you'd be the last man in the world to behave in such an absurdly old-fashioned way! To become so overwrought, all these years later, because—because there's no one to 'carry on the Grant family name!'"

Richard leaned back against the sink and stared helplessly at Molly, dumbfounded. After telling her what he'd discovered at the Army Medical Center, he'd been obliged to follow her out to the kitchen, where, moving with swift and spastic gestures, she was emotionally going through the motions of getting dinner started. "That isn't why I'm so upset!" he exclaimed.

"*Isn't* it!" She spun around him to reach into the refrigerator, then elbowed it shut with a slam.

"Dammit, Molly, *I* would have thought *you'd* be the last person to take my news so calmly! The situation has *changed.*"

Her back was to him and she was still wearing the new suit she had purchased to celebrate her recent

promotion. That fact, plus the obvious tension in
her arrow-straight spine and the back of her neck,
reminded him of many other evenings which had
begun with Molly's temper flaring. Too many other
evenings, especially the past few years. There'd
been a time when she was meek, even docile, and
he'd looked for more fire and found an earthy softness, a yielding topsoil that always gave at the
prodding of his own quicksilver temperament.
Since she had adjusted to the role of a working wife-
and-mother, however, Molly had changed. But she
rarely lost her temper unless she was already
dressed, able to rush angrily but presentably from
the house without demeaning her status as a career
woman. Precisely how often Molly had used a family
quarrel as an excuse to leave, to go God knew where,
Richard had no idea.

"There's no change to the situation," she said at
last, feigning frigid patience. She did not turn to
him. "Mark died. Mark has been dead for twenty
years now. And Mark remains dead and a bunch of
stupid government statistics won't alter the facts."

"But now it seems that Mark died because of
some terrible act of incompetence," he insisted,
pulling himself away from the sink and using his
most winning tone of voice. His shirt was miserably
wet from where he'd leaned and the stove was just
beginning to take the winter chill out of the house.
He tried slipping his arms around her waist from
behind. "An incompetence so goddamned bad that
it was practically an *epidemic!*"

"There's somebody here, trying to grate a carrot,"
Molly said softly, "in case you haven't noticed."
Her chin was lowered, her right arm energetically
pumping. "I know that cooking, like banking, isn't
dramatic enough for you, but sooner or later you'll

demand that I feed you." He caught a glimpse of a
lock of her yellow hair, independently strayed from
its businesslike placement and loose against one
pale temple, the way he preferred it. Studiously, she
avoided responding to his hugging arms. "Some
men these days, who have countless hours on their
hands, time to drive into Washington and pretend
to be secret agents, help their wives with the household tasks. Wives who *worked* all day."

"What's the matter with you?" He let go of her,
stepped to her side to stare incredulously at her.
"What in the *fuck* is the matter with you?"

"When all else fails," Molly murmured, "resort to
bullying the little woman. Use the vilest, most
common language to frighten her into her place."

He'd never consciously bullied her, never came
close to striking her. "Dammit, Mol," he cried,
"most mothers would—"

"Stop it! Stop it *right now*." She ceased working,
looked down, then toward him from the corner of
blazing eyes. "If you've chosen this evening to
begin another attack on me—to tell me how mad I
am—or if you're implying that I'm an unnatural
mother—"

"No, *shit*," he retorted, shaking his head. "I just
asked." He wished she would move because the
glare on the snow, beyond the window behind her,
was making his eyes water. "I asked you to explain,
to tell me why a woman who's just learned that her
first child was one of countless newborns who didn't
draw a *breath of life—a vastly higher number* than
average, with *no* explanation for it—wants to talk
about fucking carrots!" He'd lost his placating
mood in mid-speech, and blinked, eager to take back
his adjective. "Sorry."

"You know perfectly well why I don't want to

discuss it." Now Molly did face him. She was nearly his height and he'd always been amazed, when she was angry or naked, how distinctly unfrail she appeared. But he saw that her eyes were small in her puffy cheeks and realized she had been crying. "We went all over that just the other night, Richard. But *you're* a big deal author, *you* don't have to pay attention to my needs—because *you* have to go play Jim Bond!"

"James," Richard said. It was automatic and he followed with an apologetic grin. "James Bond. No one calls him Jim, I think." Now he wished he hadn't mentioned it. "Of course, I'm no expert, I could be wrong."

"You *are* wrong," Molly snapped. "Wrong to open up a lot of old wounds when it won't bring our Mark back to us. And wrong not even to ask me why I was home early enough to hear your fantasy and be hurt one more time today!"

He pointed an index at her eyes. "Is that why you've been crying?" Concern surged in his chest like a bad taste. "What happened, honey? You didn't get fired, did you?"

"No, I'm still on the payroll, still doing my part," she said with unhappy pride. She didn't turn her face back to the kitchen counter before he could see the fresh tears starting. "It's my daddy, if it means anything to you. We have to fly to Indianapolis tomorrow. To see him."

Richard simply looked at her, too startled, confused, and contrite to know the best thing to say. "Is it his heart?" he asked, finally, and detected Molly's all-but-indiscernible nod. He sensed his fine excitement ebbing away and let it. "Aw, Molly, I'm truly sorry. Does he have much of a chance?"

"I'm not sure, but I stopped at the cleaners and

picked up your good suit.'' She covered the dish she was preparing, moving toward the stove. ''It's lucky the girls are home for the holidays or we'd have to find a babysitter.''

It came to him with a shock that he was expected to accompany them. *Of course I am,* he thought, *Molly hates to fly.* But he had to do something about Mark; it was twenty years, and somebody had to be held accountable while there was still time. ''My work . . .''

She pivoted away from the oven and came nearly to a crouch in front of him. ''I knew you'd say you couldn't go!'' she exclaimed. ''That you were 'too busy writing' to come with us!'' She rushed to the kitchen door and burst through it. ''Well, your daughters and I don't need you and we don't want you! We'll get along just fine on our own!''

He covered the ground between them quickly, hating and fearing another of her disappearances into the night. But Molly didn't head for the foyer and front door. Instead, she started up the stairs to the second floor, and her copious tears began in earnest before she'd reached the landing. There, Mary put her arm solicitously around her mother's shoulders. Michelle stared soberly down the steps at her father, then smiled feebly and waved before ducking back into her own bedroom.

Minutes later, trying to decide whether to go with his family, Richard noticed a banking letterhead bearing his wife's hasty writing. It lay beside Molly's purse, not in it, and he picked it up curiously.

She had scribbled a morning departure time, from U.S. Air, and had done some calculations using a sum of money Richard assumed she had withdrawn from their checking account.

Any way he added and subtracted, Molly had made flight reservations for three people. Not four.

"I hope Doc Skylar is feeling better by the time you arrive," Richard offered. They were in a roped off area, the plane was almost ready for boarding, and he was starting to see in his mind's eye hideous headlines: WRITER'S FAMILY SKYJACKED was the mildest of them. A word, and he'd sprint to the ticket counter.

"Thank you." Slowly, Molly put out her gloved hands, managing a smile. He looked twenty-five in his belted car coat and fluffy cossack hat, and, with Mary and Michelle wearing their finery for the flight to Indiana, she was struck again by what a handsome family they made. But one that seemed to be coming apart at the seams. "I hope you figure out the best way to use your statistics in your new novel. I know it'll be great."

"What?" He released her hands, shocked and hurt. "Is that what you think I wanted them for? To use in a *book?*"

"Well, whatever; you know best." She stepped back, shrugging, looking at a scattering of snowflakes which turned the airfield beyond the window gray and ashen. Everything she said these days was wrong and she didn't know why. Abruptly, she longed for Richard to go with them, wished she had informed him about the money Lucille, her stepmother, had wired. Surely it was the expense of flying to Indianapolis that kept Richard from insisting he go, but she didn't want to force him; that would make it meaningless. Now the thought of being on an airplane, without him but with the responsibility of the girls, was terrifying. "Shall I phone you if—if anything—"

"If the worst happens?" Richard's heart went out to her. They'd never been apart any important length of time, only when Mary and Michelle were born, and he saw the loneliness of the Wheaton house already, beset with memories that might never be further accumulated. He wrapped his arms around Molly, reached down to include their daughters in his hug. "I'm sure Doc Skylar will be okay; he's a tough old bird. But . . . *if* . . . well, let me know immediately and I'll catch the next flight.

Then, abjectly miserable, he watched them disappear into the encasement leading to the plane's entrance. Being a writer, Richard was instantly reminded of reports given by deathbed patients who'd experienced visions of tunnels leading directly to Paradise.

It wasn't until he'd left Washington National Airport and was heading back toward Montgomery County that he realized he'd have all the peace and quiet he needed to consider his next step, perhaps a visit with the family attorney, and that Molly might have come up with her best idea.

He hadn't lied to her, not consciously. He'd never intended to write so much as a page about the astonishing mortality rate of newborn boys, two decades ago, and certainly he hadn't wanted to earn a dime in writing about their awful loss. But if there was a chance that such medical incompetence could happen *again*, threaten the lives of other dearly desired, unborn children, putting it all on paper might be the best way to approach such a revelation.

But it isn't unborn children, *it's unborn boys,* he reminded himself, falling into somber thought.

And while he didn't want to follow that line of reasoning, unless there was something physiological, medical, or chemical that he knew nothing about, the fact that *one* sex was singled out for "error" made incompetence the most modest and innocuous of terms.

Which would mean, terrible as it was to contemplate, that what had happened to Mark—and to Eddie Dugan's boy, the Italian's son, hundreds of others—was surely *intentional.* Not accidental.

But who could possibly have such a fury against people as helpless as newborn males? Richard frowned, yanked the steering wheel to force the old Camaro back into its lane as a Chevy whined past. The damnable thing was almost *Biblical!* Specifically, if he remembered his Bible at all, Old Testament—a dreadful, mindless thing belonging hundreds upon hundreds of years ago back in time when an untutored, ignorant, unsanitary specimen calling himself King could actually command the sacrifice of infant males!

But who, in this hypothetically enlightened age, could or would issue such an incredible and indescribably ruthless order?

A late model automatic was blocking the driveway as Richard drove down the block and approached his house, and there was no one at the wheel.

Someone—a woman, he thought—was standing at the front door of Richard's house, one hand raised in a gesture of rapping.

11

From any random point on the three hills overlooking them, the nature of the buildings nestled in the maternal bosom of the valley would have been anybody's guess. Each appeared to be the same height as its neighbors—a low-hung two story with a crisp, functional, even institutional ambience—and, while well maintained, it advertised nothing about its reason for existence. There were no markings or signs of subterfuge, or, for that matter, clarity. There certainly was no address on any of the buildings, not out *here*, and anyone standing atop any of the hills might have noticed that there were no rural mailboxes to be seen.

Taken alone, such facts would not have aroused the curiosity of the passerby; but there was more to report.

If that uninvited onlooker were alert, he might have observed the rather surprising, complete absence of trees where he stood. It was utterly stark; barren; without cover. Not so much as a sapling, a bush, or even a dandelion provided the chance for a covert inspection of the scene from

anywhere along the ragged ridge. The grass was
kept so closely trimmed that it would have been
impossible for anyone peering into the valley to
avoid being seen.

And the hypothetical visitor might also have
remarked upon the way most of the ground on the
precise *edge* of each hill was cleared and, even on
particularly hot days, looked wet, and soft. Very
much like mud of a kind that would retain foot-
prints.

It was particularly unpleasant to think of
standing alone upon any of the hills and staring
down. Only part of it was the considerable height,
since it would probably have been possible for a
reasonably good athlete to run down in order to
approach the unmarked, oddly squat wooden structures. Mostly it was the structures themselves—
and the fact that most men or women who looked
down would surely have sworn to a distinctly
uneasy feeling that they were being watched—evaluated; studied, identified, if possible—by more than
one set of eyes looking *up*. And that, in turn, might
have been enough to cause an onlooker to wonder
about the apparently ordinary, innocuous slope of
the hills upon which he might otherwise have
descended.

The single obvious entrance to the site was to the
east, where no fourth hill rose against the bland sky.
One could see that a road, generously covered with
large, crunchy, costly gravel, ran twistingly away
from a massive section of industrial fencing which
extended, on either side, into the hills themselves.
No entrance was instantly discoverable, from atop
the hill, but surely there had to be one; because there
seemed to be no other way for the people working in
the buildings to leave. Or, for those outside the

fence, to enter.

The twisting, gravel road itself gave a visitor to
the high hills the stomach-churning notion that it
simply vanished into the earth, a mile, possibly,
away from the heavy fence. That was illusion,
because the road had merely *begun* there, at the end
of a path from the highway which had been created
only by the impress of the few passing vehicles
which entered the site. Because they had seldom
left, since arriving, a motorist on the highway might
never have known the path leading to the gravel
road existed. Speeding along at fifty-five miles an
hour or more the person in an automobile or truck
could easily fail to notice the path, particularly since
there was no sign to proclaim its presence—there, or
anywhere at all on the highway running north and
south.

Although one might have had the impression of a
retreat, something religious and reclusive which
required no billboards or maps or public invitations
because the initiated were aware of the location, and
while it was impossible to hear that first nuance of
noise when everyone was inside the structures, there
were many people at the site, and they were unfailingly either working in the two acres of clearing
around the buildings or assembled collectively in
but one of the two story structures.

The people there, it seemed, stayed together. At
all times.

Now, they were at work in the gymnasium. Inside
it, there would have been no question about the
purpose of this particular building. Everything a
visitor might have expected to find in a well
appointed gym: a shining floor upon which no one
was permitted to walk in street shoes, weights,
basketball backboards, collapsible equipment for

exercise affixed to various portions of the walls.
And abundantly more.

Even here, however, there was a distinction, a
bizarre anomaly, to set the gymnasium and its uses
aside from most: everyone exercising in it was
naked. *Fully* naked.

An uninvited caller might have recalled ancient
Athens, or Sparta, and felt that he had
inadvertently stepped through the portals of a time
machine.

Several pairs of perspiring athletes were workng
out in the north quadrant of the gymnasium, and
while a few white mattresses were arranged for the
convenience of certain novices, most of them toiled
upon the hardwood floor.

Including the middle-sized, dark-haired man who
had both the perfect conditioning and concomitant
reflexes to see an opening left by his friendly
opponent and take advantage of it. Spinning nimbly
on the pad of one bare foot, the nude athlete brought
his swinging, muscled leg around in an arc and the
first two toes of his foot cut into the chosen target—
one special place in his opponent's throat.

The opponent, much larger, plummeted to the
floor and did not move. A steady trickle of scarlet
substance oozed from the corner of his mouth, and
his eyes began to glaze over.

No one else involved in exercising stopped, or
seemed to notice.

However, two men who had been watching from
their folding chairs on the sidelines (the gymnasium
contained no other seating, permanent or otherwise)
immediately bounced to their own bare feet and
hurried out onto the shiny floor where the middle-
sized, dark haired man stood with his head down,
panting.

One of the two, the taller and younger, dropped to his knees lithely, beside the toppled gladiator. Expertly, he touched a place in the neck where a pulse would be found if, indeed, one existed. He looked up, blank-faced, at the shorter, older naked man who was the only individual in the gynmasium wearing a hat. The information presented was terse: "It's a clean extraction. He's inanimated."

The man with the hat swung the edge of his hand toward the dark haired visitor. It was blocked with a forearm rising so fast that the fully extended and braced fingers stopped a fraction of an inch from the hat-wearer's right ear. The latter smiled, clapped the other on the shoulder. "Well done," he said. "Couldn't have done a lot better myself."

"Can I be part of the starting team, next time out?" inquired the dark haired man. He was much too unemotional to get excited about it and kept his voice level, but it would be a great deal safer once he belonged to one of the teams.

"I don't see why not. Sure; count on it. You've earned a start."

The man with the hat glanced down at where the dead man was sprawled, but the body had already been removed. He smiled approvingly. A youngster with the kind of mop used at basketball games, to wipe up sweat and spills, was running his implement over the spot. When he dipped it back into the bucket, the water became pink.

Adam Boswell paused to look across his half darkened office, fairly sure he'd heard a noise somewhere in the otherwise abandoned building. The cleaning lady, he told himself, knuckling his eyes with a Kleenex from a container on his desk. Another twenty minutes and he'd be ready to see

Marcy again. Marcy, the Vitamin E injection with the firm, hairy legs.

Boswell was burning the midnight oil, not for the first time in his career. He didn't suppose he would ever become entirely used to it and he sure as hell would make a point of never learning to enjoy it, but his constituents liked to see the lights on now and then, when they chugged past City Hall. It was a necessary part of the game and Boswell rarely complained about it to anyone except Barbara, his wife, unless he took it out on his teen-aged son. If he really *had* to go on regarding that hulking, pellucid, acne-scarred, smelly creature with so much greasy long hair he was even a fucking anachronism to his pothead peers, as the son of Mayor Adam J. Boswell.

Once, eighteen years ago, he'd shoved Barbara onto her back and told her in his inimitable fashion that they had to go on trying to have a child, despite the disagreeable facts which included five miscarriages and Barbara's four-year plunge into her personal thirties. Boswell had reached the point where he could tolerate her only marginally more than she could him, even if her disgust with sex left him in second place in *that* hierarchy.

After all, sacrifices had been foreseen and plans—plus Barbara, as often as Boswell could stomach it—laid from the start. "You're the only one more ambitious than I am, doll," he'd said as he pinned her shoulders down, "and this has always been a town with folks who prefer families. Show 'em we're normal and healthy and make the right promises and a guy like me can not only be mayor but use this place for a springboard to the governorship. Who knows how far I can go?"

She'd wanted to tell him, remind him that she was

his principle springboard, and Boswell wondered nowadays if he mightn't have come as far without Adam, Junior. Or maybe the yokels had started voting for him out of sheer sympathy.

When the door opened, without a knock, and the mayor glanced up, he thought for a moment it was Junior and his friends barging in.

Boswell's first intimation that he was wrong occurred when he realized that Junior didn't have that many friends, and he'd never seen any of them move so *fast*.

All the other clues Mayor Boswell received came in clusters of pain. There was scarcely time to wonder who the balding man was who stood aloof from the administering of his agony, a man who might have been distinguishable from the shadows he'd immediately found except for snowy gloves, which flashed as he stoically folded his arms.

There might have been three other people, or four, who took turns in doing terrible things with their chopping hands, their lethal elbows and stabbing feet. Or eleven, or twelve; Mayor Boswell quickly lost the ability to count.

He hadn't even seen a dark haired, middle-sized man in a sweatsuit who placed an immaculate tarpaulin beneath his falling body with all the deft éclat of an experienced waiter spreading a clean cloth over a tabletop.

All motion in Adam Boswell's office ceased. Except for a strangled sound escaping the lips of that bloodied worthy, it was preternaturally quiet, as well.

The man who had watched took three steps forward, and stopped before the mayor's desk. He withdrew a white glove, dusted a corner of the desk with his handkerchief, then hitched up a hip and once more folded his arms. His glance at the others was more burning, or smoldering, then piercing. After he'd checked his stopwatch, however, piercing was added to the burning and smouldering.

"You are the most goal-oriented people on the face of the earth. I'll give you that, because that's *precisely* what I have given you. You took him out soundlessly and nobody was hurt." He slid off the desk. "But your *timing* makes me want to retch. It is flat-out deplorable. Jesus!"

No one moved or spoke a word. Even the mayor lying on the tarpaulin seemed to be listening intently and had stopped writhing.

The man, still wearing only one glove, strode casually to the edge of the tarpaulin and turned, pointing. "That file cabinet was touched. There's a black hair on that yellow pad where he's written his little 'impromptu' speech; I can see the son-of-a-bitch from where I stand." He paused until the men responsible cleaned up the mess. Then he stooped, picked up one of the mayor's legs and pointed with his bare hand. "*Look* at this, dammit, somebody's mothering *sneaker* made a discernible stain on the cuff. D'you think you can get by with such carelessness on Christmas *Eve*?"

No one moved or spoke. The man dropped the mayor's leg, brushed his gloved hand against his own trouser leg. "Christ-on-a-crutch, people, you think we'll be dealing with *mayors* on the twenty-fourth? *Look* at this man, you didn't even properly inanimate him!" Shaking his head in disgust and apparent despondency, continuing to mutter, audibly, the man leaned over Adam Boswell. One of Boswell's eyes was open, the other unrecognizable now as an eye. Although the mayor could no longer speak, the opened eye was watching. "You think the worst that can happen to you people is being *left behind*?"

Sighing, he removed his other glove, and rested them both on the mayor's spasming abdomen. Still leaning, he inserted a thumb in each ear of the ruined politician, movements so relaxed, polite, and effortless they appeared courtly.

Then the thumb's knuckles snapped as they bent. He sought and found leverage by thrusting his broad shoulders forward. A torrent of bright blood gushed from each ear, but the thumbs, unstained, were already removed. As he stepped back, nimbly, impeccable, the tarpaulin turned red.

Neither the man nor the mayor had made a noise, and the latter remained silent aside from a faint gurgling sound coming from the geysering ears.

The man plucked a Kleenex from a box on the desk, and wiped each of his thumbs. He looked at the dark marks on the tissue with a blend of repugnance and professorial reflection. Then he retrieved his snow-white gloves and started for the door.

"That isn't the worst thing that will happen to anybody who's left behind on Christmas Eve," he said, never breaking stride as the office door was swung wide for him. "People, that wasn't even close."

12

Richard, irritated already because he couldn't park in his own driveway and had to leave his car at the snowy curb, slammed the driver's door hard and trotted with hazardous alacrity around the vehicle and grimly across the icy sidewalk. His imaginings on the trip home had left him moodily frightened and vaguely paranoid; and he was so relieved to find a mere woman turning to him from his front door that he did several altogether human things. The first was, he yelled at her. But the trouble was, in trying to charge up the slight rise of his front yard as the wind began to gust, like a knight reclaiming his castle, he slipped in the slush, fell heavily to one knee, and dropped his imitation Russian hat in the snow. The mishap managed to accentuate the last word of his peremptory shout: "Whatever it is you're selling, lady, we don't need a damned— thing!"

Courtney Rankin still had her gloved fist raised to rap, her serious eyes wide with surprise. Chilled because the overengineered heater in her new car had chosen to expire only blocks from the newspaper, she'd hoped to be greeted by a fatherly professor type who would offer her Danish and steaming hot chocolate in good china. She was obliged to stare, instead, at the curly haired apparition with a wet knee, a dripping cossack hat dangling from its fist, who darted past her to the door, and fumbled with a key ring while it held the storm door bangingly at bay with its elbow.

She touched the specimen on the shoulder, gingerly, despite the way it muttered. "You're scared shitless about something, aren't you?"

Richard whirled around, gaping at her. "The condition of my bowels is none of your business!" Then it dawned on him that women, these days, were into everything, including the Army and an involvement with childbirth. "You aren't a salesman, are you?" he asked hopefully.

"Salesperson," Courtney replied, automatically correcting him. "No, I'm not. I'm—"

"Yes, you are." Satisfied but miffed, Richard turned back to shaking the keys in his free hand, trying to make the right one pop into view. "The sure mark of a salesman is when she swears she's not selling anything."

"I'm Courtney Rankin. I'm a reporter." She stared at him again, watching his one-handed labors. "Are you sure you live here?"

"Of *course*, I'm sure I live here!" Richard retorted, his eyes flashing. Giving up on the sleight-of-hand trade, he clapped his Russian hat on his head and held the key ring in his left hand, immediately producing the right key. Snow turned to water dripped down the sides of his face, making his sideburns point. "I've just never been particularly mechanical." He stepped into the house, and turned to look back at Courtney. "Why are you a reporter?

I mean, why does a reporter want to see me?"

"Could I possibly come inside?" She had her arms wrapped around her sides and was starting to shiver uncontrollably. "I loathe winter."

Richard regarded her silently for a second, his anger beginning to fade. Noticing for the first time how attractive she was, he grinned and motioned. "I can relate to that," he replied, putting his hat on the register in the foyer and leading the way inside. "C'mon in."

"You've a lovely house, Mr. Grant," Courtney murmured politely, removing her coat. None of this was what she'd expected and she looked sharply at him. "You are Richard Grant, aren't you?"

"Here, let me take your coat." He hung it on a hanger, slipped it into the front closet, and added his own. He'd disappeared from sight into the foyer and called out to her. "I'll plead *nolo contendere* to that one. There's not some sort of a new public campaign to make me give back the money I earned from my second book, is there?"

He reemerged and Courtney smiled winningly as he drew near. "Not that I've heard about. To tell the truth, Mr. Grant, I wasn't aware you'd written a second novel. Has it been out long?"

"You don't measure things like heart bypass surgery or my books in an anything as mundane as time." He stopped, facing her, and felt the worse for it despite the scent of her perfume. Richard had immediately noticed she was taller. Shrugging, he started deeper into the room, motioning. "I knew it was the best kept secret around, but it's been out long enough for the famous Courtney Rankin to have heard about it."

She smoothed her skirt behind her long legs as she sat on the sofa he indicated, stalling. This was going so badly and Grant was so impossible that she felt crestfallen. "But I did read your first book, Mr. Grant. That's actually why I'm here."

He dropped into his favorite chair, nearby. Without answering immediately, he appraised her with his light blue eyes, trying to decide whether to give in to his whim or not. The inclination to like, even admire her, despite his annoyance at her intrusion, and his mental exhaustion from the events of the past few days. "You didn't even blink when I referred to you as famous, d'you know that?"

"I guess I should have said thanks," Courtney answered, seriously flustered and becoming more than a little annoyed. "Except it's probably a fact."

"Sure, it is!" He brought up a knee, leaned his elbows on it and his chin on laced hands. "You have a thrice-a-week column in a newspaper situated in one of the nation's hotspots, and half the stuff you write gets picked up by the wire services."

"Scarcely half," she said quickly. "And it's twice a week."

"You get all that exposure, you get all that fame, and when you're ready to write your book—probably a collection of 'The Best of Courtney Rankin'—the publishers will cut each other's throats to give you a six figure advance. Which your sales will never earn out, or justify, so they'll wind up getting even by peddling the remainders to Publishers Central Bureau." He paused, grinned. "Did you really like my first book?"

She froze. *I'm a reporter first,* she reminded herself; *and besides, I can be truthful.* "I enjoyed it deeply. You have absolute command of the language. You know more about how to construct a novel like that—to get in all your research so that it's meaningful, and interesting—without spoiling your storyline. I'd give up six months' salary to be the author of a book that good."

She stopped fast, but lamely, and Richard saw her expression of consternation for what it was. "You didn't mean to go that far, did you?"

Courtney looked away, abashed. But his voice was suddenly gentle and she looked back at him with a genuine smile. "No, I didn't. Didn't mean to give you the satisfaction." A frown replaced the smile. "You novelists don't understand how the rest of us who—who also have a love affair with words, well, yearn to write something enduring, of significance and length—something permanent."

"Yeah, well," Richard sighed, shifting un-comfortably in his chair, scratching his graying sideburns. Finally his glance in her direction was virtually a glower. "You know I'd like to be President of the United States for a couple of years, too. But I didn't have any earth shaking patriotism or plan for politically improving society's lot when I was in high school. I didn't work my butt off taking courses in civics or geopolitics or law. I didn't run for alderman or councilman and then state repre-sentative, or head of my senior class! I simply didn't spend fifteen or twenty or thirty years learning how to become President—the way I did certain compar-able things toward becoming a novelist."

"*Touché,*" Courtney said softly.

"Look, you have to excuse me for behaving this way." He bounced to his feet, appearing honestly apologetic and eager to get the lovely-but-tall young woman a drink. "It's just that I've been trying to get some information concerning the reasons behind the death of my son, and I suppose it's upset me more than I realized."

"Oh, God! I'm sorry I came at a time like this!" Her slender hand was at her breast as Courtney leaned forward, embarrassed and prepared to leave. "Was it terribly sudden?"

"Well, yeah, in a way." Richard half nodded. "But it happened twenty years ago!" He saw her brows rise, and the incongruity of what he had said dawned on him. Immediately he burst out laughing and, in a moment, she joined him. "Let me get you something, okay? A beer perhaps, or maybe a little wine?"

Not hot chocolate? she reflected, thinking how unlike her imagined, paternal professor this grinning, unpredictable little man was. Then she thought how delicious wine sounded, but rumpled, forthright Richard Grant was certainly a beer man and she didn't wish to appear pretentious. She peered smilingly up at him. "I'd love a beer," she said heartily.

Minutes later, he returned from the kitchen with a book beneath his elbow pinched to his side, a dark bottle of Budweiser hooded by a glass, and something for himself that didn't resemble wine or beer. Nor hot chocolate.

"What are you having?" she asked curiously as he stopped to serve her.

"Iced tea," he said. "I'm not much of a drinker, especially beer and wine." He handed her the book he'd brought. "Here. Decide for yourself if it's bad enough that you should start your own *Fahrenheit 451.*" He turned, returning to his chair. "I signed it to you."

It was his second book. Courtney opened the cover and read the inscription: "For Full-Court Rankin. Always hit the boards hard and maybe your second shot will be better than mine. Richard."

"So why does my successful novel bring you here?" he asked, before she could acknowledge his gift. "I think you said something about that. Are you actually a member of some terrorist splinter group sent here to wipe me out, the way I originally believed? The brightest and loveliest hit-man south of the Mason-Dixon?"

For the first time Courtney laughed. With her beer frothing her upper lip, with her wide and serious eyes suddenly full of mischief, she seemed much less inaccessible. "The only thing I've ever assassinated is character."

"Did you really read my book?" he demanded. "I certainly did," she replied stoutly, half-offended.

"Prove it to me. Please."

Courtney froze, looking at him. When she'd arrived at this trim, brick colonial in the Maryland suburbs, she'd have refused to play such a game with the writer. On the grounds that it was beneath her; an insult, an affront to her as a woman and as a fellow professional. Now she suspected it was important to him to know she wasn't lying, more than a rude challenge. Had he met as many hypocrites as she had? Was it possible that Richard Grant was genuine?

She placed her beer glass on the coffee table with exaggerated care, and without taking her gaze from his expressionless face. "You quoted the English writer Colin Wilson as saying that a certain kind of killing is 'not only an ultimate purpose, but also a means of self-fulfillment, a creative act.' That kind tends to be done in public, or to public figures. It is the 'cerebral' murder, the 'typical crime' of our times."

"Excellent," Richard interposed.

"Don't interrupt. Seen in that light, an assassination—an act of terrorism—is something other people find it almost impossible to understand—"

"Because that terrorist claims he is completely innocent," Richard assisted her, "and that it is society which is at fault."

"Which infuriates us, of course, since we would not do such things, or believe we wouldn't. Yet it isn't a pose, much of the time. Incredibly enough, the terrorist seems to believe it."

"In fact, it's an integral element of his motivation," Richard agreed, nodding. "Wilson wrote, 'He is punishing society. He feels he is *in the right.*'"

"And these acts of terror, of outwardly mindless killing, have become what your idol Wilson termed 'an explosion' since the end of World War II." Now she wasn't trying to meet any challenge; she was involved with the subject the way he was. "From 1940 to 1954, violent crimes in America shot up quite a bit—"

"Thirty-five percent," Richard filled in.

"But in only *two* years, between 1968 and 1970, the murder rate *alone* rose more than fifty percent. And there's evidence to suggest it continues to rise." Suddenly she stopped speaking. She snatched up her beer and sipped, half-grinning around the lip of the glass. "Do I pass?"

"You get top marks on that part of the exam," Richard agreed. Smiling, he brought his own glass over to where she sat on the couch and lowered himself into a place beside her. "Remember where history first heard of assassins?"

She nodded. Her chestnut hair bobbed at the temples but she made no effort to brush it back. "They're traceable to the Persian Ismailis, in the year 1092. Or was it 1093?" He didn't answer her and Courtney grimaced. "1192?"

"You were right the first time." He refilled her glass from the bottle, enjoying her company at a time when he'd believed he might feel lonely, but wondering why she'd come to see him. "For years, any chief assassin after that was known as the 'Old Man of the Mountain,' a leader who made up his own laws and rules as he went along."

"I remember reading that." She turned eagerly to Richard, tucking one silken leg beneath her. "There was a time, then, when assassins were *in charge,* when their acts of terror were perpetrated against their own people?"

"It was a time without formal, written bodies of law," he replied with a nod.

"But why didn't the people throw them out?"

"That's an intriguing part of it, Court. While the chief might be a real sadist, he was still the bird who gave them some semblance of an organized society. Wilson wrote, 'It is difficult for us, in our relatively stable and law-abiding society, to understand the feelings aroused by the Assassins in a society where stability was newly acquired. They seemed to threaten a return to chaos and violence. They were creatures of nightmare.' Even then, you see, they were forced to choose the lesser of two evils."

"But isn't that what Americans started feeling after John F. Kennedy was shot?" She was animated, beginning to have the impression she'd known Richard for years. "I mean, there were hundreds of conspiracy theories, right? Including the suggestion that terrorists and assassins came directly from within the government? We *did* begin to fear a return to chaos and violence, didn't we?"

"To this day, I think, many of us believe there's a secret leadership—an 'Old Man of the Mountain'— making up the rules as he goes along." His voice lowered and Courtney had to strain to hear him. "I put something in that book which worries the hell out of me, but I'm afraid it's true: 'Behaving like so many busy children's toys, going through our mechanical motions as if each of us had forever, we've wrapped ourselves in pretty tissue paper and made out a tag which reads, Don't Open 'Til Civilization Comes.' Frankly, I think old Colin was wishful-thinking on that one, but then, he's British and their wrapping paper is tougher than ours." Richard's grin was wry. "No, Half-Court, none of us fears a 'return' to chaos. We're afraid somebody will rip away the fancy tissue and reveal us—*each* of us in turn—for what we actually are and always have been. Wells put it best: 'Civilization is a race between education and catastrophe.' ''

He finished his iced tea.

"Did he mean guaranteeing an equal education for everybody?"

"Not just for what we used to call 'the great unwashed,' no," Richard answered, shaking his head. "Learning the basics about ourselves, our natures; finding ways to stop kidding ourselves about what we really are, then channeling our aggressions into creative and constructive avenues. I remember Nietzsche noting that with a society in the state of becoming, there's room for an adventurous man. Later, society seems so stultifying and frivolous that the adventurer feels he has no place in it. And once he's thwarted, he remains inventively virile, so he becomes disgusted and holds society's appointed leaders in contempt."

"My Daddy used to love Will Rogers. He quoted Will, 'You can't say civilization don't advance, for in every war they kill you a new way.' '' Courtney swallowed the rest of her beer in a happy gulp, then realized she was getting light headed.

"Look, lady," Richard began, appreciating the color in her classic cheekbones but endlessly curious, "why'd you come out here?"

With a measure of difficulty in expressing her thoughts without sounding thick-tongued, Courtney told him about the seemingly random deadly attacks upon apparently minor public officials. "I've put together eighteen separate assassinations," she continued, "but so far as I know, I'm the only one who thinks they may be connected."

"What do the authorities say when it happens? The police?"

She shrugged. "They don't tell everything they know, of course, but the general suggestion is that professional hit-men are doing it. Because each attack is executed so damned efficiently, with a minimum of fuss and bother. And blood."

"And you don't see it that way?" Richard prodded.

"Well, when gangs hit each other—if I followed that part of your book correctly—they aren't customarily so neat and tidy." She looked him in the eye. "It's when they hire pros, assassins, to take pot-shots at us upstanding white hats that they work hard to cover their tracks."

"And if they were merely vigilantes, like some of these people who have appointed themselves private aides to the authorities," he remarked, "they'd still be amateurs. And again, they'd have a tendency to leave clues behind, however clever they were." Idly, yet with a strong suggestion of impulsive affection, Richard lightly put his hand on hers. "So where do I fit into all this?" She was even lovelier than he'd first imagined. The excitement welling inside, he realized, was peculiarly similar to that he'd felt in the records hall.

"I want to know what you've heard through the grapevine!" Courtney said swiftly. She'd left her hand, and his, where they lay. "What kind of theory can you evolve to cover the known facts?"

Richard chuckled. "I haven't heard a damned thing about it," he said promptly. "As for a grapevine, I've never had such a thing. Novelists who are starting out rarely have luxuries such as newspaper expense accounts. We just hit the libraries hard and make a few phone calls." He saw how disappointed she looked, and sensed her rancor over his crack about expense accounts. "It isn't that I'm not interested, Back-Court; I am. Maybe, when you crack the whole story, it'll make a sequel to my first book."

"I'm sorry I bothered you." She said it stiffly, obviously readying herself to depart.

But Richard was thinking over what he'd just said. *Maybe it would make a sequel, at that,* he reflected. *Maybe that's the theme for my third book.* He knew he didn't want her to leave and wondered if it were only because she'd offered him a potentially valuable idea. "Look, I'm not exactly the world's greatest fan of psychology. But sometimes it's possible for a shrink who's truly intuitive—even while he'd never admit that could enter into it—to develop a sort of *profile* of a killer. It's theoretically possible—"

Courtney flushed. "I already had a psychotherapist acquaintance of mine create just such a report." She began rummaging in her purse, anxious to impress him. "Damn! I didn't bring it along!"

"Well, do you recall what he said?" Despite himself, Richard was growing excited. Wilson had written that "the assassin always walks alone," yet

Courtney Rankin was insisting that a whole *group*
was operating at numerous sites throughout the
United States. Or was it conceivable that they were
led by *one* genuine Old Man of the Mountain, some
great, unbalanced intellectual who had convinced
the others of society's collective guilt?

"He surprised me. He predicted I'd find there
were no organized crime or run-of-the-mill terrorists
involved in it at all." Feet on the floor, staring
straight ahead, she was remembering it carefully.
"Oh, they're efficient, all right!"

"Go on," he prompted her.

"I don't know the shrink's reasoning, but he
really astounded me by what he said." She felt his
impatient gaze, looked with a stare back at Richard.
"He believes that the terrorists are young."

"How young?"

"Doc likes ball-park figures; I'm sure he wouldn't
care to be held to this." She gave in to Richard's
rising annoyance. "He thinks they're seventeen to
twenty years old."

For a timeless instant, he regarded the lovely,
talented, fashionable reporter without seeing her.
Instead, he pictured an unidentified colonel of the
United States Army, face shadowed by dimmed
lighting in the corridor of a military hospital—and
concealed, as well, by the single-minded concern of a
badly shaken, wounded young veteran of Vietnam,
concern for a guileless, unsuspecting young bride
and the baby she would never hold in her arms.
Richard did not quite hear Courtney when she
added, in a hushed whisper, "Mr. Grant, he says
they're just *boys!*"

Gradually her alert, intelligent features came into
focus. Richard took her hand in both of his. "Marco
Polo did more than steal the secret of spaghetti from

the Orientals. It was he who reported the existence of the Ismailis, those first assassins we were discussing. And he recorded the awful thing Aloadin, the original Old Man of the Mountain, said to those young men he sent out to terrorize the land: 'Go thou and slay,' he commanded, 'and when thou returnest, my angels shall bear thee to Paradise.' "

He ceased speaking, unable to go on.

"What's wrong?" Courtney asked. She saw the grim set of his lips and the haunted look in his light blue eyes. She squeezed his hands. "You know something more about this, don't you—something I should know?"

He shook his head, no words coming to mind. He couldn't explain, not yet. It was too bewildering, perhaps too monstrous and shocking to put into words.

He'd found that his son was only one of many who'd been said to have been born dead, and that had made him want to seek vengeance upon the incompetent fools who were responsible. But was that as far as it had gone? Were there, in point of fact, no fools and no incompetence—but *something else?*

And no deaths?

It might not be a question of seeking revenge, not now. It could become a quest—for all the facts, however menacing or dismaying they might be to accept.

And for the missing, tragically unspoiled part of a family that was disintegrating even further as he turned back to the fascinating woman who had given him fresh hope, and inexpressible dread.

PART THREE

AS THE TWIG IS BENT

"Every male brought into existence should be taught from infancy that the military service . . . carries with it honor and distinction and . . . that even death itself may become a boon when a man dies that a nation may live and fulfill its destiny."

—General Douglas MacArthur

13

For at least two substantial reasons, any neighbors
chancing to glance between the morning curtains of
their homes at the tall man and the sleek, muscled
dog on a leash, should have registered surprise. The
fact that human and beast whipped past, giving
every impression of hurrying, the tall man appearing to drag his well-trained Doberman, was not one
of the major reasons. Neither was the fact that this
particular, commonplace event of man-walking-dog
occurred just before the ashen Hoosier dawn, or that
it was repeated each morning, without fail, even on
disaffectingly freezing days such as this.

Neighbors didn't register surprise at the sight for
the simple reason that few of the people living along
this bleak stretch of White River, at the northern
perimeter of the venerable Indianapolis suburb
known as Broad Ripple, arose before dawn. It was
precisely because of the yearningly creative,
possibly Bohemian characteristics of so many area
residents that the rushing man and his somewhat
reluctant dog generally went unnoticed, unseen; as
today.

And the first significant reason for surprise was the fact that, even at a glance, neither human male nor the canine unimaginatively named for one Ludwig Dobermann seemed quite appropriate to Ripple Village. Here, that new-old kind of person who strove to subsist on craftsmanship, art, or knowledge of the present market for special interest paperback books—and on reputedly organic foods—preferred late night conversation to early morning exercise. With the exception of the periodic, enthusiastic experimenter with Asiatic, Egyptian, or even Atlantis germinated jogging. Few of the tall man's neighbors possessed any of the qualities quickly evident in him: athletic good trim; age somewhere in the well-kept sixties; a hint of both breeding and sense of superiority in every movement; tailored clothing—

And the look of *terror* apparent even through his palpably unnecessary sunglasses.

For that was the second, substantial reason why his neighbors in the Village would have been surprised if they're arisen, as the man had done, before anybody except farmers and especially early shift factory laborers willingly arose, including most murderous terrorists.

He and the Doberman whom he had once named Hans, and who would not answer to the new name given him when they moved eastward to Indiana, resided in the last house at the end of a curling street which, because few of the neighbors owned cars and because the craft-art-and-used-book business was poor, had little traffic. The man had chosen to buy his old one-story frame house partly because of that; a passing automobile was as alerting as a Mercedes or Jaguar in a Detroit parking lot. They headed there now, human and unhuman, one sweating from urging the other on, the other perspiring because he *was* German, and obstinate. To the rear of the house was a tangled woods which appeared daunting unless one learned its complex ways and the path to a service station on the other side, as the man had been at pains to do. He kept his own car there, for a monthly stipend to an owner who knew him as Mister Carter. Occasionally he and the dog he determinedly addressed as Lance, with no discernible recognition on Hans' part, used the path in the woods both to make sure that the waiting vehicle was gassed up and running smoothly and to remind the Doberman of the training he'd had as a puppy. At such times, the human male wore specially padded, massive gloves and felt great relief in knowing that Hans-Lance would cheerfully rip out his throat at the slightest sign of significantly relaxed discipline. They weren't friends; old Hans hated him as much as he hated the beast. But a dog who longed to slaughter his own master would be merciless to an unwelcome stranger, especially if it heard the code word selected for all-out attack, *Ewigkeit*.

Passing through a series of rather clever locks, Hans a shadow at his side, the man was cautious to avoid setting off an alarm. It wasn't that the alarms would notify the authorities, because they would not. *Although*, he mused, *they might be loud enough for the police to hear.* He only intended for them to go off once, if that; to warn him in sleep that his existence was hideously imperiled. If the alarms were ever triggered, he knew, there would be no time for any authorities to save him, except perhaps the Almighty. Right now, he just didn't want the entire neighborhood to come running.

In the kitchen, the man rested a sack of groceries

he'd bought from an all-night supermarket on a white, plain metal tabletop, and told Hans to Stay. From it, a package of meat was withdrawn and unwrapped, revealing three two-inch Porterhouse steaks. Aware of Hans' eyes following him even though the short-cropped, menacing head had not itself moved, the human being put one steak on a plate and then into his refrigerator. He placed the second Porterhouse on the cracked linoleum floor of his kitchen, only feet from the dog's snout. Hans, while motionless, seemed to tremble, his short, dark hair rising inconspicuously.

The man sat down in a chair at the table and turned his head to look at the alarm clock already there. Folding his arms, crossing his legs, he watched the Doberman, whose front legs were thrown out in apparent relaxation but whose haunches were taut, readied. Ten minutes later, the tall man slowly stood, left the kitchen, and went into the bathroom. He relieved himself, washed his hands, dried them, and peered into the mirror over the medicine cabinet. For perhaps the thousandth time, he considered the possibility of plastic surgery. But it was costly, it was the kind of thing that drew attention; it wouldn't help.

When he returned to the kitchen, he saw without surprise that Hans hadn't moved. The two-inch steak remained on the linoleum floor and a roach, overwhelmed by the opportunity of its lifetime, consumed by cleverness, was zigzagging toward the meat. Its maneuvers were exotic, well-executed. But the tall man above the roach was empyrean, too rarefied or removed to be alarming; he was unnoticeable, as loose rock atop a mountain is unnoticeable, or tornadic winds building up. Behind him, Hans yawned. The man squashed the bug but only after

leggily pawing at it, repeatedly, like a horse counting to four. Cheeks burning, aware of Hans' clinical
appraisal, he sat in the chair at the table and lit a
cigarette with trembling hands. The dog watched,
expressionless. Eyes narrowing above the unfiltered
Lucky, the man blew smoke in the animal's
direction and let two words go with them: "Hans!
Ewigkeit!"

Hans was upon the steak with no visible expendi-
ture of time. When he tore into it, flecks of silver
spittle flying, his muzzle lifted and his eyes were on
a line with the seated man. The human, briefly,
looked away, picking at roach specks on the sole of
his shoe. Within seconds there was no fragment of
the remaining steak substantial enough to satisfy a
Pekingese—but Hans had eaten none of it. Moved
by special canine joys, he'd simply ripped the meat
to nothingness without swallowing a bite.

The word *Ewigkeit,* in German, means Eternity.

From the center of the chipped metallic table, the
tall man produced the third Porterhouse steak.
Languidly, he tossed it in the Doberman's direction.
Hans caught it neatly in mid-air, heard the
command *"Eat,"* and began chewing it with
deliberate thoroughness that would have done
credit to the most hedonistic epicure.

The tall man did not get up, did not move in Hans'
direction. Only one thing would have sounded more
horrifying to him than going over to pat his powerful beast, and the component parts of that one
possible happening were the sole reasons he did not
have Hans destroyed. As things were, they were, in
their way, inseparable. *It's a lovely arrangement,
old boy,* he reflected, winding the alarm clock and
glancing at the lazily masticating killer. *A perfect,
modern friendship.*

"Now then, when we get to Grandfather's house in Indianapolis," Molly said, as conversationally as she could, "you must not climb all over him." Molly had planned this; to avoid frightening them. There could be no reason for broaching the unsociable topic of death so she wouldn't mention it. "Grandfather is getting older, you know."

"I am, too," replied little Michelle,· happily kicking the soft pastel heels of her good shoes against the back of her seat. "Grandpa won't believe how much I've grown!"

"Grandfather is ill," said the older Mary, and her upper lip curled but faintly as she looked at the sister in the next seat. Then she glanced quickly, nakedly, at her mother. "Can we order something else from the stewardess?"

"Your real grandmother, you may recall, died years ago." Molly was vaguely aware that her elder daughter had asked for something, but a request then was inappropriate to Molly's mood. She pretended not to have heard. "But you must be very polite to Grandfather's *second* wife, Lucille. If she wants to kiss you, you can turn your cheek."

"I remember Lucille," Michelle said, dreamy-eyed. "She's such a *pretty* lady."

Mary's look at her junior was stony. "Lucille married Grandfather for his money," she said, glancing to Molly for approval. "Isn't that right, Mother?"

Molly blinked, brushed back a stray strand of fair hair. *Well, isn't it, Mother?* she asked herself, suddenly regretful. When she spoke, it was only partly for young Mary's benefit. "The Bible says, 'Judge not lest ye be judged.' "

Mary's similar features screwed into a frown of fine thoughtfulness. Then they were masked and she said nothing for a moment. Molly, who rarely delved for any understanding concealed much beneath the surface, was startled by her thought: *There are three times when our children are older than we. The instant they are born, the instant when they first see through our lies, and the instant they look down at our dead remains.*

The girls were watching her and Molly, feeling flushed, looked through the nearest window and saw nothing whatever. She'd always detested flying because the remove from earth and the marless, unfathomable emptiness of the sky made her feel that she'd sent her prayers into an abyss. Prayers offered as a spoiled yet overlooked girl, as a timorous bride, as an expecting and as a deflated mother, and thereafter, a blurring of pleas. Airplanes appeared to Molly to extend a life lived in fairy tales and fantasy, the way they gave no suggestion of great speed or of the fact that the pilots even remembered air disasters. She'd have been happier if the unseen man at the controls—even his existence, his appearance, was something one had to believe in; he could be *naked* in the cockpit, even utterly *mad*—had begun the flight by reciting the latest crashes and pinpointing what had been done to guarantee their current safety. Pilots, she thought, reached their impossible destinations on little more than *faith*— on the very kind of belief Molly found evaporating from her, a day at a time.

"D'you think Grandfather will like me—*us*—this time?"

Molly, startled, looked at Mary. She was tugged back not so much to the present as to the past. Her past, Mary's and Michelle's past, everybody's past. It felt unreal just as the bleak and horizonless sky seemed unreal through the unblinking eye of the jet's windows. This daughter who so resembled her might, with a different turn of fate, be a boy, just out of his teens. Named Mark. "I'm sure your grandfather loves you both very much," Molly lied. She'd wondered exactly the same thing, ever since learning of her father's serious illness.

Michelle, busily picking a scab on her knee, paused to stare silently at the grown woman. Beside her sibling, centuries away, Mary led a strand of hair between her fine white teeth and munched on it. "I dunno," she murmured doubtfully.

"Of *course*, he loves you!" Molly exclaimed, her voice traveling.

Unacquainted passengers gaped at her as if overhearing a prayer, then looked elsewhere. No one spoke.

Molly leaned from her seat and peered into each blank, pale face. "Girls," she hissed, heart pounding, left to defend Doctor Conrad Skylar the best way she could, "Grandfather is *dying!*"

Michelle nodded and resumed her scab-picking. "I know." Mary's expression was solemn, but there was no prefiguring of tears. "As you said, Mother— he's old."

Breathing hard, Molly pressed back against her coat. A stewardess was approaching, bestowing benign smiles as she came. Molly stopped her gladly, requested three soft drinks, and won approving smiles from the two female children seated with her. She stared after the crisp, uniformed back of the stewardess, whose professionally effortless glide was betrayed by a certain, tensed bracing at the thighs and fleshless ankles. Molly's shiver was an awful spasm. Why did they keep these damnable machines so *cold?*

* * *

He took the news that his daughter and his grand-children were flying in to see him in much the spirit he'd accepted his own well tested self-diagnosis. He didn't want to see Molly and her brood but there wasn't much to be done about it.

Today was one of his good days, the way he'd come to measure things in recent months. At the age of thirty, he would have regarded how he felt as sick-as-a-dog and spent three days in bed. At twenty, this level of health would have made him neurotic.

Conrad Skylar forced his neck to allow his head to turn, no more arthritic now than he had been ten years before but truly and lastingly fed up with its pain. He'd been a physician of prominence most of his life and the one discovery he could leave posterity was as foolish, as unscientific, as it ap-peared to be accurate: nature saw to it that a person began adjusting to death just as soon as possible. If you didn't get the customary raft of childhood sick-nesses that old Mother planned for you, she'd break your bones in athletics or automobiles. If you even avoided such minor disasters as those (which, if you did, automatically lengthened your personal long-evity) nature always had middle age to work with. She'd start you out with worsening vision, or loss of hearing, soften you up with the first twinges of arthritis or such, and get at your soul by killing off your weaker loved ones, thereby giving you a gut-full of poisonous guilt.

Doctor Skylar looked at what he'd turned his head to see, the photograph on his chifferobe of a strik-ingly lovely young woman and a little girl with a vulnerable face and eyes that could melt rock. If you stared into them much, which Conrad Skylar had not. The woman was his first wife and he was again bemused by the fact that he was increasingly forgetting any of the realities about her. Today, she looked less familiar than some of the pretty girls he'd seen recently on the television.

But he'd logically purged himself of his guilt where she was concerned. He'd done that by marrying Lucille and treating her exceedingly well. It was questionable whether anybody, including his younger second wife, understood his reasoning and he'd be damned—for this, as well as other things, no doubt—if he'd care.

Because it was all so simple even a fool should be able to perceive his logic. If a man neglected one wife until she died, as much of loneliness and boredom as for any proper medical reason, and he had the common decency to feel bad about it, he could set things straight by enabling his next wife to live like a queen. Women, after all, were meant to suffer. They'd been put on this earth to do the dull drudgery, the dirty work, and that was no fault of his. God hadn't sought him out for a vote, but he had an obligation to accept the evidence of his own senses. After a fashion, women were actually identical, interchangeable; they were sisters-under-the-skin, all that nonsense about feminism proved as much. So if you did one wife wrong because you were busy making something of yourself, establishing your family name as one of lasting merit in the greater society, you'd cancel out your heavenly debt by moving one hundred and eighty degrees in the other direction with Wife Two.

Besides, Wife One hadn't given him a male-child to carry on the upstanding ambience he had presented to the name Skylar.

She'd given him a daughter. And Molly Skylar Grant was the cause of his dying. That guilt he'd hauled everywhere, even to Indianapolis, even into his second marriage. Because Molly's firstborn had fatally poisoned him. The hell with whether it made medical or psychological sense, he knew all too damned well how he felt.

But if he could straighten things out somewhat, clear his thoughts of this last responsibility, it might be possible to order his dying precisely as he had commanded most of his long life's important events. Might even wind up looking forward to death; he'd told his own terminal patients to order their affairs that way and adjust to reality.

Shakily, false teeth fastening in the bloodless hinge of a lip, Doctor Skylar dialed a number on his phone. He remembered it more easily than he did his first wife's smile. He drummed his fingertips on the bedside table while he tolerated the drone.

The other party didn't identify himself but he didn't have to. "Now, don't tell me I'm not supposed to telephone and *please* don't hang up!" Skylar rose awkwardly to a seated position, legs knotted in the sheets; the act of speaking bluntly, as he always had, envigorating him. "You gave me your number years ago so I could use it in an emergency. I'm dying now, Wayland, and that'll have to do." He paused. "Never mind all that horseshit, it's merely the reason behind my emergency. I am going to tell my daughter part of the truth when she gets here. No, not all; just the part that directly concerns her." His agate eyes flicked to the door of his bedroom, which was opening. They remained expressionless as he stared at Lucille Skylar. "You can't threaten a dying man, 'Lt. Colonel.' And you needn't thank me for the warning, either, if you get around to considering the amenities." He saw the concern in Lucille's eyes clearly as she drew near, already reaching out to take the phone from his shaking hand. "I wish you well, Wayland, but to be candid about it, I think it's a moot point as to who will welcome whom through the gates of hell."

Without argument, he allowed his wife to slip the phone from his weakening fingers. He sank back against his several pillows, exhausted but peculiarly detached. He squinted at the corona of jewels glittering at Lucille's slender throat, and chuckled at his thought: who said you couldn't buy love with money? The chuckle subsided to the level of a raspy, dying motor as he told her: "I always knew that if Mother Nature didn't get me, old Ma Bell would."

"You mustn't overdo." The lovely, anxious face lowered to him but became cloudy as he coughed heavily, rackingly, for the first time that day. The blood bubbling into his mouth tasted metallic. It was as if the rampant cancer that had followed hard on the heels of his heart attack was attempting to fashion something lasting in his body. A loving cup from the regional office of the A.M.A., perhaps; in recognition of having duly sacrificed his family upon the altar of medical self-interest.

There was a growling in Doctor Skylar's ears, too —as if the busy little black cells required more room to work.

It reminded him of his old confidante's man-eating Doberman. Hans and his own devouring cancer had a lot in common.

But not nearly so much as the bald man who had terrified Wayland, and Conrad Skylar, for two decades.

14

Tightly gripping a note with the scribbled instructions she'd been given by her stepmother, Molly Grant hustled the girls into a taxicab outside Indianapolis International Airport and felt her firm foundation of personal acceptances drop reassuringly, even vibrantly, into place. The instant the three of them had joined a bustling, bobbing crowd flowing like some meaty soup in hot, collective pursuit of their luggage, Molly's in-flight feeling of alienation had begun to fade. The girls, prodded into motion, were again her replicas, whatever private views they possessed tucked safely away beneath their curls. Now Molly reclined gratefully against the back seat of the lurching taxi, thanking God they had all made it safely to the Midwest.

Mary, the elder of the two daughters, risked a careful inspection of her mother. Molly's fanning blonde hair and languid air gave her the ambience, at a glance, of a slowly aging, angelic being composed of starlight and meteoric dust, bruised perhaps by something rising carelessly from the earth. Her eyes were tightly shut, the thin, ivory skin above the bridge of her nose creased in a delicate but relatively intentional frown. Clear indication that Mother, while she always seemed more youthful with her eyelids sealed against society's sights, had another of her excruciating headaches.

For quite a while it had seemed strange to Mary that Molly Grant suffered no headaches but those of the excruciating ilk. Still, the child was beginning to understand the way grown-ups exaggerated to win a point and imagined she could be effective with the technique herself. Actually, Mary was starting to understand a number of things; and if there was nothing wrong with such education, *per se*, it still lacked a balance furnished by techniques that were more overt and less calculating. With Molly's tacit endorsement, she had become Mother's Girl; but she might be far too much smarter than Molly to become as easily forgiveable.

Little Michelle kept her pale face against the snow glazed window of the cab, but only during the first mile of the trip. She'd been freezing since stepping out of the airport and the big-eared cab driver had made it worse by speaking warmly of the unbearable cold. Michelle, more like Richard Grant than her sister, wondered if Indianapolis people welcomed the challenge of the curious, sinking-through-skin climate, or felt that praising it made them an accepted and snug part of it. Eventually, she gave up trying to find anything intriguing about the interstate and sat back, shivering with arms folded, wishing her daddy had come. For her, Daddy had a way of making almost everything interesting. He might even have urged the man at the steering wheel to take them through the town itself, instead of heading east on this big, dumb road. Why were

grown-ups always so efficient about things that
didn't matter?

Mary, reading road signs and signs on buildings
they passed, was remembering being in Indianapolis
once before. Mother and Father had both been
along, that time; she had been a little girl. For the
life of her, she couldn't recall if Michelle had been
with them, or if Michelle had been alive. The brat
seemed to materialize one day, all big eyes and
strident voice, and had merely gotten larger all over.
But Mary remembered how Grandfather Skylar had
treated her as if she were invisible, unworthy of
being talked to. Sighing, she glanced at her suffering mother and admired Molly's insular techniques.
Dry as a stick, Mother could appear so washed out
she looked positively drenched.

There was time yet for Mary Grant to develop
decently, but someone would have to notice her as
an individual soon—let her know that was all right,
and encourage her to discover her own interests,
opinions, and skills. She was abominable at trans-
lating those of others.

Molly didn't have a headache. She'd playacted to
get a last time by herself, in herself; to gather her
resources and to stake out a claim to those
memories she once had regarded as essential; *hers*.
Then she would face a father who'd gone forlorn and
feeble, the worst physical image she had seen in her
mind's eye since trying to picture the stone-cold,
emergent Mark. Imagining Doctor Skylar as
anything but commandingly erect, imperious, and
confidently authoritative was simply an impossi-
bility. But Molly wanted to forearm herself with a
rough sketch.

Spending much time in conversation with that
grasping second wife, Lucille, was nearly as unbear-

able to think about. Sooner or later, Molly feared,
they would have to have it out. Lucille was plainly
too direct and unevasive, as Molly remembered her,
for the two women to escape open warfare at such a
time. Privately, she smiled, puzzling her daughter
Mary without knowing it. Dad had always claimed
that quarrels and bickering were "the swiftest way
to reenact our early, evolutionary stages and cast
aside years of hard-won civilization." He loathed
arguing, unless he'd started it himself, and was an
integral part of it.

Richard was always saying nice things about a
dead writer named Thomas Wolfe, and Molly, lazily
picturing her husband with less clarity than she did
a father of her youth, knew Richard's hero was
wrong. You could go home again, if you felt that
home was wherever your loved one was. The
question was, Who in hell wanted to? Dad had no
more authorized her marital choice than she had his;
maybe that was what had annoyed the old man.
He'd told her privately that Richard Grant was an
ineffectual, effete, time wasting dreamer. Later,
Richard smiled at the description, saying Doc
Skylar wanted a man of action for her. "If you'd
picked the kind of creep Doc approved, Mol, his
womanizing and refusal to come home would have
corroborated your father's married life."

By the time the taxi deposited them in over a foot
of clinging snow, spun off to leave them seeming
feet beneath a collapsing gray sky, none of the
females lugging their suitcases up the lane to the
front door knew what to expect inside the house.
Even the structure itself was a surprise, because
Doctor Skylar and his wife had moved here since
Molly's only previous visit. Instead of the overwhelming mini-mansions in which she had been

raised, the old physician's final residence was little
more than a well-maintained bungalow. It reminded
Molly, after she'd knocked, of a pleasant cabin on
Klinger Lake, in Michigan, which the family had
owned when she was a girl. Inside, dutifully following Lucille Skylar upstairs with no more conversation than would have been exchanged with a maid,
Molly openly gaped at the way the elder Skylars had
shoehorned into their small house the possessions of
one man's lengthy lifetime. Costly objects which her
mother had insisted upon keeping in one place or in
a particular room were shoved and indiscriminately
mingled against walls, or stacked in corners; a single
wall dangerously supported some ten or eleven of
the original oils Daddy had procured during his brief
art-as-an-investment phase. It might have been the
beginning of a museum, but one which had been
abandoned after the preliminary purchases.
Nervously padding up the steps between Michelle
and Mary, with Lucille urgently leading the way,
Molly glanced back at the family possessions of her
past and wondered why such valuable things had
been so casually handled.

She was further surprised by the appearance of
her father and the way he reacted to their arrival.
Across the bedroom, Conrad Skylar was abed but
uncannily the same as he'd been several years
before, when he and Lucille had driven to Washington. As she approached him, layers of lifelong ruse
fell away and her heart began to ache. Her father
was like one of the portraits of Skylar men, and he'd
always refused to pose, himself, on the grounds of
wasted time, and vanity. The old man's cheeks were
pink as a newborn's, his lips red as a satyr's; while
the vanilla gums he showed when he grinned—the
teeth seeming recently inserted in them, like candles

in a moist cake—matched the sunken flesh around his canary eyes in colorlessness. Incongruously, the enduring fringe of hair which had enabled him to look approximately fifty-eight years old for ages—or was that only Daddy's special magic, the way he'd determinedly forced everyone to see him?—remained shaggy, wiry. It made Molly think of the oily black sticks in Michelle's boxes of crayons.

His eyes, she believed for a second, were feverish. Then she saw that something else was wrong with them, something that was the product of his dire illness in combat with his medication. Or possibly it was only the way his vision was no longer fixed quite fully in the present.

When he motioned to her to bend, to kiss him, his hand amazed Molly most. It might have become part of a long decaying tree on their abandoned property, back home, trembling in the impossible cold of this foreign city. *Oh Daddy, why did you leave home; and why did the last loved ones we chose have to drive us still farther apart?* His bony cheek, against hers, emanated no warmth; it sheathed hard, marbly substances which seemed to roll when she gently hugged him, and watered the dying garden of his sideburns with her tears. Over her stooped back he was motioning to the girls, her daughters, and Molly straightened, smiling bravely, praying that Mary and Michelle might somehow forgive her terrible, deficient parent.

Her other surprise came then. "Why, sweet Mary," Daddy said, "you're becoming a young woman!" His hard fingers grasped the younger child's wrist as his head turned to her and she did not protest. "And Michelle, heavens, you're even prettier than I remembered." He seemed nearly to

be feeding from them through his long postponed
acceptance, and his amazing, awful eyes raised. "I
think you've done a fine job with these beauties,
Molly," he praised, stealing the rising jealousy from
his daughter and granting his only meaningful gift.

"He asked me to tell him again their names, and
who was older," Lucille Skylar said softly when she
was seated with her stepdaughter. She'd helped
Molly put the uncomplaining, emotionally drained
girls down for a late afternoon rest, then led the way
to a second story room not much more than an
alcove. Lucille had converted it to a sewing room
and it was full of sunshine from a wide, high
window. Little else was kept in the tiny room but a
table and two nondescript, amazingly comfortable
chairs. "Conrad wrote it all on a note, then studied it
with a lot of his old, tigerish ferocity." Her mouth
curved faintly, whimsically, at the sides. "He had it
hidden beneath his covers while we were with him."

"That's like him," Molly replied ruminatively,
"and not like him. He used to remember absolutely
everything but he always had to stay a step ahead of
everybody." She sipped more hot tea with a
measure of relief, vaguely attempting to place the
pleasant, tart taste. It was oddly familiar. She
watched as Lucille refilled her cup from a silver
service, astonished that her stepmother was, while
uncommonly attractive, distinctly middle-aged.
Why had she thought the woman had the power to
stay young for her aging father? "Thank you, it's so
good. And familiar, for some reason."

"It's the only way your father will let me fix it."
Eyes whose lashes had batted in apparent flirtation
were grave behind the thick lenses of the myopic.
Lucille held Molly's gaze. "It's your mother's way
of making tea."

"How lovely." Molly, heartbeat accelerating, slightly, lowered the cup to the table. A few drops splashed on something Christmasy her hostess was finishing. "Does it still appear to be as serious as you originally believed?"

There was a pause as if Lucille hesitated to say what she was thinking. The lips Molly had considered coarsely sensual, inclined to tremor with some withheld, scatalogical quip, seemed thin and Molly realized that trembling was a nervous habit. Only a decade or so her elder, Lucille Skylar was clearly exhausted and quickly aging. "I noticed the way you looked at the things from the old house, the way we piled them up in one room, willynilly. I'd like to explain."

"Oh, *no.*" The words were honestly felt, automatically elicited. Molly shook her head. "It's none of my affair."

"But Molly, it was none of my business either— none of those things." Lucille gestured to indicate the alcove, her vivid hanks of paperbound yarn curled like uncountable strands of cartoon spaghetti. "This is where I live—and where Conrad is. This is my place and, as you can tell, I really don't require much space." Her profile, as she smiled and raised her head, moved into the day's final rain of wintry sunlight, looked vibrant, youthfully glad. "I liked the simplicity of your father, you see; how he left no doubt about the way he wanted things. I required someone without doubt, without endless remorse that bound me to a past I couldn't possibly share with him. All those wonderful, expensive possessions we stacked up in the other room belonged to a Conrad Skylar I never knew." Lucille looked at Molly, lips working. "The doctor says he won't survive a week."

"What doctor is that?"

The older woman looked down at her china cup, a finger with the nail nibbled short tracing an ancient design. "Doctor Conrad Skylar," she said.

When Molly heard Lucille excuse herself and move out to the kitchen to prepare the evening meal, she went upstairs to awaken the girls, get them to wash up and comb their hair. Enroute, she stopped long enough to peer through the bedroom door at her father. She froze, temporarily frightened. Then his chest beneath the covers moved like earthquake ground, the rumble of a deep cough informing her that he still lived. Biting her lower lip, Molly drifted the rest of the way down the corridor to the room in which she had left Mary and Michelle, feeling like a ghost who had lost the directions to her home. Rapping gently, once, she opened the door an inch, then pushed it wide with growing alarm.

The girls weren't in their bed. The window was wide open upon the rear of the lot and booming, icy wind added to Molly's shudder of concern.

Inaudibly whispering their names, she rushed across the bedroom floor, glancing about the room, reaching for the top of the window—

And saw the men, rooted in place like tall, menacing hedges, at the entrance to the Skylar garage.

Four of them looked up at Molly as she gazed down. Each wore street clothing at which no one would give a second glance. Each appeared young, formidable, unmoved by the biting chill of early evening. One of them, at this distance no more individualistic or remarkable than his fellows, lifted his hand. He did it with an exceptional lack of haste, both as if he had all the time in the world and as if he had no fear of being observed, no doubt that he

would be obeyed. Molly saw the back of his fingers
and hand, *gripped* by them, then saw the motion
and fully, instantly understood the gesture.

Come down, it said. *Come down and find your
children.*

Disregarding her first impulse to climb out the
second story window and reach the quartet of stoic
men by the swiftest means, she whirled and flashed
from the room, darted back down the hallway with
her high-heeled feet awkwardly splayed, and half
ran, half tumbled down the stairs. *Lucille's in the
kitchen*, she thought, as she picked herself up at the
foot of the steps; and, without wondering what
inferences her unconcious mind had drawn, Molly
ran to the front door and through it.

Briefly she lost her bearings on the unfamiliar
property and felt hot tears begin to pour. Quickly
she recovered, however, jumping the steps to the
hard-packed earth and losing a heel as she darted
around the edge of the building, into the cutting
gravel of the driveway.

There! They'd remained at the front of the garage;
it hadn't been a hallucination, a horrid dream. Tears
stopped by the necessity to think clearly, gasping
for breath, Molly pounded painfully toward the four,
staring men, her thoughts totally centered on her
missing daughters and their well-being.

She was *to* them, nearly running *against* the
nearest of these terrible beings who'd suddenly
turned her life upside down—putting out her hands
to brace herself and instinctively, maternally
digging her nails into the closest man's shoulders.
"Where *are* they?" Molly demanded. "*Where are
my babies?*"

"You really ought to keep a better watch on your
children, Missus." The voice, a toneless tenor

devoid of passion, and menace, was as unexpected—
as inappropriate, as explanationless—as the rest of
the nightmare. The sun had almost gone down completely, now, and Molly neither thought to see the
faces of the men nor did. Not in any sharply lucid,
memorizable sense. "Do you see how easy it is to
take them?"

"She isn't thinking, it won't work this way."
Another of them was peculiarly nearer, though
Molly hadn't seen him move. He wore a baseball
cap, and glimpsing an unsmiling, youthfully handsome mouth, she immediately expected compassion
from him. Without warning, he slapped her smartly
on one cheek, and when her head bobbed back,
repeated the action with his other hand. She saw
tears. "You must hear what we're saying, Missus.
It's important."

"I do, I'm *listening!*" She blinked away tears,
tried to perceive their purpose. She had slapped each
of the girls in precisely the same fashion, for sassing
her or Richard, and recalled her regret as she saw
the splotchy, red marks appear on their pretty faces.
At once Molly knew these men would feel remorse
for nothing. "I do hear you. But please—"

"Killing is a function." The first man, with the
toneless, mechanical tenor. His plain, inexpensive
flannel shirt and gray slacks looked new, she saw, as
did the garb of the other three men. "Dictionaries
say the meaning of 'function' is the specific, the
proper, or the natural action of anything. Follow
me? Functions do not bring joy, they simply
happen, they are. Do you understand, Missus?"

Molly, as eager to please as a bright student,
nodded her head. "You'll kill me if you think it's the
proper thing to do but it won't bring joy." She swallowed, aware that none of them was holding her,

aware they knew there was no need. "The *natural* thing."

"Or your daughters. Inanimate them." It was a man who hadn't spoken before. Shorter, chunkier, black, he could have been the sixth-man guard on a college basketball team. "If it's our function."

"Now, killing won't be a function, in the case of you or your children," continued the man in the baseball cap, his smile reasonable, "if your husband and the lady reporter do not interfere."

"I don't know what you *mean,*" she replied truthfully, fresh tears beginning.

"But you will." The first speaker stopped, gripping the handle of the garage door, hesitating. Molly saw his face clearly and felt confused, utterly without clue to why they were doing these mad things. She had never seen a cleaner-shaven, more normal looking young man. The distant notion that she must surely recognize them—know who these threatening people were and what they wanted, six hundred miles from home—vanished. Her terror mounted, as the prayer for some comprehensible reason went unanswered. "We want you to see how easy it is. But remember, we were never here. There is no point in phoning the police. But if we come again, our function will be to complete what was begun. The authorities will never believe it was anything but an act of perversion called rape."

He raised the garage door, then, with a lithe, effortless motion and no more drama or heat than if he'd held the door for his grandmother. As the whining and clanging of the thrown-back door vibrated, and old snow from an earlier day broke like pie crust and dropped to the ground, Molly stared at what she saw inside the garage and scarcely stifled a scream.

They were alive; she knew that almost at once, because the terror in the eyes above their gagged mouths could only come from creatures with life. Mary, her budding breasts bare, left in her best skirt, was tied by strong rope with her back pressed to Michelle's. Michelle's Sunday dress was ripped from neckline to hem. The children were hanging by the taut tail of the hemp from the center of the garage ceiling, the rope knotted cruelly around their waists.

Looking back with an inwardly shrieking fear mixed with thirst for vengeance, Molly was in time to see two of the four men disappearing into the distance. They gave the impression of melting through a neighbor's fence.

Lucille Skylar's astonished face appeared at the kitchen window. *"Help us,"* Molly cried, darting toward her children.

15

His bare feet were slapping the freezing, similarly
bare floor of his cabin—he was up for the day—at
least twenty minutes before the mechanically timed
phonograph began to play. In both intent and effect,
the recording served as Pardoo's alarm clock.
Actually, he had required it only during the first few
self-questioning mornings, immediately after his
desertion.

Generally, the combination of the strong little
man's long years of disciplined routine and a keen
awareness that his life was regularly in daily danger
were enough to haul him bouncingly from his cot,
erect and staring, intently looking for the slightest
evidence that his efficiently planned security had
been breached. So far, the scariest thing that happened was a lethargic wildcat Pardoo'd found upon
opening his front door.

But he left the apparatus which timed the phonograph's playing on, anyway. It had been an integral
part of his routine forever, or so it felt—that much
loved, recorded music.

Twenty minutes later, when Jackson L. Pardoo

had taken his traditional quick shower, and donned a clean work shirt and fresh inexpensive jeans which still retained their store-bought blue crispness, the recording began its scratchy rendition.

The squat, muscled, red-faced little man with the close cropped gray hair came to unmoving attention and then stayed precisely that way until every note of Reveille had been played.

It wasn't that he'd ever regretted his choice of career, twenty-four years ago. Pardoo didn't hate the Army, the military life, and never would. Might as well hate God because He let it snow out here on the western tip of nothingness.

He hated the bald man, instead, those behind the Colonel, and everything they stood for. None of which, in the cautiously revolved view of Jackson L. Pardoo, had a lot to do with his own treasured concept of military service. Like so many puky things these days, great gommy handfuls of shit had been symbolically thrown across the countless bright ribbons decorating his old Army tunic, and he'd had to make the same kind of decision for which he'd loathed elements of America's current youth, back during the Nam years. In a way, Pardoo saw, he'd arrived at the kind of decision they had— probably too late to save anything but, if he was lucky, his immortal soul.

Which most certainly did not make his the same motivation of the cowardly youngsters who'd cut out for Canada then. He'd never ducked honest combat to save his own skin, never would; he genuinely believed, as he had when the bald man sought him out, that conscientious objectors were frauds at best, nonexistent at worst—sissies and fairies who hid their timorous ways and soft little butts behind fancy words, in order to sidestep the

God-given duty they had as the most fortunate citizens on the face of the earth.

But it was undeniably true, Pardoo confessed again to himself, as he tugged on a pair of polished but scruffily worn boots, that, like the fainthearted faggots, decorated hero Jack Pardoo had finally reached a truly terrible impasse: he could neither condone what he was seeing around him, nor allow himself to speak out against the worst, the most awful situation he'd ever known.

With more eagerness than he'd expected to feel at the time he planned his desertion, Jack Pardoo slipped a live clip into his M-16 rifle—actually, it was the property of the United States Army, but Pardoo had been using the weapon for years and hadn't been about to leave it behind—and strode lithely across the sparsely furnished cabin to the door. The M-16 used 223 caliber ammo and there was always the possibility of hitting small game head-on, without adequate range, and blowing the animal to inedible bits. But it was all Pardoo had, aside from the side-weapon he'd also ripped off, and he found himself mildly pleased over the prospect of hunting for his own food. It had taken him three hungry days to bag anything upon his arrival at this carefully rented cabin in the woods, but he knew he'd get better at it. Jackson Pardoo, even approaching sixty years of life on the planet, always improved.

Closing the door and leaving it rigged so that he could detect, at a glance, any sign that he'd had visitors while he was in the hills hunting, Pardoo crunched through the icy crust to the edge of the forest, then craned his neck to inspect the range to the west. *If they've found I'm here,* he thought, gripping the M-16 tightly and frowning as he

squinted, *they'll probably come at me from there—
straight through the trees. If I ever relax at the
wrong time, even for a second, I'll never hear 'em
until they're into the cabin and on me.*

Idly, he turned his head to make out his jeep—
same definition of tentative ownership—where it
was camouflaged, just beyond the gravel driveway
which became a rugged road, unmarked and, except
for the cabin owner and a few of his buddies,
unknown. He made out the general shape of the
vehicle, thought of checking to make sure nobody
was concealed in it or had removed part of his full
tank of gasoline, or purposely damaged his brakes;
told himself that paranoia was as heavy a risk here
as the bald man. It was lonely, up here; he was just
finding out how goddamned lonely. There weren't
any smartass punks around to vandalize, and the
Colonel wouldn't need to do anything fancy, like
chopping up his brakes.

Suddenly Pardoo felt cold, thought of Christmas
coming, made himself knock it off. He felt his old
love/hate ambivalence for the bald man surge up,
couldn't stop it, quite. Truth was, Jackson Pardoo's
own training methods added to the Colonel's game
plan had created arguably the most ominous, lethal
war machine since the automic bomb had been
dropped upon Hiroshima and Nagasaki. They'd
been quite a team, if you kept professional about it,
detached and dedicated; and then this bristling old
veteran topkick had realized just how great his own
contribution was.

Frowning again, Pardoo let his M-16 droop until
it was rather aimlessly pointed toward the trunks of
some old trees bunched like leery old ladies a few
yards into the forest. The mood he felt, more
severely than before, was one of absolute futility.

There was nothing he could do to stop them, if they found him; might as well shout the bald man's name and run right into his arms. Pardoo sighed. A few scraps of his last kill remained in the cabin, enough to make do for another day. If he filled up on water. No sense in venturing deeper into the forest, complex yards away from his rented cabin and the cheering handful of booby traps he had scattered, knowledgeably enough, inside and just outside of it. Pardoo thought of lessons he'd learned in Korea and the Mekong Delta, incapable of telling them apart; but the main thing was that hunger tended to be a blustering bully who couldn't take it. A man couldn't know how little he was able to live on until he found out. Good, professional self-discipline and common sense would handle the problem of his lying, cheating appetite, at least for one more day; they might even *guarantee* the existence of one more day.

At the cabin door, Pardoo stopped and turned slowly to look back up at the range of hills, which looked like a fleshy woman lying beneath a sheet. They were just slipping beneath the low cloud-cover of winter, and Pardoo shivered. It was like the old Army saying he'd heard countless times in fighting back and forth across the 38th parallel, "It's got to get a whole lot worse before it gets a little bit better." Time was when he'd chattered that to himself, used it to cheer himself; because it promised improvement if he could take it. Nam had the other, newer saying among the troops, some mere sound of derision or lunatic buoying-up that Pardoo couldn't get the hang of. Others were too pointedly perverted for a career soldier like Master Sergeant Jackson L. Pardoo. But they were sure as fuck the kind that fitted this situation here, today, he decided. Sighing, he went back inside and began throwing bolts, adjusting locks, checking his special devices.

Pardoo sat awhile at the window, staring out of it when the snow began again. It fell with that stealthy, silent persistence which advertised it would be around awhile. The snow, the bald man, and Pardoo. He held the M-16 in his lap, wondering if anybody else had come to the same conclusion he had just reached.

Today, when the snow got too thick to see through easily, when a man had to keep his fire going or freeze his balls to his legs, why, it would be a perfectly adorable time—militarily speaking—for them to come after him.

When the timer clicked again, and the recording began playing Taps, Pardoo wearily worked his way to still-booted feet with the realization that he'd just dozed away another day of life. Man reached a certain age, he shouldn't ought to do that. He couldn't count on there being enough left to waste. Besides, now he'd be up most of the night, which meant the nerves would be back and maybe they'd bring with them that old jealous-lover's kiss of remembered malaria.

But shit, he'd made it through another day, hadn't he? And he knew the bald man was, if not bored and horny and periodically terrified as he was himself, at the very least pissed off and hurting. The way a great leader, used to giving orders, felt when he couldn't have his own way.

That nearly made this waiting—this interminable, life-on-the-verge-of-extinction stalling of the inevitable—worthwhile. It made Pardoo decide again against the alternatives he'd devised, which ranged from somehow phoning the President to writing his congressman, from going to the newspapers to suicide. He smiled as he rewound his apparatus; to Reveille. After a fashion, things were equal with the bald man, when you threw in things like group stress and individual tolerance. The Colonel would never stop searching for him—not with what old Jack Pardoo could tell the world if he had enough evidence to risk it. Not if it came down to putting his own word and his glowing service record on the line. So far, only his life was on it now and he wanted to keep it that way a while longer.

Was Terry all right? The thought came to him out of seeming nothingness. Was there any chance that the boy knew his father had disapproved so greatly, that Terry might somehow strike out on his own?

Old woman, he told himself scornfully. Probably the bald man would never allow it to happen with two members of the same family. He had the kid under surveillance right now, Pardoo was willing to bet.

Maybe, though, there wasn't anything wrong with letting himself taste a tiny spoonful of optimism. That officer Wayland knew and he'd made it all the way to the Midwest, Minneapolis or somewhere. And there was the score-tying fact that Jack Pardoo would go on hiding, struggling to keep alive, so long as he had breath in his lungs and hair on his nuts—with just as much day-to-day determination as the Colonel, who knew it, who detested the knowing. Maybe he himself was driven to cover like a starving mutt, half mad with loneliness and want. But he also made the bald man marginally madder, too, and perhaps that would cause mistakes, snafus that would lead to exposure.

Pardoo wallowed a large bite of dried meat around in his mouth. It still had some flavor of rabbit left to it

and he forced himself to swallow and get it down.
Drinking water steadily, he peered out the window
at blackness, tried to see the peak of the distant hill
and failed.

Later he did energetic calisthenics on the floor of
the cabin, half talking to himself, talking it up. Not
any of that newfangled shit they put in books for
gullible women and fat-ass desk-jockeys but good
old hardnosed ballbusting timetested grab-your-
socks military PT. Pardoo drove himself the way he
had other men whenever he'd sweated away all the
perspiration he had, till it had dried on his small
body composed of muscles shaped like perfect
throwing stones, kept at it until the new perspiration began oozing through his large pores—

Until the silly, swift, tinny sounds of a strident
bugle burst against the walls of a rented cabin and
no one could have told the aging man's perspiration
from his freely flowing tears.

The pair of pretty women, each aging and each
physically far older than she'd been that morning,
stepped quietly from the old man's room and even
more quietly pulled the bedroom door to.

"I never thought I'd do anything like that," whispered the younger of the pair. She wore an expression of astonishment, but there wasn't a shred of
pride in her awed eyes or in the way she left her lips
parted, mouth faintly trembling. "I never thought
I'd have to."

"You had no choice, Molly." Lucille Skylar
glanced toward her dying husband's room, then
took her stepdaughter's hand between her damp
palms. "Not after I told you the few things I knew
about . . . your firstborn."

It was true, Molly thought, nodding vaguely as

the two of them padded softly toward her daughters' room. After Lucille had seen poor Michelle and Mary hanging, half-naked, from the ceiling of her garage, she'd spontaneously told Molly about Doctor Conrad Skylar's surreptitious phone calls over the years—and the way he'd always clamped his jaws together in silence whenever the subject of his daughter's stillborn son came up.

I don't want you to be sick, Daddy, and I don't want you to die, but you know something about what happened to my poor little Mark, and you have to tell me! Now, before—before it's too late! Her words were replayed in her mind with as much clarity as if someone had recorded them, and meant to torture her with them for all the years she had left.

He'd told her, gagging it out around the worst coughing she'd ever had to hear, that he had intended to tell her what he knew when she arrived in Indianapolis. Immediately he'd shown that hurt look of his in his rheumy eyes, one Molly remembered that he'd used whenever he wanted to reprove her mother for some imagined failure to venerate him properly. She understood that he'd seen disbelief in her own face, and while she had no desire to hurt him or even to get even, on behalf of Mama or herself or anybody else on the planet, she hadn't been able to refrain from telling her father the truth. "Daddy, that doesn't matter now, don't you see? Whether you wanted to—to make a clean breast of it or not is unimportant after what's happened to the g-girls." Her voice had broken then. "If you want me to remember you lovingly, father, you must tell me what you know—immediately!"

Molly eased her children's door shut behind her, and followed Lucille across the room to the bed.

Making herself look down and seeing their expressions, especially that of Mary, who was older and who had some understanding of what had nearly happened to her, was the hardest thing Molly had done in years. Both girls had insisted upon bathing with their mother standing guard at the bathroom door, then dressing all the way to jackets, shoes and socks. Now, any old enmity between them forgotten, they lay a foot apart on the bed with their little fingers touching. "So how is everybody feeling?" Molly asked as cheerfully as she could. "Better?"

Four embarrassed, frightened eyes looked up at her and away, the expression in them glazing and distant. "I'm fine, Mom," Michelle piped with some of her former sunniness. Mary inhaled as if it hurt. "We'll survive."

Mary used her most empathetic, brave smile. If either girl had been unconscious when she'd found them, or obviously assaulted, Molly would have had no choice except to telephone the police. Both of the girls, however, were alarmingly, keenly conscious. They'd told Molly and Lucille exactly what had happened. Despite the fact that pubescent Mary had been stripped to the waist, none of the four strange men who had forced them into the garage had touched her. "Not at *all*, Mother," she'd said wonderingly. "While one of them held me from behind, another . . . took my things off, using just his fingertips and being careful not even to touch me." Michelle, who appeared more humiliated than lastingly terrified or shocked, explained that one of the strangers said, "Pardon me," before he tore her Sunday dress down the middle. He, too, had not permitted his fingers or hands to graze her skin.

Which meant that the leader had told the truth,

and, in a way, that made it worse. Because he'd also
given his word that they'd return and make their
actions appear unmistakably like rape, if Richard
didn't stop "interfering"—whatever that meant.
There was, Lucille had whispered after they had
Mary and Michelle safely in the tub, soaking, only
one way she could imagine "making things seem unmistakably like rape." The same way you made a
person seem absolutely ready to be buried.

Lucille had said other things, too; that she had
read several books about rape and its victims and
that the terrible men were probably correct in what
they'd said about the authorities. If Molly or she
contacted the police, now, or in the event of the
actual ghastly attack, the official tendency would be
to chalk it up to the work of local perverts, known
sex offenders whom they would arrest, and from
whom they would probably pry enough evidence to
take them to court and clear the docket. "If you tell
them you suspect they were from out of town, and
that you know they're using rape as a warning,"
Lucille had told Molly, "my bet is that the police
will automatically place you in a file labeled
'Neurotic Mother.' "

"And if I am right, that they came here to
threaten me," Molly answered, astonished to find
that she and her daughters might need to defend
their own integrity to the authorities, "the police
will never find or arrest them. Because that would
mean they are from another city entirely, while the
local officials were only checking out Indianapolis
files."

And that was when Lucille, haltingly, had told her
a neurotic belief of her own: that the mortally ill
husband she adored had withheld information from
all of them about Mark, the Grants' first child who'd

been born twenty years ago. "There's probably no connection at all," she'd added as Molly determinedly headed for her father's bedroom; "but the fact that they mentioned Richard and a 'lady reporter' makes me wonder if everything mightn't be bizarrely linked, somehow."

Whether it was or not, Molly decided, Richard had to know what was going on—and considering what she'd heard from Dad Skylar, the whole thing made some kind of weird sense. Kissing each of her children tenderly, reassuringly, she went downstairs with her stepmother at her heels, eager to call home. *People's lives don't normally have a lot of dark secrets tucked away,* she reflected as she punched out the area code and then the familiar numbers, *unless they're involved with extramarital affairs. Espionage novels are always about professional spies from Russia or people who appear ordinary at first, then turn out to be ex-Nazis or CIA double agents.* Listening to the droning buzz from her Wheaton house, feeling it had been weeks or even months since Richard drove them to the airport, Molly realized for the first time how mature, how controlled she'd been until now. For her, at least. Rather proud, she decided she would not allow herself to burst into tears when her husband answered. No matter what, she would remain as collected, as cool, as the sensible stepmother whom she was beginning to respect.

"Yeah?"

He'd taken his time picking up the receiver and sounded rushed, brusque, as if he wanted the caller —any caller—to know he was busily at work. It flustered Molly badly; his tone of voice was so normal that it was incongruous at such a moment. "This is me," she said in a small voice.

"Oh, hi." How affable; how like a friend, or a next-door neighbor, he seemed! "What's up?"

A spark of temper was dampened by all the things she had to tell him and Molly gasped, "Oh, Richard, it's *awful!* You have to fly to Indianapolis right away."

A pause, a muffled sound. Was somebody there with him? "Right now?"

"As soon as you can catch a flight!" Molly exclaimed, suddenly breathless with apprehension. Perhaps he was still mad at her, perhaps he wouldn't come! *"Please."*

"It's Doc, right?" Something abruptly softened in Richard's voice and he was speaking only to her now. "Did he—?"

"No, not yet," she wailed. She began sobbing, leaning over the phone table as her yellow hair fell forward as if she felt it would envelop just the two of them. "He talked to me, Richard! I mean, he told me things"—abruptly she remembered his own fascination with some silly statistics he'd uncovered— "things about *Mark* an Army friend told him. Richard, you were right!"

"Mol, what are you saying?" The impatience again. "You aren't making any sense. I was right about what?"

Molly clenched the telephone between both hands, her gaze locked with Lucille's above it. "Darling, Mark wasn't born dead—he was born alive, just the way you figured it!"

His hand, Molly could tell with amazement, was again covering the mouthpiece; someone, clearly, was with him and Richard felt comfortable to confide in him. Or, her. Back with Molly, he sounded as if he were holding his breath or possibly withholding his thoughts. "We're leaving immediately."

Molly pictured him standing, eager. "We'll be there just as soon as we can get a big bird in the air."

For seconds, Molly continued to hold the phone tightly, even after she had heard the click of disconnection and the returning mechanical drone. *I didn't have time to tell him about the strange men and the girls,* she thought, seeing nothing as she stared into space. *And I don't know if a reporter actually did contact him.* But at least her Richard was coming!

"Will he leave soon?" Lucille asked, brows raised.

Molly smiled gladly. "They'll be there as soon as they get a big bird in the air," she quoted Richard.

But who in the world were "they"?

The boot in his strong, square hand shone like the sun but that wasn't bright enough. Not for the Colonel and not for him. The people out there—civilians—stopped when they achieved perfection. That was what set them apart, the outsiders and the insiders, and it was why the outsiders had to be protected and guided, even reprimanded at times. The other men and he looked for that which was beyond perfection, and he was starting to believe the ideal was attainable. Because the Colonel, the bald man, had gone about it properly, had avoided filling their heads with a lot of needless garbage about relationships, nonmilitary history, fancy books and crap like self-expression. Single-mindedly educated and trained, he was the best of his kind, and he owed it all to the Colonel. *God,* he loved that bald man! Emotions such as love were frowned upon, but he simply couldn't help the way he felt. He'd do anything in the world for the Colonel, anything! All he had to do was ask. Tell him.

For a number of minutes, he'd been alone, sitting

on the edge of his cot, so locked in polishing his
boots that he hadn't heard the noises coming from
the corner. It was a very rare event, to be alone, and
it gave him a queer feeling. Worse, the silence of the
room seemed to permit the clamor of his thoughts to
surface, to focus, and he was finding it hard to do
what he was ordered to do: keep mentally as well as
physically active at all waking moments, to avoid
the same kind of wayward notions, emotions, and
questions which plagued the civilians from getting
at him. He vaguely recalled parts of the speeches
made by the Colonel and the other officers to the
effect that there was a scientific reason why human
beings who allowed themselves to ponder in
idleness, found themselves doubting or even asking
questions about the basic necessities of the world's
vital doctrines. Challenging the essentials that
maintained order, a chain of command, and the
passionless commitment to regulatory excellence at
all costs.

But now the nerve-wracking silence was broken
by sounds from the corner, and he felt grateful,
relieved that he'd been spared a continuation of the
disloyal questions he'd found coming into mental
focus. Questions of no importance, to a single unit of
a great, dedicated body, about his origins, the male
who'd sired him and the female who'd birthed him.

A second passed, as he froze into total immobility,
and he saw the source of the sounds. A middle-sized
gray mouse foolishly ventured into the bare floor-
space at the foot of anther bed, sat upon its tiny
haunches, and sniffed the air—presumably for food,
since he paid no attention to the unmoving, quiet
figure seated some fourteen feet away.

"Fool," he whispered, hurtling the boot and
following it in his stocking feet. The shiny boot

narrowly beat him to the rodent which, struck with stunning accuracy by the heel, dropped in its tracks, seeping blood.

But it wasn't dead. He realized that at once, picking the mouse up by its tail and raising it against the nearest bare light bulb. It breathed, shallowly, and its small eyes were open, staring in wounded terror at him.

Funny, he mused, bouncing it in the air a bit, *what little lies between life and death. It proves the Colonel is right, not to believe in a deity. If God existed, if life was important, killing would be much more difficult and beings would have armament, like tanks.*

The word "pet" came into his mind, then, from where he had no notion. But he had a distant idea of what *pet* meant, and the emotional frivolity of it informed him that he was letting himself wander, intellectually, again.

He dropped the injured mouse, caught in between both palms as it fell, and ground his hands together. Something warm was pleasant to the touch and he parted his palms, dropping the hank of gray fur and crushed bone into a butt can.

Then he peered curiously, for an instant, at his reddened palms and the roots of his fingers.

No different than a human being's blood, he thought, restoring the expressionlessness of his features and going into another room to wash his hands.

Returning, he perched once more on the edge of his bed and shined one boot until the beauty beyond perfection seemed marginally more attainable. Rising, he went after the boot he'd thrown at the mouse.

Dab of blood on the heel. He overcame a frown.

Have to start over, he thought in a distant way, and walked back toward his bed.

Then he turned on the radio to hear one of the command's round-the-clock programs—a speech, the way most of the programs were, had been since his childhood—and listened intently as he buffed, blew upon, and ragged the stained boot.

That turncoat Wayland was next and it was important for a man to look his absolute best when the honor of an inanimation ceremony had been bestowed upon him.

16

Courtney Rankin's first appraisal of the short, curly-haired man slumped beside her on the plane to Indianapolis told her that Richard Grant had unaccountably fallen asleep.

It was a lie.

Her second, deeper inspection of the writer informed her that he was only pretending. "Playin' 'possum," as her late grandfather might have said. When the slinky stewardess with the impressive mammarian development paused in the aisle to stoop and whisper, asking Courtney if she'd care for something else to drink, she detected Richard's eyelids narrowly parting in interested appraisal.

They snapped shut again when the girl with the bod had passed.

The lovely Washington reporter started to speak, to josh him; then she said nothing at all and settled for looking with mild, professional interest at the other passengers aboard the small jet. Many of them seemed Christmas-minded, as befitting the season; the elderly man and woman several rows up where like twin snowcapped peaks, and a boyish

priest was deep in his Bible, presumably addressing
the Real Meaning of Christmas. Courtney risked
another glance at Richard, thought he saw his eyes
wink shut again, and she frowned. A person had his
right to withdraw into thought or, so long as she
wasn't questioning him for her paper, even into
outright, evasive privacy.

But for her own part, Courtney was so excited she
found it hard to sit still. What the wife of the quick-
witted little writer had told him, and he'd passed
along to Courtney, filled her with fresh adrenalin. It
was true that the Grant boy being born alive did not
directly connect with her own interest, the unidentified terrorists who were slaughtering junior-grade
politicians. In point of fact, there was such a
tenuous tie-in that a new reporter would have
wished the writer luck and returned to the newspaper, seeking a fresh angle. And besides, the
United States Army consisted of ordinary men;
mistakes were made, and as any reporter knew,
instinctively covered up.

There were, however, certain things they didn't
teach you in journalism school—certain odd, even
inexplicable facts which could never be written
down without sounding foolish. Courtney had been
a capable pro long enough to take such anomalies as
articles of primary faith: if you went in quest of
deeply buried data, hidden information, and
instantly found the entire story handed to you on a
platter, chances were you were being deceived. Oh,
not necessarily by the human beings linked to the
case but by certain mischievous elements of nature
which never gave anything worthwhile away so
readily, so cheaply.

On the other hand, if the story was complicated,
covered considerable time, involved the suppression

of secrets and a lot of people who would lose their
shirts if a good reporter got the facts, then even the
slightest sign of progress—the tiniest shred of
evidence—probably would put you closer to the
truth than all the breathtaking, convenient tips.
Because if you really looked closer at what was happening, you discovered a different kind of serendipity entirely. Witness her decision to drive out to
meet Richard Grant. She might just as easily have
telephoned one of the other experts on terrorism,
and completely missed this intriguing lead.

"D'you see those grandmother types, down the
aisle to your left?" Richard's tense whisper almost
made Courtney jump. "The ones with the angelic
faces, who look like a Norman Rockwell Christmas
card?"

She leaned her ear closer to his lips. He kept his
eyes closed; he was still slumped in his seat, seemingly asleep. Her heartbeat quickened. "Yes?" she
whispered urgently. "What about them?"

"They," he replied, raising a magazine from his
lap and moving his lips behind it, "are the Dubuque-
Keokuk chapter of the Mafia." His brows waggled
meaningfully. "Killers, every one. Great disguise,
though."

"You!" Courtney yanked his magazine away,
slapped him on the forearm. "Damn you, Grant, you
were studying *me*. I thought *I* was watching *you!*"

He yanked the magazine back. "Never try to
outsmart the old, gray fox," he said with his eyes
wide and knowing, tapping his temple with an index
finger. "Al Capone tried, and look what happened to
him. The Kaiser's spies and the Peerless Plotters of
Juan Peron tried, and they're dead. The SS thought
they'd fooled me, and the NKVD, the CIA, CBS and
the A & P—*all* those dreaded initials!" Richard

sighed wearily, gave her a smug grin. "But the old, gray fox survives all, forever stalking the evildoers of Gotham City."

"I thought that was Batman or the Lone Ranger," Courtney smiled.

"It was," Richard admitted, lifting the magazine for cover again. "But my mask's at the dry cleaners."

"Idiot." Despite herself, Courtney found her gaze drifting back over the snow-topped elderly couple, past the youthful priest; paused at two rows of conversing wise men in business suits, settled on two military types in the row just ahead of them. One wore civilian garb, the other a Navy uniform, and they were discussing the gifts they'd bought for their small children. With difficulty, she stopped reviewing the other passengers and looked back at Richard. He was erect, now, motioning to the busty stewardess. "I had the impression you were depressed or something and that puzzles me. Aren't you happy to hear your son is alive?"

"Who said that?" he asked her sharply.

"Well, your wife—"

"—Told me her father, Doc Skylar, had an Army friend who informed him that something mysterious was going on, and that Mark hadn't died after all." He glanced at the approaching stewardess. "Which does not, I'm afraid, mean he's still alive. I'll have another one of those things you brought me last time."

The stewardess, challenged for the first time that flight, looked pained. "Sir, I'm afraid I don't recall what you ordered before."

"Well, that's okay," he replied, his appreciative smile dazzling. "Bring me whatever sounds good to you. Surprise me." He waited until the young woman walked away, beaming at her when she glanced back with a smile of her own. "Back-court, the military complex is even more gifted as passing the buck than the D.C. pols on your beat. We have no guarantee that we'll be able to trace my kid, even after we interview my father-in-law. Hell, they've probably changed his hand and given him to another family, in order to hide their mistake."

"I don't think it's a mistake," Courtney said subbornly. "I think we're onto something important."

"Obviously you believe that," Richard said, staring at her with twinkling eyes. She was, he thought, the most interesting woman he'd met in years. "Why else would you run up your expense account by going with me to Indy?"

"Perhaps it's nothing but your irresistible charm, Richard," she said, half smiling. "Who else do I know who contradicts everything I say and makes me feel like a copygirl or a stringer just starting out?"

"By gosh, that might be it!" he exclaimed, seizing her hand and giving it a brief squeeze. "Maybe you think I'm the cutest little bugger you've ever met this decade and you're starting to fall head-over-heels in love with me!"

Aloud, she answered him. "What a surprise it is, after all these years, to find out I'm a masochist!" Squeezing back, she retrieved her hand.

And maybe you've guessed the truth, Courtney reflected, turning to the stewardess and taking Richard's drink, handing it on to him. *And maybe you know you have, you clever little runt.*

When they disembarked at Indianapolis International Airport, the snowy-haired elderly couple and the two military men were greeted by their families.

Richard, leading the way with Courtney at his heels,
spotted Molly waiting for him and failed to
recognize her expression of dismay when she looked
past him to Courtney. The two rows of businessmen
repaired to the nearest airport lounge, for fortifica-
tion. The boyish priest, catching the eye of three
youths wearing inexpensive new street clothes,
nodded, went into the men's room, and removed his
clerical collar.

*His dogtags rattled and clinked until he put on a
tie and left the rest room, heading for the appointed
rendezvous point.*

Molly, at the wheel of her father's car and trying
to follow road signs, felt the bewilderment and fear
of the last few days beginning to catch up with her.
The flat, dispassionate words of the men who had
harmed her children and issued their warning in a
manner she could never forget—a warning that her
husband and a lady reporter *must not interfere*—
intruded on what Richard and the woman (*what* was
her name? Courtney something?) were saying.

"So Courtney doesn't know if there's a connection
or not," Richard was finishing, staring straight
ahead at the highway, "but she felt that she had to
check it out."

"If there isn't room for me at your father's house,
Mrs. Grant, I'm sure I can find a motel nearby."
The reporter had insisted on getting into the back
seat, alone, and Molly, watching her in the rearview
mirror, noticed for the first time how attractive she
was. "I'm glad to hear your son may still be alive."

"He wouldn't even know me," Molly replied,
always inclined to say what came into her head. She
glanced at Richard, anxious to be alone with him,
infuriated by this woman. "Besides, how could any

of this be? Such a thing as kidnapping, with no one finding out?''

Courtney, seeing Richard was not replying, glanced from husband to wife. "No one knew about President Nixon, and Watergate, for two years, Mrs. Grant. Or President Kennedy and his . . . women—for twenty years."

"And those who knew," Richard put in, "didn't talk. And what about Hitler? 'Peace in our time,' Neville Chamberlain predicted after meeting him—and ordinary people living only a few kilometers from concentration camps swear they never heard of Nazi atrocities. Tell us again what your dad told you," he prompted Molly. "Everything you can remember."

Us, Richard said; *us!* Molly had been away a couple of *days*. But how could she tell him about the attack upon his own children with that—that Lois Lane type in the back seat? "There isn't a lot to add," she said at last. "All I know is that some friend of Dad's confided in him that a number of newborn boys, who were reported dead, were actually alive. For a while, he simply assumed they were malformed infants, or had brain damage; and he didn't want, I guess, to get involved. Then, when it seemed to be happening to me—to us—and our Mark was reported stillborn, well, Daddy hit the ceiling. He demanded that his friend learn the truth."

Richard looked infuriated. "And that's when he found that his own grandson was alive? Why in hell did the old man wait twenty years to tell you?"

Molly looked away to avoid his ire. Richard's anger frightened her. She felt constrained, again, to defend her father. "I am not quite sure, but if I understood Daddy correctly, he seemed to imply that he had been threatened."

"It certainly must have been a very effective threat," said the tall woman behind Molly. Her tone, without passion, was gently inquiring. "I understand that your father is a widely known and respected physician. That he was then."

Molly squinted in the rearview mirror at her surprise visitor's face. She couldn't decide if the reporter's observation was a criticism, or if it tacitly supported Doctor Conrad Skylar. "The rest of it is that my father's friend, whose name is Wayland, also tried to keep quiet. He—"

Richard's astounded face was inches from Molly's. "That's his name? Wayland?"

"Yes," she replied, flustered, conscious of the fact that Courtney Rankin had also come forward in her seat, "and he lives in a suburb of Indianapolis called Broad Ripple. Well, he was associated with them, apparently, and—"

"This Wayland," Courtney interrupted, sounding breathless, "lives here? In this city?" Her glance met Richard's over the car seat.

"If you two will just allow me to *finish*," Molly snapped, the threat of tears strong in her tone of voice, "you'll get the rest of it." She drew in a breath, abruptly cold in the borrowed car. She hadn't been able to figure out how to adjust the heater. "Evidently Wayland was in the Army himself, maybe under another name or something—"

"Did Doc say that?" Richard interjected. "Did he mention the man's real name?"

"It was just the way Daddy said it," Molly retorted. "He's very, very sick, you know, and I did the best I could."

"Hey, I'm sorry, Mol," Richard said gently. "Please finish."

She relaxed slightly, patted his hand on the seat between them. "Well, Daddy told me Wayland came to Indianapolis because of some trusted old contact of his. He got a job at Fort Harrison, where they hired a lot of civilians. I guess this Wayland is in computers or something."

"If he knows the truth about what happened to all the newborn boys—whether they were kidnapped for experimentation or whatever—then whoever it is Wayland is running from may well be looking for him even now." He turned to Courtney with a meaningful expression on his youthful face. "And since we know about it, now—part of it, anyway—maybe they wiretapped Molly's father or one of us. We can't waste any time in speaking with Wayland."

"Absolutely not. We'll have to get out to Broad Ripple soon, and question him." Courtney reached over the seat, lightly pressing Richard's shoulder. While she kept her voice controlled, subdued, Molly heard the undercurrent of intense excitement and shivered. "This might be the lead we've both been looking for!"

"I can't wait to talk with Doc," Richard declared. He was almost shivering with anticipation. He sensed that he appeared different to his own wife—overstimulated; maybe manic—and couldn't bring himself to care. "He may know quite a bit more."

Molly turned the car into the block where her father and stepmother lived. She slowed to a crawl, letting the motor idle. She had never felt more unbearably apart from her husband; her own job at the bank, six hundred miles away, might have been a dream, a fantasy. "There's something else but I don't know if it will help or not." Her glance to the other two was eager. If she hadn't known better, she would have had the impression that Richard and the reporter had been friends for years. Molly yearned, if nothing else, to be a part of their cloister. "They have a name for what happened to the baby boys, apparently. Daddy said he'd heard Wayland mention it, once; it was . . . project something."

"Project what?" Richard and Courtney demanded simultaneously.

Molly jumped, felt ganged up on; then she saw that the Skylar house was only yards in the distance. Lucille was outside, oddly; she stood at the front door, so soberly. And all she'd donned, in addition to her indoor garments, was a sweater. Blank, Molly asked Richard to repeat his question.

"I remember," she said, thoughts moving off, drifting elsewhere. She braked the borrowed automobile in front of the house, opening the car door on her side with rising anxiety. She called back, "It was *Project Romulus.*"

Then she was scrambling up the walk. She imagined, at first, that her stepmother was grinning. She saw in an instant that the pretty, aging features were drawn into a grimace instead. Husband and guest forgotten, Molly rushed toward Lucille Skylar.

Several feet away, however, she stopped.

"He's gone," Lucille managed.

Words only confirmed it.

They'd known how important it was when the Colonel, personally, ordered them up before dawn and double-timed four crack squads to the unheated artificial lake. Enroute, junior officers and cadre harassed them, shrieked in their ears, often so close that noses touched shrinking flesh and mint-scented breath enveloped the troops as if they'd been exposed to pretty smelling gases. The running didn't bother them; most of them liked it, loved it, because they had always run, if not always in full combat gear as they were this freezing morning.

From behind them, the squads of soldiers heard their Romulus mates otherwise engaged. Shouts of LOUDER, YOU LADIES; CRAWL, YOU PIG; KILL! KILL!—this, from a nearby bayonet drill— and the report, steady fire, and sputter of .45 automatics, M-16 rifles and mortar fire, as well as the rasping repetition of .30 caliber machine guns and the blast of the light anti-tank weapon (LAW, its unamusing acronym), sounded nostalgically comforting to men being driven to another, and presumably harder, water test.

The soldier called Mark saw the priest, standing beside the Colonel, the bald man, on the bank of the artificial lake. He recognized the priest at once; they'd talked and made jokes together during a couple of G.I. parties. But he wasn't a priest, and he'd quit making jokes and now he'd completed an assignment for the bald man himself. Just as Mark had donned civvies and a stupid baseball cap to accompany three other troops for the trip to warn the Grant woman. Except that the youth in the priest clothing had been trusted to go on his own. Trying not to shiver in the early morning breeze, Mark felt a rush of admiration, of envy, for the other soldier.

"The troops who went to Indianapolis," said the Colonel. "One step forward."

Mark did not wonder about the order until he had obeyed. It was too late to wonder, then. It was too late in any case.

When the four soldiers had been marched into a tight line and were standing on the bank of the unnamed, artificial lake, the Colonel told the other troops that they were there as observers. To the quartet of erect young soldiers, from behind them, the bald man spoke more softly. "You haven't learned intimidation, gentlemen. How to instill fear. And the best way to remember it is by experiencing it. Eh?" Smiling, he paused, just to Mark's left and to his rear. "The civilians are still searching, gentlemen. You did not adequately frighten the mother, or even the little girls. One by one, you will jump into twelve feet of water. The nature of this morning's exercise is this: The hypothetical enemy plans to execute the first man who surfaces. The enemy will shoot the second man rising in the *face*—not a mortal wound, but a disfiguring one. The enemy will shoot the third man who lets show any part of his gutless anatomy in both kneecaps, rendering him a cripple."

None of the four men twitched or discernibly widened his eyes. The Colonel was so silent that, for an instant, none of the troops was certain he had not moved away and all four of them were praying that the bald man was changing his mind. To a man, they really did not want him to announce his intentions— the enemy's intentions—for the fourth man.

"Stand ready!" For the first time, Mark—he had no other name that he knew of—looked down. The water was inky, quiescent; deep. Only his eyes had moved, and his slightly bending knees. "The fourth man up will personally escort or carry the first three back to the facility," called the Colonel, for the first time letting the dozens of other soldiers hear a part of his exercise plan, "and will be permitted to escape inanimation. *Jump!*"

They jumped—submerged—as one. To his right, Mark heard a strangled sound, realized that Enos, the black troop who had accompanied him to

Indianapolis, had lost his balance and, frightened, was inadvertently propelling himself to the surface. A distant report. Silence. And Mark sought to make out the location of the remaining two men without success. Now, at the floor of the manmade lake, he realized that fear had prevented him from inhaling as much air as he might have and knew, simultaneously, that the bulk of his combat gear would hold him down almost as long as he wished. Distantly, like noises heard in a dream, he believed he heard another of his companions thrusting desperately, madly, toward fresh air. He remembered the names of the others; one of them came closest to being a friend of all the troops Mark knew, and he hoped it was not Alan who had panicked.

Then the silence was that of a watery tomb and young Mark's mind raced for a solution, strained to hear the movements of the remaining soldier. *If I hold out, he'll still be lucky*, Mark told himself. *He'll never walk again but he'll still be alive.*

A moment later, his lips moved as if kissing the cold waters, showering the killing force with affection. Heart thundering in his chest, he found that he was squeezing his eyes shut, becoming dizzier by the moment, tasting the brackish water as it slipped into his throat and his lungs. Why didn't that sonofabitch surface?

Lazily, he pawed with his arms, floating, unconsciously thrusting, faintly. The thought of trying to swim out into the center of the lake, away from the bald man's fire, occurred to him; but no one he'd ever known could fire a piece with the bald man's accuracy. A face, a woman's face, filled his mind that moment; he saw pretty, golden hair—and remembered slapping her face, bringing tears to her eyes; and wondered why. Why he had slapped someone so nice . . .

He began parting his lips in awful anguish and
dread as he thrust up, flailing his arms with the last
of his failing energy, burst to the surface and into
the air—

Colonel Albert Caull was three yards away, kneeling, looking straight at him, his .45 automatic
leveled.

Instantly, Mark fought his way to the ground,
clasping his knees as best he could as he floundered
to earth, wholly without a sound of fear or protest,
his terrified eyes fixed on the bald man as the latter
pivoted, slowly . . .

Then, chuckling, holstered his piece and made a
broad, sweeping gesture. He did so with the air of a
magician revealing the climax of his spellbinding
act.

Enos, face down, wasn't moving. The soldier
who'd been in command, when they traveled to the
Midwest, lay on his back with his hands clasping the
places where his knees had been. His thighs and the
earth around his squirming buttocks had turned
red.

The third man, his friend, Terry, was unconscious
but arguably alive, until shock set it. He didn't have
any face to speak of.

"Men, I love the beauty of early morning." The
Colonel, ignoring Mark, addressed the erect, blank-
faced observers who stood at parade rest. Pale, but
observing. "Especially when I'm in the company of
real soldiers!"

17

Richard stood at the foot of the stairs, helplessly watching Molly rush upstairs with Lucille to her father's bedroom, anguished because of her loss but thinking, too, what a tapestry of fantasy had been woven around death. People couldn't believe other people died until they saw the body with their own, living eyes, and even then the fact of death wasn't fully accepted until time passed—time during which the deceased person no longer visited or sent Christmas cards or was available on the other end of the phone. Once, when a slightly older friend had died, Richard didn't accept the news as a fact until, on a rise of emotion, months later, he dialed the friend's phone number and heard a stranger answer. *Get out of Buddy's house,* he'd thought, angry even as the reality of it came into focus in his mind.

And the reality of it was that, to Richard, Buddy would always have that telephone number, always live in the house he sometimes saw ahead of him in his headlights before pressing down on the accelerator and tugging an edge of the fantasy sustained tapestry around him as armor against the cold facts.

He wasn't sure whether the girls knew about their grandfather's passing, or not. When he heard Michelle join Molly in loud weeping, and pictured the obsessively self-controlled Mary doing her best to remain the detached observer, he found out. Awkwardly, he turned to Courtney.

"I'm sorry to've dragged you into this emotional scene," he said softly.

"You haven't dragged me anywhere," she said, touching his arm. "Never apologize because your family is normal."

"How normal is it," the voice made them turn, look up, "to cry because a man who seemed cold, stern, and unapproachable—a sideline father and grandfather—dies at an advanced age?"

Lucille Skylar, Molly's stepmother, was descending the steps slowly. Still a handsome woman, she seemed neither frigid nor hypocritical despite her question. Richard smiled, assisted her down the last few steps. "Very normal indeed, if you're a person of compassion," he replied. He added, close to her at the foot of the stairs, "I think."

"You're absolutely right," Lucille told him. "I forget, sometimes, that we cry as much because of how things might have been as because of how they were. It's good to see you, Richard." She turned her head slightly. "I don't believe we've met."

Courtney, flushing, put out a slim hand. "I'm assisting your son-in-law with research for his next book," she said. Lucille briefly held her fingers. "About a group of assassins terrorizing minor politicians around the country."

"That's why I left Molly and the girls upstairs. Because I wanted to tell you, Richard, that they seem to have paid a visit to Molly and the girls."

Her eyes shone with unnatural brightness. "If you wonder how I can talk about it when my husband has just died, you'll understand how worried I am by what happened. I thought you should hear it from me."

Seeing Richard's stare of frightened anticipation, Lucille quickly told them what had happened outside—and inside—the garage. "You had to know about it," Lucille added; "I felt you should expend your outrage on me, instead of Molly."

"Those—those *bastards!*" he exclaimed, nearly shouting. "What's been done about it?"

"There was nothing to be done. I'm sure Molly will be telling you more, but at least, now, you're prepared."

"Richard." Courtney lowered her voice, not conspiratorially or shutting Lucille out, but pointedly nevertheless. "We must be on the right track and they feel we're getting too close." Her voice was controlled, she seemed passive, but her eyes glinted with professional excitement. "We aren't chasing after ghosts."

"Pardon me if it's none of my affair," Lucille Skylar murmured, "but none of this makes sense to me. What makes a Washington reporter fly to Indianapolis? And how does it connect with those terrible people who threatened Molly and the girls?"

"Would you explain it," Richard asked Courtney, "while I see my children?" He caught her nod of agreement and started up the stairs, full of fury and fresh doubt—not the doubt that he and Courtney were on the right track, but whether they were inadvertently plunging the family into danger.

He forgot about it when he saw the kids. Michelle clung to her mother in tears of grief for Doctor Skylar, but Mary sobbed quietly alone. She'd slipped out into the corridor, apparently unnoticed by Molly, and stood with her face to a corner, hands clenched at her sides, tears sliding noiselessly down her cheeks.

"Baby," he whispered. She turned, went into his arms without a sound.

He couldn't recall the last time Mary had done that; he found himself smiling above her shoulder, adoring the moist tears on his cheek and feeling a strange sense of gratitude to an old man, for dying.

That evening, an aftermath of loss settled around the Skylar house and gradually, grudgingly, the surviving relatives spoke not only of the man who'd died but of those things that had to be accomplished before Lucille, the widow, could go on.

But after they'd tentatively touched upon the need for a casket to be chosen, a minister and all the other articles necessitated by obeisance to dark routine incumbent upon families when they could least tolerate such logic, the widow looked up from the sewing things in her lap and faced them with solemn eyes.

"Richard knows what happened to the girls, Molly," she said evenly. "It isn't safe for you to remain in this house more than a day or two."

"She's right," Richard said. His concerned gaze found Molly and he rose to go to her to kneel and take her hands. "Darling, I had no idea what Courtney and I did would place you, Mary, and Michelle in jeopardy." He touched her cheek lightly. "Did they . . . harm . . . any of you?"

"No." Exhausted by sorrow, Molly was only starting to grasp the implications of what he was saying. "But they warned us you should let it drop. Richard, who were they? What you two were discussing in the car—is that . . . ?''

Courtney Rankin explained, fact by fact, to spare
Richard the further torture of suggesting that the
Grant son had been taken at birth. He sat listening,
at Molly's feet, grateful for Courtney's unemotional
explanation.

"It's so hard to accept, this—kidnapping," Molly
whispered. "Without the public finding out." She
shook her head. "I know what you said, but still . . .''

Courtney smiled warmly at her. "Your husband's
talented; smart. But even he has a lot to learn about
. . . reality. Especially a journalist's brand; my kind.
By and large, people don't want to know about these
things until it's tied up in a package on the news,
and somebody is doing something about it.''

"Imagine the power any branch of government
has, to conceal their plans," Richard said to Molly.
"Power, and money you and I can't even dream of.''

"That's why," Courtney said softly, her shrewd,
kind gaze sweeping the others, "I think we'd better
drop it. Your family's security is in jeopardy. That
power argues that we forget everything we've discovered, and—''

"*No.*" Even before he could react to the reporter's
startling advice, Richard saw Molly leap, flushed, to
her feet. "No, you have to keep going. You must get
the facts, the truth. And stop them!''

"I can't believe this," Richard said, wide-eyed.
"You were the one who couldn't bear the hope that
Mark was alive. Now, we could find that he was
killed. Or used in some awful way.''

Molly Grant swept back a straying strand of the
golden hair, smiled at him and at Courtney. "The
men, here—they prove you are right. What's worse,
my father kept the truth from me!" She stretched
down her fingers to him. "If you don't find out what

happened to little Mark, I'll never be able to forgive
my father!''

Richard stood, and held her as she began to cry.
"We have no way of knowing that the men who were
here have anything to do with Mark," he told her.
"Yet if we could get you and the girls to safety, we
might just find out."

"I believe I have an idea," Lucille said, erect in her
chair, remarkably composed. "Let me think about
it, tell you tomorrow. Before you go to talk with
Wayland. As for the matter of my husband's prepar-
ations, I've already asked a friend of his, our
attorney, to take care of them." Her voice trailed to
a whisper at the end of her remark. Her eyes had
filled with tears. "I'm aware, Molly, that you never
believed I loved your father and now you have seen
how . . . self-controlled . . . I am." She looked away,
whipping her head to avert her eyes. "That control
is starting to vanish, and it's all I ever really had, to
deal with life. But I assure you, I loved him." They
had to strain to discern her final words. "I'll miss
him every minute the rest of my life."

Before retiring, Richard arranged to borrow
Doctor Skylar's car and leave with Courtney before
dawn, in the hope that anyone watching the Skylar
house would be caught napping, or think the driver
was an associate of the late doctor taking his Olds
for safekeeping.

Knowing he desperately needed rest, Richard
decided to bed down with Molly in the bedroom
previously assigned to her. He, Molly, and Lucille
left Courtney in Doctor Skylar's library. "I'm too
restless to sleep," she'd informed them, "and books
are the best company during sleepless nights."

Richard perched on a chair to unknot his shoe-

laces, waiting for Molly to return to their room from
the bath. Down the hall, ten minutes ago, he'd heard
the not-so-wicked stepmother padding toward her
lonely bedroom and softly closing the door. He
wondered if Molly, too, was beginning to see that
her father had done something right when he'd
taken Lucille as his wife.

Too weary to rise, he pulled down his trousers and
tugged them from his body a leg at a time.
Courtney, he reflected, was quite a woman. Her offer
to abandon the case, potentially the biggest story of
her career, seemed to him generous beyond belief.
Had he imagined it that she was responding to him,
liked his humor, his personality? Despite himself,
Richard, for the first time, found himself admitting
to himself how drawn he was to the woman journalist. There were ways in which he had more in
common with her than any woman he'd met. In the
back of his inventive, author's mind, he'd been all
but making love to her in the things he said; and he
knew that he wanted, very much, to make love to
her in fact. He wondered if—

Molly, above him, naked. Richard started guiltily.
He'd begun, thinking of Courtney, to respond
physically.

Now he draped his pants across his lap, suddenly
aware of how absurd he looked with his shirt still on,
his hairy legs entubed in socks and his penis
pushing toward erection beneath the protecting
trouser-cover. He sensed the way it relaxed, sharply,
from the guilt, because his wife was there.

And then it tensed, anew, became increasingly
taut as he realized that his beautiful Molly had
remained where she stood, wanting him.

Startled, because she had been grief stricken, he
let his gaze travel up the undersides of her sleek,

globular breasts, down the fall of her torso to the
inset eye of her navel and down farther to the
familiar but always enigmatic tangle of yellow pubic
hair. He thought, unaccountably, of the yarn he had
seen in Lucille Skylar's sewing room and simultaneously of how real blondes had always appeared
unreachably girlish, oddly unfinished, richly desirable to him. As if they required, over and over, what
he could provide for them so that they might be
suspended longer in tentative womanhood.

But there was nothing immature about the way
Molly's hands caught in the hair of his head and
drew him, fiercely, to her; nor was it the sound of a
female child when she began to gasp, above his
head, her hair tumbling forward, his fingers
threading yarn to press his lips where his lovely wife
wished.

An instant later Molly slipped to her knees before
him as though her pale, perfect legs could not
support her. Her face was full of a searching need
Richard did not understand and she said, full voice,
conversationally, "I need to know I'm alive and all
right on my own." But before he had a chance to
reply, she was seizing that which protruded against
his shorts, freeing it, almost humming as she lipped
it—at the root—and ran its length moistly, rimming
it briefly and then, holding it just inside her mouth
while her long, pink tongue probed a delicate half-
circle caresses beneath its head. Molly's fingers
entwined beneath her feeding mouth and slipped up,
down, up again until Richard gasped. Looking
down, he saw her quiet eyes through the canopy of
her spreading, golden hair. He didn't stop her and
she took all of him into her mouth with apparent
hunger; Richard watched in total absorption, sure
that he would not be able to see anything at all if she

continued much longer.

Knowing at once what he knew and wanting more, Molly was away from him then, nimbly climbing onto the unfamiliar bed, motioning to Richard. There was a sensation of occupying a hotel room in a strange city, of the tantalizingly illicit, and Richard tottered to his feet, eagerly joined Molly. Getting into bed knees first, preceded by his throbbing erection, he sucked air as Molly thrust her head forward and again took the head of his protrusion between her lips. He'd begun to wonder why the old urgency had returned, to him and to Molly, as well, but the sharp prick of her teeth raked him, grazed him avidly, and his body rose over her and he did not wish to think. She made him trail his aching erection between her breasts and down her belly; her hands clutched, then found his buttocks and, squeezing, pulled him into her waiting, wet vagina. She's more passionate than she's been in ages, he thought, hearing her tiny squeal. She closed her white legs across the small of his back; then they moved down, crushing his hips, thrusting up at him simultaneously with that feminine power that had always amazed Richard, told him woman's frailty and lack of will were only additional lies.

At the instant he saw her face in a splash of moonlight, when curtains at the alien window swayed as if in empathy, he forgot completely about Courtney Rankin and was more truly joined to Molly—part of her—than he had felt since before she became pregnant with their lost son Mark.

There was, in her pale face, the fundamental involvement in an act of loving sex that he'd almost forgotten and knew, then, he had sorely missed. The way her skin glistened, the tightness of it over the forehead and her cheekbones, the way her lips

parted as if she somehow still sucked between them
his aching penis, the way her eyes had become restless, damp slits, seeing nothing or perhaps a world
no man was permitted to see, brought Richard's
passion to heights he'd forgotten. Now, at last,
Molly was devoid of the mother-daughter softness
of workaday concern, transformed into complete
Woman, working with him and beneath him, around
him in some way.

Shoving, writhing, prodding, he paused to rise
over her, and her face suggested she was leaving on
some strange metaphysical journey—giving herself
to astral travel, perhaps—yet taking him along, if he
could come. He touched some ephemeral spot deep
inside of her, some demandingly secret place even
Molly could not consistently summon, and
answered its insistence with his own. Immediately,
Molly's fingernails pierced his back and then he did
not know if he imagined the sound of the female call
in capitulation or in mutual triumph. All he could be
certain of was how they thrashed, the woman he
loved and he, pummeled one another until the time
when he was frozen by his own spasms—and
nothing was defeated, only victory was achieved for
the two of them . . .

Of course, Richard thought, finding again the
ability to think, and to see. Panting, pumping the
rest of it for both of them, he collapsed slowly, his
upper body covering Molly's. He liked the faint,
dual pressure of her breasts beneath him and how
moist she felt everywhere; and he loved her arms
going around him in the old motion that was nearly
one of comfortable camaraderie. Her roughened lips
nibbled the lobe of his ear, playfully, and her belly,
when he felt it between them, was wet. *Of course,
it's fine for us tonight. And true . . .*

* * *

Courtney, wearing her slip, tried to adjust the
sheet and blanket Lucille Skylar had brought,
turning in contortionistic movements on the sofa in
the doctor's library and cursing. She'd been a fool to
refuse a cot in the Grant kids' cozy bedroom. It was
apparently true that the dead man had once
designed this aging house to include places in which
sleepless folk might seek solace in the wee hours.
The leather chairs and sofa were comfortable
enough, if one meant only to read.

The problem, mainly, was the books. Most were
either medical tomes or classics and near-classics of
fiction as well as nonfiction, well maintained,
lastingly and deservedly important works—but the
kind a real reader had read, and the majority barren
of prior, caring touch. They were the books a person
collected because he had bookshelves. They were the
bookshelves of a man who understood that they
were proper and served his image.

But Courtney was a real reader. She'd always
liked any book that appeared massively used, read
and reread and loaned out and returned to the
shelves with a prayer for partial amnesia, so that
the owner might read it fresh, again, one day. A
loved book.

The titles in Doctor Skylar's library, while most of
them had won love once, adorned books which had
been touched only long enough for them to be slid
away and occasionally dusted.

What she really detested were modern bookshelves which could just as easily be used to hold
decorative vases, artificial flowers, built-in tape
decks or photo albums. Doc Skylar had stopped just
short of such abomination.

After a while, giving up sleep, Courtney stood,

stiffly. Flowerlike in the slender stem of her white slip, her dark hair puffy, she had no idea in the world how lovely, how garden-fresh she appeared. Bending and cramming herself into a squeaky leather chair beside a floorlamp, she retrieved the one book she'd found to read—to re-read, of course. She opened *The Great Gatsby* at random. "An hour later the front door opened nervously," she scanned, "and Gatsby, in a white flannel suit, silver shirt, and gold-colored tie, hurried in. He was pale, and there were dark signs of sleeplessness beneath his eyes."

Oh yes, Courtney flashed, the day Daisy would see, spread before her wondering eyes, all Jay Gatsby had acquired—by every means necessary. Meant, in its entirety, for her alone; to impress only Daisy. Her fond gaze traveled: " 'Nobody's coming to tea. It's too late.' He looked at his watch as if there was some pressing demand on his time elsewhere." And later, so effectingly Courtney Rankin could not read it without tears rising: "She turned her head as there was a light, dignified knocking at the front door. I went and opened it. Gatsby, pale as death, with his hands plunged like weights in his coat pocket, was standing in a puddle of water glaring tragically into my eyes."

Courtney smiled sadly. She knew how Scott Fitzgerald had ended his book, and it was right and unhappy and she arose to replace *Gatsby* upon the shelf. She felt glad, though foolish about it, that she had bestowed more affection upon that copy than the poor thing had received before. It would feel warmer, in the hand, the next time someone took it down.

She heard the squeak of springs, above her, in the house, and raised her chin, peering at the ceiling with cheeks reddening in vivid imagination and

strong, envious need. Was it safe, now that
feminism's roots were down, to be a woman and
empathize, just a little, with Jay Gatsby?

But she could not prepare a place for Richard,
could not even imagine that he needed the possessions Gatsby fancied would charm his Daisy.
Storied houses, daring dresses and the burning of
torches belonged to a time decades before either she
or Richard had been born. If one wanted another
person, whatever the circumstances, one *asked*,
today. Rejected, she would find another warm body
elsewhere. If one did not notice the eyes, the face,
the speaking heart of another person, neither did
one tie herself to him by bits of threads that come
unraveled over the course of time.

Tomorrow, she and Richard would drive together
to a suburb called Broad Ripple. They would cross-
examine, as best they could, a frightened man about
his part in a two decade old enigma. Those events
might or might not be connected with the attacks of
terror occurring across the nation, but she,
Courtney Rankin, would be at Richard's side. And
they might, Courtney realized, they really might be
close to the end of it, then.

According to the rules, when it was done she
would return to the newspaper, Richard would
return to his writing and to his family in the Washington suburbs. According to the rules of current
custom, she could say she wanted him and they
would probably make love.

None of that seemed enough.

Courtney walked slowly back to the sofa, and
shivered. Was there danger ahead of them? She
shook her head, half doubting it. Well placed
modern reporters with some fans tended to walk the
most hazardous streets anywhere in the world, an

impervious shield preceding them. It was made of public awareness that the journalist, in any media, might one day be needed by an element of the public which suddenly wanted its own views, fears, and desires publicized.

I am a person who belongs to everyone who reads me, Courtney mused, *but I am also invisible and untouchable.* It was impossible to slaughter a front page.

But there was another danger, another risk. The kind poor Gatsby had confronted.

He'd told Nick Carraway, when harsh reality impinged upon his beloved fantasies, "This is a terrible mistake." It had been; deep down inside, surely, he'd known it all along. Because, as Fitzgerald wrote at book's end, the dream "was already behind him, somewhere back in that vast obscurity beyond the city . . ."

Not that she loved Richard. She doubted Jay had loved Daisy. But what they shared was the way life had conspired to keep them from learning if they loved, to keep them from having a chance to do, with confidences and kisses, those sweet and enduring things that transformed fantasy to reality. She needed the philosophers' stone, and knew no one, at all, who had found it.

It was Courtney Rankin's essential and sole secret that she had become a journalist because believing in romance was her requirement. She had to live as if romance might have slipped into the late 20th century. She had regarded her clever exterior and the probing questions of her craft as ideal complements, wary partners to the warmly throbbing heart of Possibility; and most of her stories had been a quest for the philosophers' stone.

Where she was able, she'd seen romance.

And she'd simply never seen it so clearly as she had upon meeting, and getting to know, Richard Grant.

18

There was, the tall, panting man realized with only mild surprise, something distantly exhilarating about dashing quickly and decisively through a pitch-black and tangled wood, so late at night it was almost morning. Elements of his peculiar joy, he could understand at once. When all other pleasures were cut off from a modern man, his customarily far-flung horizons were narrowed, turned in upon themselves. Because humankind's well publicized curiosity, ostensibly so different from that of other animals, was partly based upon his latent perfectionistic drive and an innate yen to be recognized by others as a natural appreciator, he must sooner or later find something, anything, to be enthusiastic about. It was true even in the most restricted, mundane kind of life, such as his had become.

The December air was barbed and gingery, so persistent at his back now, on this return trip home, that Wayland believed he could nearly fly. Breathing lightly, without effort, he felt better conditioned than he had since his ancient days as a raw recruit. Even so, he ruminated, there was rather more to deriving pleasure from this arboreal jaunt than his narrowed sphere of opportunity. Something about being up and around and full of important secrets while the rest of the world slept; something, too, perhaps, about being chosen by a powerful, dedicated, elite group of men as their special target. Wayland smiled, remembering, and quickly passed through a small clearing into another seemingly unmarked complex of trees. The handful of people who actually enjoyed warfare, throve on war, did so because of an ego similar to his and that of the bald man. Because, in a frighteningly basic way, such modern gladiators felt wanted. They even experienced an involved love/hate relationship with their opposite numbers across the trenches. He had heard of officers and enlisted men alike who went into major conflict with the solidest erections of their lives; and they stayed throbbingly hard until others fell—any others—to permit their gloriously fulfilling orgasms.

Wayland wondered idly when he'd started taking pleasure in this, since he had never grown sexually excited because of blood, maiming, or the realization that he had survived. Some civilians, obliged to jog to the closed service station where the car was supposed to be full gassed, oiled, and waiting for his last second getaway, would have regarded it with a mixture of paranoid panic and a sense of nuisance. Even if they'd managed to grasp how essential it was to make certain that the car—unrigged and unbugged and unbombed—was still there, they'd probably have failed to perfom this chore with Wayland's regularity and thoroughness. Such folks, such Americans, were spoiled, precisely as the bald man claimed; they'd never been in any danger from which daddy's loan or a twenty-five cent telephone call would not extricate them.

Even other soldiers Wayland had known well had grudgingly admitted to a mood of incipient terror when they'd had to rush, alone, through the kind of forest habitat which had once been natural to all men. Now, of course, they were partly "civilized," busier at erasing all memory of the collective past than they were at anything else; now, a woods or a jungle was merely symbolic, to most men, of human-kind's fantasy filled subconscious mind. That was another place the Colonel had been correct. Such soldiers feared foreign snipers and land mines, not this personal terror on good American soil. Not a ruthlessly efficient danger which obliged them to memorize every lightning struck trunk, every clump of bushes which might bear a fresh human footprint, every new growth of weeds which could misdirect you deeper into the woods.

Of course, to be on the level about it (Wayland reminded himself), he was not alone. Oh, no. Expert jungle fighters, even revolutionary guerrillas, rarely knew the kind of mobile security which he drew from the soft, snuffling sounds rising from the direction of his scampering feet and legs, and from watching the effortless racing motion of the animal's bristling back: the bought and paid for protection of the menacing mercenary, Hans—more than ready to attack anything or anyone, upon command.

Wayland slowed, stopped, and stooped to unleash the Doberman, whose legs tensed as he peered coldly into the tall man's eyes. He hadn't brought with him the special padded glove or other equipment which would enable Hans—Wayland had given up on making the animal answer to the name Lance—to enter one of his deadly practice sessions. He thought the animal, still young, might enjoy

romping awhile, unfettered. The appreciation of
freedom and awareness of its importance for living
things were what had guided Wayland to an abrupt,
early retirement. He'd had to flee the unacceptable
orders of the bald man, or cross the final line and be
just like him.

Wayland squinted into the gloom at his bounding
attack dog, conscious that furtive fingers of light
were groping the sky. Now that old Doctor Skylar
intended to inform his daughter about a part of
what the bald man and he had set up, two decades
ago, it wasn't unlikely that the Colonel would get
wind of it. His intelligence network was first rate,
always had been. If so, he'd try to prevent any
further leakage of information prior to Christmas
Eve, when Romulus matured. Since the Colonel considered Wayland a renegade, he'd never believe him
capable of keeping his mouth shut. Which would
leave the bald man one option, to maintain adequate
security—assuming that he'd finally succeeded in
discovering his old staff officer's whereabouts. It
behooved Wayland, therefore, to keep Hans
fundamentally on his side, to whatever extent
emotional commitment might be aroused in the
sadistic beast's breast. He sighed, watching Hans
skulk in the weeds, then vault playfully at insects as
well as imaginary opponents. What a shame it was,
when you had time to think about it, that man
willfully turned his best friend into a killer. There
wasn't often time to think about it. The unspoken
excuse was that times arose when humans and dogs
alike must be encouraged to revert to their savage
origins, to fundamental, murderous type. To
maintain for others the pretense that either man or
dog had ever been remotely civilized.

They were too greedy for that. They'd never learned

to share, unless there was something in it for them.

Hans moved into action with so little warning that Wayland wasn't aware anything was happening until the Doberman, growling now, turned to the path leading to the old one-story they shared and Wayland saw his ears pressed back, his sleek, powerful body launched like a torpedo toward home. What did Hans scent, or hear?

Wayland saw the beast burst from the edge of the woods into the street, propel himself forward without pausing toward the uniformed figure of a dairy routeman standing at the front door of their house with his fist lifted in a gesture of knocking. The tall man swore; he hadn't even shouted *Ewigkeit,* code word for attack, at Hans; if he harmed the damned milkman, the courts might have the dog destroyed.

Two things, one internal, one external, happened then. Wayland realized that Hans was no longer attacking, simply loping across the street toward the man with the bottles of milk—and he saw the milk truck coming, gathering speed from several houses down the block, *headed on an angled line which was calculated to meet the Doberman head-on.* "Hans!" Wayland shouted.

And the front bumper of the white milk truck struck his dog just behind the muscular right shoulder, crushing the ribs, probably breaking his back.

What Wayland realized then formed a bewildering, frenetic kaleidoscope of facts which brought his run to a halt, twelve feet from the walk leading to his house. He realized that Hans had been propelled a yard or two into the air before toppling to the ground, hard, his head on the curb and his crumpled body in the gutter. He realized that the man in the milkman's uniform had clapped his hands together sharply, in the familiar command of summons. He realized that Hans had made no sound, despite his obvious pain, and that the man in the milkman's whites was not a milkman.

He realized that the truck, after intentionally hitting his dog and appearing to stop, had only paused. Now it was bearing down upon *him*. He realized that the man who was not a milkman was the bald man—the Colonel—who had actively participated in the training of Hans and other dogs. He realized that no one on the block was up and around, that if they had been it would not have made a penny's worth of difference. He realized that he was all alone and facing death, and that the damned milk truck seemed maniacally *alive* that instant, bent on doing to him what it had done to his attack dog.

He *reacted*. He hurtled his aging body sideways to the sidewalk, not far from his dog's broken body, rolling lithely in the insubstantial sheet of snow and ignoring the jolting shock of pain as he brought his old legs beneath him for the trained-and-instinctive sprint back into the woods he'd learned so well, to run pell-mell for the automobile so lovingly prepared for last-ditch escape.

But the men who filled the back of the truck in lieu of milk bottles were pouring from the open doors, then flowing over him with such astonishing alacrity and nimbleness, such wholly numbing efficiency, that Wayland did not think to appreciate their expertise until his house keys had been wrested from his torn pocket, the front door speedily unlocked, and he was jammed into a corner of his living room like some baggy suit of clothes crammed into a closet.

His initial recovery of his own trained aplomb

started with the first carving chop of a hand to his
unprotected head and throat; he saw in memory a
Japanese POW camp in which he'd been held prisoner
and was brought to a state of disciplined detachment by the ancient recollection. *They do nice work,*
he thought, gagging from the blows to his Adam's
apple and under one ear. There was such a blurring
of human bodies before him that he could not quite
count the youths although he tried to count arms
and divide by two. *They're like one,* he praised them,
mentally, trying to cover up but yanked away from
the wall so that they could work methodically on the
other parts of his body. When he became aware of
the pain, *as* pain, Wayland's detachment fanned out
from the center of his iron will and he saw what a
tribute this was—that the Colonel had taken an
entire squad to silence him. He smiled unvoluntarily
and one soldier, seeing the opening, chopped out his
upper row of teeth with the unthinking effectiveness
of a machete slicing off the heads of tall weeds.

The Colonel didn't take me lightly, Wayland
thrilled; *he valued me enough to take me off-guard,
to impair my ability to react.* He understood then
what they were doing, exactly: breaking every
significant bone in his body. Guaranteeing that,
sooner or later, his detachment and will to ignore
agony would be supplanted by shock and sheer
physical collapse, as pierced organs ceased to
function. *How nice.* Wayland managed a crooked
smile. *He's letting my body die at its own pace.*

He found himself lying on his back. No one was
chopping at him any longer, which meant that each
soldier was confident that he had performed his
own, precise, anatomical mission. Now the pain
was amazingly dispersed and Wayland was aware of
it, but crying out would be such a miserable

242 Wards of Armageddon

intrusion upon their dispassionate activity that the
thought of doing so reminded Wayland of the
Japanese camp, how disgusted he was when his
friends screamed or howled in the midst of calm
foreign troops who'd only done their job as they saw
fit. The trouble was that he had the choice now of
clinging to life, and encouraging the most hideous
pain, or promply dying and saving them all from
embarrassment. It wasn't an easy decision.

"You poor fool. You might have owned a piece of
this planet."

The crisp baritone was as familiar as his own
voice, even if Wayland hadn't heard it for years.
He cranked open a matted eye, willed it to focus;
he wanted a last look at his fine old comrade in
arms.

He saw, through a sea of viscous scarlet swirling, a
highly polished boot beneath the route man's cotton
trousers, saw that his jacket had been unbuttoned
to reveal an expensive, fawn colored blouse cut in
good military lines. The Colonel, close by, folded
muscled arms across his chest and let his cap dangle
from one strong hand; was it a gesture of respect?
Wayland noted that he wore the same tight smile of
old nightmares; the leathery skin showed only
marks from smiling, and scowling. Wayland craned
to look up. He saw that the Colonel's head was
shaven completely now, and that it looked girlishly
smooth—soft as a woman's breast was soft.

There was no gentleness yet in the grim set of the
jaw, which had never adequately healed after the
fracture given him by a North Korean's rifle butt. It
seemed to Wayland that it had been he who bayon-
eted the geek before the geek could do the same
thing to the Colonel; not that that had anything at
all to do with *now*. No, Wayland was troubled by the

unblinking gaze from the crystal-clear, turquoise
eyes. They'd always had the quality of seeming to
look at him from the sides of the bald man's head, as
if he might have been more bird, than man; offspring
of falcon, or hawk. Now the quality was so entrenched and noticeable to the dying Wayland that
the cunning, staring eyes could have been the
optical equipment of a bee, an ant.

Wayland closed his eyes against the inhuman
gaze, ready to concentrate upon the acquisition and
acknowledgment of pain, and death.

"*Men!*" snapped the Colonel.

The attackers, turned to marble, were at attention.

For a moment it was quiet in the Hoosier house's
front room. Restful, as if the heads of the household
were reading the evening newspaper. When the
incongruity of silence registered on the ruined man,
he tried to open his functioning eye once more,
vaguely annoyed by sticky substances drooling
from a mouth that would no longer close.

*Colonel Albert Caull and his men were smartly
saluting him.*

Old instinct engaged the muscles in the dying
man's arm; he willed his right hand to leave his
heaving side and move, briskly, to return salute. He
was so thrilled, his adrenalin was flowing again.
Perhaps it is still America, after all, he thought. But
his arm had refused the command utterly. He
twisted his lips into a smile of ghastly apprecation,
formed two words that were audible only to the
frozen-erect Colonel soaring above him: "*At ease . . .*"

A heavy *thump*, on the other side of his wrecked,
prone body, drew Wayland's pain-bewildered
attention. From the corner of his eye, he saw that it
was his dead dog. Looking ahead, and up, he saw

that Caull was smiling.

He had underestimated the Colonel, at the last, Wayland realized. What would it take for people to stop doing that?

Maybe normal men like me are incapable of understanding the Albert Caulls of the world, Wayland thought, a moment later. He focused his eye where the Colonel had been, realized that they had all left some time ago. Noiselessly.

But now, as the shock poured in, he was caught midway between life and death, between admiration and loathing, and the hard decision was taken from his hands. It was a matter of moments, but Wayland fought to use them.

To their amazement, the front door was not only unlocked but open, several inches.

Courtney, ready to dart passed Richard, shoved the door wide. He thrust out his arm, before her waist, waited until she'd turned her head to glare at him.

"Me first," he said insistently. "And don't give me that liberationist jazz, that stuff about moving faster than a speeding bullet or something."

Squeezing around her, he saw the two motionless forms simultaneously.

But she had seen them, too. "If you tell me not to look," she whispered, thinking of old movies, "I'll demonstrate what I learned while interviewing one of the officers of Women Against Rape."

He paused, then grinned. "Be my guest." He made a courtly, sweeping gesture. "If you really groove on corpses, sweetie, I'll be happy to remain here and breathe fresh air."

She moved steadily, alertly, through the short hallway to the front room entrance, then stopped

above the bodies of Wayland and his Doberman.
Her hand went to her mouth and Richard heard her
gasp.

He closed the distance between them quickly,
looked down, and then pressed the reporter against
him for reassuring, living comfort. Just for an
instant, he shut his own eyes. "I've seen this
before," he said under his breath. "There are some
historical examples, largely from the Far East, but
it was . . . in Nam. The Orientals originally
developed this method of breaking bones, one by
one, as a matter of respect; they didn't want to
invade the body with a foreign property, such as a
knife, and the theory is that the pain is so wide-
spread, a man with great willpower can remain alive
indefinitely. In terms of minutes, that is; even an
hour." Richard felt Courtney shudder, and sighed.
"His soul will then tell him when it's ready to leave
the body."

"It's barbaric, and you know it!" she squealed,
breaking his embrace and rushing blindly out of the
room.

"Who's arguing?" he called. "Hey, I doubt that
the assassins are still around, but keep your eyes
open, okay?"

She wasn't sure whether she agreed aloud or only
in her thoughts. She found herself in the kitchen, ran
across the linoleum floor to the sink and eagerly
turned a faucet. Minutes ago, before arriving, she'd
been trembling from the cold. Now she bathed her
face and mouth with frigid water, gratefully, and
slowly turned, leaning against the sink as she
inspected her surroundings.

The kitchen reminded her of what she had seen
subliminally, in the living room. How bare the house
was, how devoid of anything but the minimal

pretext of a normal life. It dawned on Courtney that
what she was seeing was functional, basically necessary; nothing more. She noted the old refrigerator, a
stove so aged it was practically an antique, a
massive pet's bowl filled with water. Property of the
dead Doberman, Courtney decided, spasming again
and suddenly wanting out of the house before the
police came. She'd always had pets, especially dogs,
and while she had never thought Dobermans were
an attractive breed, she detested the idea of its
agonized death. What had happened to Wayland's
pet to make him appear as if his insides had been
pulverized? Surely they hadn't methodically
chopped the Doberman to death; not if it was
intended as a lunatic means of letting the soul select
its exact instant of departure. Maybe a car struck it,
outside, she theorized, and it was—

"Courtney, get your tail in here!"

She frowned at the writer's use of terms but went
hurriedly back into the front room, anyway, pausing
several feet from where Richard Grant knelt.
Approaching the dead man from this direction—she
did not for a moment doubt it was Wayland—she
could detect the bizarre and hideous formations of
blood he had spilled. Instead of a single, spreading
pool, Wayland was oozing away *splotches* of his
life substance. Seven or eight small spillings, from
punctures caused by the tip of shattered white bone,
appeared to her like so many tipped-over bottles of
red ink. She took another step, and froze.

Wayland was looking at her!

"He's still alive! He's told me all about it. Filled
in all the pieces of the puzzle." Richard, kneeling
beside the dying old man, drew her horrified gaze
and seemed to exist in the midst of a baffling,
steaming cloud. But his grim excitement also drew

her, wobbly kneed, into the tableau; she pressed
back her dizziness to perceive what he was saying,
and the cloud disappeared. "The regular Army
veterans were sick and tired of the people protesting
Vietnam, and calling them baby killers. They
especially loathed the younger Americans,
particularly the ones taking off for Canada, and
saw them as yellow, as effete turncoats. A lot of men
returning home nearly went into the parade and
after the folks carrying the signs. And officers like
Wayland, here, and a balding Colonel who was the
one who got Wayland to thinking, believed the
United States was doomed. That Americans were
getting so cowardly, there'd be no one fit to defend
the nation in the event of an attack."

"No more . . . Koreas," gasped Wayland. The back
of his head was cradled in Richard's hand, which
was turning pink. A red ribbon ran from the corner
of Wayland's partly toothless mouth. "No—more—
Nams!"

Richard nodded. "What he means is that military
commanders couldn't tolerate the notion of ever
again entering a war in which no winners and no
losers would be permitted." Frowning, he glanced
down at the older man. "That's why they began kidnapping newborn boys from the wives of Army men
—of guys like me, who'd had a decent war record
and might produce sons with an edge over other
newborns."

"I don't quite follow," Courtney said stumblingly,
doing her best to look only at the writer.

"Sure, you do. Don't forget that war is forever,
that military types are the most oldfashioned people
on earth." He looked at her. His outrage and an
ancient sense of deprivation were scarcely banked.
"The bastards seized our kids to create a special

unit of young soldiers intended to become an obedient, supreme fighting machine. Nothing else." He took his hand from under Wayland's head and wiped it on his pants. "Kids who'd never know a mother or father, boys who'd know nothing of family life, or going to a normal school—or even any kind of dating." He looked into Wayland's wrecked face. "Unemotional, ruthless, ideally trained human automatons who practice on crooked pols in preparation for . . ." His voice trailed away. Then, hands knotted, he shouted straight at Wayland's unmoving eyes. "Americans, 'special troops'—including my kid Mark—who are supposed to take over the government itself on Christmas Eve . . . while the rest of us are mellow and half our defenses are shut down or at half efficiency!"

"Don't! Don't hit him."

"Why not? Why in hell not?" He was screaming and didn't care. "Because he wised up, found a conscience after it was too late? He didn't tell anybody but his ol' buddy, Doctor Skylar! He didn't try to stop it!"

Courtney yanked at his arm. "Richard!" She saw him turn to face her, blinking. Courtney touched his cheek with her fingers. "Richard—he's dead."

He looked, felt, blank. Slowly, he straightened; an old, familiar pain lanced his leg. The one he'd almost lost for no reason he'd been able to fathom yet. "I say we leave this bastard where he is, take it from here ourselves." He glanced up at her with moist, insulted eyes. "I hate to sound paranoid, Court, but I don't know who's trustworthy right now. Who'd help."

"I'll phone for the police," she said softly, as if they had agreed on that much. She stepped away.

"Wayland began rambling. As if he were saying

what he'd longed to say to a military court—or his God, for all I know. I don't think he knew, then, I was even here." His voice began to level out. Courtney had stopped, near the dining room. "It doesn't look as if all the military is in on it. Things of this sort, they're for the privileged few, the elite."

"The believers," she said.

Richard nodded. "From what I pieced together when Wayland here became hysterical, or lost somewhere in time, this Colonel Albert Caull and his people believe other military types will fall in after— it happens."

"On December 24th, you say?"

"I gathered that a few bigwig Pentagon officials plus several Congressmen tacitly agreed to this Project Romulus from the beginning. How else could they house or feed and train all the children they seized." He said "children" as if the word were razorish and might cut.

"Did he mumble anything about the Pentagon higher-ups who are involved?" Courtney had drawn closer; her wide, intelligent eyes shone with horror. "Do you have the names?"

He didn't answer at once. His gaze was fixed on the two bodies dead on the floor. "He mentioned . . . a town. Sunridge. That's about it and I may not have got that straight." He swallowed hard, worked at finishing as he began to stand up. His knees felt locked as if they were warning him. "Christmas Eve —is like graduation. It's the start. Wayland barely coughed it up, but I could never have misunderstood those words of his." He took her arms in his hands, caught his breath. "It's something about a nuclear first-strike."

PART FOUR

QUEST FOR A SON

"I am tired and sick of war . . . war is hell."

—General William Tecumseh Sherman

19

Neither Richard nor Courtney knew exactly what to do next, nor where to go. When they had left Wayland's house and its fearfully still inhabitants behind, he drove the vehicle belonging to his mother-in-law in nervous fits and starts, in many directions. He'd light on one course of action and head down the apparently logical Indianapolis street for that step, only to turn frantically right, or left, and wander aimlessly fresh boulevards of the unfamiliar town.

To Courtney, the decisionless journey through neighborhoods she'd never before seen had a nightmare quality to it, especially after watching Wayland die. Sagging snowmen starting to melt became ominous, spectral scarecrows—or scarepeople, perhaps—for her. Solemn, staring black men starting the day stepped from street corners with an imagined air of menace, and she pictured them drawing exotic weapons to impede her progress and Richard's.

By the time they had crossed West 46th Street and were approaching what seemed to be a college campus, both of the terrified people in the wander-

ing automobile knew that they'd rather not phone
the police about the slaughtered Wayland. The
minute the news was flashed on the nation's TV
screens, or shortly after the wire services picked it
up, the mysterious "bald man"—Colonel Albert
Caull—would know Wayland's corpse had been discovered. The names of Richard Grant and Courtney
Rankin might even be released to the public and, for
all they knew, that could be just enough information
for Caull to order another, unguessable attack. Perhaps, they felt without discussing it, directly
against *them*.

To the right, they noticed a handsome building
identified, by sign, as Clowes Memorial Hall. A line
of people stretched from one door, presumably filing
in to a box office. Swinging around to the left,
because the campus ended at a woods, Richard
halted the car at the curb and glanced at his watch.
Not even eleven o'clock yet. Turning, he looked past
Courtney, inspecting an aging, well kept structure
to their right. This university, he saw, was Butler;
the building itself was the Student Union Building.
Through a window below eye level he saw young
people snacking, and realized it was a restaurant.
Richard grinned and opened his car door. He supposed every university had a place similar to this,
convenient for students between—or cutting—
classes. "There's bound to be a public phone booth,"
he told Courtney after getting out.

"You're calling the police?" she asked with
dismay.

"Nope. I'm calling no one." He straightened from
the car window, tugged up his collar against the
December morning chill. Then he strode briskly
around the front, displaying a reasonable replica of
his customary, airy dash. "I want to look in the

Indy phone book for the closest AAA Motor Club."

He didn't explain his reasons, and Courtney, watching his slight form bound up the steps and into the building, mused, *He looks like just another student.* Exiting male students paid him no attention. Her eyes gleamed; her lips turned up, privately. *Richard's the kind who never really ages a day until that one crisis comes up that he can't handle. Then he'll look sixty the rest of his life.*

She slipped restlessly down in her seat, propped her knees against the dashboard and lit a cigarette. The skirt slipped back from the knees and she let it, let it slip innocently and naturally, trying, as she had a thousand times, to appraise her body as she knew most men did. *Not bad knees for an old scribbler,* she told herself, knowing perfectly well she wasn't old, or getting older discernibly, and amused by her thoughts. She'd always kept her head screwed on properly through the faculty for finding herself amusing—somewhat overdrawn, inclined to pomposity, to severe principles and self-demands she sometimes transposed to others—and it was the very way she identified her faults, however secretly, that informed her she was Okay.

Making the tiniest of personal movements, she spread her propped-up right leg apart from the left. The skirt's obeisance to gravity permitted her a brief evaluation of the right leg's inner thigh, which was pale, unlined, obviously soft. *Maybe a pinch of surplus or so,* she notified her brain memory banks, *but still kissable.*

Instantly, she frowned. Why had she thought that? Making a face, she slapped her legs together, tightly, the sound a sharp, fleshly report. Unsought recollection of a very young, male face lying between those thighs—the first visitor to them, his successors few in number and unmemorable—embarrassed her, made her skin tingle. Why in the world did men ever want to kiss her there? Eyelids fluttering, she raised her gaze to the car window, and beyond, seeing Richard's image with a rush of mixed affection and hot excitement before she closed her eyes, and made his boyish face evaporate.

Then, restless, she glanced again to the sidewalk between the car and the Campus Club, momentarily recalling her four years at a New Jersey college. Like someone drowning, she saw a succession of pictures in which she remained only an observer. Most of the time, conscientious because she was there on a journalistic scholarship and had only gradually elected to pursue a newspaper career with similar zeal, she'd lived like a nun. Instructors, the Dean of Women, an older girl who was editor of the school paper and an adversary when Courtney became editor of an annual lit magazine, were what she'd seen mostly at college and saw, now, in her mind's eye. There'd been little time for friendships, no time for the frivolous. She'd written home regularly until Daddy died, then found Mother's letters too depressing to sustain the correspondence or even to allow her to return, after graduation, to their Connecticut home. Daddy'd left her some money in a trust but she'd never spent a cent of it, and privately meant to leave it untouched until and unless she married, and required it. It was merely a form of vaguely remembered security, less meaningful to her than what she recalled about Daddy, his dignity, wry humor, substance, insistence upon independence with responsibility. The fact that he'd died before most men of his generation had seemed entirely right, to Courtney, a tidy acceptance of the only responsibility Dad had seen as worthwhile—

the responsibility to be true to himself. Which was precisely why she missed him so badly there were still times when, unaccountably, she wept at the most inopportune moments, and why she was out here, in the Midwest, testing her own sense of obligation to what she'd chosen to become.

Two kids in skirts stopping above the knee—their skimpiness so conspicuous it was as if they'd run out of material for their dresses, or fiercely slashed away the hem—passed Courtney. One, nineteen surely; the other, older, in experience and attitude if not age. The latter's gaze met Courtney's, fleetingly, without enough awareness of her existence to report, minutes later, having witnessed a thirtyish broad seated outside the Campus Club with her legs in the most inelegant of postures. *Well, the hell with her,* Courtney decided, purposefully sinking lower in the car seat and encouraging the skirt's flirtation with gravity; *I am a journalist, a famous columnist from a leading Washington paper—*

And I am falling in love, with no more common sense than you little broads reveal when you screw half the basketball team, with a man who has other fish to fry. A skilletful of family, career aspirations, and hunger to add to his own responsibilities with an increment of One. Courtney blinked, wondered if she'd really said much of that aloud, and hoped the passing girls had not heard her. She stared fixedly at the purse she clenched in her rather strong hands, pressed it against her lower stomach and knew it would not stop the churning sensations she'd suddenly, freshly identified.

Richard's return—he seemed to bounce into view, outside the driver's side—was oddly wonderful, a materialization. He gripped a scrap of notepaper between his teeth as he hurled the door wide and dropped, grinning, into the seat.

"Got it! Triple-A isn't far from here, and some professor type with ivy practically crawling out of his ears gave me directions!" He fired up the engine.

"What are you trying to accomplish?" she asked, slowly sitting up and gaping at him as the car squealed away from the curb.

"I need to check the name Wayland gave," he said, looking at her so long she automatically looked at the street to make sure he wasn't driving into another vehicle. "The name of the *town*." He glanced back. "You didn't have to pull your skirt down for my benefit," he added with a wink, and refused to say more until he'd located the nearby AAA Motor Club.

This time, he was back quickly, even more exuberant as he got back into the car. "I found it!" he cried.

"Found *what?*" she wailed.

"Sunridge." He'd started to restart the engine, but turned to her instead, to explain. He leaned forward to kiss the tip of her nose. "Back-Court, I scoured lists of cities and towns in every state—and there's a place named Sunridge in Utah! The only town with that name!"

Courtney shook her head. "We're going there, then?" She almost believed it.

Richard produced several maps from inside his jacket, nodding. "It's only thirty-six miles or so out of Salt Lake City!" Looking feverish, he began busily unfolding and folding his trophies, his enthusiasm contagious. "Triple-A says it's a hole in the wall, and the map makes it look like it's the kind of place people drive through without even seeing the signs saying you're leaving."

"Then that has to be," Courtney said in hushed

tones, pausing, "where they train the young men."

He nodded at her. "And where they've raised and kept my son, Mark—if he's still alive." Much more soberly, he turned the key in the ignition and sidled away from the curb.

By the time they'd returned to the Skylar house, Courtney had made up her mind to involve her paper. Maybe she couldn't help becoming fond of Richard, and maybe propriety demanded that she place Molly's children and her grieving stepmother first; but she still wanted to cover and to break *all* of this remarkable story, not just sections of it. "I'm going to call my editor," she told Richard as they headed up the walk to the house. "If we do go, we'll need as much support as we can get and I'm going to try to see if a good photographer and a particularly musclebound stringer I know can lend us a hand."

Richard put his hand on her arm before they went inside. "Can you depend on him not to break the story about Wayland?"

She gave him a self-satisfied smile. "Believe it or not, Richard, I have a certain standing in the journalistic world. If he printed a word of it without my byline, I'd walk, and he knows it!"

While Courtney strode determinedly in search of the Skylars' telephone, Richard found Molly coming toward him, her face pasty with concern. "My God, honey, you look like you've seen a ghost!"

He embraced her, mustering a grin and guiding her into the Skylar front room, where Molly's stepmother sat. "Not a ghost; only a new student at the haunting academy." Sitting beside Molly on the sofa, he began telling what he and Courtney had discovered.

"Thank God none of those terrible men were still in the house!" she said when he'd finished.

"That's for sure," he agreed with a nod. He'd left out a detailed description of the way Colonel Albert Caull's former co-conspirator had been murdered. But he knew he had to get Molly and the girls to a place of safety, soon. "You must understand, Mol. Even if Mark is with them, he's been trained, along with the other kidnapped boys, to follow orders. He's an efficient, very deadly killing-machine and how I approach him, how you and I ever bring him back to normal, are things I haven't figured out yet."

Molly paled. Clearly, he thought, she hadn't thought of Mark except in terms of the normal twenty-year-old he might have been if he hadn't been taken from them. "You mean, he might actually *attack* you? Try to *harm* you?"

Richard nodded, took her hands in his. They were cold. "If his C.O. tells him to. And I doubt that I'd be able to defend myself." He frowned, shivered. "Hopefully, we can formulate some sort of plan— some way to shut down the base, or at least to get Mark out."

Molly had begun to cry. Perhaps the sound of her weeping reached the children's sharp hearing, because Michelle and Mary came into the living room.

"It has precedent," Lucille Skylar said.

"What do you mean?" Richard inquired, hugging his daughters.

"It's as if these boys were victims of a religious cult," Lucille murmured. She looked exhausted; presumably she'd been thinking of funeral arrangements while he was away. "If they're ever freed from the protective cocoon of those crazy Army

men, you—and the other parents—will have to . . .
debrief them. Whatever it's called."

"Deprogram," Richard helped her, smiling.
Michelle was her usual sweet self, content to cuddle
between Molly and her father. But Mary, on the end
of the sofa, seemed more drawn to Richard than
usual, her serious eyes never leaving his face. "And
yes, Lucille, you're probably right. It's going to be
very difficult."

"No more difficult than dealing with a managing
editor!" Courtney, flushed, came angrily into the
room. She looked in appeal to Richard. "He doesn't
believe what's going on! The bastard claims I'm
imagining things, that normal military men would
never conceive such a scheme!"

"Normal military personnel wouldn't," Richard
retorted. "But Nam wasn't a normal war requiring
normal military men or procedures, and there was
nothing normal about the way returning servicemen
were treated." He felt a rise of sympathy for the
journalist. "What exactly did your editor tell you?"

Courtney's redness deepened. "He said, 'Get your
splendid little ass back to D.C. posthaste and then
it's a week in the Islands for you!' He said I need
rest, the miserable —!" She stopped, aware of
Mary's and Michelle's presence.

Richard got to his feet. "Then it *is* up to us," he
said softly. "I guess it always was." He leaned down
to kiss Molly's temple. "We all have to clear out of
here. There's precious little time until December
24th so we'll have to work fast."

Molly gazed up at him, thunderstruck. Then she
reached out for her daughters' small hands. "But
those are the same men who threatened our
children!" She jumped up. "Richard, you can't go!
It's too risky!"

"Mol, there's no time to convince anybody else of what's going on!" He grasped her arms at the bicep, squeezing. "Anyone in the military whom we attempted to persuade might be part of Project Romulus!" He saw he was hurting her and released one arm, stroked her blond hair. "Don't you see, babe, that this is a crisis? That these guys mean to *overthrow the government?*"

"You're simply starting to live your silly books!" Molly exclaimed, pulling away from him.

"I'm afraid he's right," Courtney said in her low, controlled tones. "We're all alone in this." *He isn't even* mad *at her for that crack,* she observed, oddly aroused, and hopeful.

"And we," Lucille said quickly, rising and going to Molly, "are innocent civilians who are in the way. You and the girls and I, we have to get somewhere safe so that Richard and this young woman can do what they have to do."

"Yes, that's the first priority," Richard said gratefully. "Isn't there a cottage—a place in Michigan?"

Lucille turned to him, expressionless. "Klinger Lake," she said. "My husband used to take his first family there during the summer." She glanced at Molly, who nodded. "We can go there in one car while you and Courtney take the other and drive to Utah."

"That's it, then," Richard said, rubbing his palms together briskly.

Molly looked up at him, sadly. "Yes, I guess that *is* it." Her eyes filled with tears. "For all of us."

"I think we'd better get some rest," Richard said, ignoring his wife's depressing implications. "Then leave at night." He glanced at Courtney, who slowly nodded her agreement.

Molly stood, taking the hands of her daughters. The three of them headed toward the stairs, young Michelle staring back at her father with confusion. Molly stopped at the foot of the steps. "The world's gone mad, and my husband has become a character in one of his own books." She sighed. "It wasn't meant to be this way."

Richard was too restless to remain on the couch. Alone, later, in the darkened living room, trying to give anyone observing the house the impression that everyone had retired for the night, he sat up and ran his fingertips over the platter Lucille had left on the coffee table. But he'd already finished every crumb of the sandwiches she'd prepared. Yawning, stretching, he hoped the others had also eaten something, then got to his feet. Instantly, the old part ache, part painful throb in his leg sent out signals of discomfort and he stood in place, kicking his foot. What kind of fool had he become, he wondered, to think that he and a woman who hid behind her press pass had the slightest chance of taking over a military command post? Why didn't he do what most men, these days, would probably do, the way they did most things? Assert, plainly and not unreasonably, that the whole mess was too complicated and involved too many bigshots and muscle for any single man to provide a meaningful stumbling block?

Yet fathers still exist, he reminded himself, *who run into burning buildings to save their kids. And my kid, my firstborn son, has been living in a world of militant hellfire since they swapped his diaper for fatigue pants.*

Richard scratched his ribs, then the crown of his head, and decided to take the bare platter out to the kitchen. His watch didn't have a luminous dial and he needed to check the hour, to learn if it was time to rouse the house and, by doing so, place the only people he loved in the worst danger of their lives. Sighing, platter in hand, he took a step away from the couch—

And heard, beyond the bay window, a distinct rustling sound. From the bushes at the front of the house.

Immediately, he dropped to his knees, left the platter on the floor, and crawled toward the window. One end of the curtain had been left lying on the sill, providing an inch or so of bare windowpane.

He peeped through the glass, and caught his breath.

There, down at the juncture of the driveway and the pavement, crouching, only a single, gleaming boot catching the rays of moonlight—a man waited. One, silent, well trained, perfectly deadly *Watcher*.

20

Richard passed through the darkened house like a hollow, an insubstantial man, and paused in the kitchen to decide what to do. He knew he'd moved soundlessly, that he had reacted as he'd been trained, more than twenty years ago. The instincts were rusted, possibly tarnished, but they were still with him, a part of him. He could still kill.

Richard's heart seemed to have moved into his mouth and it was pounding as if Buddy Rich had just innovated at new drum solo. Leaning against Lucille Skylar's kitchen counter, aware at the outer fringes of his consciousness of the incongruity of this exciting moment, he realized that he had not felt as fully, brimmingly alive in decades, and the realization swept all other considerations aside. Somewhere he'd read that the untold reason for what dare-devils did had to do with just such an invigorating impression of coming truly alive, at the moment of high peril, of life-endangering hazard. His creative writer's mind saw further that what one lost, as he began to age, was not youth itself but the vitalizing threats which youth tended to confront. It wasn't so much that a mature man ceased to take chances, however much he preferred to tell himself that and applaud his wisdom; it was that a middle-aged man perceived that most of the danger he faced was sheer bluff—and that, try as hard as he might, the mature man cared marginally less for life and could not react, as thrillingly, to the peril of death.

Not, at any rate, the pallid imitation of it represented by asking the boss for a raise, quitting one church for another, the augury of another birthday, the distant IRS or even the brief pursuit of a traffic cop on a motorcycle. He turned noiselessly to a drawer beneath Lucille's counter, carefully opened it, and put his questing hand inside. The threat out front was not pallid, and it was not imitative. It could seize and mangle his life, and that was why he felt so excited now, felt a kinship approaching gratitude that the Watcher had reactivated him: the danger was unsought, and it was real. He pawed around for a useful weapon, closing his fingers around nothing more intimidating than Lucille's trusty rolling-pin.

Any old port, he told himself, picking the thing up and tiptoeing across to the door opening upon the back yard. He'd felt a butcher knife beneath his fingers but known he could never stab anybody; not now, not any more.

The garage loomed up before Richard. *The garage*, he thought, feeling the winter air carve into his shirt-sleeved arms, where this perverted kid or others like him had threatened to harm little girls. *His* little girls.

A second Watcher would be crouched against the garage, or close to it, if the bald man knew they'd found Wayland's wrecked body. Richard, immobile,

sought to penetrate the night with his eyes, cursing
Doc Skylar for not having put lights out back. If
there was no Number Two waiting to attack him,
they'd get away safely that night, all of them.

Assuming he dispatched the single, crouching
youth who did wait.

Hoisting the rolling-pin high, bent double,
Richard darted out onto the snow-splotched sheet of
grass and then began descending the faint slope of
the side yard, toward the street. Why old man
Skylar hadn't insisted the city put up a street lamp,
Richard couldn't guess. Perhaps Doc valued his
privacy so much—or thought so little of his
neighbors, his fellow man—that he'd had the lamp
removed! Smiling, sweating profusely now as if it
were summer, Richard edged closer to the street,
and the watching soldier.

There! The man's body was angled away from
Richard, partly facing the front of the house. He was
so intent in his silent watch that Richard was able to
circle entirely to his rear, step by cautious step,
moving lightly toward the man in the moonlight.

Sportsmanship did not enter into this; warfare
wasn't fair. Richard had accepted that much, the
hard way, during combat training two decades ago.
He had paid for quibbling over the absence of
Marquis of Queensbury rules with brutal tongue-
lashings and more brutal beatings by the fellow
trainees who'd lacked his passion for the niceties.
He'd learned his lessons well before going to Nam,
or he'd have been slain. He had prowled with squads
by night, he'd struck from shadow—even if he'd
never been able to stop muttering, "Pardon me,"
after taking the enemy out.

Now, Richard realized, he was confronted with a
more dangerous opponent than any he'd faced in

Vietnam. He was up against a unique, new variety of supremely trained soldier-assassin, or terrorist. In the youth's lifelong absorption of exotic Oriental snuffing techniques, years of coming to know pressure points and tender nerve ends, he stood head-and-shoulders above Richard in experience, present conditioning, and nimble years of age.

He'd never say "Pardon Me," after he murdered Richard Grant.

Knowing he'd have only one shot, and yanking the rolling-pin back, behind his right shoulder, the way a major leaguer gripped a baseball bat, Richard rushed the half-crouched young fighting man and suddenly swung the kitchen implement with all his might.

Or at least, all the might that remained as he realized with horror that he might literally kill this boy.

The rolling-pin, making good contact from his checked swing, collided against the back of the Watcher's skull with a sickening thud. Richard had caught him just below the neatly trimmed military hairline—and he went down, at once, as if felled by an axe.

"I *did* it!" Richard exulted, half shouting, jumping two inches off the Skylar front yard. "I put him *down!*"

But the soldier-terrorist did not stay down.

To Richard's consternation, the young man shoved himself to his knees, no sound of any kind issuing from his snarling lips. The hairless face lifted to Richard in the whitening moonlight seemed pathetic, at first, and gouts of gore were blackening the collar and shoulders of his inexpensive civilian shirt. But Richard's feeling of compassion was choked off when he saw the young man's eyes, burning with something far more terrifying than mere hatred. *I'm an object,* Richard realized; *he's not even mad, he just means to kill me, an inch at a time!*

The soldier's arm shot toward Richard, who said, "Oh, shit!" quite distinctly, and tried to turn around, away from the youth. He felt pressure so perfectly directed to the area of one kidney that the sensation went beyond pain to something exquisitely close to orgasmic pleasure. Then he saw the soldier's other hand, reaching for the region of his belt, saw something gleaming there—and also saw that the young man was fighting reactively, reflexively, the way he'd been trained to fight back at the moment dying began. *Take the prick with you,* Colonel Caull must have commanded.

And Richard hit the finely tuned killing-machine on top of the head again, hesitated, and thoughtfully repeated the blow twice. A dark mass formed where Richard had struck, breaking the rolling-pin apart, and it would have looked like spoiled cabbage in the moonlight except that it was bubbling.

The really bad moment came when he looked down at the unconscious young soldier sprawled at his feet, and Richard thought first, *He may be dying,* and second, with abundantly more horror, *He may be Mark.*

The really important thought came to him, then, that everybody had to clear out of the Skylar house now—immediately. He didn't think neighbors had seen the mortal combat, he hadn't noticed any lights going on or startled faces pressed to window glass; but if the police came, now, he'd have to try to explain the unexplainable.

Dragging the soldier's body up the driveway, into the back yard and then through the garage door,

Richard found his nerve starting to sour. An urge to cry came over him, a need to vary it with screams of outrage and question directed heavenward. What was a civilian, a writer on the verge of middle age, a peaceable family man, *doing* with obligations like this? *Who*, or *What*, had ordained the need for him to slip out of a well kept old house in a strange city, after dark, and beat a young boy to death with something from the kitchen?

Impending hysteria was stopped by a sudden, even worse thought: What if the unconscious, possibly mortally wounded youth lying at his feet in this unfamiliar garage . . . was the goddamned newsboy? Some lovestruck kid, unable to sleep because the neighbor girl had decided to hold onto her virginity a little while longer?

Terrified, he knelt in a small pool of oil and fumbled a billfold out of the youth's hip pocket. But one look, inside it, told Richard he hadn't killed an innocent.

Because there were no credit cards inside, no pictures of Mom and little sis in braces, no prophylactic purchased from a drug store.

There was no identification on the boy. Not even a driver's licence.

But he wore dogtags around his neck on a chain, stuffed into his T-shirt.

I'd better tie him up, Richard thought, standing and looking around for rope. He saw none, saw nothing adequate for the task.

And leaped, terrified, when the figure on the floor moaned.

Richard peered down at the soldier, took a good look at him for the first time, aided by the bare bulb dangling by a cord from the garage ceiling. Muscles on muscles, not weight-lifter sized but athletically,

functionally developed. A face, in repose, like a kid
you hoped your daughter might bring home with a
tearful look of happy news in store for the family.
And one spasm of movement, there on the blood
soaked floor, in the form of fingers starting to
clench, and unclench—as if the unconscious assassin
dreamed sweet dreams of choking life itself out of
one Richard Grant.

He doused the lights, and slammed the garage
door, locking it—would it keep someone inside?—
and saw other signs of illumination within the house.
Good; they were up, they were getting ready to
leave!

He started down the driveway at a jog, getting
cold now in the late December night, meaning to
start both Skylar automobiles. Then he stopped,
worrying, pivoted and raced back to the garage.

The special soldier Caull had sent to kill people
Richard loved was sitting up when he threw open
the garage door.

"You fucking bastard," the youth growled, dripping blood from his scalp and trying to rise.

"You aren't my son!" Richard sped across the
garage floor, kicked with more concentrated power
than he'd exerted in two decades. The assassin fell
backward, struck his head on the concrete floor, and
lay still. "Mark wouldn't talk that way."

The pair of automobiles, motors running, were
parked at the curb and faced in opposite directions.
Four beams of light extruded from them like yellow
ramps, substantial enough to climb. Michelle got
out of the car with Molly's stepmother behind the
wheel; she rushed toward her daddy, who was
putting suitcases into the trunk of the vehicle, and
begged for a hug.

He carried her back to the car, noting how sleepy she was, how bewildered. Before putting her back inside Richard held her close and kissed her drooping eyelids.

Mary, seated behind Lucille, rolled down her window. Past her, Richard saw, Molly was rigidly erect in the front passenger seat, looking at nothing. Mary's hand covered his cheek and he looked down at his elder daughter, surprised, aware of how long it had been since she voluntarily went near him. "What is it, kitten?" he asked tenderly.

Her eyes, so like Molly's yet customarily so much more self-possessed, were exact replicas now. "I want you to bring my brother back, Daddy," she intoned, quite solemnly.

"I'll try," he whispered. And heard Mary offer the small, precious afterthought that she loved him.

"I was jealous, I guess, at first." Molly, speaking through her window to Courtney, a voice and just then a face on the edges of a galaxy from which the sun had fled. Richard scarcely heard her. "But you are both, well, right for this. I don't know anyone else who could do it." A hesitation. "Take care of my husband."

Startled, Richard glanced over at the two women, one inside the car and one standing in the street, and felt as bewildered as Michelle, who was already asleep in the back seat. He began jogging, ran down to the corner of the street to look for signs of follow-up special troops, then hurried back, still on his toes but puffing. "Let's do it," he gasped to Courtney Rankin. He went toward the car they were taking, trying to conceal his throbbing, limping leg. "Let's *move out!*"

When he was seated with Courtney in the front seat, and beginning to shift gears, he looked back at his family, all of it he had left to him. Lucille Skylar was just pulling away from the curb and his daughter Mary, face small and white at the rear window of the car, was waving goodbye.

21

"You drive with a lead foot." Courtney, passing Richard in front of the car as the two of them exchanged positions, looked expressionlessly back at the little writer before slipping in beneath the steering wheel.

"I kept it under sixty," he protested as he took his place in the passenger seat, "if I was anywhere near a town or city."

"I wasn't criticizing you." Courtney slammed the accelerator to the floor, laying rubber as they spun back onto the road. She turned her head completely, disconcertingly, to him, grinning. "Actually, I drive much faster."

When he had the nerve, a mile further on, to glance at the speedometer, Richard saw that she was pushing eighty and shuddered. "It's super to know I pass muster." He slid much lower on the seat, theorizing that he was marginally less apt to sail headfirst through the windshield if his hurting body had a longer way to go. "And I may pass something else," he added, "if you keep up this speed!"

It was midmorning and both the suburbs of

Indianapolis and Washington seemed a million
light-years away. The farther they'd driven, through
the night and early morning hours, the more both of
them imagined they were driving over the flattest
plain of the planet. Here in the farm belt of the Midwest, once the beginning of the West, it was easier
to nod along with the Flat Earth Society; here, the
third planet from the sun felt squashed around the
middle, elongated in some strange, cosmic manner
that lenghtened both the distance from the horizon
and each dragged-out and dusty mile.

While neither Richard nor Courtney exactly
looked forward to reaching Utah, because there
would be no choice except locating the Project
Romulus command and then developing a plausible
means of entry to the covert Army base, they felt
impelled by an unconfessed impression of being
watched—despite the fact that they had seen no
other vehicles hot on their tracks. Perhaps they
were too much amateurs to identify some shifting
sequence of subtly exchanged cars, and that fifteen-
year-old Dodge passing Richard a few miles back
contained female cohorts of Romulus youth.
Perhaps they were being neatly bugged and photog-
raphed in some exotic, electronic manner neither of
them detected, or could begin to understand.
Richard's soldier, the one he'd left unconscious in
the Skylar garage, might have planted bugs on both
cars; if so, even now, Molly and the kids and Lucille
Skylar were being held by Colonel Caull.

Held—or worse.

Richard sighed heavily, glanced in the rearview
mirror. The notion that one was being scrutinized,
secretly, was part and parcel of the age. Privacy was
going, or gone. You went into groceries, the bank,
drugstores, and miniature cameras crawled

anxiously about, antennae alert to your arrival.
Merchants' associations, state and federal tax-
takers, interviewers and investigators and what-
are-you-eating-for-breakfast-these-days interlopers
wove a constant web of paranoia, then turned
maternal ladybug on you, reminding you for the rest
of your life about those peccadillos so submerged in
your brain that they felt like the remembered
wrongdoings of another person. You couldn't be an
individual.

The boys who'd grown to imminent manhood in
the clonish cocoon of Colonel Albert Caull, the bald
man Richard itched to strangle, quite naturally
would have become the baby arachnids or the
antlike advance guard of this society, he mused.
Parentless, and allowed no other role model than the
surrogate daddies with glittering stars, eagles, and
stripes on their arms and shoulders, the Romulus
youth would clearly have been given just enough of
the basics to become adequately normalized, functioning. Everything else would have been suppressed.

Yet his mind somehow refused to accept the idea
that these boys—*his* son—could so conveniently
have been stripped of all human emotions, all needs.
What about sex? True, the group that had so
horribly assaulted his own daughters had stopped
short of rape, with almost mechanical self-control.
But there was also the pimply faced neighbor boy
back home, with his annoying, but disgustingly
healthy, leers at the developing young Mary. No, he
decided, Caull's not going to keep *that* under control
for long, unless he brings in prostitutes, which I
doubt he'd do.

And the need for personal fulfillment? Richard
had read, somewhere, that no matter how much

dictators sought to stamp out individuality, even to give their wards gratification by rewarding them for their contributions to the larger "good," they were stymied in the end by that old, human impulse which eternally said, "But *I* want to do it *this* way!" Look at the Russian dissidents, he thought. *Born* under Communism, as these boys were practically born under one Colonel Albert Caull, yet still moved to find their own voice.

He glanced over at Courtney. Whether it was because of her, or not, he didn't know, but his next thought was—*love?* Richard Grant shook his head, inwardly cursing himself for being again the romantic he knew he often was, especially now, in the face of the hard-edged nightmare he was living through. But—he thought, grasping as if at a last hope, seemingly the most insubstantial of all, yet the one that somehow made the most sense to him— if I find my son, even though he's never even seen me, won't he still love me? Won't there be something in his eyes, and in mine, that will wipe out everything that's happened since he—"wasn't"— born?

Richard shifted position in the seat, then chuckled to himself. I'm a dreamer, he thought. Even if I do get Mark back, he'll probably rebel against me in a couple of years. Sons against fathers—that's the way it goes. But suddenly the writer felt something, a door opening in his mind, which made him sit up straight, causing his female companion to look anxiously in his direction. That is the way it goes, he almost said aloud. And *I'm* real—*not* that madman Caull!

"What's the matter?" Courtney asked. "Still afraid I'll crash us into a telephone pole?"

"No," Richard replied, with new assurance. "It's

just that I've figured out how we might win."

"Want to tell me?"

"No."

"I didn't think you would. 'Just drive, lady,' is that it?"

"No, not at all. But there are some things—"

Courtney Rankin looked straight ahead, wondering again at the whimsical but somehow courageous little man she'd chosen, for now, to entrust with—her life; who wasn't like anyone, in physical attractiveness, in "power," she'd known before. What is it about him? she thought. And then she knew.

He has something I don't—not yet. I'm not tracking a story—I'm helping him find his child.

The man couldn't remember a time when he'd felt so *fit,* so on *top* of things, or so satisfied! It was true that, for reasons he couldn't quite understand, so far, he'd been conscious of an underlying sense of irritation and a tendency not like him—not at all like him; it was surely the thrill of anticipation and need to wait, even as he'd had to wait forever for orders to come, telling him and his superiors in Korea that it was time to advance; that had been literally maddening—to behave a trifle hastily. The way he had with the young trooper he'd just dismissed, after frightening the soldier more than he'd intended. Which was by no means a mistake, of course, since every man jack serving under him in Romulus knew that he always looked out for them, always did what was best for them, even if they were too young and inexperienced to realize it.

The bald man glanced out the window of his CP, nodding his approval at the whirlybirds which hovered above the ground like deformed moths,

drawn by the light of his own plan, his own genius.
It was working precisely as he'd laid it out for
Middleton and Rathbone at the Pentagon, exactly as
he'd conceived it over all the arduous years since
he'd earned his command. And it was entirely all
right that they'd left things as they were, it was *fine*
that they'd provided everything he required for 24
December except overt tactical and troop enhance-
ment, that they wouldn't commit themselves to a
thing until he had pulled it off. Because there'd be
no question, no question at all, about whose mission
it had been or whose command deserved the credit.
Let the paper-pusher Middleton and Rathbone, with
all his ties to the Central Intelligence Agency,
shuffle their feet now and Colonel Albert Caull and
his Romulus command would be firmly entrenched
by the time the Pentagon realized what their
cowardice had permitted. And by then, the seat of
government, television and the press, and half the
ranking members of Congress would stand beside
Caull and his boys!

    Rubbing his hands together briskly—hands that
appeared oversized, white and crablike for a man of
ordinary dimensions; hands that somehow gestured
and exhorted almost without Caull's willing it, as if
they'd become swollen from all the things they'd
been asked to do—the bald man resumed his spastic,
short-stepped pacing. He was genuinely astonished
by how marvelous, how A-OK and how powerfully
fit he felt. Once he'd believed it best not to lead the
attack, that he'd need to general the troops from the
rear. But now he was so eager to show them personally, in real life, how you took a man out and got a
second man with the same cut of the bayonet, how a
unified team could inanimate dozens or even
hundreds of the enemy in a matter of quiet min-

utes, that he kept seeing pieces of his life's long dream rising before his vision like snippets of film from a favorite old flick. But this action movie hadn't been filmed yet; he'd only dared to tell one or two people at a time, over the years, the entire grand plot and he'd never dared to tell anybody but Wayland and Pardoo how the story ended . . .

For as long as he could remember—and he by-God remembered things with scrupulous attention to detail; he had a mind like a trap, he'd always known that; he never made those ignorant come-back-to-haunt-you errors that other men made, because he'd trained himself mercilessly, he'd pounded the disciplines of observation and exacting memory into his brain while the other junior-grade officers had gone off to their filthy brothels in Seoul, and later in Saigon—he'd heard that middle age was something a man had to fear, that you were sloughing off two million brain cells a goddamned day and it was a fucking miracle that any man reached sixty without enduring the humiliation of incipient senility.

Which was, wasn't it, an interesting assumption, right, a powerfully interesting assumption if you considered that most presidents of the by-God United States of America were *over sixty, well* by-God over sixty, when they started making the most important decisons of their lives! So who was slipping, stupid or crazy, when the American people voted such mature men into office? Laughing aloud, Caull paused in his pacing to smooth imaginary hair over his immense, tanned, bald head, amused and appreciative as usual of the utterly fascinating connections his trained mind made—and also thinking that when you considered some of the commanders-in-chief under whom Albert Caull had served, they made a far more powerful argument for early senility than Caull did! It was the fault of those inexperienced, book-taught, civilian note-takers called writers. Jesus, how he loathed reporters, and writers like young Grant's father who sat back in their cushy goddamned studies on their cushy goddamned asses and had the nerve to take potshots at the fighting men and their leaders who made by-God history! And the fault, too, of the soft underbelly of the American system of government that allowed second generation citizens, uneducated savages, kids who weren't even twenty-one years of age, and women—*women,* who'd never seen any worse war than a squabble between their goddamned brats!—to vote for a series of spineless sissies scared of their own shadows!

That would change, Caull assured himself. Qualified people—men—would do the voting in the future. Men who understood that "peace" was just another buzz-word, like "senility," "welfare," and definitions of democracy never conceived by the founding fathers. Clichés that left America vulnerable, left her incapable of taking charge in the world the way she'd always been meant to, would change—clichés such as "Americans don't make *preemptive strikes.*" And there'd be a change in a lot of the records, too, especially those records that Middleton and Rathbone sat on at the Pentagon, kept to hold Albert Caull away from the greatness for which *he* was intended, and his General's stars, records saying he'd brutalized his troops in Korea and citizens of the Republic of South Vietnam. "Brutalized?" What did those fuckface fatcats in the Pentagon and the pussywhipped public think war was all about? It was *intended* to be brutal, it was one of the reasons he and half the CO's he'd known had remained in the service of their country!

It was also the basis for his original, powerful
concept more than two decades ago, although
Albert Caull had never told about it and knew he
never would. Because the American public had been
emasculated, it had lost its guts, and halfway
through his own second tour of duty in Nam the
bald man had realized, as if visited by an inspiration
direct from God, that future generations of young
Americans were going to lack any stomach for
brutality, for war—if all of them were reared by
civilians! Caull had seen quite clearly that the
reason the United States government went on
building up a nuclear stockpile was that any incoming White House administration would have to face
the facts that (1) we lacked the right kind of young
man to throw into combat and (2) we could win
World War III only by pushing buttons and letting
machines and electronic devices fight the righteous
battle for us! He'd put down his rifle, that day,
Albert Caull had, knelt behind the lines with tears
streaming down his cheeks, and seen clearly that it
was up to him to create a force of fighting men so
powerful, so free of Communist indoctrination, so
liberated from women and womanish men
—so prepared; disciplined; suicidal; *brutal*—
that it would be their command that stopped the
enemy *finally*, the one way it could be done. By
annihilating them. By inanimating a whole nation.

It was only in these past, harder months—thirteen or fourteen of them, he calculated—that Caull
had seen his plan could not be fully implemented
until his troops, those boys he had chosen and
trained, had altered the entire course of American
history.

The moment hadn't been as electrifying, as aglow
with revelation as the instant when he'd knelt on the

blood soaked earth near Haiphong Harbor; it had
felt right, just that. It had become a matter of duty.

Which was basically why he had called young
Grant on the carpet only a short while ago. Told him
his last name—the first trooper of Project Romulus
to be so apprised—so that he could further tell the
soldier that the interfering civilian who'd fathered
Grant was trying to locate him, to ruin the
campaign of 24 December. He'd hated to tell the
soldier after the splendid, manly way he had taken
his punishment down at the lake. But it was an obligation, a duty. "I want you to perceive, Mark," he'd
told the lad, "what Romulus has saved you from.
Parents who made no effort before now to discover
your whereabouts, who waited twenty years to
search for you—*now* that you're a man's man and
they won't be saddled with your needs. The way I've
taken care of all my lads."

The boy had taken the information about his biological father well. He had remained steadily at
parade rest, staring ahead of him at the framed
photographs on the wall. There was, perhaps, the
most minute flicker of emotion in young Grant's
eyes—surprise, certainly; that was understandable
—but since he hadn't been given permission to pose
any questions, Grant hadn't asked any. Perhaps he
was a better trooper than his envelope had suggested, prior to the lakeside exercise. There'd been
signs of weakness, at times, in the relatiatory hand-
to-hand drills and an impudent, independent question or two, according to instructors who'd filled the
folder now on Caull's desk.

"Because of your blood parent, soldier, your parti-
cipation in the December 24 mission has become
dubious, extremely dubious," he'd continued. "If
your mind was centered instead upon that man who

was your biological sire, you could conceivably endanger the others." And the mission.

"Permission to speak, sir?"

Caull's prominent brows had raised. But his frown had shifted, somehow, to a smile of curiosity. The lad had guts. "You're out of order, Grant. Permission granted nevertheless."

"I've never . . . met . . . the person in question, sir." Grant tucked his elbows into a strained, still-stiffer posture. "And this is the first time I've heard his name. It was not mine, until now." Grant paused. "It has been enough to have the honor of serving the United States Army, our nation—and *you*. Sir. I think—"

"Yes, yes; I understand." That moment, Caull had liked the boy, felt certain of him. There'd been something attractive about his inquisitive, soft eyes, his expressive mouth, even his slender form. "However, you were narrowly selected for the elite company, in any case. Your recent marks in automatic rifle fire drills and your execution of Tai Kwando leave much to be desired; much." He had fingered the folder before him, glanced toward the door. "You are, under the circumstances, to be replaced, Grant. You'll get new orders tomorrow."

For a moment the lad's eyes had wandered. "The woman," he said; "in Indianapolis. She—" At last he had probed the Colonel's face with his young eyes. "Am I to—to *meet* this man called Grant, sir? His family?"

"That is enough!" Caull had snapped, feeling pressured. "If you ask another question, I'll see you on the parade grounds at oh-six hundred!"

And he'd watched the way Grant's shoulders bowed, after he'd saluted and been dismissed, and found himself unable to stop thinking of the soldier.

The questions posed were out of line, and ludicrous.
If the boy had thought about it even for five
seconds, he'd have known Richard Grant would
neither locate the Romulus command nor, for that
matter, the state of Utah!

But it bothered Colonel Albert Caull that young
Grant's responses, inwardly, were clearly emotional
in nature. The fact that he undoubtedly wanted to
participate in inanimating his father didn't make it
better. Whatever killing was done under the bald
man's command was professional, detached, emo-
tionless.

And any of the feelings Caull thought of as
emotional had always disturbed him, because he
was unable to relate to them even to the slightest
degree.

22

While Richard bustled energetically into the stylish offices of the Wanderers Motel to register for the waning afternoon and night, Courtney remained worriedly outside, arms folded, eyes restlessly scanning the detached rooms of this sprawling, modern Kansas facility.

The town, Thessalia, was one neither she nor Richard had ever heard of. He'd suggested with a clever expression on his face that the town's lack of renown was precisely why he'd selected it.

"Anybody from Project Romulus who's on our tail will figure that we'd choose some unimportant little burg, instead of a well-known place on the outskirts of Topeka or Kansas City," he'd argued as they drove into the lot. Then when she'd started to protest, he'd held up his palm, finishing his ratiocinations. "*Then* they'll figure that we're smart enough—because you're a big shot Washington columnist and I'm a professional writer—to deduce *their* reasoning and head straight for K.C. or Topeka!"

She'd glanced at his expression of intense self-satisfaction and frowned as he parked. "Then why didn't we stop back there a mile, at that ramshackle joint with the old-fashioned lights on the roof?" she'd pressed him.

"That fleabag? Norman Bates' Motel?" He'd shuddered comically and winked at Courtney as he headed toward the Wanderers office. "It looked just like the joint in the *Psycho* flicks, that's why! If you took a shower in that place it'd be a toss-up whether Norman got you first or you turned to rust because of the water!"

Molly may have been right, Courtney reflected, turning away from the series of detached motel rooms to hide her smile. *Richard is starting to live his work!*

Her restless gaze took in a bucolic sight just off the property of the Wanderers. A pond that might have been the site of the very primordial ooze from which human beings were supposed to have sprung could be seen at the bottom of a dip in the earth. Despite the fact that there was no snow on the ground and it was unseasonably pleasant for a late December evening, Courtney was mildly surprised to see a man clad in floppy, ancient boots and rude work clothes concentrating with apparent intensity as he lobbed a homemade fishing line over the pond. Seeing how young he looked, Courtney smiled, remembering her own independent outlook where weather was concerned. Once, back home, she'd played tennis on an outdoor court during the month of February, and she'd always been the first one to shuck her winter garb before spring had anything but the calendar on its side. This was probably catfish season, she considered, or the best time to fish for some wriggly delight indigenous to the state of Kansas.

"I didn't get single rooms," Richard said to her elbow, startling her. He was whispering hoarsely in her ear. "They'd figure us for that but I signed us in as husband and wife."

Then he was past her, winking back as he led the way around a lane fringed by flower beds to Number 12. She wasn't sure where to begin correcting him, whether to point out that he had a lot of nerve to assume she'd spend the night in the same motel room with him, that he'd forgotten to get the luggage from the trunk of their car, or that his reasoning sounded badly flawed to her. In any case, Richard didn't give her the chance to voice any of her criticisms; he was too busy prattling on about his ingenuity in playing Sherlock Holmes to Colonel Caull's Professor Moriarty.

"I was careful not to make any of those dumb mistakes people always make in movies and books," he assured her, unlocking the front door. "Idiots like that either check in as themselves, as Mr. and Mrs. Smith, or they use the same damn initials. You know, like 'Mr. and Mrs. Ronald Glickstein' or something."

Courtney, despite herself, was curious. "Who are we, then?" she asked.

"Scott and Zelda Fitzgerald," he answered promptly, scooping her into his arms. He grinned proudly into her astonished face. "I told 'em we were newlyweds, so we have to look the part. But don't worry, kid, I'm not James Bond; your honor isn't on the line." Heaving, awkward, he propelled them through the doorway and kicked the door shut with his toe. "Crap, woman, you must have put on weight breathing gasoline fumes! Next time we do this, in consideration of your ardent feminism, you can carry *me* over the threshold!"

Depositing her rudely on her feet, Richard gasped for breath, then plunged his hands into his jacket pockets. "Here, Mid-Court," he said, pulling his hands back out and extending his arms to her. "I popped for dinner. It's from a machine in the motel office and there's almost enough mayo on them to hide the taste."

She peered down in surprise at a pile of five extremely flat sandwiches wrapped in paper, each bedecked with a generous sampling of lint and presumably unmentionable microscopic life from Richard's pockets. "*Ugggh!*" she said, making a face as she looked up at him. "I'd get dysentery just unwrapping these things! I assume the odd number sandwich is yours, because you're a man?"

"Not actually." He'd slipped out of his coat and hung it on the bathroom doorknob before breezing inside and closing the door. "Number Six is somewhere in my jacket. I might have stuck it between my wallet and checkbook."

"Never mind," she said with a curling lip, placing the sandwiches on a table between the easy chair and TV. "What are you doing?"

"That's a hell of an inelegant question for a slick Washington reporter!" he called. The toilet flushed and his voice rose above the noise. "I have to shave or else get a dog license. Little guys are proud of their beards, you know, especially if they're dark and wiry like mine. Makes us feel more macho."

"We don't need any more macho in the world," she answered. She brought in a small overnight case from the interior of the car, containing mostly cosmetics and a hairbrush and comb, but had also packed a change of underwear plus a comfortably antiquated shirt and jeans. If they were spending only half the night in—what was it again?

Thessalia?—she thought she might as well relax and be ready to leave when the master detective considered it safe. "Not one more bulging muscle or fist raised in anger."

"That's where you're wrong," Richard disagreed, raising his voice to be understood. She heard water running in the basin. "Maybe it's time I made my own position on the military a little clearer."

Courtney, hearing the familiar pompous lecturer tone creep back into his voice, stuck her tongue out at the bathroom door. "Go ahead," she said, unzipping her skirt and letting it fall. "I can take anything."

"Well, to start with, there's no sizable organization or body of men one-hundred-percent dedicated to the common good." He paused. "Aren't you going to make me say 'body of men and women' or the like?"

"Certainly not!" She unbuttoned her blouse, smirking. "Most organizations of women are one-hundred-percent good!"

"There's somebody in here being serious, dammit!" he shouted.

Yes, I noticed, Courtney thought, openly smiling as she undressed. *That's part of your charm. You're the only man I know under fifty who has the confidence to express his own individual opinions about important matters without sounding like he's running for office, seeking a promotion, or parroting what's popular.* "There's somebody out here listening. Go on."

"I've read stuff about those old-fashioned British boarding schools—public schools, but why they call 'em that I've never found out. Stuff about headmasters who were pretty ordinary bleeders until they got so much control over small, helpless

children, without having to report to anyone, that
they became first class sadists." Richard, stripped
to the waist, was reaching into his overnight bag,
then generously lathering his face and coaxing hot
water from the motel faucet. "The point is, power is
intoxicating and our bald man who dreamed up
Project Romulus had already had a taste of it as a
junior officer. Beyond that, there's also the element
of scientific experimentation in what he's been
doing for twenty years."

"Experimentation?" Courtney's modulated tones
rose from beyond the bathroom in surprise. "I don't
follow you."

Ah, but you do! Richard thought devilishly, grinning at his Santa Claus face in the mirror. "No one
could really be sure how Romulus would work out.
It's what scientific types call a 'controlled environment' and places like that always discover a few
paranoid bad apples who think they're the ones
entitled to take charge. But Caull, *he's* been in
charge, in control of his environment, for two
decades now! I suspect he was a little weird from the
start and has become more and more paranoid,
seeing old Lesbians in train stations as sticking
miniature A-bombs in their suitcases beside their
vibrators!"

Courtney called, "You're terrible."

"So Molly tells me from time to time." He made a
distinctly macho, casual sweep at his left jaw with
the razor and saw Lime Foamy, whiskers, and a
patch of skin vanish from view. "*Ouch,* dammit-
dammit!" Courtney asked anxiously what was
wrong and he murmured, pressing a washcloth
against the side of his face, "Nothing much. Just
this serious looney-bug in here carving himself like a
turkey—which is reasonably appropriate, I'd say."

"And you were saying, before the bloodletting?"

"That you're wrong in thinking we don't need some kind of macho in the world any longer, even though it's not the warped kind Caull stands for." Gingerly, he peeked beneath the cloth, praying for coagulation. "I hate to think where the hell we'd be today if it hadn't been for the soldiers, Marines, sailors and fly-boys—the whole military ball of wax —when war broke out in the past. And in each case, an officer was in command whose task was to decide strategy for his junior officers and the so-called private soldiers, in the hope of winning one more battle. For all of us. We even knock the R.A. guys, the standing army of hard-core sergeants and corporals who get a bad name hassling incoming recruits, but whom we all rely upon at time of war. Whether we like to admit it, or not." Cautiously, now, Richard resumed shaving. "A lot of valid, vital words have fallen on terrible times recently. Two that come to mind are 'fighting men' and 'hero'— or is that three words?"

"You hated being in the Army!" Courtney cried from outside the bathroom. "You told me that and I think you *always* suspected something strange was going on at the G.I. hospital! You can't be serious in believing there's no better way to—to solve differences between ideologies, and nations, than by fighting! *Brawling,* like a group of overgrown little boys in a playground when Teacher's gone to the john!"

"I *am* serious, goddammit!" Richard exclaimed, narrowly missing another slice of his skin beneath the right ear. "I hoped the U.N. would become strong and effective. I prayed all the Genevas, all the peace talks, would amount to something. I'm as liberal as the next man, but Communism simply keeps spreading—not to mention the new witch's brew of factions and emerging nations, not to mention the rise of terrorism!" He splashed his face with water, hastily dried it on a motel towel, then turned, pushing at the door. "Next time you see a truck or two loaded with explosives heading for you, with a crazy, suicidal driver grinning at you, be certain to give *him* your best speech about peace! Next time a ground crew with heat-seeking missiles fires at the commercial flight you booked, saying it's a 'spy plane,' *you* go tell 'em—"

He had ripped open the door to the bathroom, taken three swift steps into the bedroom, before seeing clearly through his red swirl of outrage.

What he saw was Courtney Rankin. Or most of what there was to see of her. Engaged in animated discussion with him and believing he'd stay put behind the bathroom door a while longer, she had almost finished undressing when, bare-chested, there he was frozen a few yards away, staring.

Courtney wore nothing but her black lace bra. She'd been turning slightly, as he barged out of the bath, so that one hip and the long flank of her left thigh were exposed. She had been reaching behind her, fingers working the clasp of the brassiere, and her head had whirled to him in surprise, chestnut hair spinning like autumn smoke. The connecting impact created by his serendiptious mistake crackled as if lightning had struck them both.

Then Courtney turned, quite deliberately, to face him and the black bra came away in her hand.

She stood in seeming calm, poised, arms at her sides so that he could look at her. Because it had been naked to him first, Richard stared at the fringe of pubic hair rising up from where her legs joined, like a shielding, beguiling hand—or the hair of the

head of someone who lay unseen behind her,
trapped by Courtney's properly clamped, pale
thighs. He was intrigued by how sparse the pubic
growth was, so feathery it seemed like shadow, how
much lighter of hue than her other hair; and that
reminded him, automatically, of Molly but he
fought back his surge of guilt.

There'd always been, for Richard, so munificiently
much of a nude woman to see that he'd tended to
prefer looking at a distance instead of with the
proximity that turned ambient admiration to
sightless passion. At first, at least, only at first.
And yet he did not walk toward her, this intelligent
and talented woman who had first annoyed him and
then increasingly filled him with respect for her
persistence and courage. He could not recall when
he'd stayed so long at bay from naked femaleness;
and wondered about his forty-plus draining winters,
finally remembered he had not *seen* such unacquainted bareness, so privately, in over twenty
years—except in his imagination.

Courtney breathed, discernibly; he knew, then,
she'd held her breath and he reasoned that she was
not too experienced in coping with such a fundamentally human concern as being unclad before
another. But her breasts, when they rose—each as
close to being a separate unit as the small hands
fisting nervously at her sides—told him arousal was
somehow permissible. Then his gaze heated, became
the sight of wanting eyes, and he admired the
athletically perfect proportions of her—not in terms
of her bosom's size or her pubes', but the way her
tallish body was neatly squared off in the descending, delicious segments of her. She was not frail; she
looked sturdy, able to give as well as she took, no
dream woman of pliant softness and tearful, docile

ways but the reassuring *reality* of a thinking, feeling
human being of the alternate sex which a fantasy-
laden author needed to balance him—and tell him
real things could be okay, could be lived with.

Richard saw Courtney's eyes dip, saw that she
detected what he wondered if she saw through his
trousers and shorts. Her gaze seemed to understand
he couldn't tolerate for long the tautness, the pledge
of discomfort turning to pain, even if she'd never
know how her *otherness* served at once as promised
pleasure and ongoing affliction. He took an avid
step toward her.

"Does this mean we aren't going to eat our sandwiches?" he inquired.

He watched her affectionate grin take shape, her
beautiful head cocked to one side. In several swift,
nimble little steps she ran barefoot and bare into his
welcoming arms. "Idiot!" she said under her breath;
but her lips were parted against his and her breath
was hot, sweet, as her mouth moved to his ear and
he felt the passion of her there. Instinctively,
because "idiot" was what Molly so often called him
—what was it about him that brought such a word
to women's lips?—he hesitated to peer quickly
through the shades, guilty enough to expect to see a
charming blond his age advancing upon them with a
bald-headed colonel in her wake. They met at the
foot of the bed, which was placed against the wall.
There were two windows, curtained and protected
from the view of outsiders, set in the wall; but
when he looked through one, he saw nobody. He and
the most fully desirable woman he'd met in twenty
years were finally alone.

The heat exuding from Courtney's needing naked-
ness as she moved to fit herself to him was too
readily overpowering Richard. He held her at arm's

length, gently, cautioningly, a part of his writer's
mind fearfully expecting the kind of flaws most
human beings possessed, but hid beneath clothing.

But she seemed perfect to him. There was an
entirety about her body, a unity that spoke of how
she was glad he saw her and not ashamed. Her startlingly wide shoulders tapered to high breasts, the
large nipples tipped and rising from their mounds of
flesh as if demanding they be tasted. He ran his
open palms down her sides to a narrow waist, let
them glide across her belly until his thumbs met
above a large, recessed navel; he felt something
downy beneath his fingers, saw with burgeoning
and scarcely banked lust what he had not seen at a
distance—the way a slight tracery of fire, short,
light-brown hairs began shortly beneath the navel
and traveled down to culminate in the slightest,
softest patch of pubic hair he'd ever touched.

He started to stoop, but Courtney beat him,
dropping down with one knee on the motel floor, the
other raised, so that she could make him fully naked,
as she was. Her agile fngers grappled with the belt,
the zipper; her hands went out to his sides with a
sudden lust that amazed him and brought his pants
and shorts to his ankles in a single short motion.
While she did not put her lips to him, he looked
down at the expression on her face as she gripped
his erect member firmly in her hands, then lovingly
rested one cheek against it. He felt rising up inside
him a bewildering assembly of feelings and moods
that somehow seemed to merge with sheer, physical
longing; he felt incredible need, bafflement, want,
fresh guilt, fresh lust—and a sense that this was
right, somehow, or right for this moment.

Then he was lying back on the bed and the beautiful young woman was climbing up on it and between

his legs. Her outflung arms grazed his thighs and he
shivered, her teasing fingertips touched him
between the legs, her tongue emerged from between
her lips and moistened them, her head and body
were sliding slowly toward him . . .

*A crisp, cold snapping sound outside the motel
seemed so close that Courtney stopped moving. She
looked at Richard with the swiftest shift of emotion
he'd ever seen. A woman's rare instant of total
sexual need had turned to human fear.*

Courtney rolled away toward the wall. On her
haunches, she peered through the shades, carefully,
as Richard moved quickly to extinguish the lights.

The young man wearing the floppy boots who'd
been fishing in bucolic quiet stood ten yards from
their motel. Facing it. He'd been joined by a second
youthful male, similarly clad in plain, countrified
clothing. Carrying a shotgun. Facing the motel. And
while Courtney knew their room was in darkness,
she still felt that the youth with the fishing pole was
staring coolly and expressionlessly *straight into her
eyes.*

23

"Richard, we can't be sure they're part of Romulus," Courtney whispered, trying to be optimistic, "or that Colonel Caull sent them." She was already into her underwear and jeans and had remembered to reach for the fresh shirt.

"Well, I'll tell you one thing!" Richard, a short shadow in the room's darkness, only glanced at her as he pulled on his trousers. "They sure as hell aren't Santa's little helpers!" Unable to locate his shorts or T-shirt, he put on his shirt and felt the way his pants pressed mercilessly against his still tumescent body. He headed quickly toward her, as soundlessly as possible.

"What are we going to *do?*" Courtney knelt on the bed, lifted a hand with the intention of peering outside once more.

Richard caught her hand. "Don't do that! They probably can't see us, but we were lying down before. If they see us standing, and dressed, they'll know we're on to them." He made out the frightened look in her eyes and held her cheeks with his own hands. "God, you're beautiful!"

Then he was on his feet, snapping his fingers and racing to the telephone.

"What are you doing?" she asked in a hoarse whisper.

"I just remembered what they always do in movies at times like this!" He hesitated with the phone at his ear, then dialed "O." His teeth flashed hope to her when he smiled. "We need a *diversion!*"

Incredulously, Courtney listened to him, realized he had called the fire department! "*Help us!*" he wheezed. "We're trapped in a motel room—the *flames,* everywhere!" He choked out the name of the motel, urged them to send at least three fire engines, then hung up and turned back to Courtney. "I hope they know the address of this joint!"

"B-But there *isn't* any fire!" she gasped.

"There will be in a minute," Richard replied grimly, snatching a wastebasket near a chest of drawers and squinting at the contents: a few used Kleenex, a scrap of discarded motel stationery. "Give me that tissue box! C'mon, throw it!" He wadded up an enormous handful of tissues, crammed them into the wastebasket and tugged his cigarette lighter from his shirt pocket. Thrusting his hand inside, he rolled his thumb once, twice, three times—but each time there was a flicker of flame, the angle at which he held the lighter squeezed it out. "*Matches!*" he hissed. Courtney stood by feeling helpless. "Gimme the goddamn *matches!*"

Instead, she struck one and dropped it into the wastebasket. Instantly, fire blazed into view.

Quickly, after shoving the TV before the front door, they rushed back to the window by the bed, kneeling like children peeping into a candy shop. Richard giggled, stifled it with a hand over his mouth. "Look at 'em, *look* at 'em!" he exulted,

hugging Courtney with glee. The two men observing
the motel room were shuffling their feet, gesticula-
ting to one another, clearly catching a glimpse of
crimson flame inside. "They don't know *what* the
hell to do! The bald guy turns these kids into automatons, and if their little computers are fed something they don't understand, they start spinning
around and around like mechanical men!"

He couldn't see Courtney Rankin's obligatory
smile and doubtful glance into the front of the room.
Already the flames were spreading, engulfing the
draperies at a front window and running up the
walls like blood.

"It's getting hot in here," Richard mumbled, and
coughed. Grinning his encouragement bravely, he
kissed the tip of her nose and pointed. "Grab the
stuff we left in the bathroom, will you? We're going
to book out of here the minute the fire trucks show
up!"

Courtney nodded and started to move but faintly
shook her head. If the fire trucks didn't arrive soon,
it might be a moot point whether Caull's men got
them or the growing motel blaze did the trick.
Starting to cough, she disappeared into the
bathroom.

Letting his convincing chuckle die, Richard
turned back to the window, aware abruptly of the
terrible risk he'd taken for the two of them. The
motel room was filling with smoke and it was
getting hard to breathe or to see. Squinting, he
parted the shades, glanced outside—

—Saw only *one* man—the soldier with the
shotgun—still watching. And the weapon was aimed
directly at Richard Grant!

Then the bathroom door was slammed shut,
locked, and Richard heard a shrill sound that halted

his activity, his thoughts, his heart.

Courtney, *screaming—once!*

Too terrified for her and too frightened by the crackling flames behind him to plan it through, Richard *acted.* When he was clear of the window and the bed, a shotgun blast shattered the pane, sending shards flying in every direction. But by then, he'd darted toward the bathroom door, kicked at it with all his strength. He heard the lock snap—saw the door swing wide—he caught the shadowed glimpse of a *man's figure,* the arm encircling a fighting Courtney's neck—saw that the side of the soldier's body and Courtney's were facing him. All Richard's motions had been unconsidered, fast-flowing; now he was hurtling across the bathroom, colliding with the other man and sending them both spinning out of control. He had an instant when the soldier's startled gaze was locked with his—

Then the toppling youth staggered backward, back-of-the-knees catching the tub, falling—

And his skull was striking the unyielding tub, sickeningly, his limbs going perfectly limp. Blood appeared as if by magic from behind the young soldier's head, ran like paint down the side of the bathtub.

"My God," Courtney said shakily, unhurt, reaching for Richard and averting her gaze.

"*Listen!*" He pointed. "*Sirens!*"

Courtney heard them then, too, the eerie, uncanny rise-and-fall sound of the fire engines, drawing nearer.

"We're going to be okay!" he exclaimed, grabbing her hand. "It's gonna *work!*"

Then they saw, outside the splintered bathroom door, that the fire had spread until a wall of flame was only yards from them . . .

"We can't get out through the front door!" Courtney whispered, shocked.

He showed terror in his face for the first time. "But it's the *only* door."

Courtney whirled, racing back into the narrow bath. "*He* got in!" she exclaimed, pointing at the unconscious youth in the tub. "He got in *somehow!*"

"The window!" Richard shouted, beginning to cough. He snatched up some of their things, glanced at the plainclothes soldier—wanting to take him with him to safety—then rushed to the curtained window.

Behind it, empty space—liberty—yawned. The Romulus trooper had raised the window and left it open for his own escape. "C'mon!" Richard yelled, pushing Courtney ahead of him. "The car's at the end of the building!"

Fire was in the room behind him, Richard saw as she preceded him—already licking at the shower curtain. Richard thumped Courtney's bottom, shouted, "*Move it!*"

Then he was joining her on the ground outside the cabin and they were running, Richard glancing about in fear of the second soldier. By the time they were safely inside the car and he was firing up the motor, Richard was laughing aloud. "The good little soldier boy is watching the other side of the motel, just the way he's supposed to!" he cried, throwing the car into reverse and then forward, away from the burning building. He jabbed a finger. "Look at it, at the smoke and flames! With any luck, the bald man will be sure we both died in that inferno!" Sirens screamed constantly closer.

Courtney, nearly hysterical but filling with relief, leaned against him as the car gained momentum.

"And you're such a genius you even left our suit-cases in the *trunk!*"

He laughed with her, both of them sweaty and smeared with smudges of dirt, her hair a mess and his shirt unbuttoned over his bare chest—

The second trooper materialized in the motel driveway just ahead of them at the instant Richard switched on the headlights. He stood in the classic military posture, shotgun fearlessly leveled at the car—and Richard, at the wheel.

No time to think. Time only for what passed for instinct in the human animal, in the human named Richard Grant. Divided, uneager to take human life, he cut the wheel to the right just enough to catch the soldier with the car's fender—horrifying glimpse of young man raised into air, his shotgun firing with a sound like that of a cannon—

The car, veering, skidding—Richard, fighting the wheel, righting it as a fence loomed just to the left—

"*Look!*" Courtney screamed, twisted in her seat and staring out the rear window.

He had time, *just,* to see in the rear view mirror what she had seen. *Nothing!* The car-struck youth was gone! "Where'd he go?" Richard demanded, looking forward again as their vehicle plowed back into the road and a panel truck, passing, wailed a frightened protest. "*Courtney, where'd he go?*"

White-faced, she gaped at him. "He got *up!* He got into a car. Richard, he's *following us!*"

"Sonofabitch!" Richard screamed, slamming on the brakes, gaping as first one fire engine, then another, cut before him into the motel grounds. Because of his terror and concentration, he hadn't even heard the sirens.

Then he was jumping out of the car, standing in the dark road, laughing and pounding his thigh with glee, calling out the news to the staring Courtney. "They've stopped right in *front* of the bastard! The fire trucks have *blocked him in!*"

Reaching through the open door, she yanked the sleeve of his shirt, tugged. "Get in!" She was beginning to cry. "Get us out of here while we can go!"

Behind the rustic cabin her father had once loved, the long, perilous flight of steps down which they had come on foot from the dirt road where they'd left the car, resembled pearl buttons set against the background of a dark blouse. Molly turned away from it, crossed through the small building in which Lucille and her children slept, and went nervously out on the front porch.

She knew that she could never mount those steps to the road by night, and what lay before her was the skirt of Klinger Lake, tall pines rising at the distant edges of the water like arms thrown up in horror.

Shivering, she crossed her arms over her bosom and hugged herself, wondered beyond reason whether she should check, again, on the girls. If her life was falling to pieces once more—as it had, twenty years ago—it was no less uprooting, disorienting and frightening, for Mary and Michelle. Molly tried to focus on that, let her concern focus solely upon a peril that might not be ended for any of them. To lavish, once and for all, the maternal care she'd once saved for Mark, only to feel it harden and freeze inside, on those children who were still present. To quit being Daddy's girl, she thought, anguished.

Something with strong wings and a short, chunky body lifted itself across the lap of the lakes as if born and instantly eager to be gone. An *owl*, Molly thought, watching the bird meld with the stand of trees on the other side of the lake. *A night hunter, hungry . . .*

She sat down on the porch swing at her back without quite realizing she had decided to do it, and thought of Richard. Richard and—Lois Lane. Half smirking, half frowning, she buried her face in her right hand and shook her head. She hadn't imagined, for years, that he might not be the one, stable fact of her life, however she sometimes took him for granted or found his writing efforts so tiresome, so almost childish. That his hungers, or needs, might not have been totally fulfilled or—as Molly tended to think—given up. Surrendered, with all the other lies and illusions to which mortal flesh was prey in the hands of parents, peers, and commercial blandishments. Was it the Rankin woman's stylish ways, her smart looks, or the way she seemed ready to share Richard's creative drives?

Surely she could still trust him. *Surely.*

Molly nodded, moved the creaking, aged swing slowly back and forth. Trust, that was the word. In Richard, yes, in God—in many things.

Everything will work out, she thought, raising her face to the lake and becoming aware of how chilly it had become. *Everything will be fine, because it has to be.*

The owl returned from the woods, wings laboring. Molly stared hard at the bird.

Something that squirmed was in its claws but, as she watched, the motion died and the owl was arcing above the rustic cabin, leaving Molly alone.

24

As they flashed across the border into Utah and headed toward the central region of the Beehive State below and east of Nephi, a region of jagged peaks south of the majestic Wasatch Mountain Range, Richard glanced from his map into a guidebook, then peered over at Courtney at the wheel. "Utah's the tenth state in size," he said, "named for the Ute Indians. Fascinating, isn't it, the way we chased those people into an existence pretty well limited to the convenient compound word, then got guilty and named everything in sight after them?"

Courtney blinked acknowledgment but didn't turn her head from the road. "We left Indian-apolis, Indian-a," she said by way of agreement, "heading for a state named after a tribe. Do some of the places out here give them a similar treat?"

Richard looked back at his guidebook. "Well, I see a Hiawatha, Utah, but it looks mostly as if the towns had been named for very different reasons. Here's Ephraim, which sounds religious, and Eureka, which I'd bet a buck has to do with striking it rich—Mammoth, Beaver, Gusher"—Richard snickered—"Kanosh, Spry, Silver City and Jericho. Not to mention—what's this? Hinckley, Utah! And *Black Rock!* Shades of Spencer Tracy."

The trace of a smile moved upon her wide mouth. "I just hope it isn't a bad day in Sunridge."

"Apparently that's the nearest town to the Project Romulus base," he reported, "and it's on the eastern edge of what they call the Great Basin. A 'massive depression enclosed by highlands.' "

"I'm developing a massive depression about going to Sunridge at all," Courtney quipped.

Richard's return smile was full of appreciation that they'd restored their former, good-natured relationship. After putting a hundred miles between them and the Romulus soldier stalled by the fire trucks' arrival, they'd "stayed alive"—as Richard put it—by sharing the single sandwich left in his pocket.

Gradually, then, as he and Courtney had realized they were alone on the road, both of them had remembered their lost opportunity for lovemaking. For many more miles the two of them had stared straight ahead without speaking, troubled both because they'd dared to consider it and because, after undressing, they hadn't consummated the strong attraction between them. Finally, exhausted, Richard had parked the car in the woods off an unmarked road and they'd slept restlessly in each other's arms. Neither had made an advance toward resuming lovemaking but they'd awakened after ninety minutes and gone back on the interstate, incapable of idle conversation until now.

We've had our chance, as in the singular. A chance, one opportunity, Richard reflected, partly aroused by the recollection of how perfect her body had been to his wanting eyes, *and I don't think*

there'll be another. People like him and Courtney
didn't take commitment lightly, or trust and responsibility; when they gave their words, they did their
best to keep them. And their transgressions
depended upon serendipity—propitious timing, an
opportunity that naturally arose, a stroke of luck
that overcame the pledges and proprieties before
either partner had the chance to focus upon them.

"This is a state that was one of the last to be
tamed," Courtney said softly, breaking his train of
thought, "or maybe 'leveled' is a better word.
Altered, surely. Changed for good from what the
wilderness Indians knew as we know our cities—
where life had been rough, but they roamed free.
Changed to that early euphemism we've always
pretended to cherish so much: civilization." She
shuddered as she overcame a temptation to swing
off the highway and explore. "I'm tempted to say
that we castrated it. Not the Amerindians, Richard;
the land itself."

"Bull hockey. That's the sort of thing liberal
newspaper people always say by rote." He gave her
a defensive, crooked smile. "According to the
Eastern press, we're all supposed to share the guilt
for what our grandfathers—our great grandfathers,
and great-great-grandfathers—did. A long, long
time ago. But y'know, Court, not all our ancestors
settled out here because they were looking for
people to pick on. They needed places to live and
they risked everything to get them, sometimes
without stopping to think that other people, called
savages, needed still more room to live."

Courtney frowned and her eyes flared. "Dammit,
don't you see you've been pushed around by the
same kind of rationalization?"

"I have?" He looked at her with genuine surprise.

"I'm not aware of it."

"You're hundreds of miles from your own home, Richard! So is your family. Can't you see what's happened? How they've turned you into a no-good-Richard-but-a-dead-Richard?"

"No, I'm afraid I can't," he said, shaking his head. He looked more amused than mystified, however.

"You're being intentionally vague! They took your boy, Richard, just as certain Indians supposedly seized the offspring of white settlers. They took him, and they raised him as their own!" She leaned on the automobile horn, swept out into the outer lane and bore down in fiery pursuit on a Corvette that had passed them. "But it was, in the long run, the settlers who captured the Indian young. By insisting, looking very holy about it, that they receive the white man's education, religion, and booze—not to mention his diseases! And we didn't stop seizing them until they were misfits, virtual slaves who'd begun to forget the ways of their own people!"

"That's sheer wordplay—sophistry!" he raged.

"Is it really? Well, you were once a free young brave, eager to do your own thing, to earn wampum and get you a squaw! But your government took you, didn't it, took you because they placed their own needs ahead of yours. Eventually they deceived your woman, and then stole your newborn *papoose* —to raise him, with the holiest of attitudes, to educate him as they pleased and teach him what they thought he should believe! And you, you ignorant savage, decided not to be stopped by the new ways; you chose to stand up for your own trusted values." Courtney turned to face him, perilously glancing away from the road, her face intense with the kind of passion that motivated her. "Richard, you killed a man back in Kansas but you haven't even mentioned it! Because you've obstinately put your own, old ways ahead of the changing times and made your enemy something less than human, just as they have you."

He thought about all she'd said until, hours later, his map indicated they were approaching Sunridge, Utah. It was late afternoon and the crawl of lengthening shadows on fringing sagebrush seemed to pace the slowing vehicle. That was when Richard had two things to say: "We do what we have to do," and "America wasn't always this way." Neither of them was certain whether he'd said something profound, or copped out.

Then he added, covering her hand on the steering wheel with his own, feeling her hand tense, "Because of how we were . . . *interrupted*, in the motel, we don't know how to handle this. Let's not deal with it with anger. If we're going to—to end it, let's not allow that to happen the way most people do."

Tears thickened her lashes, glistened in her eyes, and she had to decelerate further. Her brief glance, to the small man seated beside her, was hot with honesty and affection. "I think I've sort of, well, learned to love you, wordsmith."

He leaned over to kiss her cheek. "And I think I sort of feel the same way, talented lady."

Smiling, he looked out into the distance, finding one range of mountains which mottled and surlied the sky as twilight drew near, and another, more hilly or cliff-like, farther away. There was a sense of brooding watchfulness about the hills and mountains, as if unseen sentries squinted out from hollows or caves, observing their progress in town.

Unless a mistake had been made somewhere along
the line, he and Courtney were surely within mere
miles, now, of the paramilitary base commanded by
Colonel Albert Caull. Project Romulus, with all the
dangers it portended, and possibly his own young
son, Mark, were only minutes away!

"I think this must have been a copper mining
town once," Courtney murmured, drawing his
attention, as they entered the single long street that
was Sunridge. They were almost idling now, drifting
past a drug store, a hardware store with a placard in
the window advertising animal feed, a gasoline
station with rusted red pumps fronting upon an old-
fashioned general store. But there was also a look of
near abandonment to this street called Sunridge,
and neither she nor Richard saw many people
treading the cracked sidewalk. For an instant
Courtney had the disconcerting thought that they'd
shut down the mine thirty years before and the
independent citizens of the town, refusing to age
and to die, remained in a kind of suspended
animation by day: vampires feeding on a vein of
crusted copper too attenuated for vitality, nourish-
ing only in a narrow and atavistic sense. She
finished, mumbling the words, "The mountains here
were once rich with all kinds of minerals."

"But not enough vitamins," Richard said with a
grin, then touched her arm. "There's a greasy spoon
and I'm famished! Let's stop and eat as much
ptomaine as possible, then get gassed up and try to
figure out how to locate Romulus."

"And what to do about it once we've found it,"
she added.

They parked in an unpaved dirt lot at the side
of the restaurant, called Bracken's. Inside, around
an overdecorated yet genuine Christmas tree,

Bracken's had the stamp of uncompromising
individuality. Expecting to find red-checked table-
cloths with tanned cowpokes sprawling or fighting
over the barmaid, Courtney saw instead white linen,
clean if repeatedly patched, draping eight or ten
miniature tables with an ambience of tombstones. It
was quiet, as if everybody in the place had known
everybody else for years and had nothing left to say.
The patrons gathered at the tables reminded her at
once of a retired bankers' home, say, or a conclave of
used-up minor politicians. Mostly male, the
customers seemed universally lank or tall, skeletal
as if they'd gone to Bracken's to dine twelve years
ago and still practiced a stubborn abstinence from
food. They tended to wear string ties; a few had drab
suspenders which pinched their frail torsos and
seemed imbedded in shriveled skin. Some wore
brightly burnished boots that caught the light from
a ceiling crawling with fluorescent tubing, stealing
the illumination and giving Bracken's a sallow,
unhealthy atmosphere.

One of the only two booths was unoccupied, and
Richard, twice stepping over glittering boots lying
in his path with a look of permanency, guided
Courtney to it. Sitting down required squeezing
past a man seated alone at a table. The fellow was
possibly shorter than Richard but he'd hung his
winter coat over the back of his chair, rolled up his
sleeves, and the hirsute arms crossed at the wrist on
his table seemed nine months pregnant with muscle.

Once seated, Richard gazed around the
restaurant, conscious of their proximity to the
Romulus post. When Courtney asked him if he
wasn't going to look at his menu, he replied: "I was
casing the joint for the bald man's storm troopers.
But I don't see anybody here, except you, who's

under forty years of age."

"Maybe they took their best shot back at the motel in Kansas," Courtney said thoughtfully. She reviewed her menu again, not the kind with a hand-written "Today's Blueplates" paperclipped inside but a neatly mimeographed luncheon sheet taped to an aged printed menu-folder; deciding, she rested it on the table cloth and looked around for a waitress. "If the food is half as desirable as the prices, it'll stay down."

"What'd you say about 'taking their best shot' at the motel?" Richard stared across the short distance of the tabletop, clearly excited. "Hey, that's it!"

"What's it?" she inquired. Courtney was just realizing how hungry she was and didn't look at him.

"We never saw any of Caull's robot army following us," he replied, speaking loudly as he always had when he was excited, "*because they never followed us at all.*"

She frowned. "That's ridiculous." Then she realized how rude her remark was, and softened it with a smile. "Unless those two young soldiers were only descendants of Jesse or Frank James, mistaking the motel for a bank they wanted to knock over."

"Fore-Court, they were *waiting* for us!" Richard snatched her hand, looked above it with eyes burning from a flushed face. He'd never looked younger to her. "They knew our starting point and how we were traveling. They calculated how long it would be before we stopped for the night, then got there ahead of us—probably with whirlybirds." He squeezed her hand so hard it almost hurt. "I'll bet a royalty check or two that there were four or five two-man teams waiting at every motel or hotel in the vicinity—because they knew where we were going, better than we did!

"And with the kind of confidence they must have in their expert training," she continued, her voice rising with the enthusiasm of fresh insight, "they probably didn't have anybody else assigned to us, from Kansas on. They'd have felt sure they'd stop us, kill us!"

"And when they learned the troops failed, they'd be waiting for you—once you reached Utah, and Sunridge." A third speaker caused both to jump and turn.

Standing close to the booth—his voice had been almost a whisper, but carried like someone's at the eye of a hurricane—was the squat man from the neighboring table, shirtsleeved arms at his sides. He wore a flannel shirt and faded jeans; polished but worn boots; and the disturbing impression he gave of scarcely leashed strength was sustained not only by his bulging forearms and biceps but by how he rocked, to and fro, on his toes, balanced, and ready. His eyes were a distant, nearly tranquilized blue, the jaws lean so that the mouth appeared carved out. "I heard what you said," he stated in a laconic voice, "because you said it loud enough to wake the dead—or join them."

Richard, closest to the man—who appeared to be in his late fifties but dauntingly powerful—gritted his teeth and then sucked in air. "If you're part of Colonel Caull's command, you can tell him we've come to pick up my son."

"I wouldn't tell that sonofabitch goodbye before I blew his crazy brains out," the man replied. "My name's Jackson Pardoo and I don't guess I can do anything but warn you folks: get back in your car, or back in another plane, and clear out of here. You'd have a better chance of kidnapping your son from Reverend Moon's place in Korea!"

Courtney saw that he was looking from Richard to her. "I'm not the boy's mother. I've come with Mr. Grant to investigate." She hesitated, bothered by Pardoo's unblinking, inexpressive stare. "I'm a newspaperwoman, from Washington."

"That's great, lady," Pardoo muttered. "Then they'll give your obituary front page coverage, right?"

"Who in hell are you, Pardoo?" Richard demanded. Then he gestured. "You may as well sit down, if you weren't really sent by Caull."

Pardoo squeezed in next to Courtney, across from Richard, and managed a frosty smirk. "I'm the master sergeant who headed up actual PT and training for the Colonel, until I couldn't stomach it any longer." He paused, glanced at the woman. "My kid's the only trooper there whose father knowingly allowed it. Ain't that just swell? Ain't that the best goddamned citation a man ever took to his grave?"

"If you're telling us you deserted the Romulus project," Richard began, "what are you doing here? Here, where they can easily capture your ass and drag you back?"

Pardoo smoothed a hand across his gray flattop, chuckled deep in his throat. "I think you'd find capturing this old ass wouldn't be all that simple in a public place," he said. For the first time, Courtney, beside the sergeant, caught a glimpse of the man's holstered automatic. *With that and those muscles,* she thought, *they'd find it difficult to take him anywhere.* "But first off, I have no choice except coming to town. I've trapped or shot just about all the game around my cabin and starving to death

isn't my style. Besides, Caull probably believes by
now that I headed east, and maybe south."

"You've stayed this close to the base knowing he
wants to—to get rid of you?" asked Courtney,
gaping at him. She paused until the waitress
brought them their food. "Is that the only reason?"

"It's logical, it makes sense from a strategic view-
point," Pardoo retorted. He caught the waitress'
plump hand, to ask if his big carry-out order was
almost ready, and it occurred to Richard that the
waitress and the sergeant had something in
common. Each possessed a face that might have
been made to display merriment, and each of them
seemed likely to have smiled last a decade ago.
Pardoo gazed at Richard as he addressed Courtney.
"What other reason could I have for staying here?"

"Because you hope, at least unconsciously, to
accomplish what Mr. Grant has come here to do."
Courtney inclined her head in Richard's direction.
"To get your son out of this mess alive."

"That's stupid, lady," Pardoo snapped. "How
could I pull off a stunt like that?"

"You couldn't," Richard said tersely, "alone.
What's your boy's name?"

"Terence. I called him Terry." Pardoo shrugged,
decided to be polite. "What's yours?"

"Grant, Mark Grant," Richard replied. "That's
what his mom and I named him, anyway."

"I know him." The sergeant's head bobbed in
recognition. "Not the most polished trooper in
camp, but a good kid—to the extent that any of
them are kids by now." *Or good* went unspoken.
Pardoo saw the eagerness for information in the
male civilian's face and waved a weary hand. "I
didn't know any of the men that well, Mr. Grant.
Especially my son, Terry. Frankly, there ain't that

much to learn about them anyway. They're carbon copies, and the model they're made on—the original —is Caull himself." He lit a partly bent cigarette. "Funny thing."

"What is?" *Mark,* he thought. *My son is alive!*

"Young Grant, at first, was cream-of-the-crop. He was state-of-the-art when he was in his middle teens; one of the better recruits." A cloud crossed Pardoo's seamed face, one that might have contained a preference to be gone as well as the keeping of a secret. "Something, well, changed the kid. He ran around some with Terry when both of them were younger, what spare time there was to run around. But by the time I went over the wall, I knew goddamned well not to mention it to either of them. Your boy, Grant, he spends a lot of time to himself, thinking. But I'm not really sure his thoughts are, well, what you'd call practical. I think he's a little out of it, mentally."

Richard stared down at his hands. Courtney, overtly charming and smiling, asked, "What's going to happen on Christmas Eve? We know they plan some kind of governmental takeover—a revolution, in effect, by trained American terrorists—but not exactly what they're going to *do.*"

At the instant Pardoo, ruminating, answered by repeating his advice to them to leave Utah at the earliest chance, Richard realized with growing excitement that *this* man—this soldier too, who knew everything about the layout of the command— might be the one person who could get them inside. Who could take them to meet Colonel Albert Caull. But how to persuade him to try? "Sergeant, what is it the Colonel is trying to make happen? *Tomorrow night,* on Christmas Eve?" he inquired, repeating his own question.

Jackson L. Pardoo paused, dropped his head to reach a decision concerning the nature of truth, and its hazards; and when he spoke again, it was in an all-but-inaudible whipser. "On Christmas Eve, half of America gets positively tanked up with holiday spirits and most of the other half is going to church or wrapping presents. Not much goes on, all around the nation. Security in the government itself is at half-strength, the day before Christmas; it's not up to par anywhere. Including security at the White House!"

Neither Richard nor Courtney could answer before they'd stared incredulously into one another's eyes, and seen the answering moods of awe, and fright.

To establish the final function of Colonel Caull's command, to stop living a secret, to act upon everything he'd been planning for two decades—to take over the United States government—the bald man had devised a magnificently simple plan.

He meant to seize the White House.

25

"Here's your order."

Startled, tensing, they looked up. A man in his middle sixties, probably, six-two and beefy, hovered above the small booth. Somehow he succeeded in gripping four swollen sacks of food for Jackson Pardoo yet he remained erect, Courtney saw, ramrod straight. The waitress, wearing a sweater around her shoulders, stood beside him. She had a fifth sack and a ten-pound bag of potatoes and her plain features were arranged in a plea for assistance.

Pardoo was up, relieving the woman of her burden; the two exchanged private appreciative smiles. Then Pardoo glanced at the older, far burlier man. "Could you give me a hand outside with these? I got a jeep."

"Let me help too." Richard stood, eagerly reaching; but neither the ex-master sergeant nor the tall, large man Richard assumed was Bracken, the owner, appeared to notice him. Already they trudged manfully toward the door and Richard, briskly tagging after, was calling, "What's in the sacks, Sarge? Surely you don't mean to eat warmed-over hamburgers all next month?"

Courtney, temporarily abandoned, looked with a frown at the figures of the men as they walked further and further away. Pardoo's voice—"Mr. Bracken sold me some of his kitchen stock"—reached her as the front door squeaked open. Sighing, she tossed a five-dollar bill from her purse on the table, paying for their scarcely touched food. Then she arose, hurrying after the men as the waitress went to her station, shivering. It made sense, Courtney mused, assuming the laconic Pardoo had a freezer in his hideout. And a generator to power it, she added to herself. The Colonel's men must have routinely visited the operator of the general store, paid him to be notified if a thin but muscular man in his fifties placed a large order for food.

Passing the cash register at the front—a towering black uncomputerized clunker—Courtney saw something in a glass case and stared. The case was between two sliding cabinets with cartons of cigarettes; her heartbeat accelerated as she peered inside. A small statuette, once a familiar sight in stores as well as houses from coast to coast, had drawn her attention. She hadn't seen one like it since her girlhood: a plastic icon depicting the raising of the American flag on Iwo Jima, a crucial battle scene from the World War II Pacific campaign.

Rushing through the restaurant door into the chill, early Utah night, she almost ran against Bracken himself, who was counting a thick sheaf of bills. Payment, presumably from the sergeant for his food supplies. Bracken did not appear to notice her but Courtney, shivering, glanced back at him. She was tall for a woman but the restaurant owner made two of her.

"If Caull got the covert cooperation of his superiors simply to conceive Project Romulus as our finest body of fighting men ever," Richard was saying to Pardoo as Courtney approached, "I doubt that seizing the government is the only thing he intended to use them for."

Pardoo, squeezing the sack of potatoes on the floor in the narrow backseat of his jeep, didn't bother looking at either of them. "It wasn't."

"Then what—?"

The soldier whirled, his face against Richard's. "Suppose you tell *me* a few things? Like how you got wind of Romulus if you're only a civilian." His basso was edged with razoring menace. "I figured I had to try to scare you and the lady off, but you're still here, aren't you? And you're asking some very sensitive questions. Is it possible I've under-estimated my old C.O., *Mister* Grant?"

"*Let go of him.*" Courtney had seen the sergeant's large hands moving up, locking in the writer's lapels. Instinctively, she raised her purse, aimed it at Pardoo—and her hand was dramatically pointed inside it. "Instead of worrying about us, sergeant, maybe you should think about the musclebound Mr. Bracken. That cooperative Neanderthal. Or maybe you didn't see the Iwo Jima tribute behind his cash register?"

It grew dark on the single street of Sunridge and Pardoo's rumbling amusement issued from a field of snowy teeth. "That little statue is my surest guarantee that I can trust Rollo Bracken, lady. I guess *you* didn't notice the Purple Heart pinned to the shelf below that 'Neanderthal's' little decoration!"

"No, I didn't." Courtney kept her purse trained

on the man while Richard began to grin. "That surely means he served in World War II—and the Romulus men who are looking for you are under the control of an older man with permanent Army ties."

"Exactly my point." Pardoo, realizing he still gripped Richard, released him and smiled. "Bracken's an old non-com, like me. *Not* like Albert Caull."

"He's talking about what I was, earlier," Richard commented, realizing he hurt where Pardoo's strong hands had bruised his chest. He shoved Courtney's purse down, then kissed her cheek. Her face, dim in the oncoming night, looked perplexed. "That there are two kinds of regular Army and have been in every military service since time began. These fellows are the kind we've needed and may need again."

"Except Bracken's older and he didn't get his priorities mixed up, the way I did for awhile." Jackson Pardoo's lantern-jawed face formed a half-smile. "Lady, what kind of weapon were you holding on me?"

Courtney flushed. "My lipstick, sergeant. But it was loaded!"

All of them laughed and Pardoo leaned lazily against his jeep while she and Richard explained how they came to learn of Project Romulus. It took less time than they would have expected; nonetheless, it was December and they were both getting miserably cold by the time they'd finished.

Pardoo hadn't seemed to notice the dipping temperature. His veiled eyes trickled over them a last, ruminative instant. "Okay, you want to know what Caull meant to do once he'd trained all those kidnapped kids and planned a way for them to seize the White House? I'll put it this way. He's been the kind of officer from the start who doesn't care for the odds when the opposition attacks first."

Richard's mouth dropped open. "He's that crazy?" He saw that Courtney was similarly astounded. There'd been hints of this, yes; each of them had wondered if the bald man mightn't be capable of such a project. But Pardoo's confirmation was dazzling. "You're saying that once he succeeds in capturing the White House, he actually intends to make the *nuclear first-strike?*" Pardoo's eyelids blinked once in affirmation. "Well, then, what other uses does he have in mind for his battalions of mechanical men?"

"Those are good boys in some ways," the sergeant corrected him. Noiselessly, he moved around the jeep to drop into the front seat. "Caull has two uses for his special troops." Pardoo slipped a gleaming key into the ignition, paused. "First, when he's become acting Commander-in-Chief, he's not apt to find all the fellas at the missile silos immediately agreeable. So some of the Romulus kids got intensive training on the code system changeovers and the computer fail-safes within the individual silos. And now, once they've replaced the troops on regular rotation, Caull's kids can handle the whole operation."

Replaced the troops, Courtney reflected, staring distastefully at the bulked shadow in the small vehicle. *One day I'll start vomiting euphemisms.*

"After the strike, then," Pardoo went on, "and after the enemy's expected retaliatory strike, the Colonel's troops will, in part, become a peacekeeping force. Deployed to all the major centers of survival throughout the States."

"For 'peacekeeping,' " Richard grunted, standing above the jeep with his heart pounding, "read something like 'quelling the looting of the hysterical survivors.' "

"He must be utterly mad," Courtney said from the other side of the vehicle. "The loss of life, here *and* there—it'll be incalculable!"

"Wrong again, lady; not incalculable." Pardoo started the jeep's motor. "Because he's calculated it every day with his own sophisticated goddamned hardware. The Colonel is one pragmatic bastard. Lady, the losses you call 'incalculable,' Caull sees them as acceptable."

Richard realized with a sense of personal loss that Pardoo meant to leave them. His mind raced, searched for a way to reach him. "He figures we'll have more people surviving?"

"Exactly." Pardoo nodded. "People, functioning industry, buildings, enough unpoisoned farmland—everything but communication. And men in command never give a damn about letting ordinary folks know what's happening."

"When you've led a fully disciplined life yourself," Richard said thoughtfully, "you think of survival *as* survival. Simple, basic, rudimentary."

"Caull's his own big hero," Pardoo agreed. "Prides himself on his logic and cold common sense. A long while back, he stopped seeing raw totals, saying they were emotional *obstructions* preventing a leader from seeing the facts. He reads *ratios*—ours versus theirs. And he believes the one chance for peace comes after our first strike, when this country's alone at the top. In charge of humanity."

"We don't have the *right,*" Courtney began.

"But it makes a weird kind of sense," Pardoo murmured. He shrugged. "Most people pressed against the wall will opt for some kind of survival. And when even that is threatened—by the promise of

another rain of our state-of-the-art ICBM's—
chances are the remnant will fall into line."

Courtney glanced at Richard, thinking frantically.
He *mustn't* drive off! "What about the lesser
powers with nuclear capability—those Caull didn't
bomb? If *we've* started World War III, what makes
him think we won't be hit by one of the smaller
nations? Even by our former allies?"

"He counts first on preparation, second on shock
and surprise." Pardoo's coolly lucid discussion
abruptly became angry, emotional. "The bastard's
thorough. He's handpicked an elite squad within the
Romulus command. Guys who don't even know
they've been selected. Each member of that
squad will lead another team of regular Army
personnel to the hot spots. To 'inanimate,' as Caull
likes putting it, any opposition to the new American
rulership of the world."

"That's insanity!" Richard struck his fist on the
jeep fender. "A squad of men can't just show up and
take over another government! It's suicidal to
consider it."

"Which is why those soldiers chosen for the elite
squad haven't been told about the honor awaiting
them." Pardoo impatiently gunned the motor. His
voice fell to the level of a whisper. "I learned some-
time back that the elite squad is planned as nothing
more than a distraction. To furnish another surprise
attack and act as a stalling tactic. When the invaded
foreign power turns its attention to the squad, Caull
and the new troops he's installed at the missile
bases have the time to reprogram. To center what
ICBM's are left on each of the nations that are
otherwise ready to put up a fight."

Courtney, despite her vast experience in covering
news, found herself trembling before the enormity of

what she was hearing. "Which means that the Colonel's finest troops will be ordered to die, either at the hands of foreign security forces protecting their own leaders, or when Caull orders a strike to prevent them from disavowing American rulership."

"Grant, here, called it right. So did I, and a bird named Wayland, who also took off because he'd had a bellyfull. It's a suicide mission." Pardoo glanced at them, striving for a smile. "Who knows? The CIA seems to have controlled a government or two and these kids are perfectly prepared. Wayland and I saw to that."

"We met Wayland." Richard locked his fingertips on the door frame of the jeep. "Too late."

"They found him?" asked Pardoo.

Richard nodded. "And slaughtered him, piece by piece."

"Then I'm probably next." The sergeant shifted gears. His expression, instead of displaying fear, showed a flicker of resolve. "Go home. I got work to do."

Then he spun away, red tail-lights glowing like fireflies in formation. There was no license plate on the jeep, Richard observed, crouching in the Sunridge street. "Dammit, we needed him!"

"Come on!" Courtney was running.

"Where are we going?" He followed at a trot; it was drizzling winter rain and his leg ached with each step. "What're you doing?"

She darted inside the Skylar car, shouting, "Get in!" Richard saw her thrust the key into the ignition as he fell in next to her. "We'll follow him back to his cabin!"

Smiling admiringly, he struggled for balance in the seat as she floored it. Sunridge's handful of buildings flashed past in the gloom like frames of an old black-and-white film. "You still think we have a chance against Caull, now that we know how thorough—and how mad—he is?"

"We *must* have," she replied grimly, pointing to the two crimson lights materializing in the automobile's high beam. "Richard, it's not just Mark now, you know? It sure as hell isn't my story! It's up to us now, everything is in our hands! But we can't manage it without help from somebody who understands the way Romulus is set up!"

Abruptly, the sergeant threw his jeep off the main road and down a narrow lane into the trees. He'd done it so abruptly Courtney overshot, had to put the car into reverse and squeal backward until they could find the path Pardoo'd taken. "There!" Richard cried, bouncing off the door as Courtney swung the much heavier vehicle between a scrub oak and several dark clumps of bushes. Ahead, he saw, Pardoo had switched off his lights. But the sergeant had worn down the grass and weeds enough to leave a faint impress and Richard, barking directions, urged them on—

Until they were almost atop the jeep, charging toward it—and Jackson Pardoo, waving his arms frantically, was out of it and perilously close to the tiny vehicle.

They reeled to a halt two inches from jeep and man. Instantly Richard realized Pardoo was swearing at the top of his voice. The passenger door flew open and, to Richard's amazement, he found himself snatched bodily from the seat and flying, ramming his shoulder into the earth yards from the car.

"*You fucking idiot!* I've got half a dozen charges planted around here, all the way to my house! You almost drove right *over* the first one!"

The writer peered up at the athletic figure heading determinedly toward him and tried not to flinch. "My God, man, you've got mine-fields?"

"Well, they're not quite that exotic. But they'll do, for homemade stuff." Pardoo easily hauled Richard to his feet. "Don't go thinking I saved you because I cared about you." He glared back at Courtney, who was threading her cautious way toward them. "A blast'll make a pretty respectable cloud-cover and I don't wanta tip my hand to the Colonel. The sound'd have his troops here in minutes!"

Richard looked around. Scarcely visible above the trees, mere threatening smudges in the drizzling rain, the cliffs seemed imposing, alert. He looked at Pardoo. "Why do you have to be so damned macho?"

"I'm not. Macho wants you t'believe a man is tough. I don't care diddly whether you believe it or not but I sure as hell can prove it if I have to!"

"You can't possibly let us enter that base by ourselves," Courtney told him.

"Just watch me!" Pardoo gazed away, clearly dismissing them. He had his hands thrust forward, parting the branches interlocking two aspen.

"Jackson, dammit, tomorrow night is Christmas Eve!" Richard, dusting himself off, was desperately trying a man-to-man approach. "You're an intelligent, experienced NCO and you know everything about the Romulus base—Caull, too. It's clearly your duty to help us stop them, at least stall what happens tomorrow."

Pardoo started up the steep incline between the trees. "Don't try your mothering patriotism on me, Grant," he growled, climbing. "I've spent most of my life in service to my country. Now there isn't one military man I can trust to bail me out. And it's Jack, don't ever call me Jackson!"

Courtney trailed Richard, who persistently followed Pardoo. "That's why you need us too, Jack," she argued. "If Caull pulls it off, he can order every investigative agency in the country to search for you! He can chase you forever; he can kill you legally!"

There was no reply. Both Richard and Courtney tried to avoid the branches slapping back into their faces, felt the ground disappear into the blackness below. "I heard what you said back at Bracken's," Richard puffed. He was almost parallel to the earth now, leg throbbing with pain. "You said, when the Colonel succeeds. That means you're sure he'll take over the White House. I think you're wrong."

"Not that I give a good goddamn," Pardoo muttered without breaking stride, "but why's that?"

"Because it *can't* be that easy!" Richard snapped. "Even if part of the security and the Secret Service are on holiday leave, others are bound to have a dozen back-up methods for guarding the President."

"Oh, they *do*," the sergeant said flatly. "But that don't mean a frigging thing. Not when the fifty percent there knows how to disarm and deactivate the fail-safe systems, and half of *that* half works for Colonel Caull."

"You're implying," Courtney asked, gasping, "that Caull does have the Pentagon's cooperation?"

They had emerged from the hills and wood alike, Pardoo standing, the others struggling to their feet.

Courtney thought she'd never seen such a brown night-world, nor experienced such silence as they grouped together in the clearing. Ahead, seventy or eighty yards in the distance, she could detect the rough shape of an unlit rustic cabin. Overhead, closer, the rising cliffs were mammoth midnight palms which might close dark fingers suddenly, crushingly. She went nearer to Richard.

"Hell, I can't say how much help the Colonel has from the Pentagon. I'm just a sergeant and the bald man got close-mouthed about the details." His hard, lean features seemed camouflaged by the long shadows; but his cold, blue eyes, always fixed on unseeable horizons, as if working doglike in concert with his acute ears, were both troubled and newly reflective. "For a long, long time, he's been making a series of super cautious contacts, then working even more discreetly through them, once he's learned their private opinions, to try to hook even more brass." He looked curiously at Richard. "You served in Nam?"

Richard nodded. "I did okay."

"Then you understand that what Caull believed, back then, wasn't exactly an isolated opinion. The punks, pukin' religion and morality after sucking off Mom and Pop, stealin' dough for drugs, refusing to fulfill their duty, running off to Canada or burning their drafts cards and callin' us baby killers." He spat.

"Are you ignoring everything we know now about Vietnam, Sergeant?" Courtney asked gently.

"If you mean, did I forget it was like Korea, another war we weren't fucking allowed to win, I haven't forgotten. *That's* immoral, asking service-men to die just t'stall so us and the Commies have time to figure a way how to uninvent the atomic bomb!" Pardoo turned from her. "You two got into this recently. Like some little shit of a nation nosin' into a hundred-goddam-years war. Caull, he's had years; he's taken his own sweet time and he's had nothing else in the world to distract him."

"Nobody? Not a single human involvement?"
Richard asked.

Pardoo shook his head. "In some ways, why, I
guess Caull's the ideal soldier at the command level.
There are those around him who say he hasn't even
gotten older, he hasn't aged an hour, a minute—
since he started." Suddenly Pardoo began tromping
toward his cabin. "If his first-strike at the government succeeds, I'd bet my ass the military will
accommodate him. There'll be enough of the top
brass goin' along immediately, that what they say
goes. Then, well, it's falling dominos until everybody's in the bald man's corner!"

"You won't join him, you thought for yourself and
left!" Richard grabbed Courtney's wrist and they
hurried after the lean figure. "And *I* wouldn't have
gone along, when I was a G.I.!"

"That's more bee-ess, Grant." Pardoo was
crossing gravel now, the crunching sounds nerve-
wracking, like snapping bones, on the still plateau.
"If an officer you had respected had informed you a
new government was coming in twenty-four hours,
you'd have busted your ass to follow orders—because you *had* to."

"With your testimony," Courtney said, "added to
what we've found out, we can try to reach some key
congressman!"

"It's too late for that," the sergeant called. "And
I doubt that one senator in ten would believe it was
even possible, even after he heard the facts."

"Then it's up to us to stop them," Richard insisted.

Jackson Pardoo, spinning, jabbed his index
finger, hard, against Richard's chest. They'd
reached the cabin and Pardoo's back was to the
three steps leading to a frail wooden porch. "Us? I
told you to count me out, and this is as far as you go.

Because if you try to follow me into my house—if you even fail to walk *precisely* where I walk— both of you are goners. Blown to kingdom come. And *I'm* going inside!"

"Then why did you say a word to us back at the restaurant?"

Courtney's question halted Pardoo after he had carefully mounted the steps. He didn't turn. "Maybe I had to talk you out of it. You looked like decent people—the kind I thought I'd volunteered to protect, a long time back—and maybe I wanted to feel like I'd saved *somebody* from Caull. Or maybe I've just got a bellyfull of casualties, real and those I keep seein' when I try t'sleep."

Richard stared at the older man's slender back, the slouched shoulders and knotted fists. It was beginning to rain again and fat drops were splattering against the winter earth with deadening finality. "You know we have to try, Jack," he said softly.

"Nobody has to try the impossible." Heavily, deliberately, Pardoo turned on his unpainted porch to face them through the dark brown drizzle and he looked suddenly aged, emaciated, in the dim and shifting light. "You'll never get through the front gate, at Romulus. Not alive. If you try it from the cliff overlooking the camp, you'll either fall and kill your silly selves—or worse, you'll be outlined against the wall of that cliff like a couple of god-damned flies stickin' to flypaper. Give it up, okay? Find somewhere safe, if you can; stay there. Who knows? Maybe us old Army types are wrong, Grant, and that bald sonofabitch offers us our only hope for world peace." White teeth flashed in a sad, sardonic smirk. "If you like livin' in a graveyard."

"I'm coming up," Richard said, starting toward him.

Pardoo jabbed his finger and crouched in front of the cabin door. "I wasn't lyin', Grant! It'll *blow!*"

Richard slowed down but continued walking. "Those kids—our *sons*, Jack; yours and mine—they haven't done anything criminal up to now. They're just victims, like everybody Caull touches."

Pardoo squatted on his haunches, observing Richard's approach closely and speaking in a hoarse whisper. "You're already nearer than I'd figured anyone would make it. But it's blind luck, Grant, and blind luck runs out fast."

"I'm coming up too, Jack." Courtney walked toward Richard, fearlessly.

"*Dammit*, lady, d'you know how these things *work?*" Pardoo was sweating. He gestured at Richard. "He's a little guy, maybe that's why he's got so close. But goddammit, weight . . . *pressure* . . . that's what sets those devices *off!*"

Courtney nodded, blankly, moved a foot closer.

"There's time to get help for the boys, Jack," Richard said. His toe gingerly probed the lowest step. Then he froze, terrified; he'd sensed vibration. "For all the young guys, guys like we were, Jack, once. Except they've never had a Pop or Mom or even a girl-friend. Jack, they're the *future* if there's going to be one."

"I'll say that much." Master Sergeant Pardoo stood, pointing. The finger shook. "If you both stand on any of the three steps *at the same time* . . . why, that'll *do* it."

"Richard's right, Jack." Courtney, a foot behind Richard. She saw the way he moved, in slow motion, like a halfback in instant replay. She saw him shift his weight as balletically as possible, till it hovered above the lowest step. "Once those young guys go to Washington with the Colonel—once they're all implicated in an attack on the White House—

they're out of our reach forever."

"They stop being victims and become equally responsible with Caull." Richard moved up. Knees bent, quivering, he stood on the first of three steps leading to the porch. "Your boy is on that 'elite squad' you mentioned, right, Jack? Caull picked him, correct? Well, when they've attacked the federal government itself, they'll be traitors. All of them. They'll be executed." Richard stretched out his hand, and smiled. "Hold on, Court. I think it's going to really come down now!"

"*Damn* you." Pardoo spoke quietly. He turned to the front door, unlocked it. "Let's talk it over then. Maybe there's a way."

"How d-do w-we . . . ?" Richard whispered the question, still holding Courtney's hand. Her knee was bent; gamely, she was ready to join him on the step.

Jack Pardoo turned up an oil light he found inside the cabin. His face was yellow in its reflection as they gaped up at it. "Hell, the steps aren't mined; nothing out there is!" He smiled at their surprise, especially at Richard's expression of dawning fury. "Where in hell would I get explosives like that? But I had t'find out what kind of stuff you were made of. C'mon in."

26

"One of the main reasons the Colonel and Wayland chose this particular Utah location, twenty-some years back, has to do with its own peculiar charms." Jack Pardoo gave them a sardonic smile, golden in the illumination from his nearby oil lamp. "It's at the base of the range of jagged cliffs higher than hills but not as tall as mountains, and it faces a heavily wooded region. The boys can practice climbing—I experimented with that aspect of training, as much for conditioning as anything—but they can also spot anybody trying to climb down into the base. In addition, that fairly sheer wall of rock runs the entire width of the woods with *no* ground breaks and that makes it still easier to keep secure. Even so, we worked out a schedule of constant patrolling right along that perimeter and we always have a squad on bivouac in the woods under covert, or camouflaged, conditions."

" 'We?' " Courtney asked. She was sitting in the one bonafide chair in the sergeant's cabin. Suddenly she smiled. "Maybe we should have determined for sure whether you're entirely freed from Colonel

Caull's influence.''

"For God's sake, lady," Pardoo grunted, exasperated, "if I wasn't, you'd both be standing before the
C.O. right now. Or dead."

"Fantastic!" Richard exclaimed. "Wonderful!"

Pardoo and Courtney turned their heads to squint
at him. Richard was sitting silently on the wooden
floor, as if sulking, back against the wall, and only
his thoughtful, shining eyes were clearly visible in
the cautious, intentional gloom of the cabin. The
place had been abandoned for years when Pardoo
found it and he'd done nothing with the cabin except
make it functionally livable. Perched on the edge of
a three-legged card table supported by a stack of
kindling, the sergeant raised a brow in question.
"What's fantastic and wonderful, Grant?"

"I'm not sure yet. Toss me another sandwich,
Jack, I'm still famished." He picked it dexterously
from the air. They'd helped Pardoo bring in his
supplies and he was finding the lukewarm burgers
Pardoo'd prepared the repast of his lifetime. "That's
just one of the reasons Caull chose this site, you
said. Tell us another."

"Well, most people in the state don't even know a
natural clearing existed, where the Colonel
constructed the base. So there wasn't the usual
traffic and commotion that goes on when you clear
away a whole woods."

"I can't imagine why they wouldn't know it's
there," Courtney put in, munching.

"Weren't you listening when I told you about the
only way you can reach it?" Pardoo demanded.
"Besides that, they thought it was part of the Great
Basin which is mostly semi-desert. By alternating
the men he occasionally sends into Sunridge for
common supplies, always dressed in civvies, Caull

makes 'em look like tourists, young folks just passin' through." He wiped his hands on a scrap of paper, nearly daintily. He'd had only one sandwich. "It's goddamned hard to keep a whole town from knowing there's an Army base as near as Romulus is, but that's just what the Colonel's done."

"You sound as if you admire him," Courtney remarked.

"That's because I do, lady." He stared levelly, frigidly into her eyes. "Colonel Albert Caull's the most knowledgeable commanding officer in all my experience. I'd follow him into battle anywhere, except . . ." Pardoo let it trail off.

"Except against your own government, right?" Richard glared at Courtney, both because she seemed to make no effort to understand the military mind and because Jack Pardoo was clearly a man with a decisive and volatile temperament, and one who had been on his own, alone, far too long to remember good manners. The wrong word could change his mind about assisting them. "What if land developers ventured into—no pun intended— this neck of the woods? Or farm types?"

"Low probability, Grant." Pardoo added, dryly, "It ain't exactly Salt Lake City around these parts. Only people around here to try out for the Mormon Tabernacle Choir'd be bobcats and bears, mule deer, cougars and coyotes, wild geese and ducks! As for farming, well, Utah's almost entirely dependent upon irrigation. Less'n four percent of the land area is fit for farmin'. Winter wheat, that's just about the only crop that'll mature and most of the fertile land lies to the *west* of the Wasatch Mountains." The flat planes of Pardoo's long face were shadowed as he reached down to pick up his old canteen. He'd never drunk anything from it but water, which he now wallowed around in his mouth, studying Richard Grant. "Folks wanting to farm automatically bypass this region. You've seen Sunridge, Grant. It's practically a frigging ghost town."

"If we close down Romulus," Richard said with a flash of his old humor, "the good folk of Sunridge'll be out of business overnight and never know where the action went."

"I think that's an acceptable loss," Pardoo growled. "If it happens."

"You don't think we have much of a chance, do you, Jack?" Richard inquired.

Pardoo got up, ignored his guests to refill his canteen from a water bag at the rear of the room. "About as much chance as if we rode right up to the base gates and demanded to see the Colonel." Head cocked to the side, he glanced back at Richard. "Which is what you were thinkin' when you were making all those happy goddamned sounds a few minutes ago."

"Not exactly, but close," Richard murmured. He was beginning, he thought, to like this hardbitten old bastard. In the city, you'd call a man like Jackson L. Pardoo "street smart." What, Richard mused, did you call him out here? Survival smart, or perhaps slaughter smart? He close his words with care as he watched the master sergeant return to his rickety perch on the card table. "What *is* the procedure when somebody drives up to the Project Romulus gates, Jack?"

"Never happened." Pardoo crossed his legs without looking away. He added, pointedly, "Never will." Then an afterthought made him shrug. "Well, the Colonel and certain special squads have left and come back."

"What happens then? Surely there's some kind of S.O.P."

Pardoo watched him narrowly. "There are two guards on duty at all times of the day and night. One stays inside a small post with phone lines to the CP. One goes out, armed, to stop the approaching vehicle while the other trooper keeps an M-16 centered on the car. The man inside relays the information about the persons in the vehicle to determine clearance and, if it's okay, the trooper who went outside hops on the fender and rides the vehicle to the destination cleared for it."

"Could we get up a head of steam," Courtney asked, "and simply rush past them?"

"Yes, ma'am." Pardoo looked into his canteen, then up at Courtney. "Until the men at the gate detonate the charges your car rides over. No bullshit about *those* explosives, Miss Rankin; but they aren't pressure bombs."

"Thank you for the intelligence, Sergeant," Courtney replied frostily. "And it's *Ms*. Rankin."

"No problem, ma'am." Pardoo grinned impudently at her. "A-OK, *Ms*. Rankin."

Richard, still thinking it through, swallowed the last of his sandwich and innocently cleared his throat. "Jack, is it still accepted that a surprise operation begun at night has the best chance?"

"Generally speaking." Cautiously.

"In darkness, a civilian vehicle driving slowly, but coming out of nowhere, could catch the gate guards napping. Right?"

"If it hadn't tripped certain wires on the path leading in from the woods."

"And the location of those certain wires is something you know?"

"Of course! Spit it out, Grant." Pardoo jumped up, hands on hips. "It's damn near oh-three-hundred hours and sack-time is essential to an operation like this."

"Courtney here has reminded me often enough that, as a member of the press—the *Washington* press, at that—she enjoys certain privileges other people lack."

"Not privileges," Courtney said quickly. "Reporters, columnists, journalists in general tend to be immune because other people want to use us."

"And a smart military man like Caull would know how arrogant you journalistic types are!" Richard rose, kissed Courtney's offended nose, and faced Pardoo. "What if I buy a camera tomorrow, in Sunridge, and pose as Courtney's photographer? She shows the guards her I.D., casually says I'm Rich Grant, her lensman."

Pardoo stared disbelievingly at Richard but held his peace.

"Then she tells the guards her D.C. newspaper has learned something about Romulus through a source at the Pentagon, and we want to interview the C.O., take some pictures."

Pardoo's laugh was uncontrollable, harsh. "You'd be the last people in the fucking *world* the Colonel would permit inside. News people, capable of blowing the whole operation just when it's ready to culminate!" He shook his head. "Besides, Grant, they'd have photos of both of you posted with the gate guards, and those kids are sharp, baby, they'd recognize you immediately!"

"You're absolutely right," Richard said.

Jack Pardoo's mouth dropped open. "They'll pretend to accept your story," he said, wonderingly, "while taking you straight to Colonel Caull!"

"You got it," Richard nodded, rubbing his hands together briskly. "The device with the cameras and Courtney's press card is what they call a hook in book-writing, a maguffin in movie-making. I don't *want* them to buy our story so we won't even *disguise* ourselves!"

"Let me think a second," Pardoo grunted, pacing. "The Colonel knows you're on the way. The guards will be looking out for you, your pix all over the base. But they'll expect you to try to *sneak* onto the grounds—not be fools enough to *roll right up to the gate!*" He turned back to Richard with an appreciative smile. "You must be a helluva writer, Grant. Or maybe the military lost somebody slick when you didn't re-up!"

"From you, Jack," Richard said softly, "that's my finest praise. My best review."

"What about me?" Pardoo's excitement was breaking free but his disciplined caution was equally aroused. "They sure as hell know *my* mug and they'll also know I wasn't so dumb as to make believe I was somebody else."

"This is the one place my plan could fall through," Richard said tensely. "If a vehicle they don't recognize shows up, will they search it thoroughly or just go by the instructions from headquarters detachment?"

"As I said before, Grant, nobody's ever showed up but expected personnel. The military." Pardoo looked worried. "I dunno; it's a gamble. Call it fifty-fifty."

"Right, then you go onto the post inside the trunk of our car, holding it down in case you have to get out fast. Armed as heavily as you can be, of course."

Pardoo put out his hand. "It could work. It *should* work, but it'll be close. Look, we arrive at eighteen-hundred hours when most of the men are in the mess for supper. They'll be excited as the devil, thinking about the mission. Regular duty's done for the day and the darkness will help, just as you suggested."

"A detail." Courtney joined them, covering their clasped hands with her own. "I don't want to nitpick, gentlemen, I really don't. But once we do get inside—*how* are we going to stop them?"

27

Richard's myopic gaze again drifted, almost hypnog-
ogically, across to where Courtney lay motionless on
an old Army blanket Pardoo had spread for her on
the floor. Incapable of stopping a steady sorting of
ideas linked to the anticipated events of the next
frightening night, dramatically aware that this
might well be his last night alive, Richard was
approaching a level of quasi-consciousness in which,
he knew, the undiscriminatory cranial hemisphere of
mind-right took command of pragmatic, fact
centered mind-left. Some of the surfacing ideas were
brilliant, most were fantastically impractical. And
mixed with them were horrific, imagined images of
the bald man, memories of Molly and the girls (they
were standing on a precipice above a terrible, steep
chasm, smiling and waving at him) and sensual im-
pressions of the brilliant and beautiful journalist
with whom he'd nearly made love. Seeing her both
with his eyes and his inner vision, part of a phantas-
magoria of careening mental flashes also depicting
others, he asked himself if he loved her and knew the
answer was yes. How he loved her, and for how long,

he had no way of knowing then. But feeling
marginally aroused, then feeling the bite of winter
air stealing beneath the cabin door to mouth his face
and throat like some dumb arctic brute, raised
Richard nearer to consciousness, and present
memory.

Courtney was so stubborn, so courageously and,
to him, pointlessly independent that he was always
infuriated by her. Or so he felt now in the bleakness
of the sergeant's dilapidated house, moved by the
plight of womanhood. She'd refused the offer of
their laconic host to sleep on the cot in Pardoo's
"room," a rear section of the cabin whose line of
demarcation from the rest of the structure escaped
Richard. Pardoo'd known why she refused, too; his
angry, appreciative glance at Richard had said so.
Master Sergeant Jack Pardoo, even when he denied
it, breathed fiery, macho condescension, and he'd
made it embarrassingly clear that he doubted
Courtney's ability to get through a day without
masculine assistance. He'd intended his offer of the
filthy cot as his kind of gallant act, the sort one gave
to an infant, or handicapped person, and there'd
been no way she could accept it. Richard believed
Pardoo had known she'd decline.

Now, Richard noted without surprise, Pardoo
himself was similarly obliged to disdain the cot's
comfort under the pretext of standing watch.
Instead, confiscated Army rifle rigid on his bony
knees, he dozed fitfully in the abandoned cabin's
single chair. And Richard, not to be out-gutted, lay
upon his own O.D. blanket, several feet from the
unmoving and silent Courtney.

He glanced with mild longing toward the unused
cot, then back to Courtney, wishing he could see her
better; wishing a great many things. She was an

amorphous shadow to him but for a single, slender white arm, limp on the dark wooden floor between them. Transiently illumined by preoccupied moonlight from the curtainless window, her loosely curled fingers appeared delicate, fragile. It reminded him with cruel suddenness of another motionless feminine hand he'd come upon in Nam, during a lull in the fighting. Later, when he'd tried to tell Molly about the dead Vietnamese mother, she'd broken in to guess, with television bred insight, that the hand and arm were severed. He'd replied *No*, and frowned. Nor were the fingers curled upon the severed and smaller hand of a child. No, not that either. The woman had been perfectly whole, the front of her unmarked and blood free; there'd been nothing noteworthy about her for the network TV photographers to record for posterity, she'd just been dead. Youthful, petitely pretty, and dead. At the time, for Richard, that had been quite enough drama and its meaning had not escaped him.

No one had ever seemed to share such emotions, the few times he'd mentioned the dead mother. Eventually he'd quit trying to convey them to other Americans and had forgotten his feelings until now. Americans had seen dead women, their own mothers and grandmothers, neatly coiffed and impeccably gowned beneath soft mortuary lights, before; after a while you didn't take it so hard because it was the way of it.

The bald man, men like him, reached such acceptances sooner, with less initial drama. In Nam they'd referred to "body count" and rarely bothered with additional, mincing distinctions.

He glanced up at Pardoo, and with a rush of ferocity akin to nausea, suddenly resented him and everything about him. The sergeant's legs were

sprawled, one twitching; the booted toe of the other
foot nudged Courtney's hand and Pardoo, beginning
to snore, sounded simultaneously inquisitive and
plaintive. "Mf-f?" he asked, head thrown to one
side. "Mf-f," he said, insistently. The fly of his pants
was tented above Richard's prone head, like some
forlorn and forgotten outpost in the rocky ledge of
an insurmountable cliff.

Courtney's fingertips touched his own. He
spasmed; thoughts invaded, reality rushing to get
in. He felt surprise, seeing his own arm out-thrown;
but when his fingers instinctively closed, grasping
hers, she slid her whole body without sound over the
chill space separating them and her mouth moved
on his, tasting. She did not so much kiss him as move
on, tasting his cheek, ear, neck; and when her hand
pressed him Richard was amazed to learn his own
trousers were tented. Fleetingly he saw that her
eyes were wide; she looked obliquely into his as if
she, too, had almost dreamed but failed, and she
craved the justice of one real instant she'd made for
herself. He heard the soft metallic slither of his
zipper, felt himself spring warm and gladly free into
her trembling, squeezing palm, and drew the faded
Army blanket over her hand, her wrist, and over
him.

When Courtney returned to her own shadows,
seconds later, Richard closed his eyes in strange
peace, found them moist, and shuddered. Lifting his
head, knuckling his damp lids, he saw dimly Jack
Pardoo rising swiftly from his chair and rushing to
the cabin door. His motion had been crashingly
palpable, yet, Richard knew, barren of distinguishable noise. The fellow was outside so rapidly
Richard had no sensation of December wind coming
in. He focused, and saw that Courtney's back was

turned, her knees drawn to her chest. He spoke her name but only with his dry, unkissed lips.

Returning, gusting past Richard in the dark, Jack Pardoo had closed the door quickly behind him. Yet something achingly without warmth, something freezing, brushed against the faces of the unspeaking, wide awake people like the undone winding sheet of a spirit unacknowledged.

It was time. Jack disconnected the signaling wires in the road leading into the woods from the main highway, got into the trunk of the automobile and pulled the lid down. Richard's last glimpse of the master sergeant was of the steady, startlingly sane look in Pardoo's eyes, and the Army automatic clenched in his hand, across his heart. Richard's imagination conjured an aging, athletic Dracula vanishing into a casket, holding the wooden spike meant for his own unique murder. He hoped passionately that no one on the Romulus base held the mallet.

Sitting bold-upright in the front seat beside Courtney, Richard took the expensive camera he'd purchased in Sunridge that day upon his lap, restlessly slung the carrying strap around one shoulder. Rugged clothing they'd brought for this perilous moment remained in their suitcases, in Pardoo's cabin; instead of it, Courtney'd worn her own business outfit—an attractive but no-nonsense pants suit—and he'd settled, on Courtney's advice, on clean slacks, sports short and jacket without tie, a light meter and some pens and pencils in the pocket, plus his mussed car coat. Since they'd left the unfinished petering out lane Pardoo'd described and obeyed Pardoo's directions for finding the command post gates, Richard had found his burgeoning terror taking the form of temporary confusion.

By the time Courtney cried *"There!"* and pointed, indicating a ten-foot-high cement block structure and some path-blocking obstructive rods crossed like the skeleton arms on a poison label, he was finding it hard to remember that they needn't convince the guards of their story that they were there on an ordinary assignment from her newspaper editor. Once she had shown them her identification and they'd had the chance to match both her name and her face with the poster presumably mounted inside the guard post, it would mean either that they would be taken directly to headquarters—

Or executed, on the spot.

"Would you relax a little?" Courtney whispered, nudging him hard. She appeared unbelievably comfortable, confident, and he took heart from it. If men couldn't be macho any longer it was nice if the women would be. "You're here to take pictures of a decorated military hero, not to witness an electrocution."

"It isn't the witnessing part that worries me," he said brightly, not in the slightest intending a quip. Abruptly he realized that the high beams of their automobile were boring deep into the base, and Richard had a glimpse of low cement block buildings with a distinctly military ambience. What they lacked, however, was any logo identifying the United States Army. One, he thought, had an American flag whipping in the bitter breeze. He made out an oval patch of bare earth which he assumed to be a parade ground or one of the areas in which the Colonel conducted exercises.

But there would be no exercises, no parades, no

practice after this evening. Night was already coming fast, the night of Christmas Eve, and the sky would not be filled with eight reindeer and a sleigh driven by a jolly, bearded old man, but by Army helicopters or jets.

Courtney braked to a squealing stop in front of the roadblock, and briskly rolled down her window. Already she was waving her press identification beneath the nose of a tall, uniformed youth who'd stepped swiftly from the guardpost, doing his best to conceal an expression of surprise. *So far,* Richard thought wildly, *so good!* He'd been so deeply lost in thought that he hadn't heard what Courtney said, but he raised the gleaming camera in his lap as the guard beamed his flashlight into the automobile's interior. "Rich Grant," he said with a sureness that surprised him. He grinned at the blinding light as it moved to his face. "Lensbug extraordinaire! Tell the big brass to put on their Class A's, break out the limburger and get ready to say Cheese!"

The light blinked off, retreated. Courtney glared at him. "I didn't mean for you to relax that much!"

"Look," Richard whispered, "the guy inside. He's showing him something!" He stopped speaking as both troopers in the post gave them surreptitious stares. Fixing his lips ventriloquially, Richard muttered, "I think they've made us, Fore-Court! It's over the ten-second line in a fast break for a dunk— and we're the ball."

Both uniformed youths came to the side of the car. "This base is sealed to civilians and all personnel without the highest clearance." The closest one, sounding as if he'd switched on an internal tape recorder. Now he was pacing the length of the car, restively, aimlessly tapping the sides of it with his massive flashlight. He stopped by the trunk.

"Some big shot at the Pentagon leaked it,"
Courtney called, putting her head halfway through
the rolled down window. "Let's get with it, kid!
Check it out with the bald man if you have any
doubts."

Each uniformed man gawked at Courtney, then at
Richard, who realized he was beginning to perspire
heavily. It was as if Courtney had addressed the
College of Cardinals and referred to the Pope by his
first name; or worse. The soldier beside the trunk
returned at a deliberate gait, inclining his head to
the other. "*Do* it," he said; then, folding his arms
across his chest, he watched each visitor with stolid,
expressionless scrutiny.

The man inside gripped a phone receiver, listened,
paused to say something pointedly to the man at the
car; his words were barely audible to Courtney and
Richard. But Richard guessed the message *sotto
voce* for Courtney. "Level B Alert," he said, and
watched for the other soldier's reaction.

But the trooper near them remained impassive,
keeping his arms folded, and again growled, "*Do* it."
Inside the post, the youth did two things: he
activated the electronic lifting of the roadblock and,
while the bars climbed ponderously into the air, he
came outside and lightly sat upon the fender of their
car.

The fact that he'd unholstered his side weapon
and now kept it in one hand was presumably meant
to appear routine. Unfolding his arms, the senior of
the two troopers lowered his head, peering in at both
of them. "You have four minutes with Colonel Caull.
Private Charles will take you to him." He paused.
"Proceed slowly and watch him for hand signals."

Courtney nodded and the car moved forward. At
once, the youth perched as observer on the fender

motioned sharply for Courtney to slow her speed.
We've done it! thought Richard, squeezing Courtney's leg in his excitement: But her expressionless
glance sobered him. They'd done nothing but get
inside and the rest of the plan was anything but fool-
proof. Point of fact, he reminded himself as the
command post's flat, beetlish structures loomed in
the car's high beam, it might be full of loopholes.
Fatal ones.

All you could say for the plan was that it was the
one the others hadn't shot full of holes.

After passing the gate, getting on the base,
Pardoo was to judge how deeply they'd penetrated,
then slip from the trunk and make his way a short
distance to the Romulus generator shack. This
wasn't the first time a government's covert military
operation had not wished to utilize power from a
sovereign state. Once at the shack, Pardoo was to
kill all the lights. They could delay Caull's departure
with his special team for Washington, regardless of
their method of transport. The Colonel would have
to know what had happened, what might happen
next. Dousing the power would permit Pardoo,
who'd participated in the training of every troop on
the base and was therefore instantly recognizable,
to reach the bald man—and *kill him.*

That was the pivotal step, and the time when the
young soldiers' familarity with Jackson Pardoo
would become an advantage. Caull's major aide,
Wayland, had been slaughtered as a traitor. Wayland's replacement was a substitute, and one of the
few certainties of the plan Richard had evolved was
based on the kind of paranoia the bald man gave off
like some contagious radiation: Caull, Wayland, and
Jackson Pardoo were the only ones in command
whom the kidnapped troops had known, *trusted,*

—

always. In their bewilderment, according to Richard's plan, a Jackson Pardoo who vanquished Albert Caull would replace him—as their leader.

He saw Courtney in shadowed, bravely calm profile as she obeyed the soldier's hand signals— *God, could he be Mark?*—and added to his all-day rendition of hasty prayers.

Pardoo! *He was out of the trunk!* Out of the corner of his eye, Richard spied the sergeant through the rear window, emerging soundlessly from the distant side of the car's trunk. Compensating for the vehicle's motion, Pardoo had landed in an unwavering crouch with his arm outthrust for balance. Their eyes met briefly—or so it seemed to Richard, who wanted to applaud the oddly balletic leap—and then the writer's heart nearly stopped.

"There!"

Alarmed, Richard's head jerked forward. Charles, the soldier—presumably his first name—was *pointing* from his post on the fender.

But not at Jackson Pardoo. The boy was indicating a wide, two-story structure flying from beneath a roof overhang an oversized American flag. Richard's smile came and vanished swiftly. Only the faintest illumination showed from inside the building, as if some single, pulsing heart of strange light had been transplanted from a draconic source. Richard squeezed Courtney's free hand, for reassurance; hers and his. Then she twisted it away to strike the top of his hand, her gaze riveted to the rearview mirror. Biting his lip, Richard wriggled around on the seat to glance behind them.

Jack Pardoo's figure was dwindling with the creeping distance and poor visibility. Merely yards away from several frame structures set well back from the road, he was still crouched, still running.

But—four, five, *six* equally silent men, seemingly unobserved by Pardoo, were closing in on him—and there was no way for Richard to shout a warning.

Cool air rushed in; the car's overhead light went on. "Follow me, please," said a voice to Richard's back. Twisting, he saw the private had opened his door even as a second soldier had opened Courtney's. Each youth had a guest by the elbow, the touch light, steering firmly. *I think I could take this kid,* Richard thought, but followed Charles quietly, Courtney and the unidentified trooper from headquarters bringing up the rear. There were no lights in front of the gray two-story; it was still dark, and silent. It occurred to Richard that he'd have no way of recognizing young Mark Grant, if he were here, alive; that he had never seen so much as a snapshot of his own son.

They mounted four steps to the front doors of the building, Richard's sweat turning cold at the nape of the neck, lying against his spine like a dead palm. Then the private named Charles was holding a door wide. Richard stopped walking. "You from Utah, or these parts generally, son?"

An unreadable something flickered in Charles' sober brown eyes. "Guess you might say I'm a native of Utah, sir."

Of course. Perhaps Charles was raised, as a toddler, somewhere else; but Project Romulus—this drab, militarily businesslike slab of earth with its boring buildings and maddeningly unchanging strictures—was all the boy would know, in his life of harsh discipline. "Who do you think will make the NBA playoffs this year?"

"The NBA? I wouldn't know, sir." Charles' knuckles were white where his fingers gripped the heavy door.

"You wouldn't know about Adrian Dantley or
Darrel Griffith of the Utah Jazz, I imagine."
Richard controlled a sense of surfacing sadness.
"You're not married, I suppose?" Muscles around
Charles' soft mouth knotted; he said nothing.
"What kind of fiction d'you like, Private? No; make
that easier—what's your favorite TV program?" A
stare; no reply. "You a fan of 'Hill Street Blues'?"

Abruptly, Richard was nudged from behind.
Courtney, also, was off-balance and he saw the
impatience in the strong, adamant features of the
tall soldier at the rear. It was he who'd done the
shoving and Richard didn't care for the gleam in the
shining, healthy, hostile eyes. "Colonel Caull
granted you four minutes. He's not pleased when
he's kept waiting . . . *sir.*"

"Gotcha." Richard's head bobbed and he went
inside, saw Charles jump back in front of the procession; the tall boy held the door open, his hand above
Courtney's head.

It could have been a military building anywhere,
with its unfinished, transiently airy look, the vast
space passing for a lobby and a tentative, stenciled
information placard affixed to a wall. "This way,"
Charles stated, leading them to a flight of olive
drab, uncarpeted steps. Richard craned his neck to
see a few rooms close by with closed doors, each
bearing further stenciling, data for insiders in the
form of enigmatic numbers. He wondered where
everyone was, as Charles' heels clacked ahead of him
on the bare steps.

Second floor, exceptionally like the first at a
glance; there was no third story. And, "No Christmas tree anywhere I look," Richard announced
chattily to hide his fear, as they were urged up the
hallway. "No festive decorations to cheer our boys

away from home." He tapped the shoulder ahead of him, an inch or two higher than his own. "How d'you account for nothing Christmasy, Charles—or should I say Charlie?"

"Just Charles." The boy's stride was space-devouring. He glanced over his shoulder, expression almost friendly. "Afraid I don't know much about holidays, sir. Except they aren't very important."

Richard, camera jiggling against his chest, heart-beat rushing as they neared their destination. Their footsteps were unwelcome, obtrusive on the bare, narrow floor. "Better watch it, Charlie. Santa Claus doesn't bring toys to boys who think he isn't important."

"Who, sir?" Charles inquired without turning.

Off the corridor, rooms with open doors; Richard saw several uniformed youths as they hurried past, one man apparently in his thirties. All worked with unnatural quietness, none looked up despite the clicking heels. Suddenly, filled with the need to disturb their stoic assurance, to experiment, Richard chose not to continue marching obsequiously to their fate. He jumped from the procession, swept his camera's viewfinder before one eye.

"Now's as good a time as any to get a few pix for Perry White, our dear old city editor!" He winked at Courtney. "Right, Lois?" Turning, he focused upon a startled boy stooping before a file cabinet just inside the next office. "Smile, kid," he cried, "you're on Candid Camera!"

With daunting alacrity, the tall and impatient soldier was there, whiplike arm flailing, hand slapping at the expensive camera. It flew from Richard's hands and he yanked one back, gasping, throbbing pain in his wrist. The camera had struck

the cement floor hard and the noise clamored in the
almost deserted hallway. Pieces of it broke off, rolled
against the wall, the sound becoming a steady
clatter.

Outraged now, Richard with muscles tensed took
a step toward the tall soldier—

And a door at the telescoped end of the long
corridor slammed crushingly back, against the wall,
the reverberations rushing toward Richard as if the
perpendicular figure fulminating in the doorway had
burst the sound barrier. At this distance, the
soldier's darkly patterned camouflage suit, outlined
by viscous fluorescent lighting at his back, made it
appear that a patch of rugged jungle landscape had
been detonated from the earth and left to hang
suspended, hollowly, in mid-air. "What in *Christ* is
that racket out here, people?" Lithely, sounds
echoing toward Richard and Courtney, he moved
purposively forward. "I have specific orders that
nobody but personnel essential to the mission utilize
this floor prior to ETA! I demanded silence, goddam
your eyes!"

Courtney stood beside Richard, whose face was
haunted and terrible. "Colonel Caull?" It was a professional woman's voice, raised, faintly peremptory
and all business. "Colonel Albert Caull?"

It is *him,* Richard realized, momentarily trans-
fixed. The labyrinth had been solved at last and here
he came at them—the man who'd seized his son
more than twenty years ago, who had nearly driven
a young wife over the brink, who'd misshaped and
partly ruined their marriage . . . a military maniac
who'd *dared* to raise their child as the military's
own, who intended to become the federal government, and who yearned to place a world of suffering
humankind in nuclear jeopardy. Hard, then, not to

think of a man who thought the unthinkable as a truly monstrous thing; the fact that Albert Caull was his own Frankenstein's invention merely made it bleaker. Now the bald man approached them with no visible reaction, and nothing horned or scabrous to say what he'd become. Suddenly Richard's thrill of curiosity overcame his fear as well as his rising rage, and he gaped openly as the officer drew within range.

His skull was indeed hairless; it caught little highlights from recessed illumination close to the acoustic ceiling. Lifting slightly, in an instinctive posture of his accepted superiority, it made Richard think of a bomb gently rising from a silo.

And Richard gasped. *I saw this son of a bitch before,* he thought. *The same colonel from the corridor in the hospital at Fort Christopher . . . the night Mark was . . . born.* Caull was just older now, his soft eyes buttery as he squinted first at Courtney and then at Richard.

"Oh, yes." He nodded as if remembering. "You're Rankin and Grant." Without another word, he executed a surprising about-face and trod back toward his office, gesturing with a simple, upraised waggling of fingers. "Get in here pronto, people! I don't have much time to dispose of this problem."

Richard was jolted into moving protectively ahead of Courtney. *Dispose* of it? He was on the Colonel's heels when they flashed into the office; fractionally late with the thought, it occurred to Richard that he might have vaulted upon the tall man's back, himself attempted to capture Caull. Broad-shouldered, the bald man was no physical titan; his vitality, Richard thought quickly, could be internally centured solely, not muscularly.

Then the realization of what a dark, pleasing joy it

would be to annihilate the ghoul personally made
Richard drop a step behind, shocked by the blood-
lust such men so quickly generated.

Neatly stacked papers lay in an out basket on a
desk bearing the nameplate 1st LT. BELDON-
WOOD. Beldonwood himself waited near the
colonel's almost identical desk, tapping a fountain
pen somewhat impatiently against a clipboard
clenched in his hands. Nothing about the
lieutenant's appearance was memorable, but this
must be one of the candidates for Wayland's post,
Richard realized. Differences of rank meant little
when one man stood so exclusively at the helm.

File cabinets grouped against one wall, steel
sentries wearing flowering plants. There was a
squat, unadorned bookcase; Richard ached to read
the titles of the books there.

Two flags, one that of the nation and one presumably that of Project Romulus or its military
designations were at another wall; between them,
where the President's affably smiling photograph
might customarily have been expected, was a green
chalkboard with the traces of partly erased chalk,
and a closed door through which a more private
chamber might wait. But nothing about this room
seemed different to Richard Grant from others he
had seen during his own service career; there was
never a poster or sign to shout MADMAN! or
KILLER!

All of which left as the sole incongruity the
apparel of Colonel Albert Caull: A camouflage suit,
in contrast with the standard dress uniform of the
adjutant, Lieutenant Beldonwood. *Why, then, apart
from the likelihood that he'll try to kill us,* Richard
wondered, *does something feel askew, slightly bent
out of shape and perfectly terrifying?*

"After all your trouble finding us and getting here, people," the Colonel said, rolling his eyes from Richard's face to Courtney's, "I wish I had more suitable, impressive quarters to show you. We've had damned few visitors over the years, damned few."

"I'm sure that's been your decision, Colonel Caull," she replied, producing a notebook and searching in her bag for a pen. She gave every impression of intending to interview him. "Now, if you—"

"Which should tell you someting, Ms. Rankin, that probably will astound you: this is a command base of the United States Army in every sense of the word, a training base at which the finest fighting men in the history of the organized military system have been arduously, well trained." His lids fluttered. "We're funded by U.S. taxpayers' dollars; we serve those taxpayers the best we can, and we're ready to protect the American citizenry. There are no fascists, no martinets here, no crazy people. Just U.S. Army troopers and officers doing a difficult, even thankless job to the utmost of our ability." Again the fluttering lids, a glance away, as if his feelings had been hurt. "No one asked either of you" —he looked momentarily at Richard—"to put your civilian noses into our military activities."

"That's the neatest apologia I've heard in some time," Richard said as lightly as he could. "I don't remember, though, my congressman voting for any bills related to the funding of such a special command. And"—he kept up the ruse—"there seems to be some question, back at the paper, about the nature of the men under your command— whether they volunteered or were somehow . . . conscripted."

"Give me a look at that clipboard, Lieutenant," the Colonel murmured. His gaze remained introspectively fixed on Richard. He had a way of craning his neck from time to time, registering the mildest pain. Was it an old injury, or a nervous affliction he enchanced? Now he looked away to scan something clipped to the board; he still had not sat nor asked his guests to do so.

Abruptly, Richard saw what it was that he found personally terrifying about Caull. At a glance, the bald man was no more imposing than his quarters. One might have expected such a creature to shout, stalk around the office, wipe flecks of foam from his lips—at least to be larger than "somewhat tall." Yet more middle-sized men of common appearance had acquired the reins of command than giants, historically. If you put humanity's most evil specimens beneath the microscope, they were usually average in every obvious way.

I'm short, Richard saw, *and Pardoo*—two more unlarge men who were trying to obstruct one more juggernaut of mad change.

Yet cocksure *drama* exuded from his despot, like sweat from his pores. One could believe that Albert Caull was so absolutely enough for Albert Caull—and required no other living thing—that it could be seen, spilling over; that the man's confidence in his manic magnificence disallowed dispute, demurral, defiance, even momentary disbelief. It was *godlike,* in its way, Richard perceived. His total certainty about himself evolved from internal dramas of misapplied conviction, and duty, and it became both contagious and infectious, if you let it. Richard filed his insights away, but just beneath the surface of his mind.

"I can give you no more time." Caull gave the clipboard back to Beldonwood. Did he believe he could apportion *time?* "Obviously, people, you have some notion of what's transpiring tonight. Obviously, I can't warrant intrusion; it's that simple." His eyes glittered, sweeping them. "I know who you are, why you're here, and it's not to interview me. Why don't we get on with your plan, your scheme, and dispose of the matter."

"Oh, I don't know." Richard slipped into his party face. "Why not wait and just be surprised?"

Courtney took cigarettes from her purse, turned frosty professional eyes to Caull. "Candidly, I am disappointed. You didn't even *search* us."

"One of us could be wearing plastic explosives," Richard quickly added.

Caull laughed. He gestured, at last, for them to sit. "I'm surprised you ever heard of plastine. But this won't wash, people. You're here to locate Mr. Grant's offspring; you'll be prudent. Besides," he glanced with some curiosity at Courtney, who slipped a cigarette between her lips with an insolent expression, "you were scanned electronically three separate times. Never mind where." Without lowering his chin, he looked down at Richard. "Why aren't you armed?"

"Your reputation for thoroughness, Colonel," Richard replied. "Seemed a waste of time." He watched the older man slide into the chair at his desk. "However, we *have* arranged a small surprise for you, the way a guest brings good wine"

"Of course, you have." Caull seemed appreciative. "You were a good soldier, Grant. And you wrote an intelligent book. So you must know that the definition of tactics, military-wise, is: moving forces in close proximity to enemy forces while regulating the use of troops or weapons. The tactical system is

built upon the bare bones of efficiency; you surprise
me by understanding at least three or four purposes
of tactical operations: Moving, finding, and guarding." He showed a trio of fingers. "You two
managed all but one of the four."

Richard borrowed a cigarette from Courtney, lit
it. "You know, I think I can tell you whose tactical
procedures you've used as the basis for your takeover plans."

"That, I doubt," Caull said, biting off the words.
"Who?"

"Frederick the Great," Richard said easily, and
was rewarded by Caull's swiftly concealed look of
surprise. "In the eighteenth century, Frederick was
first to realize that unannounced, quick maneuvers
based on total knowlege of the opponent's position
and strength gave him a chance to learn its weak-
nesses. Hence, Christmas Eve."

"Commendable. But in this century, Corporal, *all*
military strategy recognizes surprise as the means
of successful attack. Colonels S.L.A. Marshall and
Harvey Shelton said, 'This can be achieved by more
rapid movement to the area chosen'—that's set-up,
people—'by secrecy and concealment, by feints
toward areas other than that chosen for the attack'
—I believe *you* entered the picture at that point, Ms.
Rankin—'and by the adoption of unexpected lines of
operation.' "

Courtney watched him preen. "I'd forgotten," she
said softly, "the literal Greek translation for
strategy: the 'general art.' " *I can dispute with the
Devil, too,* she thought.

"But *he* is merely a colonel," amended Richard,
smiling at her and then the reddening Caull. "Or do
you think of yourself in still more rarefied terms,
Colonel?"

"Such as the Macadonian *strategos*, or *sematophylax*—brainy officers assigned to special missions?" Caull returned Richard's taunting glance. "Possibly the Roman *legatus*, Corporal? The rank which they finally had the common sense to create as the commander of all their legions?"

Richard beamed his sweetest, laziest grin as old knowledge came back. "Tell you the truth, Caull, I had in mind that bastardization of Latin that the Germans devised: *hauptmann*. Nicest translation of it is 'head man,' I think."

Caull, for a second, stared at him, blank faced. Something was moving ahead now in his tumultuous mind. "I'm going to inform you that your surprise is not going to happen. I told you, remember, that you'd succeeded with three of the four intentions of military tactics. The fourth, people—which is now doomed—is . . . *hitting*."

Courtney gasped but sought to hide her nervousness by relighting her stale cigarette. "I'd say that was a really awkward, unprofessional bluff."

"*Would* you." Caull waited a beat. "That note on Beldonwood's clipboard?" He sat up straight. "Sergeant Pardoo is trapped and his inanimation is momentary." His arm shot out; Courtney's cigarette was between his fingers. He frowned, said, "Aren't you aware these things can *kill* you, people?"—and crushed it.

He'd known they were behind him almost from the instant they'd crossed the road, but he had kept moving at the same pace. His mission, that was what counted. Stopping—engaging them—probably meant his demise, and that could not be allowed—at least, until Pardoo had extinguished the lights.

The problem was, he'd trained every one of them.

Not that it was a question of affection; it was that they *knew* what he was supposed to be thinking.

As Pardoo's foot reached the first of three steps leading to the generator shack, the lead men were diving for him—one high, at the shoulders, one low, tackling him behind the knees.

Pardoo's edge was that he knew they hadn't seen his face, recognized him.

The soldier aiming for the shoulders shot over Pardoo's head. He crashed, hard, against the unyielding structure. The man at the knees found only the step with the tip of his chin and was out of it, Pardoo no longer there. He ducked through the space between the top railing and foundation of the steps and, rather than being attacked by the remaining troops, he was already moving into full attack against the other four youths.

Pardoo's trained mind was cooperative as a computer. Because it was physically impossible for more than three to handle him at once and unlikely that more than a pair could grasp an agile, moving man, Pardoo ignored the fourth troop in line, focused all his attention on the two closest. Already estimating how long it would take for the man who'd flown over him to recover and mechanically counting seconds, the sergeant hacked one youth, vertically, the heel of his hand into the nose. He used the intentionally angled pitch of his body to swing one foot at the second man. A sound like a whisper told Pardoo he'd missed and he rolled headfirst in somersault, this time clubbing the second soldier with the full force of his boot heels.

Flash of regret: Where he'd struck the boy meant the boy was dead.

Soldier Three used that fractional hesitation to close in expertly. Pardoo said "Attaboy!" while he exchanged three, lightning-fast parries and plunged the braced tips of his right fingers deep into the pit of the soldier's belly. He'd learned what he was taught and his chin came forward only fleetingly; but it was enough.

As if falling, Pardoo flattened himself on the ground. Attacker One sailed above him a second time, landing in a heap. This time he came quickly to a roll and a crouch.

"*Sarge!*" he cried in surprised recognition.

Guard dropped, he was hit in the jaw as hard as Pardoo could punch.

That mercy, however, was a mistake; it had taken a split second longer to strike with the full weight of arm and shoulder than to have chopped, then pivoted for further confrontation. Now the last of the original six soldiers had his left arm wrested up behind the back as far as it would go. Promptly, the trooper made it go considerably farther. Pain, not surprise, made Pardoo shriek.

It also made him lethal.

Assuming the sergeant would faint, or yield, the soldier released the ruined wrist and stepped back to draw his side arm for the arrest. It didn't clear the holster. Jack Pardoo's lunging feet struck the youth's torso, instantly felling him.

His pain had caused Pardoo to miss the vulnerable lower belly by a foot. Regaining his feet, arm dangling uselessly, he saw from the corner of his eye that the trooper had pulled himself erect with commendable courage—

And that the younger was his son, Terry, half his face swathed in bandages.

The first slug from Terry Pardoo's automatic struck his father in the shoulder of the already disabled arm, spun him back, hard, against the steps leading to the generator room. Blood geysered. The sergeant, bracing himself, staggered but did not go down. Instead, he ran around, then up the steps, made it to the second one before his son's second slug—*the kid remembered; he isn't wasting 'em,* Pardoo thought with fierce pride—passed completely through the older man's left leg. *He don't know who I really am,* Pardoo thought, blinking away tears of pain. Getting to his knees, he crawled forward. "Hold it, Terry—hold up! Look, it's the sarge—and I ain't no traitor!" Kneeling, gripping the railing above his head with his working hand, he saw Terry's hand faintly relax. "Listen up, Terr, okay? I'm *your father,* kid! Your *dad!*" He chuckled and spat something metallic-tasting to the ground. "You *got* it now, Terry—yeah, *I'm your old man!*"

Terry Pardoo shot the deserting soldier full in the chest.

"I can't say I count smoking among my major concerns," Courtney whispered. "Now."

Caull exposed the wristwatch beneath his sleeve. It had a naked, mammoth look and its face was ringed by what resembled indestructible alloys. "You've used up the time you were allotted, people."

"Then you're leaving for D.C. shortly?" inquired Richard. "You and your team?"

The Colonel scrubbed at his bald pate as if shining it, suppressed a relaxed yawn. "Just me. Jesus, didn't you notice we were a little short of personnel on the base?" Just slightly, casually, he turned his head. "Beldonwood, assemble three-squad outside the door. They screwed up so badly in trying to make the select team, they can—well, they can use something special for them." His buttery gaze returned to Courtney. "Pardon the French. I was saying that more than two hundred Romulus troops were dispersed gradually throughout Baltimore over the past eight days. That's thirty miles from Washington."

Courtney's lips parted in surprise, shock. Richard, watching the lieutenant's quiet exit and hearing his footsteps echo hollowly down the hallway, was first to realize *why* Caull had ordered up his third squad . . .

"I leave to rejoin my men shortly," Caull continued. If anything, he was more relaxed, even playful, as he locked his hands behind his neck.

Gotta stall, play for time, think, Richard told himself. "You're flying?"

Caull nodded amiably. "Taking a small jet, to a private strip in Baltimore." It was as if an eighty-year-old man were bravely bidding adieu to his brash, young son and knew the odds of seeing the confident prodigal again were devastatingly against. A glance told Richard that Courtney also had realized the nature of the bald man's immediate plans. "A whirlybird'll meet me, drop me off at our indicated rendezvous point in the capital." He yawned, eyes crinkling in a smile. "Figures to be a smooth operation, people!"

"I suppose your jet could *crash,*" Richard said. He blurted it out and smiled as he stared at the Colonel's head. "Sorry if I put that rather baldly."

"Running out of delaying tactics, Corporal?" Caull asked mildly. "For your information, you haven't used up a minute that I hadn't intended for recreation, anyway. And because it doesn't matter what you know or don't know, I'll admit that the select team will simply abort the mission and await further orders should I suffer a heart attack, stroke,

or anything of the kind. But I'm A-1, people; never
been more fit. Where you two are concerned, I
apologize that there's no time for a court martial;
but you're civilians and it would come to the same
thing, anyway."

"My newspaper knows where we are, Colonel."
Courtney's confident, almost smug delivery of the
lie made Richard's heart sing with pride. "If I don't
check in, my managing editor'll have reporters over
this base like white on rice!"

"My, my goodness!" The Colonel laughed out
loud, almost charmingly. "A death-squad composed
of columnists, rewrite men and typists—coming for
me!" He gave Richard a man-to-man smirk and
slight wink. "I'm lucky that your valiant team of
op-ed and obit guerillas will discover this base—
deserted."

"Now you're bluffing," Courtney said, chin up.

"Nope! Lieutenant Beldonwood has orders to
dismantle the post the instant he learns we've
assumed command. Of the government. It's served
its purpose. The residue of troops remaining on base
will report to me in Washington."

Richard struggled to sustain the light, bantering
air while his mind raced. Despite the merry expression Albert Caull wore as he looked at Richard, a
certain bizarre signal passed between the two men.
It said, *I know you must try to capture or kill me
before the three-squad gets here and I don't blame
you. You'll have your chance.* Desperate, Richard
changed his approach. "Colonel, by what right did
you kidnap my newborn son? You stark-raving-mad
old bastard, who gave you permission to take all our
sons?"

"I didn't invent conscription, Grant," Caull
replied. " 'Our only aid will be derived,' the great man

said—'from drafting . . .' " Caull's brows raised challengingly. "George Washington made that statement in 1778."

"But there *was* no conscription until the Civil War," Richard argued, leaning as if passionately involved in civilized discussion. "Not in this country."

"Why are either one of you talking about the draft?" Courtney demanded. "These were babies—infants!"

"Miniature people," Caull snapped. "John Locke explained that a child's mind is a *tabula rasa*—a clean slate. Whatever is imprinted upon it as an infant stays."

"So that's your initial premise," Richard murmured. Distantly, he heard footsteps in the corridors snaking through the half darkened military building; many footsteps. "That's where you started."

"D'you recall, Corporal, how you wondered in what 'rarefied' terms I regarded myself? My position, I saw two decades ago, was like that of the great Carthaginian. Called upon to lead an army at a time of strife, he found his people, the civilians of his day, fat and lazy with successes of a time that had passed, never to return. With damned little support from his government, he bought the services of mercenaries and employed the slaves he took from Spain, France, and Africa as fighting men. George Fielding Eliot wrote that his triumphs 'were the product of a personal leadership' that was 'transcendent.' "

Richard looked at Courtney, framed the name with his lips. Looking back at Colonel Albert Caull, seeing the dreamy expression on his rather bland, hairless face, he whispered the name of the bald man's idol: "Hannibal."

And for the first time, Richard believed that the Colonel and his devoted troops would seize the reins of American government.

They heard the shuffling, impatient men on the other side of the door and the Colonel stood, his smile, his affability, banished. "That's it then, Corporal." He re-cinched his belt and rested his fingertips with surgical delicacy on the top of his desk. "Why don't you make your play and get it over with?"

The lights in the bald man's office and everywhere on the Romulus command post went out and the world turned to darkness.

Unaccustomed, marginal hesitation had caused Terry Pardoo to miss the heart and the slug hit high, to the left of Jackson Pardoo's right breast, throwing the older man onto his back and a few feet beyond the entrance to the generator shack. His skull had struck, knocked open the door. Dazed, hurt, his functioning hand groped on the floor, found something.

Then he saw that Terry had staggered up the steps and into the shack, after him, arms outthrust, his hands sharing a piece.

Jack Pardoo saw the youth rise above him. His head and shoulders were outlined against the undraped window and the face was featureless, a blank. The .45 was centered upon Pardoo's heart and no one could miss at such a range.

"Bastard," Terry choked it out. "You people taught me the world was the Colonel, the project, my skills. That's all I wanted." It was, Jack realized, a cleansing of sorts, a purification. "I don't *have* a dad—*Sergeant.*"

He takes after his mother's side, Pardoo thought,

firing his own automatic without decent aim.

Considering, his reflexes were still respectable. The single bullet pierced his son's right eye. The near wall turned red, as if a weary painter wanting to quit for the night had thrown a bucket of paint at it.

Moments later, *all* the lights in Jackson Pardoo's world went out.

28

Partly expecting the sudden oily flood of darkness, Richard capitalized on Colonel Caull's surprise, plunging over the desk at the man, hands reaching. He struck the bald man disappointingly low, round the waist; yet the tackle dragged Caull back into his chair and both men went tumbling over the back of it, hitting the floor with stunning suddenness.

Richard, younger, leaped to his feet and instantly groped for the Colonel's side arm. He was all but shocked when the weapon filled his hand as readily as if he'd tugged it out of his own holster.

Growing accustomed to the dark, Richard saw how fortunate he'd been in their fall. He'd landed on top; Caull had struck his alopecian skull on the pole from which the national banner rose. Caull, eyes shut, was at least dazed. Gaping down at him in moonlight from the window, Richard perceived the seepage of blood from the side of the man's cranium; and for a moment, Richard thought Albert Caull was dead.

Then the officer began getting up, eyes still closed, working his boot-clad feet beneath him and thrusting, groping instinctively for his desk and support.

Richard, startled and rendered indecisive, saw that Caull was virtually unconscious. But his iron resolve, his decades of passionate training—and the lifelong objective on which he had fixed his obsessive mind over twenty years ago—somehow enabled him to function. Richard felt awe. If those stolen boys whom he had considered robotic possessed an ounce of the perseverance and mad dedication Colonel Albert Caull could claim, they were vastly more dangerous than he and Courtney had feared— and the two of them would not get out of there alive, regardless of the gun he leveled at Caull. Killing him would not stop it. More, the youths were slaves to this awful man in much the same way vampires' victims were: because, physically, the Colonel had permitted them to sip from his own poisonous blood, his own dark force, and they had become one with him. Surely they were beyond even the love of a mere father.

But, *I never believed that nonsense*, Richard thought, suddenly slamming the toe of his shoe against the rising officer's shoulder.

Terrifyingly, Caull came up fast, furious, his face contorted with rage, black in the ill-lit room. Richard, however, was ready. He jabbed the man's automatic against Caull's forehead bruisingly, crouched to aim the weapon with both white-knuckled hands, his own heart wildly drumming. This mockery of a man had existed like a prize experimental rat. He'd treated life like a masterable, mad maze, and now he had simply seized upon the first ruse occurring to him, in an attempt to catch Richard off-guard. Caull's fury as he glared balefully up from a similar crouch was that of an infectious rodent kept from its triumphant reward. But which, really, was most guilty at the last? The cunning rat, or the self-perpetuating *Zeitgeist* which had endorsed and abetted the labyrinth's making?

"Set that chair up," he told the Colonel in a breathy whisper. "Sit in it."

"No, by-God I won't!" the bald man snarled.

When he took a step toward Richard despite the muzzle of the .45 at his head, Richard edged backward in rising alarm. "Damn you, Colonel, stop!"

"Why?" Caull did pause, momentarily. He was grinning. "Why should I do what you command when there are certain documents in my desk, orders for Carrjordan with whom I'm to rendezvous in D.C.? If I don't show, the papers promote him to full command—instruct him to fulfill the White House mission precisely as planned!"

"He's running a bluff, Richard!" Courtney exclaimed. She gripped a heavy bookend in her hands and was heading for Caull. "Remember your own writing! He's a megalomaniac, Richard, he'd never let anybody else command that mission!"

The bald man straightened, glanced sharply at the woman. "No civilian—especially a female civilian— would ever understand a military operation of this scope." He looked back at Richard and put out his wide hand, palm up, for the automatic. He looked pasty and sad, then, but the expression was quickly replaced by that of apparent pride. "You remember, deep inside, what it was like, Grant. You know that the mission is more important than any one man."

"If you keep coming," Richard said softly, "you'll leave me no choice. At least you won't get to see the awful things you've done."

"Watch closely, Corporal Grant," Caull said, smiling as he sidled forward from the shadows. He kept

one hand at his side but the other, which had been
outthrust, slowly rose until it was loosely curved
inches from his well-shaven cheek. For an instant
Richard thought with horror that the man meant to
deflect the slug from the .45—or catch it! Caull's
eyes glittered strangely. "Watch, and learn what
men such as I are by-God made of."

Richard squeezed his eyes closed and pulled the
trigger.

Darkness of a different kind engulfed Richard,
blacked out his mind and seemed to devour the automatic's report. He had a sensation of dizzying movement and then a peculiarly regenerative flush of
acute pain from the base of his skull to his waist.

Albert Caull was looking down at him, reaching,
big hands bigger as they became Richard's
universal focal point. One hand seemed briefly to
caress the side of his face but the other clutched,
fastened in the graying hair at the back of his head
and he felt movement again, finally saw that he was
being lifted into the air—too late to do anything
about it except remember, crazily, times when he
had lifted the infant Mary from her cradle and
marveled at how small and light she was.

Deafness, *sounding*—a thunderclap of it too great
to quibble with impossibilities, including the impos-
sibility of either missing Colonel Caull or failing to
kill him with the bullet he'd fired. From his own
bowels Richard seemed to hear a yowl of agony, and
when he tried to get control and strike back at the
uniformed man who was methodically crippling him,
he knew it was his own pain announcing itself.

Falling! Richard, as if from Olympian heights,
landed on the floor near the office door and knew
that Caull had dropped him and spun away—that
the scuffling had alerted the arriving men outside

the door, one of whom was pounding on it—that he
was no match for Caull and that the bald man could
have finished killing him, then . . .

He cranked his aching neck, turned his head.

Across the room Courtney appeared to be per-
forming a dance by herself. She was moving back
from the advancing Colonel, one hand waving
frantically as she tried to regain her balance and the
other, still gripping the bookend with desperation,
hitting out futilely at Caull. Richard saw fresh blood
issuing from the officer's bald head; to his horror, he
saw the smear like a lipstick slash across Courtney's
mouth and chin—and perceived, like a drowning
man surfacing a final time, that Albert Caull
intended to kill her.

"*No!*" Richard shouted, fully conscious.

Somehow he was hurtling himself over the
distance between him and the bizarre ballet.

He wasn't in time. Inches from them, he moaned
as he saw the Colonel lash out with one hand, feint
with the other and strike Courtney a second time
with the heel of the first hand. Then he was there,
furiously locking his bent arm around the bald
man's thick neck, intent on snapping it.

Caull stooped.

Richard reached consciousness in an anguished
planet of pain to see Courtney, cradling his head in
her arms, her full lips become some exotic red rose
and one eye closed—

Caull, unmarked, unarmed, smiling—his arms
folded across his chest in a relaxed posture that did
not conceal his pride—leaned against his desk. "The
men aren't to enter this room until I give the order.
Wanted to be sure you both were conscious. First."
He raised his arm to point at the .45 in the corner of
the room. "I'm disappointed you imagined I'd have

armed weapons in here with you people arriving."
His eyes were feverishly bright, the buttery pupils
boiling. "That traitorous shit Pardoo had enough of
my training in him to kill the lights but you can
make book that he's inanimated by now—especially
since his son happens to have been one of the men I
had posted between here and the gates." He looked
from Courtney to Richard, a mask of altered expression concealing his next words. "That was, as a
matter of fact, what gave me the idea."

What idea? Richard wondered. But he'd shut his
eyes; he was still trying to think of a way out for
them. With Pardoo's death, and Richard really
couldn't disagree with Caull's estimation, it was
surely over. What hurt was seeing in Caull's mad
eyes the awareness that they were beaten, literally
as well as figuratively. Ashamed because he knew
deep inside that even knowing what the Colonel
believed would not be challenge enough for him to
attempt another physical attack on the bald man,
Richard avoided Courtney's eyes. He felt smaller,
seeing how she did not weep from her own pain.
From beneath partly lowered lids, he saw the lights
on, again, reflecting off the Colonel's pale skull. It
wasn't even bleeding now.

The American flag, behind the officer's desk—
after tonight, surely, the bright stars would merge
as one, army-stenciled with Caull's initials. Soon,
only the red stripes would be left, dripping . . .

Sound of the door opening brought up Richard's
gaze. A trooper had been admitted by Caull and his
bright eyes were everywhere, intelligently taking in
what had happened and made so much commotion.
The soldier wore an automatic, holstered on his hip,
but carried no rifle. *Apparently they'll do it at close
range,* Richard thought dully; *with their side arms.*

He looked slowly over at Courtney, wondering if they'd go outside for the execution or do it in the corridor. Courtney, he saw, was staring first into his own face, then at the face of the head of the appointed firing squad, and took another look at the youth.

Another time, he might not have discerned the resemblance. The soldier had no glasses; his hair was short, in a crewcut; he seemed athletic, lithely springy and strong.

And the curiosity in the young trooper's eyes was made of the same independent wonderment, even the strains of naiveté, Richard had always seen reflected from his own mirror.

"*Mark,*" Richard whispered. He was looking at a taller, younger version of Richard Grant; and the longer he stared at the boy, the more his conviction —and a tumbling, swirling cauldron of emotions— grew.

"You know, Grant, there's something by-God poetic about my idea." Colonel Caull pushed himself away from his desk, half smiling. "Poetic, and mathematically fine. Pardoo did part of his job; he turned off the lights. Then, if I'm any judge of my men, he and his son Terry died together—at one another's hands." He glanced, scantly, at the soldier beside him, chuckling. "Not that I'm going to let anything happen to Mark, here."

The Colonel wasn't stopping him from standing, wobblingly, unable to support his weight yet on that leg he'd wounded so long ago. Richard did not try to go toward his son; but he raised his hands and forearms, spread them wide, as if summoning the soldier. But as Caull had spoken, Richard had seen the youthful wonderment in Mark's eyes burn out, as if some switch had been thrown.

"This civilian," Caull said levelly, "is the one who prevented you from being a part of the elite squad tonight. Your emotions were suspect, when I had to tell you of his interferences. Now, Corporal, you heard the ruckus, right? The discussion? You know he has attempted to thwart us over and over. Do you follow me?"

Mark was at attention. "Yes *sir!*"

The Colonel clapped the boy's arm in camaraderie. "It occurs to me that you've earned a piece of revenge, Corporal. Personal revenge. Forget the firing squad! Draw your automatic."

"Don't give it to him, son!" Richard shouted, limping forward a foot.

The bald man spread his hands. "Give it to me? Why would I want it?" He spoke directly to Mark, then, in confidential tones. "Finish this phase of the operation and you can accompany me to Baltimore and Washington. I can use a soldier with real guts and I still remember you were the last man out of the lake, Mark!" He made an awful chortling sound. "I was trying to decide whether to send somebody in after you, or let you drown—with honors!"

"Mark, this man is *mad!*" Courtney was on her knees, putting out an arm to him. "You can see that no matter what you've learned—can't you? Mark, your father and I—"

"Am I to kill the female, too, sir?"

The Colonel, beaming, looked for Richard's expression as he nodded briskly, joyously. "Certainly, we've no further options. Are you ready?"

Richard saw his son snap to attention, the .45 unholstered. His own mind refused to offer a scenario for salvation; he felt stunned, drained, emotionally immobilized. He heard Mark's—the trooper's—machine-like "Ready *sir!*" and edged toward

Courtney. Her eyes were closed; her lips were moving in silent prayer.

"*Aim!*" ordered Caull, but his voice was already in another world, to Richard. Too beaten to register surprise in reaction to it, his mind abruptly filled with a picture of Molly, Molly and the girls. What would happen to them, now? Would it matter to this lunatic, after he'd taken command, that they, too, had opposed him? Richard shook his head, wishing he had time to speak on their behalf, knowing that time was ending; he closed his eyes. "*Fire!*"

A shot; Mark had obeyed.

But only after he had thrown his nimble body to one side and spun to face Colonel Albert Caull.

The bald man, at the first tensing of the young soldier's leg muscles, had run for the door. The bullet from Mark's .45 slammed into Caull's back, a direct hit in the spine; just above the trim hips.

For a moment, Caull was flattened against the door as if crucified—outflung arms twitching, spatulate fingers of his large hands woven like spiderwebs against the plane of the door.

Then he turned toward them again, alive.

A mammoth wound in the Colonel's stomach resembled a second, internal face exposed finally; it consisted of arterial blood and torn, tubular flesh, like German sausage lovingly doused with some rare, red sauce.

He seemed to be shrinking, curling in on himself. Paralysis brought his arms down and crumpled his legs, and when he finally began slipping down the door—grinning at them—it seemed to Richard Grant that he would not die but dwindle down and down into some microscopic world of fantasy in which he would be one with all the germs and viruses afflicting humanity. Mark fired again and roughly one quarter of Caull's bald skull rose as if cleanly, surgically lifted, then spattered the door and the volumes of Army Regulations in the book-case, and the shoe at the end of Richard Grant's once-wounded leg.

Richard reached out for Courtney, shielding her the best he could in the warm space between face and shoulder. His gaze trailed back to the boy with the look-alike face, and a smoking .45 automatic which surely contained additional bullets.

The well trained trooper had turned, arm raised, expressionless. Before Richard could speak, the pale face contorted and, tearlessly, mouth working, Mark advanced toward his father. "I wanted to see what you were like," he mumbled, the barrel of the automatic like a pointing finger; "to know you, a little."

"Son . . ."

"I might have done it anyway," the soldier said, as if defending himself. "But he shot my friend in the f-face. And now he's gotten him *killed.*"

Richard heard the pounding at the door, at last. He did not know one thing to say or do until the soldier's arm lowered, abruptly, the weapon dangling at his side. Richard raised his own hand to touch the beardless cheek of the son he'd never seen. "Mark . . . *son* . . ."

"What am I going to *do!*" The young man leaped away from Richard and Courtney Rankin, who'd moved soundlessly to Richard's side. Mark's arms lifted, slapped his legs in anxiety, as he glanced toward the door. "What am I gonna *do?*"

Richard took two limping, tentative steps toward the youth. The wild look in the ambivalent eyes stopped him. Richard cleared his throat. "You're the son of an independent man, Mark. I don't know your—friends. You'll have to decide what to do *on your own.*"

The .45 came up, seemed momentarily to establish a wavering aim somewhere between the two civilians. The young, similar face showed another instant of indecision, then went all but blank.

"Some of them, the other guys," he said softly, his voice an even tenor, "wanted to know—about their folks. We talked about it, sometimes; late at night." He drew himself erect, gave a tentative smile. "Besides, they were left behind tonight, like me."

He crossed the room to the door, stepping over the bald man's body. Its weight had pressed against the door. His own sidearm drooping, young Mark moved the bloodied remains away and edged the door part way open.

Courtney took Richard's hand, realized that Mark Grant was crying, sobbing, for the first time. She was washed by relief. The young man was using his pent-up emotion to save them all. "Mission's over," came the choking voice. "Aborted, inanimated." There was an immediate flood, a torrent, of questions. Some, Courtney thought, were at once furious and suspicious. Most sounded merely surprised and disturbed. "When he found out there's a story about Romulus that broke in the late editions of the newspapers tonight—in D.C.—he killed himself. Committed suicide!"

Richard, watching from deep within the office, smiled marvelingly.

"Announce it to everybody who's still on the base, okay?" Mark said against the tumult of almost hysterical reaction. "The Colonel's orders are for us to—sit tight; wait for reassignment. Got that?"

A second young face squeezed past Mark's. His shrewd eyes met Richard's, then took in the corpse of his dead commander without expression. "I'm not sure Lieutenant Beldonwood is gonna buy it," he told Mark, conspiratorially.

Mark glanced down, touched the .45 in the other trooper's hand. "Use that to convince him, if you have to," he whispered, then closed the door.

"Will it work?" Courtney asked quietly.

But Mark Grant seemed not to have heard. He had dropped to the floor at the base of the two flags and curled himself into a ball, knees to the chest. He was crying, Courtney thought. But the sounds were at once the strangest and the most touching ones she had ever heard. It was as if Mark had never allowed himself—or had never been allowed—to sob, to weep.

Unable to speak, Courtney kissed the top of the boy's head, then turned back to Richard.

He was ransacking Caull's desk and littering the carpet with official forms that fluttered but briefly, like birds dying. She was startled, at first, by Richard's burst of frenetic action, and wondered why. Then she realized that she had imagined the little writer would hug to his bosom the son he had not seen before. Instead, he seemed at a glance to have forgotten Mark's existence in his passionate search for something.

"*Nada,*" he said, looking up at her. "Zilch."

Courtney saw the enormous strain in his face that moment and the way his red-rimmed eyes darted, repeatedly, to his weeping son, only to be torn back to her own agonized face. *He doesn't know what to say to Mark,* she realized. "What are you talking about?"

"Caull's documents," Richard said shortly. "The ones he described." He snapped the lock on a thin, partly concealed drawer, using a letter opener, glanced at the few sheets of paper inside and crumpled them into a ball. "There are no orders to *anybody*. No battlefield promotion for someone named Carrjordan, no instructions for *anybody* in D.C.!"

"What? *Who?*" Mark, overhearing, peered almost incredulously up at them. When Richard repeated the name, Mark shook his head, grinning the way people do when they have heard something preposterous, silly. "That guy isn't getting any kind of promotion!"

"Why not?" Richard came limping around the desk. "Who is 'Carrjordan?' "

"The bald man's *kid,*" Mark replied, glancing from his father's face to Courtney's. "Didn't you know?"

"Know what?" Courtney demanded, frowning. "We don't understand."

"Well, it got to be common knowledge on the base," Mark said. He turned his head just slightly; clearly, the pressure of Caull, even inanimated, made it hard for the young soldier to speak freely. "See, that was the Colonel's illegitimate son; he was named Carr Jordan." Mark shrugged. "I don't know what Miss Jordan's whole name was."

"But Caull said that was the man in Washington who would take over if anything should happen to him." For the first time, she fully understood Richard's frantic search. Such a man could pick up where Caull had involuntarily left off.

"No way." Mark's eyes were wide, his expression completely candid. At his age, he still needed, welcomed, adult management, mature people who asked questions and gave orders; that much was clear to Courtney. "See, ol' Jordan was one of the first guys from the States who got it in Vietnam."

"More than twenty years ago," Courtney murmured.

"C'mon, let me help you up." Richard hauled young Mark to his feet. "The psychology behind this is fascinating. I'd make an educated guess that the Jordan boy was under Colonel Caull's command."

"And Caull felt responsible for his dying in Nam," Courtney put in.

"They've been substitutes, the Romulus kids," Richard rasped, shaking his head. While he was neither looking at nor touching his own son, he hadn't moved a foot away from Mark. "Substitutes and sacrifices, *all* these kids—so Caull could both justify his old command decisions and replace his boy with hundreds of others."

"He wanted us to be prepared, really trained," Mark said. He seemed to be protecting the only father figure he'd known before that night. "I guess he thought another war was going to come and wanted most of us to—to make it."

"He doesn't need your justification," Richard said bluntly. He raised his eyes, peered questioningly at Mark. "Or deserve them."

"No, he doesn't need them!" Mark exclaimed. Fire flashed in his eyes. Much taller than Richard, he was inclined to move with such athletic quickness and vigor that he sometimes suggested a certain menace, whether it was really there or not. Courtney, sensing the scarcely controlled violence, watched Mark warily, saw the boy's confusion as he glared at the father he believed had deserted him. "Maybe I was wrong, insubordinate! The Colonel *fed* us, *housed* us, and made us *strong*. Maybe—"

Someone rapped sharply, once, on the door.

Then they were filing inside, not boisterously in the way of active, affably aggressive young men but with the attitude of well trained military troops who lacked a leader and might need to act on their own initiative. Ten, eleven, twelve of them, with the soldier to whom Mark had whispered bringing up the rear. None of them had drawn a weapon; all of them had their hands in readiness above their holstered automatics. Tall, powerful youths highly skilled in the martial arts, they filled the regulation Army office like a weightlifter's shirtsleeve.

All twelve soldiers stared expressionlessly at the bloodied Colonel Albert Caull, and Caull stared dispassionately back at them.

"You the lady who wrote about us?" It was the shortest, seemingly slightest of the troops but he was hairless, perfectly bald. As if he had hoped to curry favor with the Colonel—or loved and admired him.

Courtney took a step from Richard, and Mark. "I am," she lied. *And I will,* she thought for the first time, *if I get out of this in one piece.*

The small soldier took one step toward Courtney. As with Caull, light reflected off his hairless pate. "Did you tell the truth?"

"Of course, she told the truth!" Richard exclaimed. He stepped beside Courtney. "Do you know who this woman is? How *famous?* She's—the print medium's Barbara Walters!"

Not one of the young faces registered an awareness of the celebrated name.

The short soldier smoothed his scalp, thoughtfully, turning his attention to Richard Grant. "Do the other families know?" he demanded.

"Not yet." He caught his breath. "But they will, when they read Ms. Rankin's story tomorrow; the wire services will pick it up." He paused, perspiring. "Why do you ask?" There was no reply. "D'you have a dad and a mom somewhere?"

The moment he'd posed the question, Richard knew how wrong he had been. "I wouldn't know," the soldier grunted. "They've never contacted me." Slowly, almost reflexively, he drew his .45 from its holster. While he did not aim it, he turned it in his hand, regarding it in much the manner of a ruminating farmer touching base with a familiar farm implement. "They didn't look for me, I guess," he said, quite softly. Richard saw the color mounting his cheeks, the muscles knotting in them. "None of the parents gave a *shit*"—the word was emphasized so sharply it was as if it had been wrenched from him, and he lifted his head and his gaze to stare, hard, at Richard Grant—"about any of us. Goddam civilians just bought what the Colonel handed out, or else we didn't matter to them. We weren't *worth finding!*"

Richard saw the handgrip of the automatic swivel into the bald soldier's palm—

And an arm went round his shoulders, fingers squeezing.

"My Dad cared," Mark Grant said. It was fractionally more than a whisper, but all the soldiers heard it. "*My* Dad found me—and *he came.*"

"To take you home," Courtney Rankin said.

"To take you *all* home," Richard added.

The muscular little soldier with the bald head was the last of the troops to leave the room. They'd gone silently, without another word, while the only one of them to speak had stayed standing before Courtney, Richard, and Mark.

At last, he reholstered his weapon, thoughtfully snapped the holster shut, and looked up at the others with shining eyes. "If there's one of you," he said, putting out his hand to Richard, "somewhere there are more who care."

Epilogue

"I have written to you, I have prayed for you, but what you will do I can't tell."—James Janeway (1636-1674), who lived in London during the Great Plague and the Great Fire and wrote of thirteen children who perished.

They came from the Army and Defense Departments, the Pentagon and the Attorney General's office, the Federal Bureau of Investigation and, it was proved later, after numerous denials, the Central Intelligence Agency. Members of congressional subcommittees especially, hastily formed to cope with such questions as the lawsuits filed against the federal government by certain opportunistic parents. Some expected the President, or the Vice-President; one or two reports were filed that one or the other of them had been flown quickly in, and quickly out.

Psychiatrists, psychologists, sociologists, educators of several varieties, church folk, and writers of many stripes—some invited, most not—came too.

To the heretofore unknown or unacknowledged site of Project Romulus.

Colonel Albert Mead Caull was gone, and with him, every vestige of privacy he had striven for more than twenty years to maintain. No one in the civilized and free worlds—they are not always the same—could avoid hearing silent details.

Courtney Rankin's status with a major newspaper based in the capital not only stood her in good stead but freed her to remain with Richard and Mark as well as to act as a buffer against all those who longed to get at them. In the main, only network and some cable news people attempted to bypass or ignore her unique claim as the journalist who broke the story. But Richard's loyalty to the brilliant woman who'd been at his side each step of the perilous way prevented TV folk from doing much more than circling the wagons of Courtney's hard-won exclusivity.

No other parents of the Romulus youths were allowed on the base.

As a consequence, Richard's observations were sought by all the visitors to this lonely spot in the sovereign state of Utah. Once, trying to fall asleep at night, it had occurred to him that only a fool could fail to guarantee his financial future, in his position, especially since he was a writer. The next day, four publishers left word for him to call them and he knew there would be others. He wondered, when he thought about it, why he couldn't focus his attention on the rare opportunity; why it did not mean more to him.

It was Courtney who enabled Richard to stay. She did not hesitate to imply that Colonel Albert Caull could not have gone so far without clandestine assistance from numerous Washington associates but made it clear that she would not pursue her conviction as long as she, Richard and Mark Grant remained on the base.

Which had to do, principally, with the delicate question of when Mark could—as every reporter enjoyed putting it—"go home."

The immediate problem on the night of the bald man's death involved the two hundred troops he had distributed over the maps of D.C., Maryland, and Virginia. It was Defense, that night, who was first to realize that they needed to be rounded up at once. Inanely, in Richard's opinion—he was to be privately considered a "damned troublemaker" over the next days—it took more than half a day of inter-departmental phone calls and meetings to facilitate the roundup. (In time, it was discovered that an early F.B.I. investigator had managed to call his office, with the result that unmarked helicopters darkened the sky the next morning, in turn eliciting public rumors of Unidentified Flying Objects "buzzing the White House.") Richard, fearful that the wandering troops wouldn't know of Caull's in-animation and were trained to fight back, had urged the first committee formed to *let* the two hundred troops come back. "It isn't just a military base to them, it's home," he reasoned. "People will be hurt if you try to bring 'em in. If you wait, however, they'll simply drift back here of their own accord."

"And why," a plainclothes general from the Pentagon had asked, his patience of manner intolerable, "will they do that, Mr. Grant?"

"They're orphans," he'd explained. "Gentlemen, there's nowhere else they can go."

He was praised on "ABC Nightline" the next even-ing but his advice was completely ignored. It

sounded too simple. And Richard Grant was both a
civilian and a writer. One of the people who day-
dreamed; used imagination. Another plan for
"apprehending the runaway soldiers" was in place
before daylight.

Three troops were located that winter night. One
was sitting on the wharf down the way from Baltimore's aquarium, on the Inner Harbor. Two were
reading great words at the memorial to Abraham
Lincoln in Washington; one of them appeared dazed,
or rapt. One trooper was caught, then returned to
Utah, without incident. The remaining two men
could not believe what they were being told about
their commanding officer's death, and ignominy.

Each of the pair, in his own way, escaped.

The first overpowered five armed, regular Army
soldiers plus a Washington motorcycle police officer
who'd been first to see him. And the second died
when he chose to run from a regular Army sniper
standing on the roof of a famous edifice. They had,
believing they were honorably defending themselves
and all they had been taught to believe in, taken the
lives of eight men. All told.

And no one ever learned what happened to the
brilliant, daring trooper who escaped alive. He
would disappear into mythology, and books by
wildly inventive authors.

By 0600 hours two days later, however, the
remainder of Colonel Caull's select team returned,
voluntarily, to the former Romulus site. They
returned individually, in twos and threes; one entire
squad marched in, came within a hair of firing upon
the new base temporary personnel, and then surrendered.

Most of the men did not ask what had happened.
Because of that and, more importantly, in the

view of the authorities, because of the eight men killed and an array of injuries and property damage, the almost two hundred troops were subjected to close psychiatric screening—always with two armed, regular Army soldiers on guard. One psychiatrist released a report to the effect that the majority of Romulus troops were "incorrigibly paranoid, sociopathic mutants"; asked, he said that they were "perhaps irreparably warped."

Richard's hope that the youths would promptly be welcomed into the wider society was dashed; clearly, they would not be allowed to go anywhere for months, and then, irony of ironies, they would probably confront the sort of public hostility he and other Vietnam veterans had been obliged to face.

His concern was vastly more particularized than general. He did not want the son he had reclaimed sacrificed to his elders' neurotic needs; and when Doctor Lenore Bianchi proved to be one Army appointed psychiatrist, he met her in the former Romulus mess hall.

Biachi pretended not to know or remember him. He understood. Once icily beautiful, Bianchi seemed brittle, and haggard. She had worked with Molly while insisting that her recollection of seeing her newborn son, alive, was fantasy; delusion.

Richard hoped Doctor Bianchi would want to make amends and, to encourage it, he went to the meeting in the mess hall ready to cite authorities from her own profession.

"Wasn't it Maslow," he began, sipping coffee and trying to seem relaxed, "who said that any institutionalized person can gain satisfaction from thinking creatively—using his brain for the good reason that it brings pleasure?"

"Well, that's quite a paraphrase," she replied.

"Come. What is it you want from me?"

Impulsively, Richard reached across the wooden table to touch her hand. "Please don't start rehabilitating these boys believing you can reach them by just offering strictly material advantages, or worse, by threatening them with how civilian law punishes violent people."

Bianchi crossed a silken leg, peered narrowly at Richard. "Would you have the analyst say that society aches to welcome and comfort them?"

"Certainly not!" Richard flushed. "We always make the mistake of letting our kids think the world hungers to shower them with opportunity."

"Make your point," she said shortly. She hadn't touched her coffee.

"I'll let a guy named MacDougald do it for me." Richard's mind raced. "He's associated with an Atlanta group which advocates attitude therapy."

"I'm acquainted with them." Now Bianchi smiled. "It was MacDougald who learned that the root for 'love' defined mental attitude, not feeling, alone. And who established that accepting the concept of law first depends upon loving a higher being—such as God."

Richard glanced away. "I take it that you don't agree."

"On the contrary," the psychiatrist replied, standing. "That is precisely how Colonel Caull manipulated them." And the interview was ended.

So it was that the rehabilitative progress was fast for some of the former Romulus troops, difficult and not nearly so fast for others. By and large, however, there was no instance of violence. Some educators whose assistance was sought in order to acquaint the young men with common facts withheld from them by Colonel Caull's staff even complained that their students were "excessively docile" and "overly inclined to accept the word of any authority figure." By March, an official estimate released to the media stated that thirty-one percent of the youths in the compound had accepted the nature of what had happened to them with remarkable alacrity and displayed evidence of readiness to be released to their families.

Among that number was Richard Grant's son Mark. He was permitted to spend two or three hours with his father daily and a bond rapidly formed between them, Richard striving to convey to his son everything that had happened to the Grant family since Mark's birth and, in a few sentimental cases, before.

When it seemed likely that Mark and several other clearly well-adapted young men would be given permission to leave, however, both print and picture journalists quoted a "source who wishes to remain anonymous, but highly placed in the activities at the Utah command post" as claiming that the ex-troopers had been hazardously brainwashed. Their minds, it was said, were set "like traps" by an Albert Caull whose ingenuity was, retrospectively, becoming legendary. The media claimed, citing the "unnamed source," that Caull had hypnotically and permanently turned his youths into mercilessly deadly fighting machines. Some columnists and news analysts recommended that the youths be "studied," or "evaluated," for a longer period of time, instead of being "unleashed upon their families and the general public."

Courtney Rankin had remained with Richard as long as possible. "I've written every word of every column about what happened here and there's nothing left that I can't handle from Washington."

It was almost spring. They were sitting together near the small airstrip at the rear of what had been the Romulus site and a plane was perched like a mosquito beneath azure skies. From where they sat, it hummed, not unmusically. Richard's hands were clasped between his legs. He didn't turn his head to see her when he asked Courtney's plans.

"Uncertain, wordsmith." She shrugged. "Perhaps I'll join you between covers."

"I hope it's more satisfactory then when you tried to join me between sheets," he said, and smiled. They laughed briefly. "I read up on something, Back Court. They have a good military library. And what the Colonel said about the Carthaginians was largely true. But he seemed to have forgotten that when the invincible Hannibal finally lost, at Zama, no one could take his place. With Hannibal vanquished, the Carthaginian state collapsed."

"I'd forgotten." She lit a cigarette, took a drag, pressed it between his fingers. The touch lingered a moment longer than necessary. "He committed suicide, Hannibal. Didn't he?"

Richard nodded. His gaze rested on the mosquito-like plane, reporters crowding around it to see who might be aboard. The passengers, if any, were being held up. "Caull killed himself too, in a way."

She peered directly at him, drawing his eyes to her. "I've never fully understood why he chose Mark to execute us. He went out of his way to make sure Mark knew who you were."

"Eight hundred years ago, in France," Richard said, returning her cigarette, "a boy named Stephen led thousands of other boys and girls on a march to recover the Holy Land. He said he'd make them walk on water, that nothing could stand in their way."

"The Children's Crusade," Courtney said with a nod. "There were thousands of German children, too, most of them from the lower classes."

"Correct. And when they found they could not walk on water—when they learned that the sea would not part—they either went quietly back to their homes, or wandered the Mediterranean, the prey of slave dealers. That little jet." Richard inclined his head. "That's yours, isn't it? You're taking off when it leaves?"

"I hate goodbyes."

"And Molly's on it, right? That's who that blonde woman is, trying to part the journalistic sea?"

"I arranged it," Courtney acknowledged. "But I couldn't arrange for the girls, too. I had to give them up to make the deal."

Before Richard could comment, he caught a glimpse of Mark, making his way toward them with the scarecrow look of refugees Richard had seen in the sort of pictures one put down hastily. He'd taken the boy into Sunridge that morning, and the first civilian clothes Mark wore as he approached them looked more like a uniform—as civvies always did on old troopers—than fatigues had. A breeze blowing across the airstrip was deceptive, part reality and part fantasy; it felt warm, at first, but its source was relentlessly cold.

He took Courtney's hand in his as he turned from the boy and the blonde woman whose paths, without the awareness of either of them, were about to converge. One by one, he folded her fingers over his hand, close to his lips, as if impressing them for another day.

She pulled free, before he kissed them, turned and strode toward the humming jet without a backward glance. Molly's eyes had found him and did not see the dark-haired reporter, Richard saw both women simultaneously, with striking clarity; and as Mark drew within range, Molly saw him, too, and broke into a run.

So long, Back Court, he thought. Aloud, Richard called, *"Mark! Molly! Hullo!"* And inwardly, remembering the lost years: *It's been . . . so long.*